Sin & Salvation

Also by K.F. Breene

Sin & Salvation

By K.F. Breene

Contact info:
www.kfbreene.com
books@kfbreene.com

Chapter 1

ALEXIS

"**B**LAST US JUST enough to knock us on our asses, but not enough to severely damage us," Bria instructed with her hands up, as though she were a bank teller and this was a hold up. The muscle-bound men lined up next to her shot her dubious looks.

"Why'd Zorn put her in charge again?" Jack muttered to Thane and Donovan. Demigod Kieran had assigned half of his elite task force, the Six, to train with me today.

I shifted from side to side in my small backyard, which the Six had cleared of weeds and straggly bushes. We now had somewhere to train in the back of the house where nosey neighbors wouldn't stop and gawk. And by 'we,' I meant myself and my two teenage wards, Daisy and Mordecai, who were picking up their lessons *much* faster than I was.

In my defense, my magic was a lot more nuanced than simply shifting into a wolf, like Mordecai did, or learning to be sneaky, like Daisy was doing. I had to work with the power from the Line for larger jobs, and that could get dicey in a hurry. A simple *sorry* didn't cut it when you accidentally ripped someone's soul out.

Not that I had, yet. A person's soul had built-in protections, it turned out, which felt something like a psychic steel cage surrounding it. Whenever I reached someone's steel cage, I chickened out and backed off, losing my momentum. So far, I'd only successfully gotten to the soul of one person—Demigod Kieran. That had happened in a very intimate moment, and I was pretty sure he'd let me do it. Not a repeatable occurrence, and not helpful in my training.

The experience with Kieran had also had an unintended side effect—I'd somehow connected our souls, allowing us to share magical abilities and keep tabs on each other. Very intimate tabs on each other.

He seemed to think it was a good thing, but as Bria constantly reminded me, getting romantically attached to a Demigod on a warpath was a terrible idea. Especially because Kieran had made it clear I shouldn't waste my heart on him. A heart that fluttered every time he walked into a room or texted me goodnight.

I was such a fool.

I blew out a breath, forcing myself to focus on the wall of muscle facing me.

Bria licked her lips. "Just real easy-like," she said, her hands still raised. "Like last time."

And the time before that. And before that.

Two months had passed since I'd set Kieran's mother's spirit free—and my fast progress in the beginning had swiftly plateaued. Daisy and Mordecai attributed it to age, as though being twenty-five meant I was geriatric and incapable of learning. They'd quickly stopped being my favorite people.

I drew on the power of the Line, a doorway of sorts, where spirits crossed from the world of the living into their own realm. With the appearance of a black hole stretched thin, slapped onto a backdrop of bruise-like colors, it repelled the mind. The feel of it, though, comforting and welcoming, gently called to the soul.

A light wind caressed my face and ruffled my hair.

"Here we go, boys," Donovan said, his dirty blond hair standing up in a stylishly messy halo.

Jack nodded, grim, letting his hugely muscled arms hang loose at his sides. Thane tilted his shaved head from side to side like a boxer gearing up for a match. I grimaced at his thick, brown beard, holding a stray crumb from his breakfast.

"Have I mentioned that it's weird we can see the wind from the spirit plane actually affect her physical person?" Bria mumbled.

"Yes. At least three times," Thane said, bracing himself. His muscles rippled and his eyes sparkled with malice.

A tremor of fear shook my spine—a reaction to his violent energy. All of Kieran's Six could kill me six ways from Sunday, and while my mind knew they would never try, my flight reflex wasn't so sure.

"Can you stop that from happening?" Bria asked me, her wariness at what I was about to do melting into an expression of contemplation. "You don't want to give away what you're capable of before you actually do anything."

"One thing at a time," Jack said through clenched teeth.

"We don't have that luxury," Bria said, her eyebrows lowering. "You heard what Henry said yesterday. Valens is planning something. Something big. We've got precious little time before he realizes Kieran is an enemy and not an asset. If we don't get the jump on him, he'll direct all the firepower he's been assembling on us. He's nimble like that. We have to get Alexis up and running."

My belly fluttered and Jack's lips tightened. He knew Bria was right. We all did.

I took a deep breath to calm my anxiety and focused on the strange wind. Logically, it didn't seem possible that it would affect my living body unless I could physically cross the Line, which I was pretty sure was a no-go. Not that I had time to experiment.

I dragged my teeth across my lip, focusing. As I

drew in more power from the Line, the pleasant breeze became more of a gale. My soul flapped in my body and my hair blew back from my face. The guys tensed even more, and pained expressions crossed their faces. Their physical bodies weren't affected by the wind, but their souls sure were.

I squeezed my eyes shut, holding on to the feel of the Line, and envisioned slamming a door on the wind.

That didn't help at all.

"Bria, I need your Necromancer tools, I think," I said, opening my eyes again. "I need to see what I'm doing."

While Bria couldn't rip souls from living bodies or pull power from the Line, she could work with parts of the spirit world (and stuff those parts into dead bodies). Her various tools allowed her (and me) to see the magic inherent in our shared trade.

She jogged forward immediately and snatched her camo backpack from the ground near my back door. Moments later, I was surrounded by scented candles and triangles of incense.

"We're rollin'." She hopped up and dusted off her ripped jeans before falling back in line.

Squinting through the scented smoke from the various candles and incense, I pulled power from the Line into the yellow haze around me. Tendrils of green and blue magic curled upward, and then I saw it—a throbbing cord of orange amidst the other colors.

"Huh," I murmured. "There are, like, different strands of my magic."

It was one of life's little jokes that I was a visual learner with a nuanced magic better suited for feeling, but here we were. I catalogued the different feelings associated with each of the strands, then pulled at the orange cord specifically, pushing the others aside. The wind died down before cutting out, but the power of the Line still pumped through my blood, ready for use.

Donovan let out a noisy exhale. "I know she'll be a game changer, but man, I'm not loving this part of the job."

"Same," Thane said. "Being the guinea pig for this shit is rough."

Without warning them, I slapped my magic against their souls' steel cages. All four of them gasped and their power surged, something I could now sense because of my connection to Kieran. It was their primal reaction to my attack.

The guys grunted and wobbled where they stood, visibly struggling not to take a knee.

Bria bent at the waist. "Ouch," she said. "It's hard to get used to that."

"No shit," Thane murmured.

More power and they would've dropped like rocks. It was hard to focus on normal things, like standing, when someone was attacking your very soul. This offensive move I had down.

In discovery mode now, I bumped up against Thane's steel cage, guarding his most precious commodity. I stroked the hard surface before giving a firm poke, looking for cracks or weaknesses. I didn't feel any. How the hell was I supposed to get in there?

"Nope." He jumped up and down, shaking out his hands. "Nope. I do not like that, Sam I am."

"Hold steady," Bria said.

"She's tap-dancing on my threshold," Thane replied through gritted teeth.

"Hold," Bria commanded.

"Why doesn't Zorn do this?" Donovan asked with tight eyes. "He has the best constitution for fucked up shit."

"He doesn't trust himself not to react," Thane grunted out. "Ain't that a bitch? Here I am, with a magic known for reacting, and *he* doesn't trust himself."

"What magic is that?" I asked, giving that steel cage an exploratory jab. The guys had always been strangely tightlipped about their magic, and I'd never been overly curious. It now occurred to me that that might've been a mistake.

"Bullshit," Bria said, ignoring me. She straightened up painfully and put her hand to the middle of her chest. "Zorn just doesn't want everyone to know he isn't made of metal. He doesn't want to admit that Alexis could reduce him to his knees and make him say uncle."

She'd know. I'd say they were the unlikeliest couple imaginable, but Kieran and I probably held that dubious honor.

Tuning them out, I thought back to those different threads of power. I wrapped the blue—spirit—around Thane's hard casing, before giving the orange cord a yank. A thick wave of the Line's power screamed through me.

Before I could back off, Thane jumped and made a sound like "heh." A blur of movement preceded him surging toward me.

My heart pushed up into my throat and I staggered backward, caught off guard.

"Hold, dammit!" Bria lunged forward at an angle to intercept. "Get a hold of yourself, Thane."

I blinked rapidly, not sure if this was a drill, or if he was really losing it. The other two guys hadn't reacted, though, which meant it couldn't be that bad.

I batted down the fear and surprise and focused. Going off gut instinct, I wrapped the orange power around the blue, covering the hard box containing Thane's soul. I squeezed, feeling for any give. There wasn't any. I squeezed harder. Still nothing. Like an egg in the palm of a hand, the vessel's design withstood the pressure. This wasn't the way to his soul.

Thane pushed Bria to the side, closing the distance between him and me at extreme speed. He swung an arm, fist closed, aiming for my face.

"Holy shit birds." I flung myself backward, lashing out with my magic.

Bria pivoted and kicked, clipping Thane's moving ankles. His feet swept out from under him. He fell, eyes widening. He had barely hit the ground before Bria was on top of him, her knife poised to strike.

"Jesus, she's vicious," Donovan said with a gleeful smile.

"Uncle," Jack said, clutching his chest. "To all of this. Uncle! I want to go home."

I took another jab at Thane's steel cage, trying to poke a hole into it. Like squeezing it, nothing happened.

"Hurra!" Thane's word took no real shape.

He bucked up, a surge of strength and power that sent Bria flying, arms windmilling, knife catching and throwing the sun.

"She getting to ya, bud?" Donovan said, a full smile covering his handsome face. "Just need to hear that *uncle*."

"Don't taunt him," Bria yelled.

"Why?" Donovan asked. "He's been through worse than this."

"She is"—Bria hopped up like she was on a spring—"messing around"—she grabbed the back of Thane's shirt—"in his shit!"

The fabric ripped but held, Thane now dragging the knife-wielding Bria behind him as he attempted to get to me.

My body stilled and adrenaline pumped into my bloodstream. Without thinking, I slashed my magic through him. But I hadn't increased the power.

Thane staggered but didn't go down. He huffed through his nose, like a bull, and a shiver went through his body. The smile dripped off of Donovan's face. A curse slipped from Jack's lips.

Thane was about to reveal his magic, and I was no longer sure I wanted to know what it was.

Chapter 2

ALEXIS

"HE'S NOT A minotaur, right?" I asked with a tremor in my voice. "You'd tell me if something that dangerous and off-balance were participating in my training...right?"

"Drop him, Alexis," Bria shouted, stabbing with her knife. The blade dug into Thane's side.

He didn't so much as twitch.

His heavy footfalls crashed onto the ground. His breath came out in hard pants. His rage-filled eyes shone with malice.

"Drop him now before he turns!" she yelled.

Cold dripped down my spine as another shiver traveled Thane's length. Donovan stepped forward, and I felt his power pulse.

Like a panicked woman trying to fit car keys into the ignition as a masked madman revved a chainsaw nearby, I reached for more magic. The Line pulsed, promising power aplenty, but I had to keep some semblance of focus to use it properly.

Thane's body grew, straining at his white T-shirt and cotton sweats. Muscles bulged along his frame, so big they were inhuman.

"Turns into what?" I demanded with a high-pitched screech.

Donovan shoved his hands forward. Thane jolted to the side, his face reddening.

"Don't do that, it'll just piss him off," Bria hollered.

Donovan lifted his hands this time, and Thane rose up into the air.

"Donovan is a freaking Telekinetic?" I asked, jogging to the side of the house. I was no hero—if Thane was about to freak out, I was happy to get out of Dodge.

Donovan ripped his hands down, and Thane crashed into the ground. Jack jogged up on the other side, ready to help.

"Alexis, dammit, slice through him," Bria said with her bloody knife in hand and legs bent.

A strange growl, like that of a rage-filled beast, rose up out of Thane's chest. His eyes, beating into me, gleamed crimson.

"What the hell is he, a cross between a shifter and a vampire?" Fear tightened my throat as I hunkered down at the corner of the house.

"Calm down, buddy," Jack said in a smooth voice, his hands out. "She'll fuck with your head, but she won't kill ya. You gotta have faith."

"The boss trusts her, bro," Donovan said, and he lifted his hands into the air. Thane rose ten feet off of the ground, his ridiculously large muscles flexed, ready for action.

"Quit knocking him around," Jack berated. "Let him get his head straight. He can still come back from this."

Another low growl started in Thane's chest, shivering up through his body and gaining strength and volume as it did so.

"Fuck," Bria said softly, drifting closer to Jack. "Alexis, you'd sure be a lot of help right now. You know, *if you used your fucking magic.* Don't worry about hurting him. He might be past that now. Just worry about taking him down."

"He can come back from this," Jack insisted. "I've seen him come back from the brink. He has the most incredible control of any of his kind."

"What should we do, run?" Bria asked.

"From a Berserker?" Jack yelled. "Are you out of your fucking mind? They love a chase."

The color seemed to drain from my reality as Donovan magically lifted Thane a little higher. I barely heard him say, "I got it."

"Did you say...a Berserker?" I asked through suddenly numb lips.

Berserkers were basically mindless killing machines. They were faster and stronger than an average man, and could rip through shields, magical and otherwise. On the battlefield they were hard as hell to kill, and once they got going, they didn't stop until everyone was dead.

I'd just set loose a Berserker. In my backyard.

With the kids in the house.

Thane threw his arms wide with an agonized roar. Fabric tore across his shoulders. Red infused his cheeks and anger burned in his crimson gaze, still rooted to mine. He convulsed and arched, letting the roar build until it filled the backyard.

The sound stuck my tongue to the top of my mouth and fear rooted my feet to the ground.

Thane thrashed in the air, ripping and tearing at the invisible hold. Glowing red whips of magic lashed out, crackling through Donovan's magic.

"Never mind. It's not fine." Jack took a step back. The panic I felt laced his words. "Call Demigod Kieran."

"I got him," Donovan insisted. He backed up, distancing himself from that lashing magic.

A glowing red whip glided delicately through the air before savagely cracking Donovan across the face. He jerked back and Thane lowered dramatically.

"We have to stop him." My voice was no more than a whisper. I could barely feel my shaking legs. "The kids are in danger."

My heart, already galloping, kicked up its pace. I ripped my foot from the ground and struggled it forward, toward the enormous man-beast. Then the other foot. A strange primal fear gripped me, and I fought through it with gritted teeth.

Thane pointed his toes in the air and stuck his fists out to the sides before a roar-scream erupted from his mouth. Magic shimmied around him. The ripped remains of his shirt fell away, revealing a torso so lumpy with muscle it looked unnatural. His skin shone, almost metallic, and flares of magic whipped out in all directions, electrifying the air.

Those whips merged into one thick line, sizzling like a live wire. It rose, almost lazily, before snapping out at lightning speed. The end sliced across Donovan's right arm, opening a large gash. Blood oozed out a moment later.

Donovan screamed and staggered backward, his right arm dropping. Thane's body jolted downward. One foot touched the ground. His huge band of magic whipped again. The air crackled as it struck, but Donovan dove away, barely escaping the attack.

Thane's second foot touched the ground. He staggered forward.

Bria dashed in with her knife, raking it across Thane's wide chest. It didn't leave a mark. Steel couldn't damage a Berserker once they shifted.

"Shit, I forgot about that," she said before throwing herself to the side, away from one of Thane's huge fists.

Donovan grabbed the air with both hands, one of them trembling. Thane roared and shook, magic sizzling around him, and threw off the hold. Jack dodged in, ducking under a fast-moving fist. He grabbed Thane around the middle and tried to rip him to the side.

Thane barely budged.

He clapped his enormous hands on Jack's back before grabbing and flinging. Jack flew ass over end, like a doll, into my fence.

"Holy…" I struggled with my foot, trying to override the intense desire to step backward again.

The back door swung open and a confused Daisy stuck her head out. "What in the hell is—" She caught sight of Thane at the exact moment he caught sight of her. "Is that Thane?"

"Did the beard give it away?" Bria said, gesturing wildly. "Get out of here. Close the door. Run!"

A huge wolf, larger than its natural counterparts, slipped out from between Daisy's leg and the door frame. It loped into the scene before stopping near Jack with its lips pulled back from its teeth in a silent snarl, Mordecai's signature.

"No!" I yelled, and sucked in the power of the Line. "Kids, get back in the house!"

A manic laugh rose from Thane before morphing into a ghastly roar. Jack and Mordecai flinched together—the primal response of shifters whose instincts knew something bigger and badder was in the vicinity. Thane braced, and I knew one moment of sheer panic.

He was going to charge my kid.

The colors in the backyard shifted to the surreal palette of the spiritual plane, turning the space into a sort of comforting nightmare. The Line pulsed, high and off to the left, out of the way. Shadows swirled around us, the shapes of people floating behind the veil, which was more translucent than I'd ever seen it.

Calling up the wind of the spirit world, I lifted my hands and yanked it down in a way I didn't totally understand, ready to direct it solely at Thane.

He ran, faster than a blink, straight for Daisy standing in the doorway of the house. To get there, he'd have to go through Jack and Mordecai.

Oh, hell no.

I harnessed a huge swell of magic before slashing through his middle. The force of the spirit world hit Thane dead center, blasting through him in a way that would surely freeze him up. My magic cut down deep, clanging when it hit his soul's casing. His soul flapped wildly, pinging around the inside of its casing, pulling at the bindings that held it in place.

He tried to push through it. Tried to fight the effects of the Line. But his feet dragged. His head bowed.

Still, he kept moving.

He needed a bigger push or he'd reach my furry kid.

This time, I braided the power from the Line together with spirit magic before wrapping them around the impregnable casing of his soul. I might not be able to break in, but the pressure would sure suck. I squeezed as hard as I could before sending another slash of magic through him. Then I slashed once more for good measure.

The human-beast howled in agony. He gripped his massive chest before his ghastly body crashed down onto the ground, its size reducing before my eyes. He clawed at dirt before flipping over and hugging his middle.

"Uncle," I heard, his voice a raspy wheeze. He rolled from side to side. "Uncle!"

Chapter 3

ALEXIS

"I'LL BE DAMNED," Jack said, rising slowly.

"See?" Bria pointed at a panting Thane, his hands still clutching his chest. I closed off the Line and let the magic dissipate before sagging where I stood. I wasn't sure if it was from using the magic, or the excessive adrenaline, but I was exhausted. "Zorn is freaked out he's going to end up like that." She stowed her knife.

I ran my fingers through my hair. "Would someone mind explaining to me why a freaking *Berserker* was involved in my training?" I hadn't meant to yell. "What if I hadn't been able to stop him?" Or screech.

"But you did." Bria nodded at me in pride.

My flat stare prompted a better explanation.

She sighed as Jack squatted by Thane's side. "Look," she said, "Thane's the most balanced of the Six, and has the most control of his kind *in the entire world*. He's trained to handle a lot of situations, but you don't fight like anyone else on the planet—" She paused for a moment. "Probably. I mean, I don't know what the Hades Demigods get up to, but—"

"You're losing your point," Jack said softly.

"Right, right. Berserkers are scary, sure, but labels are misleading." Bria started dragging me toward the back door. "I don't have to tell you that. Soul Stealer, hello?" She shoved Daisy out of the way and pulled me into the house. "Kieran knows Thane is in these trainings." She stopped short. "Dang it, I forgot my backpack. Hang on…"

My feet felt like lead as I trudged down my small hallway to the round table straddling the line between the living room and the kitchen. When Bria returned, she grabbed my fabulous Burberry handbag, a gift from Kieran, and shoved it at me.

"As I said, Kieran knows Thane is in these trainings," she continued. "He's cool with it. He trusts Thane."

"Berserkers…"

I jumped at Daisy's voice. She passed me into the kitchen before grabbing a glass out of the cabinet. Her plain red T-shirt was streaked with dirt and something blue. Chalk? Lord only knew.

Mordecai padded in behind her. Changing form took a lot of energy, and apparently it also hurt for the first handful of changes, so he wasn't keen on shifting back and forth too quickly.

"Ew." Daisy kicked at him. "No dogs in the kitchen. Get out! Shoo!"

"Daisy, don't kick—"

Mordecai growled, a deep-chested, rather terrifying sound.

"Mordecai, don't you growl at your sister," I admonished him. "Honestly, one of you can't even talk. How can you *still* fight?"

"Lexi, he'll get hair everywhere." Daisy inspected the ground behind him. "See? A dog hair."

"He's a wolf, Daisy, and you leave hair all over the house. You make the bathroom look like a Sasquatch's murder scene."

She huffed and filled her glass. "Anyway, as I was saying before Fido came nipping at my heels... Berserkers are hard to take down, aren't they?"

"Yes." Bria nodded adamantly. "When they're really rolling, they're hard as hell to stop. Their brain shuts off, rage takes over, and they destroy. That's their one function—*destroy*. They make one hell of an ally in battle. Thane was only just starting to get rolling."

Silence filled the room, thick and gooey. Daisy stared at Bria, unblinking.

"And Lexi was able to take him down?" she finally asked.

My mouth dropped open. "*That's* what you took away from all that? Daisy, Berserkers are incredible war machines who stop thinking when the rage takes over. They stop thinking. That's really dangerous to have around a couple of teens only a few months into training. You didn't get a good look at him out there, but he was terrifying."

Mordecai growled softly.

"What's that, Lassie? Timmy fell down the well?" Daisy smirked at him.

"Daisy, would you stop picking on your brother?" I asked, exasperated.

Daisy crossed her arms over her chest. "Lexi, your magic is stealing souls and leaving dead bodies in your wake—"

"We call them cadavers," Bria corrected.

"—and you're not trained. Sometimes you sucker punch Mordie and I through the chest when you're pissed. You don't even know you're doing it, but it still hurts like hell." She held up a finger. "Hell isn't swearing, remember?"

We had an agreement that if she swore, I'd punch her in the face. It was terrible parenting on my part, but the threat sometimes worked. More often than not, however, she'd offer a compelling explanation for why she'd broken the rule.

"At least Thane knows what sets him off and can usually avoid it," she finished. "You just flail around, invisibly slicing people in two."

"I'm learning to control my magic, and I can't steal souls yet," I said in my defense. "He is ruled by rage. He would've ripped the house apart to get to you, then ripped you apart."

Daisy rolled her eyes and drained her glass. "That Demigod you always have hanging around—"

"You mean my boss?"

"He could kill us all, rage or no, and get away with it. And not just him. Every one of the Six could take us down. Zorn wouldn't even make a sound while he was doing it. The whole crew is dangerous. I don't know what you're getting all bent out of shape about."

I ran my fingers through my hair. I hated when the kids stomped on my reasoning. "I'm just worried about what would happen if I couldn't stop him."

"Right." Daisy pushed forward and pointed at me. "Let's get back to that. You did, actually, stop him? All by yourself?"

"She did." Bria nodded with a smile. "She's making strides. And let's remember, she also started it. That'll sink in soon. She's not quite there yet, but it'll happen."

"What'll sink in, that she is more dangerous than a Berserker?" Daisy asked. "Or that Soul Stealers have a worse reputation than Berserkers?"

I scowled at her. I couldn't think of anything else to do.

"Look..." Bria paused in order to open the front

door. "Today was a learning experience. For everyone. This won't be taken lightly, trust me. All of the guys will be thinking about how they could have handled it differently. Kieran definitely will be. He would lose his shit if anything happened to you. He coddles you far too much." She pursed her lips, and I knew it was because she thought I was an idiot for getting involved with him. "But no one—and I mean no one—will take a harder look at this than Thane. He's gone over three decades without a mishap. The guy might look like he's in his lesser thirties, but he's more like sixty. These bastards don't age normally. Thane will beat himself up for this. The very last thing he needs is for you to make him feel worse."

I opened my mouth, but what could I say? She was right on so many levels. I *had* caused the problem in the first place, and it *had* been a learning experience, albeit a terrifying one.

"Come on." She jerked her head at the door.

"Where are we going?" I asked in confusion. I looked down at my Burberry medium buckle tote, in pink, hanging from my forearm like it was on display.

"There is a bar close by, and I'm pissed I only recently found it." Bria jerked her head again. "Come on. I need a libation after that shit-show turned awesome situation. We can discuss what happened."

"You *would* want to hang out with a bunch of derelicts in a dive bar," Daisy muttered, refilling her glass.

Bria gave Daisy a gooey, Bambi-eyed smile. "You get me."

Daisy's eyebrows lowered. "Ugh."

Bria motioned me out of the house.

"Oh, it's you," Frank, my resident poltergeist, said from the middle of the walkway leading to my front door. His watery blue eyes shifted to Bria, narrowing as they did so. His gray comb-over didn't move in the small breeze.

A month ago my yard had been full of spirits who'd followed me home from a haunted house in the magical zone. If it hadn't been for Kieran, who could now see ghosts courtesy of our soul connection, they'd still be loitering on my lawn.

But one whipcrack of command from him, and most of them had found somewhere else to be. The rest had been hauled away by John, a very able-bodied spirit who hated Valens as much as we did.

The only one who'd stayed was Frank. He, for some reason I didn't want to think about (which likely had to do with my mother), thought of my house as a place of comfort. He wouldn't leave. Unfortunately.

"Why is she always hanging around?" Frank asked, staring at Bria.

"One could ask the same thing of you," I retorted.

"Is that Frank?" Bria asked, stepping onto the walkway. She was able to feel stronger spirits, but Frank wasn't one of them.

"If I've said it once, I've said it a hundred times: you don't need riffraff like her hanging around," Frank said, bracing his hands on his hips. "She's a bad sort, make no mistake."

"Yeah, it's Frank." I followed Bria down the walkway toward him.

"I have a lovely cadaver for you, Frank," Bria said with a wry grin. "A real nice one. You've always wanted to have a vagina, right? Didn't I hear Alexis say that? The breasts aren't there anymore, but you can always pretend."

Frank's expression soured. He backed away from us. "She's vulgar. Why do you hang out with such foul-mouthed women, Alexis? Think of what your mother would say."

"A vagina and breasts are parts of a woman's anatomy, Frank," I said dryly. "Fifty percent of the adult population has them. How is that vulgar?"

"Snatch. Now that's vulgar," Bria said. "Do you want a snatch, Frank? I'll stuff you into a body good and tight. That's why you hang around, isn't it? To be shoved back into the world of living in a different skin? How about a granny? Do you fancy coming back as a granny?"

"Wretched woman." Frank reached the sidewalk

and went left, which was, unfortunately for him, the way we were headed. "Repulsive. A skin, Alexis? Has this woman no respect for the dead? Well, I won't have it."

We turned his way and he sputtered, about-facing and walking faster.

"No, I will not," he muttered. "I will not tolerate such a woman."

He flickered and then disappeared, probably heading home to the house he had died in. Ms. Merlin, his roommate, unbeknownst to her, would not be pleased with the slamming doors and mysteriously opened cabinets. She was a crotchety old woman, though. They deserved each other.

"So that's why he always takes off when you're around," I marveled as we sauntered down the sidewalk. Shadows stretched across the cracked cement and leaned heavily against the run-down houses we passed. "I wondered."

"Spirits can sense what I am."

"Then they can surely sense what I am, too, but for some reason they choose to hang around."

"That's because you're nice to them. Stuff them in a cadaver or two, control them in a way they surely won't like, and watch them run." She hefted her backpack a little higher on her shoulder. "Been there, done that, don't wear the T-shirt." She glanced my way. "It got too old. My left nipple popped out through the hole."

It was impossible to tell whether she was joking.

"Where is Henry that he's getting all the intel from Valens's people?" I asked, thinking on our situation. Nervousness fluttered my belly, something that was happening a lot lately. "No one ever mentions what he's doing, exactly."

"He's here and there." She held up a hand in response to my eyeroll. "I'm not being evasive. The guy is all over the place. He's the only one of the Six that isn't extraordinary for his magic. Don't get me wrong, he's high in power, but he's a Reflector." She gave me a knowing look that I perfectly understood.

Reflectors could push a person's magic back on them. Sometimes that was extremely helpful, like if a Fire Elemental blasted a Reflector with fire. But when in combat with other magical beings, like a Shifter or probably a Berserker, it wasn't useful at all.

"Henry's skill lies in his ability to blend in to his surroundings," Bria went on. "He's been exploring the government building and the warehouses, making house calls to Valens's bed bunnies—you name it. Hell, he's been using those secret tunnels you found in Valens's house to eavesdrop. You remember those?"

How could I forget? I'd nearly plummeted off a ladder, and after listening to the live-in ghost bicker with his long-dead mistress, I'd almost welcomed it.

"He has a knack for charming information out of people," she continued, "and a real skill in being in the right place at the right time to overhear pertinent information. Valens and his people underestimate anyone they deem less powerful. They discount Henry for being a Reflector, so they hardly notice him hanging around. It's perfect."

"But he has no idea what the big plans are, and how Kieran fits into them?"

Bria ran her fingers through her hair, and for the first time I could remember, wariness crossed her features. "In short, no. No one has anything concrete. But I've heard the guys speculate, and what I've gathered is"—she glanced around at the empty street before lowering her voice—"Valens wants to make a play for more territory."

I let out the breath I'd been holding. "That's not news. And it's not abnormal. History is filled with rulers, magical and otherwise, trying to expand their empire."

"History is also filled with genocide." She gave me a sidelong glance. "What I've pieced together is, Valens wants all of San Francisco. *All* of San Francisco. He's pushing for legislation that repeals the Peace Accord Treaties."

My stomach didn't just flutter this time, it dropped out and rolled around on the ground. "So, in essence,

Valens wants the treaties stripped so he can essentially wipe out the non-magical population, without repercussions, in pursuit of their land?"

"Does that sound so far-fetched?"

A strange heaviness filled my middle. No, it did not. And Valens wouldn't just stop at the non-magical area. The dual-society zone would go right along with it. If Valens got his way, my little family would be ripped apart—and not just mine. No human would be safe, and considering his attitude toward low-level magical people, he'd probably go after them next.

"I don't know any of this for sure," Bria said, probably reading the rage and uncertainty on my face. "I've never heard so much of a peep about this from Kieran. It's just the guys speculating. But…"

"There's no way Valens could get those treaties revoked," I said with a rush of logic. "He has a lot of power here, and it has clearly gone to his head. In places like Los Angeles, where there aren't nearly as many magical people, the non-magical would easily reign. They'd wipe out the magical people in no time. Why would other rulers take that risk?"

"But the ruler of magical Los Angeles, a class four…" She stalled. "See? I don't even know what magic he has. He's a nobody. He has no power. And in the Magical Summits, when you have no power, you have no voice."

I shook my head, unable to believe this. "When magical people first revealed themselves, they had to fight for a place in society. The whole world was at war. History books describe it as a walking nightmare. For *everyone*. Those treaties were the only thing that restored some sense of order."

"But now magical people have their place carved out, and in some parts of the world, like here, they have enough power to take what they want."

I sniffed. "And he's under the impression Kieran would help with any of that?" I pointed to get her to cross the street.

She chuckled. "That's clearly a case of wishful thinking on Valens's part. He apparently thinks a child ends up the way a parent wants them to. Boy, could my mother set him straight on that one."

I shook my head. "He'll never get the repeal passed. There's no way. The world would go right back to war. Non-magicals still have nukes hidden on this planet somewhere, and if the magicals take over enough territory, they might use them. Desperation makes people do crazy things. He may be powerful, but he's just one Demigod. The others won't allow it."

"Except...he's gaining favor with a few power players. At the moment, the only thing really stopping him is a certain headstrong ruler from Sydney who has the lockdown on cockblocking. A lot of people are wary of

Valens, and just kinda…get out of the way. Or are made to. Not Dara. She politically gets in his face, and helps everyone else find their courage. If he were to remove Dara, say with a large army he was amassing…"

Bria's implication slammed into me. "If he took out Dara, he'd have more power than any other ruler in the Magical Summits."

"He certainly would. Factor in the other rulers who are already in his pocket, plus those who think like he does…"

"And we all get shit on in a big way," I mumbled, thinking of Daisy and what would happen to her. Of Mordecai, with no pack and no hope of finding one in this area. Of me, and my need to keep my power hidden. Of Kieran…

My worry peeled away slowly. I took a deep breath.

"But Kieran isn't under his control," I said with a surge of confidence I wasn't expecting. I smiled, warmth infusing me. "And he's not the type to just get out of the way."

Bria laughed as we turned the corner. "No, he is not, and boy-oh-boy will daddy dearest get a rude awakening. I hope someone gets Valens's face on camera when he finds out—I'd love to see his 'eating shit' expression. He'll blame Kieran's mom, too. You watch. He'll point a finger, bet you anything."

I opened my mouth to ask her about this army Valens was amassing, and whether we had a hope in hell of competing, but all the breath left my lungs in a whoosh.

There it was, up ahead, the exact same as always: Lucky Charmz, an Americanized Irish Bar with the unfortunate name of a sugary cereal. I hadn't visited since taking the job with Kieran. I supposed it was time, but the thought of walking through the doors gave me nervous flutters.

Miles, my ex-boyfriend, ran the place, and we had a long-standing, unspoken arrangement: he used his success to make me feel small, and I used his delusion to get free drinks.

For some reason, it just didn't feel right anymore. And it wasn't because I was making a bunch of money, either. I didn't mind handouts now any more than I ever had, especially from that yahoo. But the thought of getting drinks from a man I'd once been intimate with…didn't seem right now that I was intimate with someone else. Something about it tap-danced on my "not awesome" nerves.

Stupid morals.

We neared a small strip of buildings in what was probably the most run-down set of businesses in all of San Francisco. A brick wall rose up to the left, beyond the sand-swept clearing behind the houses, blocking off the magical zone. The rumble of a crashing wave drifted through air that carried the smell of sea foam. Someone groaned loudly from the gutter up the way.

"I found this place when I was out scouting the area," Bria said in an unneeded but fitting hush. She weaved between the cars lining the sidewalk, her gaze taking in each one. "Looks like a shit-hole. My kinda place. You'd be surprised how much people know in a shit-hole."

"Not this shit hole," I said, slowing as we neared the familiar worn door with the dull metal handle. "No one knows squat in this place, alive or dead."

She narrowed her eyes at me before yanking open the door. "How do you know?"

I gave her a dry look before forcing myself to cross the threshold. "It's four blocks from my house and I have no friends. Of *course* I know this bar."

The same stooped figures I'd committed to memory over the years lined the bar, some with beers in front of them, some without, all of them dead. I walked behind them, along a series of empty tables to my right, and rounded the bend to my usual seat at the end of the bar, next to the surliest Irishman I'd ever met in my life. He was a living resident, and his horrible attitude (which I found humorous) kept my seat vacant from the living and dead alike.

"Let me get this straight..." Bria's gaze roamed the row of what probably looked like empty seats—drunks didn't make for strong spirits—before darting to the pool table in the room at the back where anyone even remotely cool and/or normal gravitated. It was too early for the party crowd coming back from better bars to seek out their neighborhood dive, however, and the balls lay strewn carelessly across the green velvet. "You'll let me into your house to have a few drinks after a hard day, but I'm not a good enough friend to bond with over a speedball at your local dive bar?" She huffed over the imagined offense, her gaze sticking to Mick, who was hunched over his drink, leaning his forearms against the bar. If memory served, this pose meant it had been a long day of beer drinking, and he'd either head home shortly or tuck into the whiskey and fall asleep where he sat. Bets could be placed on this constant dilemma of his. "You think you know a person."

"I haven't been here since I've known you," I murmured, stopping behind my seat and putting my hand on the chair back. "Hey, Mick."

"Well, how's things?" he grunted, not looking over. I was the only person he ever said hi to. In his mind, I'd probably forced my friendship on him, and now he just had to roll with the punches.

"Jesus," Bria said, staring at him. "What's with the Irish Crypt Keeper?"

"He's a pillar of the community, what do you mean?" I edged around my seat before pulling it out to sit.

"The whole bar is open, and we're going to crowd into the corner?" Bria swung her gaze down the seats again before following my lead. An old man with a grizzly beard gave her the stink-eye before flickering and disappearing. "I find myself delighted and mystified by how odd you are, Alexis. Even here, in a place I should be infinitely more comfortable than you—since I've made dive bars my *thing* since I was twenty-two—you out-weird me. It's shocking."

I didn't see how dive bars and out-weirding someone fit together, but let it go.

Liam, an older bartender without a fuck left to give, made his slow way down to us.

"Here's what else I find shocking," Bria went on, resting her forearms on the bar like Mick was doing. "You're dressed in that expensive training gear Kieran bought you, with the glowing skin and shining eyes from all that fancy skin cream and good sex, and yet, you still fit into this place better than I do. I'm wearing a fucking dog collar. I should be the one who fits in here, not you."

"First, I think you are taking this too personally. Fitting in here isn't a good thing—"

"Fucking right it isn't," Mick muttered. "Shit hole."

"Second…practice," I said as Liam reached us. "Lots and lots of practice." I half smiled at the bartender.

"Guinness, please."

He stopped, turning his gaze to Bria, and waited.

"Jack and Coke," she supplied.

He started to turn, and guilt ate through me. I put up my finger. "I'll... I got... I'll pay," I muttered. "I'll pay for this, not Miles."

"Eh?" Liam squinted one eye at me. "You don't want to put this on Miles's tab?"

Bria touched my arm and leaned farther over the bar. "Who is Miles?"

"No, I'll..." I circled my finger in front of us before pointing at the Guinness tap down the bar. "I got it."

"We want to put it on Miles's tab," Bria rushed to say. "Put it on the tab, just like...normal?" She shot me a questioning glance.

Liam moved his finger back and forth in front of us. "Both?"

"No," I said, shaking my head. "No, I should—"

"Yes, both," Bria chirped. "Both of us. Miles and I go way back. Just like"—I got another questioning glance—"you guys?"

Liam nodded and continued to turn, making his slow way back down the bar.

"We shouldn't charge it," I said quietly. "We should pay."

Bria turned and rested her elbow on the bar, lowering her chin to her fist. Her eyes glittered with mirth.

"Well now...that depends. Who is Miles?"

"She rode the boss," Mick said in a series of grunts. "Liam, I'll have a shot of Jameson."

Bria's eyebrows lifted. "Rode...as in..."

"Shifted. Fucked. Buggered," Mick said. "Made a bad fuckin' mistake, at any rate."

"We dated," I said, my face flaming. "He had just bought this place when we started dating."

A slow smile curled Bria's lips. "You get free drinks...whenever you want...because you screwed the owner? And you didn't invite me here first thing?"

"He's a fuckin' *coont*," Mick said in his thick brogue. "Not worth the free drinks."

"Don't mind him," Liam said, reaching us with the Jack and Coke. The Guinness sat under the tap, resting. Liam hooked a thumb Mick's way. "He's a fan of the ol' gargles." He shook his thumb at his mouth and leaned back like he was drinking.

"I'm a fan of the ol' fecking whiskey." Mick spread his hands wide, growing surlier by the moment. "I'm dyin' of thirst. Any day, man."

Liam thinned his lips, the effect giving him a dimple on his right cheek, before turning back.

"Young man, young man, young man," Mick muttered, and though he'd randomly said it as long as I'd known him, I'd never figured out the context.

"Does Kieran know about this?" Bria asked, indicating the bar at large.

"Yes," I said, remembering when I'd first seen him in this bar. He'd done his homework.

"You don't…" Bria moved her finger back and forth above the bar. "You don't still bump uglies with the owner, right?"

"No." I huffed and smoothed my hair. "He's just an ex-boyfriend who wants to lord his good fortune over the harlot who broke up with him. These are pity drinks, as far as he's concerned."

"Oooooh." Bria grinned while nodding. "I get it. Because"—she leaned closer with a smirk—"Miles would be dead now if you were screwing both him and Kieran at the same time. Demigods don't like to share their prized possessions."

There was that word again. I scowled at her. "I'm no one's possession."

"Fuckin' right," Mick said.

Bria clucked her tongue. "I'll admit it. I can't believe Kieran knows you get free drinks from your ex and hasn't pitched a fit. What dimension am I living in? Is this an alternate reality? I even mentioned this bar to him! He must've known I'd drag you here, and he said nary a word." She huffed out a laugh. "I am tickled."

I opened my mouth for a rebuttal I hadn't quite thought of yet, but she held up her hand.

"No, no. Don't say anything. Just let me soak in the

shock for a moment. Somewhere, a pig is flapping its wings, taking to the sky. This is history, and I am witnessing it. Hark."

"What is she on about?" Mick asked, looking over.

"I haven't a clue." I took a sip of my Guinness, barely sparing a glance for the woman who'd just walked in and looked around. This was clearly her first time in the bar, and Narnia had turned out a bit different than she'd expected. I'd seen the same expression—unsure and a little disgusted—a million times.

Bria studied the new arrival. "What's her game? She's in the wrong place."

The new woman sat down at the other end of the bar and waited patiently for Liam to approach her. Her posture screamed confidence, from her slightly upturned chin to her glimmering eyes. Bria was right—this woman wasn't at home in dive bars. This woman expected people to do things for her, and do them quickly. I could see it in her soft scowl as she waited. In her tapping fingers as Liam took his sweet time. She was used to being kowtowed to by underlings.

So what was she doing wearing an outfit that wouldn't have looked out of place in my pre-Kieran wardrobe?

"Maybe she came here on business and is trying to dress like the clientele so as not to get mugged," I muttered, answering myself.

"Those clothes fit her too well," Bria said quietly, lowering her gaze to her drink. Something in her tone, plus the set of her suddenly stiff shoulders, set me on edge.

"How do clothes fit someone *too* well?" I asked, following her lead and lowering my gaze. "Some people are great shoppers."

"Cheap clothes are made to fit a wide range of body types. They're generic. That's why, before Kieran fixed you up, you always wore high-water pants and your tops looked like second-hand acquisitions from a circus. You have a pretty standard body for someone who's in moderately good shape, but you're an Amazon. Nothing on the racks fit you well, let alone perfectly.

"This woman's cheap-ass clothes mold to her body perfectly. Nothing is too loose, or too tight. Based on the size of those—very expensive—fake boobs, that is a damn miracle. No." Bria shook her head and upended her glass, draining it dry. "She had those cheap-ass clothes tailored to fit her body. Odd, right? She probably spent more on the seamstress than she did the clothes. Hello, sore thumb."

Surprised Bria had caught so much from a crappy outfit, I flicked my gaze back up, careful not to make eye contact or stare for too long. I didn't want the woman to know I was checking her out.

Her durable yellow cotton shirt cinched in at the

waist like on the mannequins in the stores. Except, as I'd learned the hard way many times, mannequins always have the excess material clipped in the back. The V-neck showed just enough cleavage of the woman's large, perky breasts to be sexy while still practical. And the color, one that should fade quickly in the wash, was still a vibrant yellow. Bria was absolutely right. There was no way a top like that would fit this well. I'd always looked like a square.

"Her slacks are the same way," Bria continued, staring at Liam as he picked his nail. "They end above cheap runners that will give her blisters if she intends on chasing us. Someone thinks we're idiots."

"Dressing the part…to chase us?"

"Yeah. Unless Mick has a big secret?" She glanced over at him.

"Feck off, that's my secret," he grumbled.

"That's no secret, bud. It's almost a shout." Bria jiggled the ice in her glass, attracting Liam's gaze. "She's here for us, I'd bet my next drink on it."

I licked my lips, fear tickling my gut. None of Kieran's spies had heard a peep about the ghosts we'd freed—or the missing employees who'd kept them prisoner—since. But only a fool would think Valens hadn't noticed. The silence was deafening.

"But still," I said in a hush, lowering my gaze again, "maybe she's just trying to fit in so she doesn't get mugged."

"What's her magic level?" Bria asked, spinning ice cubes around her tumbler. Liam headed off to make a new one.

I bowed my head and closed my eyes for a brief moment, tapping into the ability I'd picked up from magically connecting souls with Kieran. Immediately, I felt the pulse of the woman's magic. Strong and sure, fairly powerful—a solid class four or a little less. Not as strong as Bria, who was a class five, but strong. I said as much.

Bria nodded, accepting another drink from Liam. "What bullshit." She took a large gulp. "I wanted to spend some quality time in here, getting hammered."

"What do you think she does?" I asked quietly, hesitant to drink any more. If I needed to react quickly, alcohol would make things difficult.

"Spy."

I started at hearing Mick's raspy voice.

He reached for his whiskey. "She thinks we're daft." His lip curled into a snarl as he lifted the whiskey to his mouth. "She works for Valens. Should have his bollocks cut off, *duh coont.*"

Sometimes it didn't even sound like English.

"Do you know her?" That was the last thing I'd expected to come out of him. The absolute last.

"No, I don't fecking know her." His spit pummeled

my face. "Don't need to. You seen one, you seen 'em all." Mick shot back his whiskey and slammed the glass down on the bar. "Ahhhhh," he said, much too loudly, while looking aggressively at the woman down the way.

"We're going to be great friends," Bria said with a smile.

The woman's eyes darted up at the noise, and stalled on Mick's hostile-eyed stare. Her jaw set, and I could see her weighing and measuring her opponent. The Six did it all the time—even Mordecai and Daisy were starting to do it. No question about it. This was no civilian.

Her gaze flicked to us, hitting me for a fraction of a second before lingering on Bria. She then jerked her gaze down to her drink, slumping her shoulders as if submitting.

"It's me she is interested in," Bria said quietly, finishing her second drink in record time. "Let's see if she'll follow me. Come on, Alexis, drink up. Let's reel in this fish."

Chapter 4

VALENS

"Sir, I have eyes on the subject," Flara said through the cellphone in a sultry voice.

With the phone against his ear, Valens glanced at his son, sitting across the expansive living room with his gaze rooted to the smear of vibrant colors streaking the evening sky through the darkening window.

"Oh yes?" Valens said, pushing up from his seat. The movement drew Kieran's notice, a slight question in the depths of his eyes.

Despite Valens's best efforts, the boy had turned out more like his mother. He dallied around all day setting up government aid for the sick and the poor, people who had no place in Valens's city. He was even organizing a magical fair, of all things, dragging him into the squalor of the dual-society zone. If it wouldn't severely strain their already tense relationship, Valens would have ended that accursed fair and demanded his son stay in the magical zone where he belonged, learning the ropes of government. He had plans for the boy.

Valens made a light gesture with his hand, indicating the call was nothing, before retiring to his library. He had been about ready to make the move anyway.

"And where is that?" he said into the receiver as he climbed the stairs.

"The Necromancer is in a decrepit bar in the dual-society zone near the ocean."

"Decrepit goes without saying in that waste of an area," he murmured, stalling the conversation until he could sequester himself in his library. His son never ventured very far into this room. His disgust for Valens's hunting conquests was plain, though that was probably because his son didn't understand the cunning and endurance required to bring down some of these beasts. A manticore, for example, was a formidable foe. The creature had nearly taken Valens's skin.

Or maybe it was another example of his son's weak constitution.

Right now, Valens's allies were giving Kieran a pass. They were letting the boy breathe to mourn his mother. Soon, however, they'd start to wonder if Kieran was hard enough to take Sydney. They'd wonder if Valens could execute his plans for expansion with his son as his partner.

Valens was starting to wonder that himself.

In another few months, Valens would be forced to give his son an ultimatum, one with possibly devastating consequences for both of them: continue the family business, or you will cease to be useful. He had not spent his life creating an empire to see his wife's weak blood ruin his efforts. She'd weakened him once—he would be damned if he allowed her to do it again from beyond the grave.

Valens walked around his desk, checking the doorway to make sure Kieran hadn't followed him, and then sat in his chair.

"Who is she there with?" Valens asked Flara. He'd chosen her for this lowbrow task because she was decent at blending in, powerful enough to hold her own, and rarely, if ever, professionally engaged. He didn't like his bedmates bruised. Her greatest asset came when she spread her legs. Not to mention all of his elite staff were assigned to higher level duties, at present, getting his complex plans into action.

"She showed up at the bar with a female in her mid-twenties, and they sat next to an older man with a staring problem. The older man is a drunk and is trying to pick a fight."

"Ignore him. The other female—do you recognize her?"

"No, but I've had the team run her face. She's a lower-level Ghost Whisperer living in the dual-society zone. She's a nobody."

Valens clenched his fist and leaned against the

dragon scale desk. A desk he'd commissioned after stalking and killing one of the most fearsome creatures in the magical wild. It was said that a man who could take down a dragon could do anything. But here he was, nearly two months after his employees had disappeared, and he still had no clue who'd done it, or why.

They'd already ruled out a crime of passion. The complete lack of evidence indicated a cool head. The bodies hadn't turned up, and there was no sign of foul play.

It had to be someone with access to the government building. The security footage had been expertly manipulated. Three hours had been cut out, and footage from a different day with the same time stamps had been spliced in. His team had nearly missed the anomaly. The security booth was rarely empty, but this person had managed to get in unnoticed, which spoke of someone with access codes and familiarity. And yet, all the checks had come up clear.

How had the perpetrator even known what those particular employees did? There had been rumors of them calling ghosts, but he'd kept a tight lid on their true function. Not even all of his Elite knew about the spirit trappers. He'd grilled those who did know mercilessly, enough to feel confident they hadn't let the information slip. Someone must've figured it out for themselves.

The Necromancer—Bria Stevens—was a strong class five who couldn't keep a job. She had a problem with authority and a penchant for unlawful behavior. She bounced from place to place, living in squalor and dressing like an inmate. No one with any pride would hire her.

Or would they?

She was the only stranger in his territory with the right sort of magic.

"That Ghost Whisperer," he said, thinking through this new information, "what is her power level?"

"The file says she's a class two."

He leaned hard on his desk, frustration eating at him. A Ghost Whisperer, even a powerful one, didn't have enough tools for something like this. Their skillset as a whole was lackluster. Mostly worthless.

"She is dressed well," Flara went on, "but she doesn't wear the clothes like she was born to them. She's pretty—she's probably someone's plaything."

He fisted his hand. His staff had been incredibly incompetent of late. He was starting to lose his patience. If it got out that someone had killed two people under his protection without him having a clue how, or even why, it would undermine his position in the magical hierarchy. Add in his wimpish son, who had the power, but not the blood, of a Demigod, and he'd be subject to ridicule.

Ridicule was unacceptable at any time, more so considering what he was planning.

"Follow the Necromancer," he ground out. "Find out where she goes—who she speaks to. Whoever put this together is higher level, but the fastest way to find that person is to lean heavily on the staff."

"Yes, sir," Flara said, her purr getting under his skin.

"And come here when you're finished. I have a need for you."

"Yes, sir," she said in a breathy whisper.

He tapped his phone off and tossed it across the desk. He'd ride her hard tonight. Hell, maybe he'd just break her and toss her aside. He needed to relieve his frustrations.

His mind turned back to that Necromancer. What other lead did he have? She was the only logical choice, especially since she clearly wasn't trying to fit into his magical society. Only crooks and derelicts hung out in the dual-society zone. She had secrets.

And after he got her in front of his highly experienced torturer, he'd pry out each of those secrets until he found one he could use.

Chapter 5

ALEXIS

"THE MOST IMPORTANT thing is not to freak out," Bria said, finishing off her fourth Jack and Coke. She'd been shotgunning them in anticipation of being followed. The woman had no sense of self-preservation. "The second most important thing is not to let her know we're on to her. Which might be a little difficult, since your Green Isles friend over there has been staring the shit out of her face."

"Good, yeah, get nice and drunk before we have to fight for our lives. Great call." I wiped a sheen of perspiration off my forehead.

I took a deep breath as the woman with the yellow shirt settled on her bar stool. She'd just come back from having a smoke, and she had the pristine soft pack and a box of matches to prove it.

Mick huffed and took a sip of his whiskey. "They sell lighters right there on the counter when you're buying the pack of smokes," he muttered. "Buy the fuckin' lighter, girl."

Yes. I'd had the same thought. Say a smoker lost their lighter—they'd probably have a few matchbooks swiped from random establishments. They wouldn't carry around a small box of camping matches from the grocery store. How weird was that?

"She must've just checked in with her boss," Bria said, reading my mind.

I chewed my lip nervously. "Who do you think her boss is?"

"If we're lucky?" Bria picked up her empty glass, frowned at it, and set it back down. "Some thug-nobody who thinks I stole his grandma's carcass."

"Why would someone think—"

"Been there, done that," Bria interrupted. "I mean, the lady was way across the Line. What did she need with her body? I have no idea what he'd be so worked up about."

Mick laughed, his body shaking with each loud "Ha!" He slapped the bar before picking up his whiskey. "To your granny's unneeded corpse." He took a gulp.

Bria hooked a thumb Mick's way. "That guy gets it."

"Okay…so if it isn't a thug-nobody who's rightly pissed that you stole his nana's dead body, then what?" I pushed wisps of hair out of my face. "Who do you think sent her?"

Bria frowned at me, silently calling me an idiot. "Why, Valens, of course. Zorn figured I'd be the first target. Who else would he suspect?"

"Kieran, for a start," I whispered.

"Well yes, him, but for some reason, Valens hasn't latched on to Kieran's rock-solid motive. I haven't a clue why, because—"

"Here's the thing about drink," Mick began as the bar door swung open. "You get louder the more you drink. Drink enough, and you roar your business down the bar."

Bria ticked a finger at him, tapping the air. "Noted, Senator. Good looking out."

A man walked in, his dark brown hair cut short and his deep-set eyes cloaked in long black lashes. He scanned the bar quickly, and I groaned and sank in my seat.

"Hello, sir," Bria said softly as she eyed the newcomer. She sat up a little straighter.

"Miserable *coont*," Mick grumbled.

"Of all the nights for Miles to drop by," I muttered.

Miles spied me and his eyes sparkled in recognition. He started our way.

"Just once would he not come over to gloat?" I said quietly. "I've got enough problems."

"He's not coming to gloat," Bria whispered out of the side of her mouth. "He's still into you."

"No, he isn't. You'll see," I said in annoyance.

He stopped next to Bria, leaning against an older

gentleman who'd barely moved all night. Hell, he probably hadn't moved for decades.

"Alexis, great seeing you. I haven't seen you in a while," Miles said, then glanced down at his exposed forearms. Goosebumps covered his skin. He no doubt felt the spirit he was crowding. "What have you been up to?"

A shit-eating grin lifted Bria's cheeks. "Hey, Miles," she said, sparing a glance for the woman across the bar, who hadn't so much as taken out her phone to pass the time. She stared down at her hands, clearly listening in. Someone hadn't paid attention at spy school. "How's it going? Remember me?"

Miles frowned, taking in Bria. His gaze flicked to the chain dog collar around her neck, her spike bracelet, and then her Led Zeppelin T-shirt. When he shifted, it was slightly away.

"Uhhm…" he faltered.

She put her hand to her chest. "Bria. Remember? We went out for a slice a while back, then went back to your place." She lowered her volume and leaned closer to him. He leaned back. "The fuzzy pink handcuffs and the nipple clamps, remember?" She chuckled softly. "That was a wild time. I wasn't sure about the strap on, but you seemed to like it. You still into all that?"

His face paled and his jaw went slack. He stared at her with wide eyes and shook his head quickly. "Wasn't me," he said, knocked firmly off of his high horse.

Despite the situation with the spy, I couldn't help a grin.

"Oh no?" Bria feigned confusion and blinked down at her empty glass. "You sure? I could've sworn I took you to task with a bullwhip. The dirty sock gag was weird, but your scream was so high-pitched that I didn't mind muffling it. That wasn't you?"

"Anyway, Miles, we were just leaving," I said, pushing Bria's empty glass to the edge of the bar.

The haughty expression I knew so well crossed his expression. He noticed my clothes. "Trying to move up in the world, Alexis?" His gaze darted to my drink, then the bare bar surface in front of it. It was a cash-only bar, and everyone usually left their pile of money within easy reach for Liam. The fact that I didn't have any cash out meant I'd used Miles's generosity. Again.

For the very first time, his triumphant smile annoyed me.

"Found someone who will dress you up, but he won't give you a little spending money, huh?" He tsked, leaning his elbow against the bar, settling in. "Pity."

Suddenly, this was all very, *very* irritating. It rankled, even. I wasn't poor anymore. I wasn't a nobody. Sure, I didn't really know how to use my magic, but at least I had some. Kieran might've gifted me the clothes (sorta), but I worked my ass off for my paycheck. I'd freed his mother's ghost, for cripes' sake, and dozens of others. I trained constantly. I confronted my fears. I'd even forced the world's most controlled Berserker to lose control, and then made him cry uncle.

I was no longer the muck layering the crack between the societies. I was a training fighter, ready to do my part and topple the magical dictator of San Francisco. I deserved a helluva lot more than this dickface clown talking down to me.

I dug my hand into my expensive handbag and pulled out my cheap wallet. "Liam, what's the tab? I'll take care of it now. We're leaving."

Liam started, and Miles huffed in condescension. I nearly held my breath, praying Liam wouldn't remind me of our earlier conversation. A moment later, thank all that was holy, Liam pushed forward and headed toward the till where he'd written down our drink orders.

"It's fine," Miles said smugly. "You don't need to prove anything to me, Alexis. I know the score."

Anger burned through me, urging me to defend myself, but I didn't want to attract attention from the woman across the bar. Bria cut out the need.

"Hog-tied." She snapped. "It was definitely you, Miles. Remember? You asked to be hog-tied and pegged? I didn't know what 'pegged' meant at the time, but then you explained about the strap on." She laughed. "My eyes were opened that night, I'll tell you that much. What a lunatic."

"Jay-sus," Mick muttered.

"Too much for me, though." Bria pushed away from the bar and swung her legs off of the stool. "Too much."

"Twenty," Liam said, starting over.

Miles stood there, frozen and red-faced, staring incredulously at Bria.

Chuckling, I took out some bills. That amount was much too low for all Bria had drunk, but I wasn't going to stand around and argue. Maybe Liam enjoyed seeing his boss taken down a peg.

"Is mine twenty, too?" Mick asked, shakily standing from his stool. He dug his hand into his pocket before bumping against the wall.

"Thirty-two," Liam said without reflection. Apparently, he just called out arbitrary numbers.

"Well, Miles, it was great catching up," Bria said, standing behind her stool. "I hope the burns from the candlewax healed up okay."

"A-Alexis, come on." Miles ran a hand down his face, trying to ignore Bria and get his bearings. He had his work cut out for him. "You don't need to leave in a huff. Just because you had a couple drinks a while back with Dem—"

I magically punched through his middle, smacking his spirit box to keep him from saying Kieran's name. I should've known he'd bring it up. He was probably jealous to no end.

Miles jerked hard and fell against the bar. His face lost the rest of its color and his expression closed down into terror as he grabbed his chest. "Help!" he bleated. "Help me!"

"Holy—" Bria grabbed him around his chest and wrestled him onto the stool. Mick paused for a moment with a wad of crumpled-up bills in his hand. The very disgruntled old man ghost dissipated with a scowl. "You okay, man?" Bria asked. "What happened?"

"My…" He scratched at his chest. "I think I'm having a heart attack. Call… Call someone."

"Just let it take you," Mick said, laying out a couple green balls of money. "Go with it. It'll hurt less."

"Would you stop?" I asked Mick, unable to hide a smile.

"It's probably a panic attack. You're fine." Bria patted Miles's back and stepped away. "C'mon, Mick, we'll walk you home. Power in numbers. We wouldn't want the little beasties of life to get us."

"Shut up," I seethed through gritted teeth, shoving Bria toward the door. This whole situation was spiraling out of control. The woman would know we were on to her for sure. "Just go."

I gingerly left my money on the counter, including a generous tip, before tucking my wallet back into my handbag and following Bria.

The woman at the end of the bar touched her cross-body bag as the bar door swung open. I held my breath, only to let it out again when a crew of barely legal guys and girls tramped in. Laughter and noise quickly filled the bar to bursting. The group of ten stumbled toward the bar, already drunk before seven in the evening. It would be a messy night. Thankfully, I wouldn't be a part of it.

"Hold on," Mick said, rolling a few more dollar balls onto the bar's surface.

"This night keeps getting weirder," I muttered as I glanced back at him. Since when did he leave before having his fill of whiskey, followed by a nap on the counter? And since when did he accept someone's offer to walk him home?

When I stepped outside, the cool air and soft crush of the distant waves welcomed me, coating me in comfort. I'd always liked the sound of the sea, but after bumping souls with Kieran, it downright sang to me. I wanted to frolic in the waves and dive down into the mysterious depths.

"Why'd you sucker punch Miles?" Bria asked, stepping to the side and waiting for our drunken escort.

"I'm pretty sure he was about to say that I'd had a couple drinks with Kieran. Which I did."

"Ah." She nodded before bending over her phone.

"Good reaction, then."

"Miles really took that hard," I whispered, thinking back. "I only used a sliver of magic, and he nearly collapsed."

"We keep trying to tell you—your magic is startling. It's arresting. The first impulse is to curl up in a tight ball and protect your middle. Even your overprotective lover feels that way, and he's at the pinnacle of power."

The door swung open and Bria braced herself, hands at her sides, probably ready to dip down and grab the knife out of her ankle brace. If the woman had followed us out this quickly, we were looking at a fight.

Chapter 6

ALEXIS

L IKE FRANKENSTEIN'S MONSTER, Mick took a hard step on shaky legs, lumbering out into the encroaching night. A loud exhale deflated my lungs.

"I thought you'd never get out of there," Bria said, starting forward. "I was about to leave you behind."

"Had to dig out those last two dollars," Mick grumbled. "Those Kerry men are as tight... If the Titanic were that tight, it wouldn't've gone down, boy! They're that feckin' tight, boy."

I knew he meant tight-fisted. Clearly the huge discount he had already gotten wasn't enough. He'd wanted to stop at paying thirty.

I pushed it out of my mind as we crossed the street, hurrying in front of an approaching car. This was the moment of truth. We'd left the bar, and we were moving slow. It would be easy for the woman to follow us, and just as easy for her to catch up and engage. I was pretty sure we could take her, but what if she had left the bar earlier to organize reinforcements?

A horn blared, making me jump. I turned around just in time to see Mick stagger out of the way of the oncoming car, nearly clipped by the bumper. "Ah, ya cheeky fucker, ya," he mumbled before pinging off the front of one parked car and then the back of another.

He stepped up onto the curb but hadn't lifted his foot high enough. His toe hit cement and his weight pitched forward. He slammed into a parking meter.

"Ya feckin' ol' bag!" he hollered. I wasn't sure if he knew he'd hit an inanimate object.

Bria laughed as I caught movement near the bar.

The door slowly swung shut. There wasn't a soul in sight, though there was one on my radar. Whoever had just walked out had slipped into the shadows at the side of the building.

"She's out," I whispered. "I can't be sure it's actually her, but who else would it be?"

"It's her," Bria said quietly before stubbing her toe and jogging forward to catch her weight. "She nursed that one beer the whole time while listening into our conversation. If it's Valens, he must be grasping at straws. Clearly he sent a lackey."

"She's powerful, though."

"I don't know what her day job is, but it ain't spyin'."

The soul moved, coming up the other side of the street. I barely kept from looking.

"We're being followed," I said, my mouth going dry.

"Okie dokie." Bria rubbed her hands together as Mick finally caught up to us. "Her efforts are laughable, but being a target is interesting, at least, so let's not look a gift horse in the mouth."

"Why can't you take anything seriously?" I muttered as my heart sped up.

"Are you kidding? I could write a book on this. It would be called *So, you're being followed.* Sub-title: *Tips and tricks to keep you alive.*"

Mick snickered.

"First thing is," she said, "and this goes doubly for you, Lexi, because Mick is much too drunk to be afraid—don't panic."

"Working on it," I said. My stomach flipped over. "Crap, I never got a chance to text Kieran."

"Second thing is, figure out who the primary target is."

"'S you," Mick slurred. "She kept lookin' at ya. Worst spy I've ever seen, boy."

"*Shhhh,*" I said, making a shut-the-hell-up gesture with my hand.

"What?" he asked, his voice ringing out across the quiet street.

"Third thing is, figure out how the primary target should engage."

"I thought you said not to engage," I said, monitoring the soul across the street. The woman was a ways behind us, keeping our slow pace instead of overtaking us. Given the distance, I doubted she could hear anything other than Mick's random shouts.

"I'm pretty sure I said not to freak out. I really don't remember saying anything about not engaging. If you'd contacted that lover of yours, then we'd know for sure. As it is, I'll have to make an educated guess."

"No, no." I pulled out my phone. "I'll text him right now. See look: spy came to the bar. She's now following—"

"It's good. I got this." Bria rolled her shoulders and veered around a sidewalk sign a business had left out.

"Liquid courage," Mick said. "Just tell me where the—what da *fuck*?"

A loud crash made me whip around, just in time to see a fallen Mick pulling the sidewalk sign down on top of him. He lashed out, swinging a wild fist, missing the object directly above him.

"Good call, waiting for him," I said, risking a glance at the other side of the street.

A flicker of movement caught my eye, but I didn't dare look harder. I could feel her there, waiting. Watching.

"Let's get moving," I murmured.

"Yup." Bria ripped the sidewalk sign away from Mick and put out her hand to pull him up. "Let's split up."

"Terrible idea," I said, my thumbs flying across the screen of my phone. "You've had a lot to drink. You'll make poor decisions."

"I had a lot to drink so I *wouldn't* make poor decisions, actually. It'll muddle my cat-like reflexes. Now I'm down to her level while pleasantly buzzed. It could be worse."

The person moved, creeping a little closer. Nearly within earshot. "Where do you live, Mick?" I asked a little louder than necessary.

Bria cocked her head, clearly picking up on my signal. She closed her eyes for a brief moment, then shrugged. "Still can't feel her," she whispered.

Dawning understanding made my thumbs still. "Would she know a class-five Necromancer's range for feeling souls?"

Bria's eyes narrowed as Mick struggled to his feet. "Probably," she said. "Even a useless spy or assassin would know that much. Zorn can mark the distance to within half a foot. She's probably just gauging a rough estimate, if she's thinking of it at all." Bria clapped Mick on the back and raised her voice. "All right, buddy, which way are you going? I'll escort you home and make sure no sidewalk signs mug you."

"Feck off," Mick muttered, staggering on.

"Head home," Bria said to me quietly, her body loose but her eyes tight. It was as though all the alcohol had magically evaporated from her system. "I am ninety-nine percent sure I'm the target. You should be fine. If any muggers or rapists come out of the wood-works, kill them. In this part of the world, no one will care. But if I'm wrong, and she goes after you, com-municate through text only. If she tries to engage, run like hell. Don't use your magic with her if at all possible. If you do have to use your magic, aim to kill. Do you understand?"

"I don't know how to kill with my magic," I said, tremors running through me.

She smiled. "I have a feeling you'll figure it out. Worst case, eye gouge and take off. Just get home safe. If something happens to you, nothing in the world will protect me from your overbearing boyfriend."

"What about you?"

"Come the fuck on," Mick shouted, swerving from side to side on the sidewalk up ahead before stopping and turning back.

Bria chuckled. "I train with Zorn. That bitch ain't got nothin' on me." Her expression turned serious again. "Just keep *you* safe, okay? Kieran will probably send the brigade to scoop you up. I'll text you when I'm...where I end up."

"Ew. It better not be in Mick's bed."

Her expression soured. "Good God, Alexis, what is wrong with you?" She shook her head before jogging after Mick.

It was a fair question. That had been a pretty gross

thought.

"You didn't need to stop," I heard her say when she reached him. "You go as far side to side as you do forward. I could give you a half hour head start and still beat you home."

"I'm getting my exercise," he grumbled as they turned the corner.

I hurried past them, crossing the street and slipping into a patch of darkness on the other side. Their voices trailed away into the night. A car motor revved somewhere ahead. Behind, a shoe scuffed the sidewalk.

I chanced a quick look back. The dim light fell across the woman's yellow shirt as she hurried diagonally across the street. An unlit cigarette stuck out between two fingers. Her prop was at the ready should she be noticed.

I lurched forward, walking quickly, putting distance between us. I needn't have bothered.

After stalling briefly to take a look around the corner, the woman slipped after Bria and Mick.

The hush of the late evening wrapped around me. Someone called out in the distance, disturbing the quiet, before the distant crash of the waves invaded the scene once again.

I opened up a little to the Line, then expanded my magic as far as it would go. People sat in houses, going about their lives. A few spirits wandered around, and one sat in an upstairs bedroom. No one else was waiting to intercept me. Bria had, as expected, been the target.

The soft sting of guilt prickled my conscience.

If anything happened to Bria, I would never forgive myself. I was the one who'd released the spirits, after all, not her.

My phone vibrated in my hand.

Kieran: *Where are you?*

I bent to my screen.

Me: *Three blocks from home. The woman went after Bria. Bria needs to know what you want her to do.*

Kieran: *Zorn is handling that. Jack will pick you up. Get to a hiding place.*

I rolled my eyes and slipped the phone into my pocket. Truth be told, I did like having someone look after me. It was a nice change from always having to look after myself and others. Someone cared about what happened to me, and it gave me a warm, happy feeling in my middle.

But there was a big difference between looking after me, and thinking I needed rescuing all the time. Ever the knight, Kieran did not see that distinction.

My phone vibrated again.

Bria: *I figured out why Kieran didn't stop you from going to that bar.*

I blinked at the text for a moment before replying. *Why the hell are you texting? What's going on with the woman?*

> **Bria:** *I'm walking in zigzags like I'm drunk. I've taken three wrong turns so far. The so-called spy has shitty shoes, remember? I'm going to make her feel it before Zorn gets here and forces me to stop.*

My pricks of guilt evaporated.
My phone vibrated again.

> **Bria:** *Kieran wanted you to put Miles in his place. He wanted you to pick a side. Him.*

I opened my mouth for no real reason. The deepening night welcomed me, throbbing all around. I was still drawing power from the Line, just in case, and I could feel it slithering in the darkness and filling up the cracks.

> **Bria:** *He must've known you would push back eventually. That guy Miles was hot, but a real dick. He was trying to make you feel like dirt so you'd beg for a compliment. Joke is on him.*

I frowned at the phone. I had never gotten that sense at all. Nor had I ever felt like dirt.

> **Bria:** *I can't think of any other reason Kieran would refrain from interfering. That's not his MO.*
>
> **Bria:** *It must have driven him nuts, knowing that*

another man was providing for you. But he left you to handle it. The dude trusts you, yo. That's cool. Don't tell anyone I said so.

Bria: *This bitch is looouuuuddd. You got any Jack Daniels left? I'm walking off my buzz.*

The texts stopped for a moment, and I realized I'd also stopped, too engrossed in her rapid-fire delivery to keep walking. She was clearly not someone who should be put in a potentially dangerous situation without a clear plan of attack. She was like a dog chasing its tail.

I started forward again, readying my thumbs to text back, though I had no idea where to start, when yet another came in.

Bria: *Zorn is on scene. He's shadowing me. Close, too. So close I can smell his deodorant.*

Bria: *He smells so good. I love that smell. Spicy and warm, like pumpkin spice in the fall.*

A soul bleeped onto my radar, moving slowly. Almost at the same time, a car rolling down the street caught my awareness. Headlights off, the streetlight's glow slid across the top of dark blue paint. The wheels turned slowly, giving the driver plenty of time to scout the sidewalks.

My chest filled with ice. Maybe I should've hidden after all. Kieran often knew things I didn't.

Without thinking, I opened myself further to the

Line, debating whether or not to make a break for it. But honestly, while standing in this dark pocket, movement would be worse than just standing still.

Then again, I'd never been very good at the spy game.

My phone vibrated again, but I ignored it.

A slight breeze ruffled my hair before fluttering my soul. Magic pulsed around me, flowing through the grass and crawling across the concrete. It was as beautiful as it was strange, a comforting nightmare. I could barely focus on the car, although the flare of red taillights indicated the driver had seen me. That couldn't be good. I knew I should run.

But my legs wouldn't move.

I could feel the world beyond the Line, a place without dimension. I felt both like I was in a trance and like I was completely lucid for the first time. Shades of bright violet and blue fizzled through the night, outlining houses and seeping into the cracks in the sidewalk. My soul fluttered again as power built around me.

Spirit was everywhere.

I had no idea what to do with it.

"What in the bloody hell are you doing?" Jack stepped out of an old Toyota I'd never seen before. He still hadn't flicked on the headlights. Oh. "Get off the sidewalk and get in the car, you whack job. Do you want the neighbors calling the cops?"

Chapter 7

KIERAN

K IERAN WAITED IN the front living room, looking out the window at the black beyond, trying desperately to focus. A million things needed his attention. The hard numbers were coming in regarding his forces, and his numbers were sorely lacking compared to his father's. Valens wasn't a well-liked man, but he knew where to spend his money and the widespread fear he cultivated served him well. Few people were brave enough to stand up to him.

Then there was the issue of transportation. Kieran needed to move large quantities of people at possibly a moment's notice. That would require vehicles on call. But a single person purchasing a fleet of buses or vans would be noticed, not to mention he'd need a warehouse to store them all in. He had to figure out the best way to camouflage his actions.

The ocean was another problem. A Demigod grew in power the longer they lived. Though Kieran and his father were both immortal, Kieran was practically a baby in comparison—Valens had been alive for centuries. One on one, his father would almost surely beat him. Age had made Valens stronger in Poseidon's magic. Faster. More adaptable. He did things on their "leisurely" swims that widened Kieran's eyes. Kieran had a lot to learn, and through micro-aggressions and power plays, his father loved to remind him of that fact. If at all possible, he needed to stay on land. That, or he needed to post people in the ocean.

He massaged his temples. A million things needed his attention, but his mind kept slipping back to one.

He tapped his fingers against the arm of the chair.

For one heart-stopping moment earlier, when he'd read Alexis's text incorrectly, he'd thought his father had sent someone after *her*. That she was the target.

Fear such as he'd never experienced had deluged him, and he'd nearly jumped up and run for the door. It would've been rash beyond belief. She could've easily protected herself against minor threats, and if the spy had taken her into custody, he could have devised a plan to get her back.

But where Alexis was concerned, he lost all sense of logic. All reason. Nothing else mattered—not his duty or his vengeance. Just her.

The bell chimed, pushing him out of his reverie. Sodge, his father's ancient butler, who would probably rather go to bed than stay up to take care of his master's disappointment of a son, was surely on his way to let Zorn in.

Sure enough, a few minutes later Sodge slowly walked into the room, his loose jowls shaking and his lips slightly turned down. Zorn followed.

"Sir," Sodge said, his tone flat. "Master Zorn is here to see you."

"Yes, thank you, Sodge. That'll be all."

"Of course, sir." Sodge turned, paused for a moment, then left the room. He was an odd one, and would surely be delighted when Kieran was out of the house for good. So would Kieran.

"Sir," Zorn said, staying where he was.

Kieran rose from the cream-colored chair. "Let's speak outside."

He led the way to the double doors that opened out onto the back deck. The moonlight shone down, highlighting the dark waters of the ocean far below. The salty breeze ruffled his hair and sang to his heart, asking him to dive down deep and swim until he forgot all his woes.

If only that were possible.

Before Zorn could speak, he altered the winds and the violence of the ocean below. Any words loud enough to be overheard would be whisked out to sea. Not that his father or Sodge would concern themselves with him. They both thought he was useless.

"News?" Kieran asked.

"Nothing new from our efforts, assuming you read Henry's last report about Valens's spies in the non-magical government?"

He nodded. Yes, he certainly had. Over a dozen of his father's people had infiltrated all levels of the non-magical San Francisco government, one as high as an advisor. Had the mayor decided to fall in league with Kieran, that advisor would've been in on the ground floor. Kieran's battle would've been over before it had begun.

His father excelled at the long game. For years, he'd been weakening the non-magical sector of San Francis-co from the inside out. His spies in the government reported any shortcomings to him, so he always knew when to step in with aid. In the guise of keeping the region strong, he had skillfully created a dependency. One day, all he'd have to do was pull away the aid, and the non-magical government would come tumbling down.

The man had absolutely earned his cunning reputa-tion. His strategy was just shy of brilliant. His spies were everywhere.

If Kieran hoped to take him down, he could make no mistakes.

"I assume your father is otherwise engaged?" Zorn asked as he lowered onto the patio couch.

"Yes. He's having someone over tonight. He asked Sodge to ready the...party room. He'll be in his bathroom, freshening up."

The party room was basically a sex room with good air freshener and regular cleanings. It was the only room in the house Kieran had never entered.

He expected Zorn to say something about the woman who'd followed Alex and Bria from the bar. Instead, he straightened his spine and said, "The results from the test came in. I got a call right before I had to go bag Bria."

After discovering Alexis's true magic, which meant she could only be the child of a Demigod in Hades's line, they'd taken a DNA sample from her to discern which of the three Demigods had fathered her, a large undertaking since they didn't want anyone to know of her existence. They'd had to make a lot of new friends, many of whom had not been cheaply bought.

"Who is it?" Kieran asked.

"Our worst nightmare. Magnus."

The breath left Kieran's lungs in a whoosh.

Magnus came from a time when the norm was for children of Demigods to rise up and attempt to tear their fathers down. That was, of course, Kieran's goal, but he was after good, old-fashioned revenge rather than power and territory. Magnus thought he could prevent any such uprisings by killing his offspring. And so far, he hadn't been wrong, which was why he'd never changed his stance. Have his baby, and he'd kill the kid. Everyone knew the stakes, and because of that, he had remained child-free for decades.

Crazy didn't just go away.

"You're sure?" Kieran asked quietly.

"Positive." Zorn paused. "What are you going to do?"

Kieran shook his head. "He doesn't know about her. I'll need to keep it that way."

"You can't keep her from this fight. You know that. And when she opens up and uses her magic, everyone will take notice. Everyone. In the world."

Kieran leaned forward against the wood railing. "I can force her to hide."

"Like your father did your mother?"

Rage blistered through Kieran. "It wouldn't be like that."

"The intent might be different, but the result would be the same."

"It's the only way I can protect her."

"No, it isn't. And, excuse me for speaking plainly, but you can't fully protect her. Not her. She and her wards won't step down. They don't care that they're half-trained and mostly ignorant about the magical world. They have convinced themselves they'll be the turning point in the battle, and without them, you'll lose."

Despite the situation, laughter bubbled up. "You have to admire that confidence."

"You do. And yet, they aren't totally wrong. The only way you can protect Alexis is to teach her to protect herself. That's the best leg up you can give her. Then fight beside her when everything goes sideways. She's a damn fine asset to have."

Kieran stared out at the ocean for a quiet moment.

"She...made some strides today," Zorn said.

"Oh yes?"

"Yes. Firstly, she found a hidden pocket of the spirit world here on our plane ..." Zorn shook his head. "I don't really understand it, to be honest. Jack said he found her earlier, standing in the middle of the sidewalk with her hands out, looking up at nothing. She expanded her magical reach with the help of the Line. That's when she picked up...another realm."

Kieran shook his head. "Have you ever heard of this?"

"No, but I know very little about the spirit world. The Hades Demigods would probably know something."

"If only that were an option."

"If only."

"Did she know what use it might be?" Kieran asked.

"No. But she started experimenting with it almost

immediately. The gremlin is not pleased. She's not a fan of spirits." Zorn pushed up to standing, catching Kieran's attention. He had a feeling he wouldn't like whatever was coming next. "Alexis prodded Thane too hard earlier. He went active."

The words trickled around Kieran but didn't quite seep in. The situation Zorn referenced shouldn't be possible.

"Come again?"

Zorn clasped his hands behind his back, a submissive move for him. "Thane felt his limit approaching when training with Alexis. Not long after, she pushed him over."

The words still weren't making sense. "Pushed him over..."

"Thane went berserk."

Fire rose up in Kieran's middle. He had okayed Thane training with her and the kids, as long as Thane was sure he could stay in control. So far, that hadn't been a problem.

"He was pushing his limits, and he didn't *walk away*?" Kieran demanded.

"Bria told him to hold. She was in charge. He followed orders."

"You put her in charge."

"And you put me in charge."

Without consciously planning it, Kieran took two

fast steps and clutched Zorn's throat. "Thane is one of the most powerful Berserkers in the world. You remember what happened when I had to subdue him. You remember how many people he hurt and killed—how many *trained adults* he had hurt and killed—before I made it to the scene."

"Yes, sir."

"If he'd made a complete change, you wouldn't have been able to back him down. He would've torn through Alexis's house. Her kids. Her neighborhood." Fear choked him for the second time that day, his primal need to protect her overpowering his senses. His fingers tightened on Zorn's throat. "He would've torn through Alexis."

"He did make a complete change," Zorn squeezed out, his hands still behind his back and his eyes calm despite his dwindling air supply. "Donovan, Bria, and Jack tried to back him down," he continued, his voice hoarse. "It didn't help. The kids came outside, which triggered Alexis, and she made Thane submit. She took him to the ground, all by herself. I was told that he said, 'uncle.' Literally."

All Kieran could do was stare. The words didn't compute.

"That's impossible," he finally uttered. "She's not fully trained."

"And yet it happened."

Kieran peeled back his fingers from around Zorn's throat. He forced himself to return to his position at the banister. Zorn stayed where he was, his hands kept behind his back. He was taking responsibility for what had happened with Thane.

"She won't go undetected for long, sir. And the only training that seems to work for her isn't exactly inconspicuous. She can't stay in the dual-society zone much longer."

Kieran had a solution for that. But it would require him to leave his father's house, and doing so would start the countdown. Once his father was onto him, he'd have to move quickly. Quicker than the time it would take for his father's allies to back him up.

He needed more time to prepare.

When he didn't respond, Zorn walked over to lean on the banister beside him. "Alexis told you where she was earlier tonight. At what bar."

"Don't start with that. I'm barely hanging on to control as it is."

"Alexis paid the bill. She told her ex-boyfriend to shove it, then hit him with her magic. She reacted just like you said she would."

He took a deep breath, and something tight and sharp loosened in his middle.

She'd reacted like he'd *hoped* she would. There were never any assurances when it came to Alexis.

"You made the right choice, letting her stake your claim," Zorn said. "Bria expressed a grudging respect for your decision, which doesn't mean much, but—"

"It does," Kieran responded. "It means a great deal, actually. She's been leery of me since day one."

"She's warming up to you."

"So it seems. Bria was a good choice to mentor Alexis."

A sly smile crossed Zorn's lips. He didn't respond.

"We'll move them into the new house tomorrow," Kieran said, grudgingly making the decision. "It's time. If she tries to refuse, we'll work on the kids. They'll bend her to their will. I want us all in the same location."

Zorn nodded and dug into his pocket. He pulled out his phone as Kieran was turning back toward the house.

"This is who was following the girls." Zorn held up a picture.

Adrenaline ran through him. He looked over the woman's face, then waited as Zorn swiped to show him a body shot.

Flara wasn't without talent, but she was too polished to blend into low-income areas.

"And now we are certain—my father has noticed his employees missing."

They both knew Valens used her, in all forms of the word, exclusively.

"So it seems." Zorn slipped his phone back in his

pocket. "He's caught scent of the trail."

"Not yet. That he sent Flara means he's still sniffing. But he's headed in the right direction. Things will start moving quickly now."

"Yes, sir."

Kieran paused. "You saved this for the last piece of news. It would've cut our conversation in half. Why wait?"

Another sly smile curved Zorn's lips. He shrugged. "Curiosity. I wanted to see what you'd do with the other information before I…pushed the agenda."

"You're ready to go to war."

"Been ready, sir. All we have left is the details."

Kieran turned, lead in his middle. "Wars are won and lost in the details."

And he intended to win.

Chapter 8

ALEXIS

*G*OOD MORNING, BEAUTIFUL.

A smile graced my face as I read the message on my phone. Kieran was smooth, I had to give him that, and right now, I needed it. It helped me ignore the lingering feeling of impending doom from the night before. Bria didn't seem that stressed considering she was being watched by a Demigod, but I was plenty freaked out on her behalf.

Filtered light bled through the fog outside my window pane. Just because it was the nice time of year clearly didn't mean the fog was an ancient memory.

I glanced at the time. Nine o'clock. The kids would be up getting their breakfasts in early so as not to throw it up during training later on. They'd finally learned that lesson the hard way.

I zipped back a return text, though I couldn't bear to end my salutation with *handsome*. Or hot ass. Or fucking godly. The man already had an ego problem—I didn't want to make it worse.

But good heavens I did want him in my bed. It had been nearly a week since I'd seen him last. Nearly a week since I'd felt the rush of his kiss. My body ached for his touch.

"Time to get up, Alexis," I chided myself, desperately wanting to spare the time to let my hand slip down south and take care of some of the pounding.

My phone vibrated.

Kieran: *Wait until later when I can participate.*

Shivers ran through me and a slow smile curled my lips. The pounding between my thighs intensified. Sometimes I hated that he could feel me through the connection I'd forged between us. And sometimes, when we both had quiet time, I loved it so hard.

I blew out a breath while throwing back my covers and swinging my feet over the mattress.

After getting dressed, I walked down the hall in time to hear Daisy say, "Tell me how that is a bad idea."

She sat at the table with a half-eaten omelet in front of her.

"Did you make one of those for me?" I asked, stopping next to her. Mordecai looked back from the stove, a black apron around his waist and a spatula in his hand. "Isn't the rule that we have to be up for you to make us food?"

"Yup, that's the rule," Daisy said, cutting off some

of her omelet. "Now she is, so you have to make her one, Mordie."

"When did I become the house cook?" he demanded.

"You're a guy." Daisy shrugged. "Everyone knows the guys cook around this house."

"Since when?" Mordecai asked.

"Since we started eating real food, that's when. Hello?" Daisy turned so she could glare at him. "How little do you pay attention?"

Mordecai flipped what would now become my omelet. "That's gaslighting."

"No, it's not. It's a fact."

"Okay, you two, knock it off." I crossed to the fridge. "Daisy, stop gaslighting your brother."

"I wasn't—"

"The Six are the reason we have real food," Mordecai said, sliding the spatula under the omelet. "Just because they also started cooking for us, and also happen to be guys, doesn't mean—"

"Ah ha!" Daisy jabbed her fork at him. "You just proved my case. Now do as the lady says, and mind you don't burn the omelet."

"Daisy, that's not nice," I admonished her out of duty. "What were you guys talking about? What's a good idea?" I crossed to the cabinet and took out two glasses.

"Daisy thinks this whole situation with Kieran is a hot mess," Mordecai explained, "and we need to enlist more help."

"From where?" I set the glasses on the table. "Craigslist? Upwork?"

Daisy rolled her eyes. "I heard Jack and Donovan talking last night—"

"Do you constantly eavesdrop now?" Mordecai asked with a scowl.

"Um"—Daisy lifted her hands—"yes. That *is* what I'm training for, idiot." She shook her head in annoyance. "Anyway, apparently Valens has at least three times as many forces as we do. Three times, Lexi! He has more Elite, too, that he controls pretty tightly. If we don't think of something to help, we'll be steamrolled."

"Kieran is working it out," Mordecai said. "He knows what he's up against."

"Kieran is only one man, and up until recently, he was a rich playboy mostly confined to an island. A small island, at that. He's never led an army, or organized troops, or—" Mordecai turned around to give a rebuttal but Daisy stayed his argument with a hand. "No, I haven't either. What I'm saying is, he's in over his head. He needs help, and someone has got to step up. Since you and the Six are content to blindly follow him, that leaves me."

Mordecai slid the omelet onto a plate and nudged it

in my direction. "It's all meat. No veggies."

I frowned at him, momentarily distracted from what Daisy was saying. "Even shifters need vegetables," I said, taking the plate. I was going to say canines, but that was a touchy subject, and also Daisy's favorite button to push. "You need—" I stopped when I noticed him pointing at the pan resting on the top burner. "You made collard greens to go with an omelet?"

"I don't like vegetables interfering with my meat dishes," he said as though that made sense.

"Okay. Parental crisis averted. You may continue, Daisy."

Daisy was utterly convinced that our little untrained and mostly unknowledgeable family would save the day. Which was probably why she felt responsible for overseeing his efforts.

Daisy pointed at me with the business end of her fork. "You told us that Kieran said the magical ruler of Sydney doesn't get along with Valens, remember?" She paused for my answer. I nodded. "The fire thrower lady, remember?"

"A nod generally means yes," I said dryly.

Daisy scowled. "Gross." She scoffed but continued. "Kieran was going to move us into the fire lady's—"

"Fire Elemental," Mordecai supplied as he mixed eggs in a bowl.

"—territory to keep us safe because she would get

pissed if Valens tried to stick his nose in her sh—stuff."
Daisy pressed her lips together after her near miss with
swearing.

"She's a class-five Fire Elemental, and I remember
all that." I reached for the orange juice.

"Well, if she hates Valens, and Valens hates her, she
might want to join our cause," Daisy said. "It's certainly
worth asking. The research I've done tells me that she's
fierce, a strong leader, and well-liked and respected by
her people. She'd be a good ally, right?"

"Yes, but it's not for us to initiate that connection."
Mordecai peeled two strips of bacon from the package.
"We're nobodies. You're not even magical. We can't go
randomly contacting world leaders."

"Peel off a couple more, would ya?" I asked. "I could
do with a side of bacon. And Mordecai is right. She's a
ruler and we're basically trainees under an uncrowned
Demigod taking on an active Demigod of a prestigious
magical city. It's a delicate situation. If anyone ap-
proaches her, it should be Kieran."

"Right. I agree with you. It should," Daisy said after
she finished chewing. "But when I asked Zorn about it,
he ignored me."

"He always ignores you." Mordecai pulled the package of ham closer to him.

"Yes, genius, I'm aware of that." Daisy pushed her
plate away. "But you don't have to be part dog to read

body language."

"Low blow, Daisy," I said around a full mouth.

"Zorn discounted me," Daisy said. "He might as well have called me an ignorant girl."

"Except…" Mordecai shook his head as he put the eggs into the pan. "I mean, I don't want to start anything, but in terms of the magical world, you *are* an ignorant girl."

"Since when don't you want to start something?" I asked. "All you two do anymore is fight."

"He said that to tell me he's serious," Daisy explained. "He's not just busting my chops. And yes, Mordie, I am ignorant, but this is glaringly obvious."

"Kieran got no love from the non-magical mayor of San Francisco," Mordecai said.

Daisy threw up her hands. "So? Kieran shouldn't give up looking for more allies because one butthead turned him down. Everyone knows the mayor is a crook, just like Valens."

"I just think we should leave the networking to Kieran," Mordecai said, plating his omelet.

Daisy huffed loudly, stood, and grabbed up her plate. "That's just the problem—everyone thinks everything should be left to Kieran. It's one thing to have faith in the guy, but at some point, we have to take a step back and acknowledge he's terrible at delegating."

"The thing is…" Mordecai sat at the table. "Kieran

has gotten a lot of training, he's talked with powerful people, and he's been preparing. There's a reason everyone is turning to him. He's a lot more qualified to make these types of decisions than me. *Or you.*"

"Spoken like a follower and not a leader." She dropped her plate into the sink. It clattered against the porcelain. "What do you think, Lexi?"

I paused in my chewing. "It's a dicey situation. On one hand, I can absolutely see what you're saying." Daisy beamed and I held up a finger in warning. "But you're also being short-sighted. Joining the fight against Valens means picking a side. If Kieran loses, she loses. And if he pursues her as an ally and she doesn't want to get involved, she'll know his secret information. How much would that be worth to Valens? Mordecai is right, it is an extremely fragile situation."

"No." Daisy crossed her arms over her chest. Her usually pale cheeks were stained red. "What's fragile is *our* situation. Zorn is amped up when he talks about it, and I can tell he's trying to psych himself up because he suspects an unfavorable outcome."

I widened my eyes. I knew she trained with him, so she had better insight into his moods, but I'd never seen him look more emotive than a zombie.

She slapped on the water faucet to rinse her dish. "Everything you said is true, Lexi, and I get that, but as soon as Valens knows what we're doing, none of those other concerns will matter. I'm not saying the fire lady will engage, but it's worth a shot."

"Except, as soon as Valens knows about us, it'll be time for battle," Mordecai said. "How can you expect another ruler to make a decision and mobilize her forces that fast? She lives across the world."

Daisy yanked open the dishwasher, dropped in her dish, and slammed the door shut again. "Look. The bottom line is, we have no way of knowing unless one of us tries. I have a nice little life right now. I don't want to lose it." She paused at the edge of the kitchen and held up her hand to me. "If we're throwing our lot in with Kieran, maybe we should do more than hope he has all the answers." She stomped from the room.

"You'd think she was a battle commander instead of a fourteen-year-old non-magical girl who knows literally nothing about the magical world," Mordecai mumbled.

I slowed in my eating, vaguely staring after her. "No, she's a fourteen-year-old non-magical girl who was fucked by the system, left for dead, and now has a real appreciation for surviving. She might have a point."

Chapter 9

ALEXIS

A KNOCK AT the front door brought me out of my trance. The colors in my room disintegrated into the normal dull beiges and browns of the living world. The Line drifted away, and I swore I felt a sort of *goodbye* as it did so.

Until recently, I'd always thought the world of the living was the big deal—the origin of life—and when we were done living, our souls needed a place to bugger off to. Hence the spirit realm.

I'd had it all wrong.

Spirit was the bedrock of the living world. It lined every fiber. Every particle. Every crack. The souls residing in our bodies relied on it.

The Line was a safeguard. Its purpose wasn't to keep the spirits confined in the beyond, but to keep living bodies *out*. Its dark, bruise-like colors spoke of death, and drew on our fears of the afterlife. The effect was off-putting, purposefully so. Our living minds hated the very idea of it, because our living bodies weren't welcome. Only when we shed our shells were we free to roam.

I rubbed my eyes and pushed to my feet. Another knock sounded, echoing down the quiet hallway.

A glance at the clock said I was late for my training.

"Crap," I said under my breath, tying back my hair.

Halfway down the hall, I heard soft muttering from the living room. The kids sat on the couch, staring at the laptop screen.

I stopped short, then ducked into the kitchen and checked the time again. I grabbed my phone while I was in there.

"It's eleven," I said, confused. They looked up at me, Mordecai with raised eyebrows. They hadn't realized that, in addition to spouting the time like a watchman, I was also asking for an explanation. "What are you doing here? Shouldn't you be training?"

Daisy went back to the screen. "No one showed. Did you piss off Kieran?"

"I…" My phone didn't have any new messages or texts. "I don't think so. He texted me like normal this morning."

"He texts you every morning?" Mordecai asked in disapproval.

"You need to pay better attention." Daisy held up a finger to forestall Mordecai's reply. "That wasn't gaslighting."

"You guys need to look up what gaslighting means," I said, walking closer. "Did they text or call?"

Mordecai scanned the surfaces around them. A moment later, Daisy joined him.

At Bria's persistent urging, Kieran had gotten them cell phones. But being that they had no friends and no time, not to mention weren't used to having phones, they rarely used them and often lost them around the house.

"Didn't you think to check your phones when no one showed up?" I demanded, my no-nonsense tone hastening both of them off the couch. They knew when to push back, and when to get moving. Now was the latter. "They could want you to report to them."

"They would've told us last night," Daisy said, dashing around me and into the kitchen.

"Given you are still here, and they are not, clearly they didn't tell you *something* last night. Something they probably thought they could relay via text. Oh wait, *no one thought to check their phones!*" Mordecai raced down the hall. "Weren't you guys saying *this very morning* that you want to stay in this fight? Well, that'll be pretty hard if you don't get training, won't it?"

Daisy jetted out of the kitchen, around me again, and took off toward her room.

I followed them, my voice rising. The key to really driving your point home was to become a loud, extremely angry moving target.

"If you go in like you are, you'll both die," I berated. "Then where will you be?"

"Got it," I heard from Daisy.

"Found mine," Mordecai said. A moment later, he mumbled, "The batteries are out."

"You say that it's dead, moron," Daisy said, appearing in the doorway bent over her phone. "Training is postponed." She smiled, out of breath, and held her phone up high as if finding it were a praiseworthy accomplishment. "It's postponed. We didn't miss it."

Mordecai appeared behind her, his mouth a thin line and his eyes wary.

"You lost your charger too, didn't you?"

"Yes, ma'am," he murmured, and bowed a little. If he'd been a dog, his tail would be between his legs.

I hated that now I always compared his body language to that of a dog.

"Well?" I drew out the word dangerously while lifting one eyebrow. It had taken some time to learn that little trick, but it really came in handy.

Flustered, Mordecai stepped into the space between Daisy and the doorjamb, bumping her to the side. He paused, his wide eyes on me, unsure.

"Go find it!" I hollered.

Daisy jumped and turned, all hands and jerky movements. "Mordie, I have one. I have one over here."

She got him angled in the right direction before shoving his much larger body out of the way.

"You don't always train together, Mordecai," I boomed. "What if you're supposed to be working on scent today, and Jack is somewhere waiting for you?"

"I have it," Mordecai said, his voice panicked. "I have it. I'm plugging it in."

Another knock sounded at the door. The fact that whoever it was had not yet left meant they A) knew someone was home, and B) had a lot of patience. That ruled out strangers, Zorn, and Bria.

I stalked down the hall as Mordecai called, "It's charging."

My knuckles were white around the door handle. I pulled it open.

Thane stood just off the steps to the walkway, giving me a ridiculous amount of space. His face held regret and his eyes an apology. Frank was nowhere to be seen. In fact, I hadn't seen him since Bria had chased him off the night before. I wasn't sure if I was thankful or a little sad that my annoying watchdog was gone.

"Hey," Thane said. He dug his hands into his jeans pockets. Clearly he wasn't training anyone today.

"Hey," I said, pushing the door wider open. Memories of the day before flashed through my head. "Want to come in?" I was proud of my even voice.

He glanced beyond me before turning sideways and

directing his gaze away. "Nah, that's okay. Look—"

"Don't apologize." I stepped out onto the stoop, forcing down a swell of uncertainty. Now that I had a little distance from the situation, I felt for the guy. He couldn't have scared me any worse than I'd scared him. I'd made the guy go berserk, for cripes sakes. The least I could do was put on my big girl undies and push through my uneasiness. He certainly was. "You have nothing to apologize for. If anyone should apologize, it should be Kieran for keeping everyone's magic from me."

He shrugged those big shoulders and looked at the ground. "He didn't think you'd feel safe."

No need to tell him Kieran had been right.

"I should've walked away when I felt myself nearing my threshold," Thane went on. "I knew how close I was, but I didn't back down. That's unforgivable."

"Ew," I heard behind me.

I spun around and Daisy took a big step back and held up her hands like she was being mugged. I hadn't even heard her approach. Zorn's lessons were working.

"Bria was in charge," Daisy said quickly. "None of that was Thane's fault."

"Training is postponed," Mordecai yelled down the hall in triumph. "It's postponed! We're in the clear." He jogged toward us. "Lexi, did you hear that? My training is postponed, too."

Daisy studied me for a reaction.

"In the future, *check in*," I said in a dangerous tone. "Do not wait for me to tell you."

"Yes, ma'am," Mordecai said, and I marveled at his use of that term again. It was new and kind of nice. I felt in charge and important.

"Okay."

The same lesson hadn't rubbed off on Daisy.

When I finally turned back to Thane, I had his full attention. A small smile was hidden in his bushy beard.

"What?" I asked.

"Has Demigod Kieran heard you use that tone?"

I frowned. "My mom tone? I doubt it. It's usually reserved for times when my wards"—I turned and raised my voice—"forget that they are no longer children."

"I guess this is how Mordecai learned pack structure," Thane said. "Jack couldn't figure it out."

"I don't use this tone very often. It's just that I'm right in the middle of trying to figure things out, and those lugnuts were lazing around, and you're interrupting…" I took a deep breath. "What can I do for you, Thane? Besides not accept your apology?"

His smile grew. "For the record, a true leader rarely needs to use *the tone*, as you call it. Once you garner respect and loyalty, people aim to please. Demigod Kieran could write a book on it. He has very little employee turnover. You're a natural, too. I wonder if he knows."

Hearing Kieran's name sent a little thrill through me, reminding me that I'd been feeling his roller-coaster emotions all morning. He went from aroused to anxious to fearful to excited, then back to aroused, on a constant loop. Add to that my interrupted study of the spirit world, my growing list of questions, and the incessant pounding in my core, and I was not a joy to be around.

It must've shown in my expression, because Thane's smile dwindled.

"Anyway." He took a step toward his car. "I did want to apologize. I realize that I put you and your wards in danger—"

"I put my wards in danger by working with Kieran. You're one danger of many. Forget about it. And don't think you'll get out of helping, either. We might need to take it to a wide open field, or to the beach where Jack can grab you from the water and drag you away, but I want to let that beast out again to see if I can subdue it a second time."

Fear flashed through his eyes, and I didn't know what he feared more—what he could potentially do when he changed, or me.

"Demigod Kieran won't—"

"He doesn't make the rules around here." I looked

down at the vibrating phone trapped in my hand. The face lit up.

Kieran: *Find me.*

My bad mood dripped away and a smile took over my face. Another message came in before I could scoot Thane out of my yard.

Kieran: *Bring the kids.*

My bad mood crept back in.

That wasn't my idea of a fun lover's tryst. Kids could really water down the romance of a situation.

I texted back: *Are you sure about the kids? They have chores to do.*

They did now, at any rate.

A feeling of excitement came through the soul connection, followed by a wave of heat that made it hard to breathe.

Kieran: *We'll have plenty of time to be alone. Bring the kids.*

Fire surged through me.

"Thane, I gotta go," I said, speaking unnaturally quickly as I turned toward the house. "Kids, get your shoes on. We gotta go."

"I'll go with you," Thane said.

I held up my phone. "I got a text from Kieran. He

didn't mention you." I paused and narrowed my eyes. "Does he know you're here?"

"I'm on duty watching you," Thane said. "Plus, I'd be pretty stupid to show up with you if I were trying to hide this *tête-à-tête*."

I tilted my head at his perfect French accent. "Do you guys have the ability to speak all languages like Kieran does?" I glanced back. No kids were in sight. "Hurry up," I yelled.

Footsteps shuffled off to the right. Something banged in the back bedroom.

Thane was smiling again, but this time it was accompanied by a brow furrow that looked like a nice way of saying I was stupid. "You don't know? Demigods impart certain gifts to those who give them a blood oath. It's different for each person, like a level up of the magic they already have. But certain gifts, like universal communication and enhanced strength and speed, are given to everyone. Those help us do our job."

"A simple yes would've been fine," I muttered, incredibly impatient, both naturally and because Kieran was feeding me his own impatience. I needed to figure out how to lessen our connection at times.

I prepared to shout into the house again. It was like the kids operated at half speed unless I was yelling. It drove me nuts.

Daisy walked down the hall in flip-flops and Mordecai came out of the bedroom with one of my old robes, a pink faux satin affair with red tassels.

"What's going on?" I asked them.

Daisy held up her phone. "Zorn said to change to sandals."

"I'll be working on multiple changes today." Mordecai flung the robe over his shoulder.

I pointed at it. "You're going to wear that?"

He glanced at it in confusion. "Yeah. Why? What's wrong with it?"

Daisy rolled her eyes. "Don't bother, Lexi. He's not worried about his masculinity."

"Oh, because it's pink?" Mordecai shrugged. "Pink is just a color, like any other. Besides, pink used to be perceived as a masculine color. It only became associated with femininity in the past century." He waved the thought away. "I don't really care either way."

"You should care about those weird tassels." Daisy flicked one. "But then again, you change from an animal to a human, then back again. You got the lock down on *weird*."

"Yeah, like you can talk. You sneak around in the gutter," Mordecai retorted.

"How is that weird?"

"You *guys*!" I took a step out the door. "Can't you go half a day without fighting?"

"We fight out of love, Lexi," Mordecai said, shoving

Daisy in front of him.

"A love of torture," Daisy muttered.

"What can you expect?" Thane waited for us with a cockeyed smile. "They train together, they live together—they share the same room. That's too much time with one person."

"I don't advise you ever getting married," I said, locking the door.

"No one would have me."

I expected him to laugh, like Donovan surely would've. Jack made that kind of joke with regularity. Instead, sadness crossed Thane's features.

"Because of your magic," I said softly, feeling like a real dickhead for giving Bria a hard time about having Thane around. I waved the thought away. "I'll probably have a similar problem. At least you aren't shackled to two crabby wards."

"We're right here, Alexis," Mordecai grumbled.

"Yeah. I know." I unlocked the car as we headed down the sidewalk. "Boy, do I know. Wait…" I blinked back at them, slowing as I approached my car, a shiny BMW Kieran had gifted me in the guise of calling it a company car. "Where will you be training? Is that where Kieran's sending us?"

Both kids shrugged. "My text just told me to go with you, and what to bring—*shotgun!*" Mordecai laughed and darted for the front seat.

Thane hurried around to the other side of the car, his face suspiciously blank.

"Damn it—damn isn't a curse, Lexi," Daisy said. "I'm godless, remember? So that means the idea of damn is moot." She trudged to the backseat, not waiting to hear my verdict. It was probably for the best—I was still sorting through her reasoning. "I was thinking about what Zorn would have me do barefooted. I missed that one."

"Snooze you lose." Mordecai shut his door.

"The adults should sit in the front—" But Thane was already slamming his door shut, his chosen seat directly behind me so I couldn't see his expression.

"What the hell is going on?" I murmured, the butterflies rolling through my stomach a match for how Kieran was currently feeling. It wasn't a good sign.

I didn't want to know what made a Demigod nervous.

Chapter 10

ALEXIS

NOT EVEN TWENTY minutes later, I idled in the car while the ocean crashed against the cliff in the not-so-far distance. Wispy swirls of white interrupted the deep blue expanse overhead, stretching out to meet the ocean. In contrast to the wild beauty beyond us, a broken down car without any tires sat rusting in the barren gutter of the dead-end street.

I'd followed the *feel* of Kieran to this forgotten strip of land at the very edge of the dual-society zone, backed right up against the grimy brick wall blocking off the magical zone. It was a no man's land, and it looked like people stumbled out here to die.

"I knew it, Lexi," Daisy said in a hush, pushing forward to peer out the windshield. Her hand squeezed the side of Mordecai's seat. "I knew he'd eventually get tired of you and kill you off."

"I doubt that's what this is," Mordecai whispered.

"Why else did he send the Berserker with us?" she replied.

"He didn't. I opted to come with you," Thane said, his full volume unnaturally loud in the quiet car.

"To see the massacre?" Daisy clucked her tongue. "Sick."

"This is not a murder scene," Thane said.

"Yeah right, like we can believe you." Daisy huffed softly. "You work for the guy."

I pulled down the visor, Bria's trademark surreptitious move, which really seemed to fit the moment. I made a mental note to make fun of her a little less.

"We're not here to be killed." I glanced out the window at a newspaper caught in the wind, scraping the street. "Probably."

"This place is so out of touch, it has actual newspapers," Mordecai said.

The pulse of Kieran throbbed in my middle, telling me he was away right. But the brick wall was away right, and any view of what lay beyond was obscured by enormous greenery. The other side of that wall was probably thriving and lovely. This side was that side's toilet.

"This is the perfect spot for a murder." Daisy leaned back to look out her window. "He could bury you right here. Who would know? There are four houses, and three are boarded up. The owner of the fourth must've decided boarding was too good for that ramshackle piece of *shhh*—garbage. It was just left to rot. Like we will be."

"Yes, thank you, Daisy, for the running commentary," I said dryly, pulling the car to the curb and hesitantly putting it in park. There had to be a reason Kieran wanted me in this rough part of the city. He didn't do things like this without a purpose.

"Hell, the ocean is right there," Daisy continued, almost like she was talking to herself. "He could just throw you off that cliff and have the currents take you away. He wouldn't even have to bother killing you. Your magic doesn't faze him anymore. He could throw you over his shoulder like the caveman he is, super-speed jog you to the edge, and plop goes the nuisance. Doneskies."

I tuned her out. "Were we supposed to drive into the magical zone?" I asked in confusion. "Because that—"

"No," Thane said. "You're in the right place, and this is not a murder scene. Beyond that, you need to figure it out for yourself."

A relieved breath exited Daisy. "Thank God," she said. "It's just training."

Thane's seat groaned. "Did you *honestly* think we would've spent all this time training you up, just to kill you off?" he asked Daisy.

I turned off the car and reached for the door handle. "Yes, she did. You have no idea what sort of upbringing she had. Trust is hard-earned."

I ran my hand down the center of my chest as I walked around the car, feeling the pounding connection to Kieran. I crossed the grimy sidewalk and watched my step on the uneven, sandy ground. Dune grass stuck up beside shrubbery gone wild. I neared the wall, stepping around a suspicious looking bone that I hoped had belonged to a large animal.

"I smell blood," Mordecai whispered, right behind me. "The scent is faint. Very old. But it's there."

"What would be so important about this place that the guys would postpone our actual training to bring us here?" Daisy murmured, catching up to my side. "It has to be more than a wall, right? It has to be more than a barrier. Somehow, this has to help our cause."

"I agree, but..." Mordecai shook his head. He didn't see how. Neither did I.

Divots lined the top edge of the wall. Occasionally four parallel lines slashed through the grime. They looked like claw marks. Like something big and bad had tried to escape over the wall and couldn't quite make it.

"That doesn't bode well," Mordecai said softly, his eyes on those lines.

Down the way, in the direction of the ocean, a large black crack cut through the dirty, dingy rust-red bricks. Dark spots started near it on one side, and ended on the other side, almost like someone had painted them on.

Around the line, a few bricks stuck out farther than others, or were crumbled away, like someone had taken a chisel to the wall in places. All in all, the area was just similar enough to the rest of the wall that I wouldn't have noticed the differences if I hadn't been looking for them, but now that I was...

"Am I losing my grip..." I started down that way. "Or is this area down here...not quite right?"

"You're right, it's different. It must be an illusion," Daisy said with confidence. "Zorn did it."

"Zorn can pull off illusions?" I kept my eyes on the area so I didn't lose it, worried that I'd look away and not find it again. Some of the spaces between the bricks were brighter than others, with fresher mortar. Occasionally, though, unless my eyes were playing tricks on me, the brighter spots shifted position. "Zorn's an Illusionist?"

"No, Illusionists can create nuance and detail a Djinn can't. Wait, you didn't know what he was?" Daisy asked, shocked. "You have these guys in your house, you train with them, and you don't even know what they are?"

I stopped walking. I couldn't help it. Nor could I help the smile sneaking up my face. "Zorn is a genie?"

"Yeah." Daisy motioned me on. "A Marid. The most powerful kind. Why do you think he makes such an awesome spy and assassin? He can turn into gas, for

God's sake. Gas, Lexi! He can drift through cracks in walls. And he somehow thinks I can be as good as he is?" She snorted. "Fat chance."

"He said that?" Thane asked as I started forward again, my grin bigger. "That you can be as good as him?"

She ignored him. Daisy wasn't one to tell stories or throw around her ego. Apparently, she was also having trouble believing in herself. I'd need to circle back to that.

"He doesn't grant wishes, though," she said, her voice softening as we slowly walked along the wall. "I looked it up. Only nobility can do that, and he was born a nobody. His father had a gambling problem and his mother didn't like working. They were both powerful, but they didn't do much with it. Besides beat their kid, I mean."

"Daisy babbles when she gets nervous," Mordecai said to me, as though I hadn't lived with her as long as he had. He looked up at the sky. "I smell Kieran on the breeze."

That was because he was close. Not far beyond the wall.

Why did Kieran want us in the magical zone? Even being on the outskirts was dangerous, especially for Daisy. She had no business going beyond that wall. And neither did I if I wanted to stay undetected.

"This isn't a murder scene, but is that?" I muttered, thinking of our destination.

"Still no," Thane said, checking his watch.

With a furrowed brow, Daisy reached for the patch of brick that didn't seem quite right. Her pinkie brushed against the strange discolored crack.

"I was right," she said softly. Her hand still looked like it was reaching toward brick, but as I stepped up closer to the wall, I could see that her hand had passed right through the supposed barrier.

She swung her other hand to the side and I pushed back, giving her room. I could tell this wasn't the first time she'd had to feel through one of Zorn's illusions. Her right hand jerked to a stop as it bumped against another edge, indicating there was a large hole through the magical barrier.

"Another brick wall was put in back here." Daisy stepped forward and her body disappeared beyond the crack.

I followed, in time to see her palms bump up against the second brick wall. My senses revolted again before piecing the situation together. A six-foot-wide or so hole had been knocked through the old brick wall, the original barrier between the dual-society zone and the magical zone. A new wall had been built about five feet back, connected to the old with brick on one side. The other side had been left open as a pass through, like the opening of a labyrinth. On top of that, Zorn's magic had smoothed everything together so it looked like the old brick wall was one long plane. Clever. He wasn't an Illusionist, but he'd done the job just fine.

"Do you think the guys created this hidden doorway?" Daisy asked. "Or was it here and they just covered it up?"

"We did it," Thane said. "The location fit the intent."

"What's on the other side?" Mordecai asked.

My stomach fluttered. "Kieran."

Chapter 11

VALENS

"REPORT," VALENS SAID, leaning back in his chair. Soft music played from the other side of his large office and light streamed in through the many windows facing the Golden Gate Bridge in the distance. He stalled to straighten a piece of paper before fully facing one of his best spies.

After Flara's lackluster report last night and his inability to reach climax, he'd been left with no choice but to listen to his gut. The Necromancer was a stronger lead than Flara would have him believe. He could feel it.

Amber, a name solely used when she was working, chosen at random from a list of top stripper names, stood straight and tall just inside the door. Her silky black hair cascaded over her slim shoulders. Intelligent onyx eyes surveyed him, no doubt cataloging each nuance of his tone and body language to determine his exact mood and level of patience. She'd know she was under the gun to perform.

"Bria Stevens is heralded as an excellent Necromancer and problem solver, but a lone wolf as far as the trade goes," Amber said, delivering the information like she was reading it straight from a report. She might as well have been. The blood oath she'd taken had given her exceptional information recall. "She never gets too close to anyone. She's friendly with the power players in the trade, and involved in all the right groups, but she maintains a respectable distance from the others that keeps her clear of in-fighting. She is taken seriously without being seen as a threat. In short, she has positioned herself perfectly. That takes great intelligence."

Amber paused so he could soak in that information. She was setting the stage, and that stage seemed to be filled with professionals. He'd been shortsighted in sending Flara—a decision that might've bitten him in the ass.

"Noted," he said. "Continue."

"My team is still compiling data, but so far, the Necromancer is elusive. She comes and goes seemingly at random. She has been seen entering the non-magical zone, though she has no clearance to do so, and she hangs out in the dual-magical zone occasionally. My guess is that she works at being unpredictable. She attempts to mask her movements in chaos, and she does an incredible job. If she'd played her cards like most Necromancers, she would've been snatched up by a Demigod and pulled into his or her inner circle.

"That said, she hasn't trained to compete with someone of my caliber. She moves around under the radar just fine, but doesn't dispose of the stolen cars as well as she should. She has covered her face to avoid facial recognition at moments when she shouldn't have, and vice versa. In short, she has been sloppy in places. Either that is because she is not trying as hard as she should be, or she is simply missing the mark on excellence."

"Do you think she was involved in this?"

"I believe so. Her timeline and appearances were *almost* impeccable during the period in question. Almost. But a few slips and a trip to the outpatient emergency room gives me reason to suspect she had a direct hand in the disappearance of your spirit workers."

Valens rubbed his thumb across the leather of the chair arm. *Finally* a lead. "I'll look for your report on the best way to twist information out of her."

To his surprise, Amber shook her head. "I believe she was involved, but I'm hesitant to bring her in just yet. That would set off some large alarm bells. I have a growing suspicion…" She shifted her weight, a small movement that spoke volumes. She was not a woman given to uncertainty. "Last night, the Necromancer was seen with a class two Ghost Whisperer. Soon after leaving the bar, the Necromancer separated from the

Ghost Whisperer to walk a drunk man home. I believe the man was a distraction. As was the convoluted path she took. I checked out this Ghost Whisperer. On paper, there was nothing to give me pause, but…" She shifted again and a small line formed between her brows.

Valens stilled his thumb. This was unusual. Amber looked almost troubled.

"Nearly three months ago she was brought in for a magical reassessment," Amber said. "She is twenty-five years old, with no job offer or pending application of any kind to prompt the reassessment."

"Did they find anything abnormal?"

"No. All was as expected. The new report was in line with the old one." She paused.

His impatience got the better of him. "Then what is the problem?"

"Something…seemed off. The dots weren't all connecting for me. I followed up with the staff. One of them remembered the Ghost Whisperer was tested in the surveillance room, a room usually reserved for high-powered magical workers. Another recalled that she was also seen by a high-level Authenticator, but he didn't remember why."

Valens raised his eyebrows and a thread of intrigue filtered into his awareness.

"When shown the report, the staff assumed they'd

made a mistake." There was that shift again. "The new assessment happened right around the time I brought in Dunstin…"

Dunstin was a class-five earth Elemental who'd run from his home territory in France. The man had been extremely unhinged and dangerous, but exceptionally talented. Valens had hoped to reprogram him and force him into his Elite, where he could keep the magical worker on a very tight leash.

Unfortunately, someone had tipped off Elise, the Demigod of France. Valens had been left with little choice but to give the treasure back, lest he start an altercation that would severely tax his reserves at an inopportune time. The magical person wasn't worth a war.

Regardless, the situation had been messy and, as Amber was clearly hinting, an excellent distraction.

He leaned forward in his seat, his heart quickening.

Amber nodded. "The timing seems like too great a coincidence."

"What did the mountebank who did the assessment have to say?" he asked.

"He disappeared, along with his nurse. He quit with no explanation as to why, and didn't leave a forwarding address. He sold his house, but other than that, I can find absolutely no paper trail. Neither can I find any trace of tampering in the files. It is like he and the nurse vanished."

Valens entwined his fingers, his pulse racing now. This was how he felt when in pursuit of big game. Adrenaline and excitement and a small but healthy dose of fear. The best hunts were in pursuit of something— or someone—as cunning as he. The danger got the blood pumping.

"Go on," Valens said.

"The Authenticator in question has relocated. He got a better job offer...in Sydney."

The breath gushed out of Valens. Dara. The bane of his existence.

If they some day added a class six to the power scale, Dara would rank in that small group. Her mother was a mortal Demigod of Zeus's line, torn down in defense of her territory, and her father was a world-renowned Fire Elemental, who'd gone down right at her side. Dara had survived. Later, through a connection with a man of Hades's line, she was able to use his spirit power to obtain immortality. The man had disappeared shortly thereafter.

She was a constant thorn in Valens's side, opposing his proposed legislation at every Magical Summit. The Fire Elemental even galvanized weaker leaders to stand with her. His efforts to foster and encourage non-magical dependency were thwarted at every turn, even simple motions about legalizing certain types of trade with the Chesters. The changes he wished to implement would help all magical people, something she was not interested in hearing. It was madness. He knew that if he needed to go in and extract the Authenticator, she would do everything in her power to block him.

Whoever had sent the Authenticator there would've known this.

"Let me guess, he has no listed phone number," he said.

"Correct. I could not find a way to get a hold of him."

Valens steepled his fingers. "If Dara were coming after me, she wouldn't start by cutting down two of my mid-level employees," he murmured to himself.

"I do not believe she had any part in this." Her shrug was small. "On paper, everything seems in order. But…"

"No." He held up his hand. This was why Amber was the only striking beauty he refused to lay his hands on, and why he gave her the loosest leash of any member of his Elite. Many of his employees had genius-level intelligence, but she had something extra. Her extremely potent intuition was rarely wrong. "This is wrapped up a little too tightly, you're right. It's strange that a poor class two living in the dual-society zone would be brought in for a reassessment without any reason. Even if the report of the assessment is correct, the mountebank *and* the nurse disappearing without a trace is relevant. An Authenticator leaving at the same time is also relevant." He tapped his fingers against his lips. "Very few would've delved as deeply as you have."

"Yes, sir. In addition, there is no video footage of the Ghost Whisperer's assessment. Given that it was in the surveillance room, of course, something not noted on the report." She straightened her suit top. "I'm afraid I have more questions than answers for you, sir."

Valens smiled. It was rare for Amber to admit defeat.

His smile wilted a moment later. The mastermind of this situation was a careful player, and then some. The Necromancer was good, but she clearly worked for someone excellent.

"I agree with your assessment that we should wait before bringing in the Necromancer," he said. "Shift your efforts. Get more information on the Ghost Whisperer. Nothing else has happened in the last two months to suggest we have a time frame in which to catch the perpetrators. Let's stalk our prey for the moment."

"That's not all, sir," she said.

He stilled. How much more could there possibly be?

"When she came in for her assessment, she was with a sick fifteen-year-old shifter who got assessed for what the shifters call Moonmoth disease. It's an autoimmune disease where the body attacks the magic—"

"I'm aware."

"Not long after, an 'unnamed' benefactor sponsored the boy's treatment." To Valens's office, nothing was truly anonymous. Everything left a paper trail. "The kid made a dramatic and eyebrow-raising recovery. He was a strong class four at the time of the surgery, but he's just about to get his big boost of magic."

"He'll be a strong class five, then."

"Yes, sir. He's the Wolfram boy. His father was alpha of the Green Hills pack before Will Green took over."

Valens's eyebrows shot up in surprise. "I thought that boy was dead."

"He has been living in squalor in the dual-society zone. The report indicates he was as good as dead until his 'unnamed' benefactor, Jeffrey Smile, sponsored his treatment."

"Who?"

"Jeffrey Smile. He doesn't exist anywhere but on paper. Every avenue to trace him led to a dead end. I had our best hacker on it, and he turned up empty. Whoever is pulling the strings on this is better than our best."

And there it was: the reason for all her flustered movements. The other player behind this wasn't just her match, he or she was better. They were one step above her.

"You've only had a day," Valens reminded her. Sometimes being an overachiever wasn't ideal. She thought she was failing before she'd really even begun. "In that day, you've accomplished a great deal."

"I had the whole team working overtime."

He furrowed his brow. "Why would someone this skilled waste their time taking down my spirit workers? Through Necromancy, I still have access to souls."

"If you pardon my speculation, sir, this could be a statement. Those particular employees erected the air/spirit wall over this building. Only a few of the high-powered magical workers could see it, but people talk. The staff saw the practice as an extension of your power. They speculated that you were warding evil spirits away, or that it was a force field of some kind to thwart attackers. All speculation by small-minded simpletons, of course, but it was great marketing for your reputation. In cutting down those two magical workers, the person who did this has destroyed that illusion, while also hindering your ability to raise an army of the dead. I am wondering what leg of your operation will be cut down next." She squared her stance and clasped her hands behind her back. "Again, this is purely speculation, sir. As I said, I have been left with more questions than answers."

"Noted." He brushed his fingers against his lips, his

mind turning. "Get more information on the Ghost Whisperer, and alert Will Green that the Wolfram boy is alive and well. If I know Green, he'll sort that out for us."

"Should I give him a time table?"

"Don't bother. Just let it slip that the boy primarily sticks to the dual-society zone and has a silent benefactor of some sort. Green is one of those small-minded simpletons you spoke of. He is barely hanging on to his mantle. He'll rid us of the boy to protect his placement. What remains of it, anyway. Maybe getting rid of the boy will push this Jeffrey Smile out of anonymity. Vengeance is a hardy pastime."

"Yes, sir." Amber spun on her heel and left the office.

Valens turned back to his desk, his thoughts turbulent. Tampering in his territory couldn't be tolerated. The perpetrator had to know he or she would be killed if caught. Given the level of maneuvering, his adversary had to be highly competent and insightful. Highly trained. It spoke of an experienced Demigod.

But how had he missed another Demigod's interest in him, and which one was it? He'd be damned if he'd let someone get in the way of his plans.

Chapter 12

ALEXIS

"TREES," DAISY WHISPERED as she cleared the brick wall. "All I see is thick, bushy trees."

"Are they real?" I asked, stopping behind her and eyeing the mass of green stretching from one side to the other.

"Yes," Mordecai said. "I smell them."

"Where were you on that wall, then?" Daisy grumbled.

"I smelled the wall, too."

"The gap, I meant," Daisy said.

"Gaps don't smell."

Thane chuckled, following along behind us.

Elation bloomed in my middle. Kieran's feeling, not mine. He was close. Other souls existed somewhat near him, but they seemed muted. They were inside, probably. He was outside. "There's a building or something beyond these trees."

"Very far beyond?" Daisy asked.

Remembering what I'd discovered in my room earlier, I closed my eyes and pulled magic from the Line. I boosted my awareness and then spread the extra power around me, along the ground and through the trees. This would allow me to see the ever-present spirit in the world of the living.

"What is it?" Daisy whispered. "Why are you waving your hands in the air like a psychopath?"

"*Shh.*" Pure power and spirit vibrated through my body and hugged my soul tightly. I peeled my eyes open, seeing the spirit seep through all around me. It pooled in holes and crevices and clung to branches. Soft mist rose from the ground, ultraviolet blues and purples that normal humans couldn't see.

My magical vision gave me a sort of bat-like perception of the area. Souls throbbed brightly to life beyond us, some of them within a mess of walls beyond the trees, like I'd suspected, and one floating on the other side, light and pure and waiting for me.

"Each soul gives off a different pulse," I said in fascination, amping up the spirit surging through the area. "It's not something I can see. It's a...feeling. An acknowledgment. Like seeing a face and knowing who it belongs to. Same thing. Huh. How come I've never noticed this before?"

"So...what's the plan?" Mordecai asked.

"Right, yes. Sorry." I pushed farther into the trees before stopping again. "Kieran is waiting out front of what is probably a house or office building or something. Others—the rest of the Six and Bria, I assume— are in the enclosure, also waiting. Given that this is a puzzle, or challenge, or training exercise, the right thing to do would be to check the perimeter and see if there are any traps or tripwires or lord knows what. But I'd rather not bother. Thoughts?"

"The Six will beat the living hell out of us if we aren't thorough," Daisy said. "I've learned that lesson."

"It's a hard lesson," Mordecai agreed.

"But I'm in charge, and so I'll get the heat for not bothering." I lifted my eyebrows.

Daisy glanced at Mordecai, then *didn't* glance at Thane, still standing behind us. The non-action spoke volumes. She didn't want to admit she liked my idea when a potential tattletale was in our midst.

"I can change and take care of the perimeter really fast," Mordecai said.

I thought about it for a second, trying to fight past the butterflies and excitement that gave me the mad desire to sprint through the trees, over some sort of fence, and into Kieran's arms. I had to be rational. I had to think about our training. Kieran was counting on me to step it up. There was a reason he didn't want me wasting my heart on him. He knew he needed to focus on the battle ahead, which he doubted he'd survive. We might not survive either if we didn't—

"Oh screw it, let's just go."

His services might not have originally included sex, but he'd opened that floodgate. He could deal with the repercussions.

Mordecai stopped me. "Wait...there is less tree smell over here."

He led the way, stopping at a wall of green and sticking out his hand. It passed through without disturbing the foliage. Another illusion.

I stopped relying so heavily on my vision and reverted back to focusing on the spirit around us. It still clung to trees and branches, outlining them, and showed an open space of about three feet wide where Mordecai's hand had been.

"Oh my God," I breathed, stepping in front of him. I could see through the illusion.

"Good looking out, Mordie," Daisy said softly from behind me.

"Yes, that was excellent work," I said over my shoulder. "Now that we know about this facet of Zorn's magic, we'll want to keep our eyes open."

"I can't spot them." Daisy's voice rang with frustration and defeat. "I can't do anything helpful. A non-magical person doesn't have any chance in the magical world."

The urgency to run to Kieran pulled at me, but a stronger sensation stayed my feet. I needed to look after my kid.

"Wait." I turned to face her. Her soul glowed bright and beautiful in her chest, and I smiled at the sight.

Mordecai pushed closer. "Your eyes are serious, but you're smiling weirdly. Are you okay?"

"You look really creepy," Daisy said.

My urge to smile vanished.

"Listen, Daisy, I know magic seems like a leg up. And honestly, it is. It's a cheat. That's why the non-magical section us off and live without us. They think they're safer keeping the two groups segregated.

"But here's the thing. Batman didn't have any super powers. He was a normal man who got a fright from a bunch of bats when he was a kid, then tried to overcome his fears and went a little nuts. What made him note-worthy was an excellent fighting ability and a bunch of gadgets. Other than that, he was just a slightly crazy dude in a costume. So learn to fight like no one else can, get Kieran to buy you a bunch of shit, and settle for a sidekick with a genie robe instead of spandex. *Voila.* You're golden."

Daisy's lips pulled to the side before she nodded thoughtfully. "That's true, I guess."

Mordecai was nodding, too.

Thane was looking at me like I'd just sprouted two horns while stealing Daisy's milk money. He just didn't get it.

"Remember, too." I held up a finger. "A lot of magical people focus on their specific form of magic. They train in that magic. So, sure, they're really good at that one thing, but their other skills are underdeveloped. Bria's a garden-variety psychopath without her dead bodies, Jack needs water to shift, and Thane could've ripped Donovan's head off. See what I mean? You'll only have a disadvantage in that *one* thing your magical adversary is good at. So make sure you're good at everything else, and capture that fucker the instant they're not in their element."

Daisy heaved a sigh as Mordecai rubbed her back. "It'll be a lot of work," she said.

"Yup. It will." I shrugged. "But someone else is paying for it, and what else have you got to do?"

Thane leaned around the kids to better see my face. His expression was one of incredulity. I couldn't tell whether that was a good thing.

"Okay, let's go see what Kieran is nervous about." I about-faced.

"I can't speak or open doors when I use my magic," I heard Mordecai say in a soft, comforting tone. "Changing form quickly is really tiring and painful, and so is changing a lot. I'm mostly stuck in one form or the other unless I plan out good times to change. At least you can always stay in human form."

"I guess," Daisy said glumly, but I could tell she was

coming around.

Grass met the line of trees, an expanse of it spreading out behind a huge two-story house with two chimneys. Sensor lights lined the wall behind the house and cameras covered every inch of the spacious backyard. My heart quickened as I hurried to the side, ignoring the kids' comments on the size of the place. Through the plain, stained wood gate (yes, I noticed those things now, thanks to Bria and her fixation on decorating) and around the house—

My heart leapt.

His deep black eyebrows arched over those entrancing stormy blue eyes. His sharp cheekbones and strong jaw gave his face a severity that said *badass*, but his shapely lips softened his overall look into a rugged, godly beauty. Raven hair was cut short on the sides and longer on top, trendy yet wild. A tight white T-shirt hugged his broad, muscular chest and loosened over what I knew was a washboard stomach. His stylishly distressed jeans hugged his powerful thighs.

Good heavens, the man was so freaking hot. But that's not what drew me.

An untamed, raw energy pulsed from his body, like a thunderstorm right before the lightning zapped down. He was all the strength and power of the ocean, wild and tumultuous, aching to be let free. The effect, teamed with his charisma, drew me to him and made it painful to walk away.

"You made it," he said, a sexy smirk playing across those kissable lips.

"Yeah. We would've been here sooner, but we were debating our chances of being murdered and dumped in an unmarked grave."

"We still could be," Daisy murmured behind me.

Kieran's smile increased in wattage. Fire raged through my body and I blinked in a lust stupor. He must've felt it through the soul connection because heat kindled in his eyes.

"You had a Berserker in your car, and you were worried about me?" Kieran asked lightly, but I didn't miss the flash of fear in his gaze. He hadn't taken that news about Thane's loss of control very well, I'd bet.

I laughed. "He's the only reason we aren't still sitting in the car right now."

Kieran nodded, his acute focus rooted to me. It used to be disconcerting. Then it was distracting. Now, I could admit to myself that it was enthralling, being able to command his attention like I did. I'd never seen him focus this hard on anyone else, as if the rest of the world didn't exist.

"So," I said, trying to pretend my cheeks weren't burning. "What do we have here?"

Kieran blinked, as if coming out of a fog. He tore his gaze away, but it found its way back to me.

"Your new house, obviously."

Chapter 13

ALEXIS

M Y EYEBROWS WRESTLED my hairline. I'd been in a nice little moment just then, basking in his presence. Now I was flung back into the real world, trying to make sense of what I'd just heard.

As if mirroring my thoughts, Daisy asked Mordecai, "What did he just say?"

Kieran took a step back and made a grand sweep with his hand. Thane smiled like a gobshite.

"Happy early birthday," Kieran said.

I left my eyebrows where they were and tilted my head. "My birthday isn't for two months, number one, and...what?"

"I know. I'm early. I hate waiting and I love giving surprises, so..." Kieran gestured to the enormous house again.

Playing along, because it was never wise to antagonize Crazy, I took in the home I was standing in front of.

A three-car garage sprawled off to the left with a

black BMW and Bria's old Mazda (her actual car, not one of her stolen ones...I didn't think) sitting in the driveway. Two more black BMWs hugged the curb out front. Clearly those belonged to the rest of the Six, hanging out inside like I'd thought. Two large stone pillars ran down each side of the front door, supporting stained glass windows. The door itself was embedded with one. Huge bay windows adorned the front of the house, overlooking careful landscaping.

Across the street was another large house, just as carefully tended, with Kieran's red Ferrari parked in the driveway. The road ended not far from the houses, and beyond it the cliff bottomed out in the great wide ocean. The comforting roar of the waves washed over the quiet street.

We'd just been talking about Batman, and now we'd stumbled into a rich hermit's paradise.

Two more houses could be seen at the other end of the street before a sharp corner took the road behind an array of leafy trees.

"It's a gated community that didn't take off like the developers had hoped," Kieran said, following my gaze. "About half the houses are filled, and most of those are at the front, farther away from the dual-society zone. That one is mine." Kieran pointed at the house where he was parked. "And this is yours. Well..." He spread his hands, and I had a strange urge to punch him in the stomach. "At the moment, it belongs to Henrietta Johnson, but since she only exists on paper, and all the paperwork is waiting for you inside, it's as good as yours. As soon as we are out from under my father, she can sell it to you for a dollar, and that'll be settled."

I blinked a few times, and then blinked a few more times, and then wondered why neither of the kids were speaking. Turned out, it was because they were looking at me like two starving beggars eyeing a pot of gold.

"Okay, now hold on." I put my hand up to stall whatever they planned on saying. "This isn't like him buying us food, or the guys cooking it, or free training. This is…too much. Way too much. Like…way, *way* too much. So much too much that it is on its own planet of *too much*."

"Yes, but you're one-hundred-percent in his pocket now, and he is putting you in incredible danger," Daisy reasoned. "He owes you this."

I pushed my held-up hand her way. "For one thing, he's my boss, which is different from being in his pocket, and for another, the danger he put me in is finished. The job is done; his mom is free. *I'm* now putting *myself* in incredible danger. If anyone is going to buy me a new house, it's me. He doesn't owe me squat but my next paycheck. Which I'll use to buy myself that new house…someday."

"He's protecting us by putting us in a house without

your name on it," Mordecai said. I'd just known he'd have the better argument. The guy was too levelheaded for his own good. "You'd still have your house. A house that you can move back into when this is all done."

"Right!" Daisy flung a finger at me. "The paperwork for Franny is inside—"

"Henrietta," Mordecai supplied. Kieran's smile sparkled.

"—but that doesn't mean this is actually your house. It's no one's house. We can just squat here while all this Valens stuff is going down, and when that is done and we're the victors, we can reassess."

"It's in the magical zone, Daisy," I said. "You're not magical."

"I have an I.D. that says I am," she replied smugly.

"That's why I had Zorn put in—"

"No." I moved my hand from Daisy to Kieran, silencing them both. "It's dangerous here. If Valens's people find her here, they can kill her outright. At least there are laws Valens has to follow in the dual-society zone."

"Valens doesn't have to follow laws anywhere," Kieran said, his humor dissipating. "He sent that woman after Bria yesterday, and it won't be long before he sends someone better. If he goes after you, Alexis, I'll be the only thing standing in his way. I need you here so I can protect you. This is the best compromise I could make. You'll be safer here. You all will."

"Even if they check me out, my paper matches my lifestyle," I said, ready to fight until the last on this one.

"They won't just look at your papers, baby," Kieran said softly, anxiety tightening his eyes. "They'll want to peel you apart and see what you know. They'll do it with pain." His body tightened, and I could see him struggling under the weight of that thought.

I surveyed the enormous structure in front of me. "But this…" I shook my head and took a step back. "Why not a shanty on the other side of town? This is too much."

"A shanty?" Daisy asked in disgust.

"It's not yours," Mordecai said. "We'll just stay here for a while, use the back way to come and go until the battle is finished, and then we'll go back to our incredibly cramped home in a not great part of town. This massive improvement is just temporary."

Kieran leaned into me, warmth radiating off his body and soaking into mine.

"If you stay here, I can stay with you. Or you can stay at my place," he said, his stormy eyes inviting.

"Foul play," I murmured, my gaze roaming his incredibly handsome face. Heat flash-boiled my blood and my body vibrated with desire. I could barely breathe. "But won't your dad think something's up if you move out? Won't he check out your neighbors?"

My voice had turned sultry, dripping with my aching need.

He took a step to close the distance, his body inches from mine. Electricity singed me as it passed between us.

"Neither of those things are an issue anymore." His sweet breath fell across my face. I wanted those lush, shapely lips on mine. "He's on the cusp of connecting Bria to me, I can feel it. It will all unfurl from there. Quickly." His pause was slight, but anxiety dumped into my body through our connection. "We're out of time."

He was worried but not letting it show on his face. Our fate, whether we would live or die, waited on the horizon, just out of sight.

"Which is why you need to make new friends," I heard Daisy say, but I couldn't focus—not on her, the obvious danger we were all in, the horribly shortened timeline, or the enormity of this gift.

All I could focus on was Kieran's eyes delving into mine, urging me to take his hand and let him lead me into the house he'd bought for me. To let him take care of me and the kids. To let him provide for us as he so desperately wanted to.

Silence fell around us. Souls pulsed in bodies. The delicious sea breeze caressed my hair.

Kieran's stormy eyes dared me to say yes.

Chapter 14

KIERAN

THE PHONE VIBRATED in Kieran's pocket, but he ignored it. It was probably Henry calling to update him on the status of the business license for Lionel Curtsy, a fictitious man who'd just inherited a nice sum of money and planned to start a used car dealership specializing in passenger cargo vehicles. Old school buses, vans, trucks—all things Lionel would be purchasing for the business venture to come.

Kieran would then need to come up with more manpower to fill all those vehicles. Sadly, a made-up name couldn't help him there.

He pushed the interruption from his mind. He'd deal with it later. Right now, he could only focus on the woman standing in front of him with open, honest, and frightened eyes, scared to take this plunge with him.

He couldn't blame her. He'd felt his own fears all day long, in between surges of nervousness and desire. But the second she had walked up to him, eyes alight with fire and intelligence and passion, his fears had melted. All of his misgivings about the magnitude of this offer had drifted away.

She was his. She'd initiated the connection by joining their souls. She'd cemented it by thwarting his attempts to send her away. She'd nailed it down by turning away her ex-boyfriend at the bar.

Despite his fear that he wasn't good enough, he *did* want her heart. He wanted it with everything in him. He couldn't resist her, and it wouldn't take long for her to realize that she couldn't resist him, either.

She was his, and soon, she'd give in to it. Like he had.

"I…don't know," she said hesitantly.

"Well, I know." Daisy gestured toward the house. "Let's go have a look."

Fear flashed through Alexis's eyes again, and she opened her mouth to protest. But honestly, what choice did she have? Everything he'd said was true. Her fear of giving in was the only thing keeping her from seeing that.

"Come on," he said, reaching out his hand with a smile.

Alexis blinked those deep brown eyes at him, and a stunned look crossed her face. A moment later, the stars in her eyes turned into a glare.

"I said I didn't know." She turned slightly to avoid his hand. "Take a hint."

"It isn't a hint when you just tell him. Come on." Daisy grabbed her elbow and dragged her. "I bet Bria is in there. She'll have a good take on all of this. You listen to her."

"I don't listen to her. She always takes your side, and then makes fun of me for my poor choices in life," Alexis grumbled, though she allowed Daisy to pull her away.

Mordecai gave Kieran a sheepish look before skulking off after the girls. The shifter was really shining through in that boy. He now recognized Kieran's status as alpha and acted accordingly with his body language. He'd fit into pack life perfectly. It was time he met some of his own.

Thane must've been thinking the same thing, because he fell in step with Kieran, somewhat removed from the others.

"I found that pack Jack was wondering about," he said, and Kieran allowed him to slow the pace a little. "Alexis seems dopey most of the time around those kids, but that's because the power structure is clearly defined. I saw Alexis throw her weight around earlier when I showed up at her door. It was enough to raise my small hairs. She has leadership potential."

Kieran nodded as they reached the open door. A squeal of delight from farther inside made him smile. He'd never heard Daisy squeal. That family was as good as moved in.

"Those kids were falling over themselves to do as she said," Thane went on, giving the large entryway a glance. Tiles made to look like stone covered the floor. High ceilings gave the space a feeling of grandeur and the wide staircase leading upstairs curved away right. The designers had done a great job with it, something Bria had grudgingly acknowledged. Her good opinion on these matters was hard-earned. "She is clearly the alpha, and Daisy used to be the beta."

"Used to be?" Kieran asked, hanging a right down a small, bare hallway toward the kitchen. He'd brought in furniture, but the rest of the house was a clean slate. Alexis could dress it up however she liked.

"Haven't you noticed the kids have been bickering a lot lately? Alexis complains that they didn't used to fight so much. Now that Mordecai is healthy and training, he's trying to rise up in the pack. He took the back of their line coming in here today, keeping Daisy—the physically weakest member—protected in the middle. He's probably trying to dominate her socially so as to officially move into the beta role."

Kieran grinned and shook his head as the space in front of them opened up into a brand new kitchen with top-of-the-line appliances. The rest of his Six and Bria sat gathered around the large, circular kitchen table on the other side of the island, watching Alexis and the kids open and close cabinets and appliance doors as if they were a game show audience. A swinging door led to the dining room, and a bigger, rectangular table.

"Daisy is a spitfire," Kieran said quietly, watching Alexis's eyes glimmer. His heart swelled. His chosen family was in this house, all of them. "She won't lose the intellectual fight to Mordecai very easily."

"This is true."

"Did they have any problem finding the doorway?"

"Enough," Daisy called out, putting out her hands. Everyone turned her way. Bria froze halfway to standing. "We've seen the kitchen. Let's move on!"

Bria laughed and finished standing. The rest of the Six stood up, too, joining the tour. They were all caught up in the delight and discovery of the newcomers.

"The actual doorway? No," Thane said, following the others into the dining room. "But they sat in the car for a while debating whether you planned to kill them."

Kieran chuckled and Daisy led the charge to the next room, a bright living room with huge bay windows facing the ocean. A couple of trees dotted the cliff, cutting down on visibility. The distance cut down on it a little more. The view was a pale representation of what his father got to see every day, but it was the best Kieran could do.

"Oh my God," Alexis breathed, drifting to the windows with her hand on her chest. "It's gorgeous."

Apparently, Alexis wasn't nearly so spoiled as Kieran.

"Who found the way through?" Kieran asked as everyone but Bria walked toward Alexis.

Bria crossed her arms over her chest and looked at the setup with a critical eye. "No. This is wrong. Who has an entertainment center, anymore?" Bria gestured at the piece of furniture in the corner. "And why wouldn't the couch face it? No, the TV should go on the wall, and a little—"

"It's not your house," Zorn said in a low growl.

"I realize this isn't my house, Zorn. Why else would this setup be such a clusterfuck? You might as well have designed the space. There isn't even an ocean gazing chair situated near the windows." Bria shook her head. "I have to leave this horrible room. It is messing with my chi."

Zorn's jaw clenched and Kieran held back a bark of laughter. Zorn had been in charge of the furniture placement, and it was obvious he'd been thwarting Bria's attempts to mess with the furniture in his house, which, Kieran had to admit, was just as oddly positioned.

"Alexis noticed the odd look of the brick wall," Thane said, returning to their discussion as the commotion died down, "and Daisy immediately clued in that it was one of Zorn's illusions."

"And through the trees?" Kieran watched Alexis, standing and staring at the view. It was like she was so lost in the ocean she didn't hear the kids trying to hurry her up to see the next room. It was a headspace he practically lived in at his father's house.

"That was kind of odd," Thane said, missing the scene. In fact, everyone but Kieran seemed to have missed it, including her kids, who were giving up on her and moving on without her. "Alexis found the way. She seems to have figured out another facet of her magic. I interrupted a breakthrough of some kind when I knocked on her door earlier." He paused for a moment and his voice dropped in irritation. "Which was probably why she took so long in opening it."

"Don't you want to see the rest of the house?" Kieran asked Alexis.

She turned slowly from the window, and when their gazes met, his will buckled. He stepped forward without another thought, knowing Thane would get the message and make himself scarce.

Emotion bled through their soul connection. When he neared her, she leaned in, almost imperceptibly, and he knew what she wanted. He put his arms around her shoulders and pulled her in close.

"I've always loved the ocean," she said softly, folding into his embrace. "I grew up hearing the distant crash of the waves. Smelling the salt in the air. The kelp. I've always wanted a view, like your dad has. Or like the one from the magical government building. Always." She took a deep breath. "I never, in my wildest dreams, thought I'd actually have one. Your magic makes this that much more special. It's almost like I *feel* it. I feel the pull of the ocean and how it affects the tides. I feel the power, and delight in its majesty." She sniffed. "I don't have the right words."

"You don't need the right words," he whispered, skimming his thumb along her jaw. "I can feel it through the soul link."

She nodded and peaceful silence drifted between them.

Another squeal blasted through the house, and Kieran smiled.

"Regardless of how tickled she is, we still can't accept this," Alexis said. "It's too much."

"You freed my mother, thereby freeing me. You're helping me take on my father. You and your kids will mean our victory." He paused. "I will counter and say, it's not nearly enough. Not even close."

She sighed and shook her head, pushing back. "Let's go see what the kids are doing. They've never had a good Christmas. That they remember, anyway. This will have to make up for it."

"I'm Santa, and you're the Grinch?"

"No, I'm Robin Hood. Say goodbye to anything valuable."

He laughed and slipped his fingers between hers as they followed the sounds of delight echoing through the house. Confidence and warmth settled into him.

His phone started vibrating again as he led Alexis from the room. It wasn't like Henry to be this persistent. He knew what Kieran was doing.

His gut churned. Something told him it was more bad news. News he likely wouldn't be ready to counteract.

Chapter 15

ALEXIS

"BUT LEXI, WE'D have our own bathrooms!" Daisy followed me as we made our way through Kieran's illusion-riddled backyard. In the likely event Kieran was being watched, he didn't want anyone to see us crossing the street to his house. So, we'd hiked down an overgrown trail on the cliff before trekking to the back of his house through the trees. The place was so secluded we didn't see one foot print or dog poop.

I glanced around the well-tended backyard, half expecting to see a lurker nestled within the trees. Kieran had been distracted through the second half of the house tour. He'd left for the office to make some calls and take care of a few things, so everyone had broken up to get some training in, the kids with Jack and me with Bria. I'd struggled with focus, though, worried about what I was feeling through the soul link. Bursts of emotion had been blasting me ever since Kieran left. It troubled me that Bria, who was always quick to the draw, hadn't seemed to notice.

Something had definitely gone wrong. Or maybe, something was continuing to go wrong. Kieran didn't have everything sorted out, I could tell.

It struck me that Daisy could be right. Maybe Kieran did need some serious help, and we should take it upon ourselves to make that call to Sydney. What other options did we have? If Dara really was the only person standing in the way of Valens steamrolling the Peace Accord Treaties, wouldn't it be better for us to unite our efforts?

"You don't need your own bathrooms," I said absently as I chewed my lip.

Then again, living in virtual ignorance as we were, would we do more damage than good? I'd gathered that the plans were intricate and Kieran was a master at disguising his trail from his father's people. One wrong move might unravel the whole thing…

"Mordecai stinks," Daisy blurted. "Air freshener and candles can only do so much."

"That adds to the spice of life," I said, letting us in through Kieran's back door.

The sun was sinking over the not-so-distant water, painting the sky in beautiful layers of pink and orange.

"Umm, it smells good," Daisy said as we walked through a back room, similar to the one in the house across the street, and made our way toward the food smell. "I'm starving!"

"You're always starving," I said as we entered a kitchen almost exactly like the one across the street, only a little bigger, if that were possible.

Jack and Donovan stood at the grill beside the stove, both wearing clean sweats and tight T-shirts. They were probably the most robust cooks I'd ever seen. The fan whirred and smoke rose into the stainless-steel hood as flame licked the steaks. Unlike usual, they weren't chatting or bantering. Their shoulders were tight and their movements a little stiff.

A wave of nervousness rolled through me. This time I couldn't tell if it was mine or Kieran's.

Thane looked up from the large round table, similar to the one across the street, and gave me a tight smile before glancing back down at his laptop. Working, I'd bet. Bria paused from her salad station at the island, her face grim.

"Everything okay?" I asked the oddly quiet room. The kids stood behind me, making no move to file in and claim their space, clearly sensing the weird vibe.

Bria grimaced and started tearing lettuce. She clearly only believed in knives when they were being stuck in human flesh. "There's a severe weather system bearing down," she said. "It's looking like a category five shitshow."

"We're keeping an eye on things," Thane said, flicking his gaze up from the laptop. "There are a lot of moving pieces right now. It's easier when we're all in one place."

Nervous flutters of a different kind ran through me. I tried not to think of how much the kids loved the rooms and bathrooms they'd get, or the privacy and convenience of the master suite. I tried not to think of that deep look in Kieran's eyes when he'd offered me the house, open all the way down to the soul I had linked to my own. I desperately tried not to think of how close he was at that moment, probably just pulling up to the house, and how desperately I wanted to see him and never let him go.

I tried, and failed.

Before I could figure out what to say, the front door opened and a moment later Boman entered the kitchen with a grim face to match the others.

"Incoming," he said, making his way to the counter.

Zorn's form appeared in the entryway next, vicious and sleek, gliding forward like a phantom. He was clean and fresh, dressed down like the others, but his aura of ruthless energy would have given a horror movie villain pause.

Bria glanced up, and instead of making a quip or raising her brows in hello, like she would've done with anyone else, her gaze caught his and held it for a long moment. Much to my incredible dismay, her cheeks flushed red and heat lit her eyes. She looked down again, the first to do so, and her body tightened in a way I completely understood.

And then felt.

Kieran filled the entryway. Fire burned in his eyes as he beheld me, and suddenly the room seemed too hot, my chest too tight.

"We have a problem," Zorn said to the room at large.

"How bad?" Jack asked without turning around.

I heard the front door click shut, and this time Jack did glance back, waiting until Henry strode through the door with a blank face and a laptop under his arm. Jack's eyes widened.

"I pulled Henry, for now," Kieran said, stopping beside me, his arm brushing mine and sending an arc of electricity between us. Primal energy crouched within him, emanating strength and power. Without trying, he stood out from even this group of exceptionable magical talent and fighting prowess. No one would have to ask which one of them was the Demigod—his radiance and air of command was all too clear. "Amber is active."

Henry put his laptop down on the table in the suddenly still room.

"Who's Amber?" I asked into the hush.

"Kimmie Draves." Henry pulled out a chair. "Goes by Amber in the field. She's one of three magical people heralded as the world's best spies. Her skills at espionage far outshine most. Her attention to detail and ability to sniff out discrepancies is almost unparalleled. Word is, she has her team poring through digital files and records. No one knows what she's hunting for, but she's asking questions. Specifically, she's asking about Alexis's reassessment."

My blood ran cold as Kieran stepped toward the island, putting himself in the middle of his crew. Something about him spoke of unwavering confidence, of his ability to control the situation, no matter how dire. His very presence calmed my trembling limbs. His hard gaze straightened my spine. He hadn't said a word, but I trusted that he could lead and protect us.

I understood exactly why the guys put all their faith in him. His power of leadership was such that it really did seem like he had everything covered.

But Daisy had been right, too. He couldn't do it alone. The pressure was increasing, and soon we'd be called upon to fight. We needed every advantage we could get.

"We knew this would happen," Kieran said in a steady voice. "I prepared for it. I hid our tracks carefully—"

"I could've done better these past few months," Bria mumbled, her expression frustrated. She shook her head. "I got sloppy a few times—"

Kieran put out his hand. "You've done fine. It's taken them this long without any solid leads. It'll take her a while longer to piece everything else together. He hasn't discovered us yet. Jack, check that food."

Jack started and turned.

"We're procuring transportation as we speak," Kieran went on, easily holding everyone's attention even as Jack scrambled to calm down a steak engulfed in flames. "The bodies for our undead army have been magically sealed to stop further deterioration. Our land troops are watchful and ready. We have people swimming into the area from Europe. We may not have the numbers we'd like, but we're prepared. My father is not expecting an internal battle. His strategies are geared toward politics and territory takeover. I will be a surprise to him, I am positive. That'll give us an edge."

I heard Daisy grumble but couldn't make out what she said.

Kieran looked around the room. Spines straightened within the confines of his gaze. Just a look from him was enough to bolster his men.

But they didn't feel what I did. They didn't sense the anxiety rolling off Kieran in waves.

"We can do this," he said. "We're ready for this."

Pressure settled on my chest, and Bria's hard eyes met mine. I read her loud and clear—Kieran didn't fully believe his own words, but I needed to keep that to myself for the sake of group morale. Part of leading was instilling your people with confidence in a dire situation. I'd practiced that with the kids often enough.

"We've done all we can for the moment," Kieran said, reaching for a bottle of wine. "No one is scheduled to follow me tonight as long as I stay on magical soil. We have cameras set up all around the neighborhood— if someone comes spying, we'll know in advance. Let's enjoy a meal and some downtime. No wars will be starting tonight."

His gaze hit mine, deep and open. A question lingered in their depths.

Another wave of anxiety rolled through me, and this time, it was all my own. I had a decision to make. A decision that might change my whole life.

Chapter 16

ALEXIS

INNER WENT BY much too quickly. Despite the danger nipping at our heels, the guys could banter and chitchat with the best of them. My sides split from laughing so hard.

When everyone had finished and rubbed their bellies, they stood up slowly to clear away plates.

"No." Kieran stopped me from standing with them. He shook his head. "Let the guys do it."

"Lucky." Donovan crinkled his nose at me in jest.

"She's banging a Demigod," Bria mumbled, taking her plate to the sink. "She's getting the short end of the stick on that one. Soon he'll start cutting her meat for her."

"I want someone to cut my meat for me, are you kidding?" Henry dropped some dishes next to the sink. "Feed me, too, I don't care. It'll leave my hands free to scratch my balls."

"You're considered the charming one of the group?" Bria shook her head. "And you wonder why I don't date?"

"Not with that personality I don't." Henry laughed.

Kieran stood and ran a lock of my hair through his fingers. He directed his comment to the kids. "We have ice cream and cake if you want some. I'm going to show Alexis—"

"Come on, man!" Bria cupped her hands over Mordecai's ears. "They're just kids. They don't want to know what you're going to show Alexis."

"No, we certainly don't want to know what you're going to show Alexis," Henry mumbled.

Kieran gave Bria a flat look.

"It's fine, go." Daisy waved him away. "Woo her into accepting that house."

"Boy has your tune changed," Jack said, bumping Thane out of the way to get at the cake Donovan was uncovering.

"For my own bedroom and bathroom, I'll join a chorus and sing his praise," Daisy replied dryly.

"Come on." Kieran slid his fingertips over the bare skin on my neck. Goosebumps covered my flesh and heat raged in my core. "I have something I want to show you."

"Does it rhyme with—"

"No." Henry held up his hand to stop Bria. "There are actually kids present, in case you forgot from two seconds ago."

I took Kieran's hand and let him pull me up, ignoring the tomfoolery going on around me and instead focusing on the delicious hum spreading through my body. He led me out of the room and stopped at the base of the stairs, looking down onto me.

"Do you want to go up?" he asked quietly.

I took in his handsome face and those perfect, shapely lips. "It would be awkward to strip you naked right here. Otherwise, I'd say no."

He pulled me closer in a rush and planted his lips on mine. I fell into the kiss with everything I had, wrapping my arms around his neck and hugging him tightly. His hands spread across my back, his fingers lightly pressing in, as he angled his head and swirled his tongue with mine. I moaned into his mouth and ran my fingers through his hair.

"Stop," he said, gripping my hips hard, breathing heavily. "Let's stop, or we will end up naked right here."

Face turned up and mouth open, I panted with need.

"I want you to take that house across the street, but after learning this recent development, now it'll have to come with strings—" His step back turned into a stagger. Still hanging on to him, I stepped heavily after him. He grinned sheepishly but didn't apologize.

He turned and took my hand before climbing the stairs.

"My guys will take turns staying here. If the heat turns up, I'll keep them here or at Henrietta's house. If you stay at your home house…" I knew home house was what the Irish called their parents' houses—where they grew up. Fear and anxiety bled through the soul connection, but his voice remained even and confident. "If you go back, we'll reassess the schedule. I might have two guys on you at all times, and we'll need an exit plan."

I didn't comment as he turned down the hall, so similar to the layout of the other house. He pointed at rooms we passed, all fully furnished guest rooms, just like mine—

I grimaced and squeezed my eyes shut.

Not mine. Henrietta's.

Get out of my stomach, butterflies, it's not my house!

He paused at the last door, straight ahead, and I knew from the layout it was his room. His fingers curled around the door knob.

"Are you afraid of rejection or something?" I teased, seeing—and feeling—his hesitation.

He chuckled softly but didn't comment as he turned the handle and pushed the door open. The dwindling light of the early evening blazed through the airy and artfully decorated room. It cut across a deep blue rug that complemented the palette of a large oil painting on the wall. A king-sized bed took up the far wall and a little couch and two chairs congregated around the massive window facing the gorgeous blue ocean. Way out in the distance, a curtain of white waited for its chance to drift in and cover the mainland.

The soft click said he'd closed the door behind me, and heat unfurled within me. "This is beautiful," I said, out of breath.

"I have a few less trees blocking my view than you do." He wrapped his arms around my middle and held me close. "Whatever you decide about the house, it has nothing to do with this moment," he whispered.

I closed my eyes as his strong hands curled around my upper arms. His heat coated my back and his hot breath warmed the hollow of my throat.

I sighed and leaned my head away, giving him more access.

"Stay the night with me," he said in a thick voice laden with emotion. "Your kids can sleep here. They'll be safe. You'll all be safe."

I moaned as his lips trailed up my neck and grazed my jaw.

"Stay the night with me," he said again, his hands slipping down and applying pressure on my hips.

I moaned and moved my hands behind me, feeling along his thighs until I reached his hardness. I cupped him firmly and moaned as his lips sucked lightly on the fevered skin of my neck.

"Yes," I said in a breathy whisper, massaging his erection. Waves of heat ran through me. "*Yes.*"

He turned me to face him and captured my lips with his. His tongue thrust, needy and insistent, and his fingers worked into my hair. I yanked the bottom of his button-up shirt out of his slacks and unbuttoned it from the bottom up.

He nibbled my bottom lip as he pulled one hand from my head and slid it down my torso. His fingers rolled over my budded nipple, sending a shock of pleasure straight to my core.

"Hmm, Kieran."

His hand trailed lower, dipping into my pants, and then still lower, until his fingers just barely skirted the edges of my panties. I sucked in a breath and moved my knee to the side, giving him more room. His other hand found my breast, and he massaged my nipple.

I deepened the kiss as his fingers continued to brush under my panties, driving me crazy. I rubbed his hard bulge before going back to his buttons, my hands shaking with eager anticipation. His fingers brushed a little harder, turning my insides molten, until his hot touch finally slid over my clit.

"Oh..." A scorching wave of passion washed through me. I let out a trembling breath.

His kiss increased in fervency, sucking me into that place I only went to with him. That place of no gravity and complete focus. Of pleasure and mutual desire.

His fingers slid down my wetness before pushing into my body.

"Holy—" I fluttered my eyes closed and reached down to cup his erection again, rubbing as he thrust first one finger, then two, into my depths. "Yes, Kieran."

"I can't tell you how much I've wanted this," he murmured against my lips.

He pushed my bra up before slightly pinching my nipple. The fingers on his other hand worked back up to massage my nub. Pleasure speared straight through me, pooling in my desperately tight core.

"What, your own house?"

"You in my house, for as long as I want you. Sleeping by your side and then burying myself into you the second I wake up. Serving you breakfast, and licking between your spread thighs as you eat it."

"Oh God, Kieran, please." I moved against his fingers, needing his cock inside me. "Please, Kieran."

"You writhing under me helplessly," he whispered against the shell of my ear, jerking my jeans button free. "You begging for me to fuck you again. And again."

He ripped my shirt up and over my head with one hand, then grabbed my jeans and yanked them to the floor. A moment later I was in his arms, rushing for the bed. As soon as he laid me down on the soft mattress, he grabbed my lacy panties and tore them loose. He ran his lush lips up the center of my stomach, drifting to the side to lick my budded nipple. His hands reached under me and snapped my bra clasp open. He pulled it away and threw it over his shoulder.

I arched and slid my thighs up the sides of his unnecessarily clothed body. He switched to the other nipple, sucking it in before rolling it around his mouth with his tongue.

"Oh holy…shit." I huffed out a breath and arched, soaking in the sensations.

He rose up and shrugged out of his shirt, fully revealing his delicious upper body, sculpted by the gods. Cut pecs led down into that nearly eight pack; large shoulders gave way to bulging biceps.

He undid his pants before pushing them down to release his enormous, straining cock. Once out of his jeans, he slowed down for a moment. His entrancing eyes, deep and open, leading all the way down to his soul, lingered on mine. They didn't drift away to my exposed breasts, or even around my face. They stayed rooted to mine as he said, "You take my breath away, Alexis. I am so lucky to have found you."

Warmth wrapped around my heart. It was *me* he was responding to. Not my looks or the shape of my body, but me as a person. He was looking deep down into me, at all my secrets and the weirdness I liked to hide, and pulling it out to show me how much he treasured it.

I'd never felt more beautiful than I did in that moment. I'd never felt more relevant to someone, or more cherished.

Through the haze of passion, I recognized the depth of feeling running back and forth over our soul connection. I couldn't have said who it started with, just that it was tightening the connection, bringing our souls closer together. Intensifying our feelings.

"Let me buy you a house," he whispered into the hush of the room. He lowered down and touched his lips to mine. "Let me look after you."

I ran my hands over his strong shoulders and pulled him closer, heat burning through my body, magic fused with desire. I pushed my knees up his sides and sighed when he reached between my thighs.

"Give in to me, Alexis," he commanded softly, and the fire rose.

I gripped the sheets as tight bands of pleasure wrapped around me from his sexy magic. He was starting to lose control, just as I was.

"Say you'll be mine," he said, and though his voice was still so soft, alluring, I heard the command within the words, and his underlying need to claim me as his own.

My breath turned harried, and I arched under him with need. His fingers dipped into me with a steady rhythm, building me higher. I reached between us and curled my fingers around his hard length, steel wrapped in velvet.

"Hmm," he groaned and his thumb touched down on my clit. He plunged and rubbed, winding me tighter. Drowning me in sensations.

"Take me, Kieran," I begged, needing him in a way I didn't understand. Wanting him with a fervor that didn't seem natural.

His possessive Demigod power swept into the room, rising like the tide. I lost myself in it, letting it carry me where it would. Letting him work me higher until I could barely think.

"Do you require proof that I am devoted to you? Is that what you need?" he asked in a dangerous tone that hit me in all the right places.

I gyrated up to meet his fingers, nearing the edge. Ready to jump off and crash into orgasm.

"Yes," I breathed, responding to his ministrations.

He thought I was answering his question.

He leaned farther over me, flexed and deliciously imposing. He dwarfed me with his strength and showered me in his raw, primal energy. His fingers worked me hard, but he kissed me softly, the contrast intoxicating. He moved down and flicked a nipple with his tongue, then sucked it in.

"Oh—God!" An orgasm tore through me, blasting

my world apart. I shivered on the bed as he braced himself above me, his eyes locked with mine.

"I've never spent a full night with a woman," he said, his deep voice rough and open. "You will be my first."

I barely stopped from widening my eyes. I would've thought he'd spent the night with several women. He was a Demigod for criminy's sake. They were like catnip to felines. Especially this one, who was incredibly handsome. I said as much.

He slowly leaned forward and ran his lips against my jaw. "I've bedded women, but I've always left right afterward. Directly afterward. Except with you. I would've stayed for days on end with you, but my father would've wondered who had attracted my interest. I left to protect you."

I cupped his face with my hands and kissed his lips, emotion filling me up.

"Before you, I'd never bought a wardrobe for a woman," he continued in a low hum, "let alone on two separate occasions. I'd never stolen a woman's pants to get her size so a team of advisors could pick out the perfect attire for her body size and personality. And I've never given a woman her own drawer, let alone twice, both times without her ever having stayed over. Yours is that one, by the way." He pointed to a reclaimed wood dresser stained in espresso across the room. "Bottom right. If you need more room, I can make it."

Butterflies fluttered through my belly. Warmth squeezed my heart. "And a house?" I asked with a small smile and embarrassingly glassy eyes. "Is that a door prize usually?"

He didn't match my smile. "I've never dated, in the traditional sense. Or thought of a woman every waking moment. Or promised I would protect her regardless of having no assurance she was mine to keep." He pushed back, his stormy eyes intense. "Or allowed her to stay by my side when everything in me knows I should force her to go."

"Right, yes. The ol' *don't waste your heart on me* shtick."

"You shouldn't. I'm a mess. I'm dangerous. My father loved my mother as intensely as I love you, and he ended up locking her in a castle on an island."

I froze at his words, unable to focus on the last. It was hard to breathe through the emotions welling up inside of me.

"But damn it, Alexis, I know you're meant for me. I feel it. Our first meeting wasn't a chance encounter. Not really. You weren't terrified by a dangerous stranger following you around, threatening and propositioning you in turns, because you lack good sense, but because you recognized your destiny. It was tolerating someone who would stand by you while you claimed your birthright."

I struggled to keep the emotion out of my tone. "Just *my* destiny?"

"You freed my mother when no one else knew how, and I know you'll free me of my father, too. Just when I needed you most, I found you. With your help, I'll stay on the path my mother set me on. One of compassion and morality. You make me a better man, Alexis. You'll make me a better leader, if ever I should rise to that mantle. You are not just my destiny, you are my salvation."

I blew out a breath slowly, tears clouding my vision.

"Take that house, Alexis, for you and your kids. Give them a better life. Let yourself live a better life." He paused as he stared down into my eyes. "Be mine, and only mine, as I will be yours."

I held his gaze for a long moment, and finally, against all logic and sense, gave in. Kinda.

"Make me."

Chapter 17

ALEXIS

H IS EYES FLASHED with desire. He ran his palms up my inner thighs, pushing, spreading me wider.

"There is no going back after this," he said with a warning in his voice.

I moaned as his sexy magic caressed my skin and soaked down into my body. "I know."

I licked my lips as he leaned forward. His mouth skimmed across my core before sucking in my clit.

"Oh God…" I leaned back and closed my eyes, letting my hips drift up of their own accord. "Deeper," I breathed.

He pulsed the suction while running his fingers in and out. With his other hand he reached up and massaged my breast, lightly pinching my nipple and sending wave after wave of bliss through me. I lavished in the exquisite pleasure, so close to coming even though I'd already climaxed once.

I grabbed a fistful of his hair and yanked. He groaned, sucking harder. His hand working faster.

"Holy...*fuck!*" I shook with the orgasm, arching back and floating on the waves of passion.

He didn't give me a chance to come down. Faster than thought, he settled his muscular body onto mine. I groaned as his tip slid up my wetness.

"You're mine," he whispered against my ear, and thrust.

Colors burst behind my eyes. The whole world stilled in the moment. His magic blistered pleasantly across my skin.

"Mmm," I moaned, deliciously filled.

"Mine," he said again, his rough voice sending the shivers of ecstasy down my spine. A tidal wave of his magic sucked me under to a place with no thought. He pulled back before ramming into me again, then again, hard and rough and fucking fantastic.

"Yes, Kieran," I groaned, holding on for dear life as his power dizzied me.

Something about this time felt different than all the others. Something about his magic skimming flames across my skin made my heart leap expectantly. And it made me want to call my magic and entwine it with his.

Giving in to the feeling, I opened up the power of the Line, letting it fill the room and seep into our soul connection. He groaned in bliss and thrust harder, hitting me just right.

"Yes, Kieran. *More.*"

His movements became wild. The passion rose like a storm, overcoming me. A gale force wind blew from the Line, covering our soul connection with spirit and hardening it into something unbreakable. Invulnerable. Forever.

He crashed into me with a fervor I'd never experienced. I raked my nails across his back, lost to the exquisite feel of him. Basking in his magic and power. The pressure built, higher and higher, winding through my core and tightening.

I held on for dear life as his power spun around us, almost a solid force. I cried out as I hit another high, my body unbearably tight. The pleasure so sharp it cut, so delicious I could barely breathe. For a moment, I hovered right there, at the cliff's edge, just needing a little push.

"Mine!" he exalted, and a surge of power such that I couldn't understand slammed into me. Magic seared my skin and soaked down into my body. The pleasure wrapped around me as his body drove down deep.

The room lost gravity and I lost my grip on reality. Suddenly, we were falling—then floating—weightless in pleasure, limbs entwined. The well we'd tumbled into had no bottom.

With one last thrust, he whispered, "Forever."

I exploded into so many pieces I was sure they'd never all be found. He groaned and shook over me, finishing with me. His lips lingered against mine as my body vibrated against his.

Our heavy breathing filled the quiet room. My heart thudded against my ribcage and every muscle in my body loosened, then went completely limp.

"You've outdone yourself this time," I said softly, my voice slightly hoarse. I had the distinct impression I might've been screaming instead of ladylike moaning.

Breathing deeply, like he'd just sprinted a mile, he rolled onto his side before pulling me with him. I settled my head in the hollow between his neck and shoulder and breathed a sigh as the weight of his arm wrapped around me.

"That was..." His voice drifted away. "I have no words for what that was, Alexis."

"Incredible? Fantastic? Legendary?"

"Permanent."

I looked up, surprised by the gravity of his voice.

He skimmed his fingertips across my back. "I didn't ever imagine a person could feel this way. It's exhilarating and consuming. I feel like I'm still floating."

I smiled, knowing exactly what he meant. It was like the bed was just a prop for appearance's sake, and if it weren't there, we'd still be at exactly the same height, me wrapped up in his strong arms, enjoying the soft thrush of the ocean in the distance and the warmth of each other's bodies.

"My father must've felt like this with my mother," he said quietly, almost like he was talking to himself. His breath rustled my hair. "It must've started out like this. I want to give you the world, Alexis. I never want you to want for anything."

"Two wants don't make a right."

He huffed out a laugh. "Trust you to laugh it off. I'm trying to tell you this new feeling is scaring the shit out of me."

Well that wasn't expected.

"Something just happened there with my magic," he went on. "I'm honestly not even sure what it was, but it feels…" His voice drifted away.

I shrugged. "It felt good, whatever it was. Fiery but not painful. I liked it. I'd be down to do that again."

He shook his head. "I don't think I can do it again. It's done, now. That's it. I think."

I frowned. "What is…it?"

"I don't know."

"Right…"

Thankfully, I had a lot of experience shrugging off random magical things for which I had no explanation. I'd been doing it most of my life, learned from my mother, who had always taken all my crazy in stride.

And along those lines… "I think I accidentally made the soul connection permanent. Sorry. But you were claiming me, or whatever, and—"

In a rush, he rolled me onto my back, settled between my legs, and thrust into me. I gasped in shock, then groaned in pleasure. His magic settled over me like a hot, sexy, tantalizing blanket. Fire burned across my skin again, achingly delicious.

"Found your—" I said, then I gasped again as he pumped into me before pulling back and thrusting harder. God he felt good. Better than anything in the world. Better than chocolate. "—sex trigger."

He slammed into me, over and over, and I was hard pressed to move fast enough to meet his downward thrusts. Pressure built almost immediately. His magic sizzled. I yelled with each thrust, wild. Lost. Taken by surprise and loving it.

"Mine," he whispered, and he reached down between us and massaged my clit as he stroked in and out. "Come with me."

I wouldn't have a choice. This train was smashing into the station.

"Now, Alexis. Come with me," he commanded. His magic seared my flesh in the most gratifying of ways.

"Oh!" The wave of pleasure crashed, sweeping me along with it. For the fourth time that night. A girl could get used to this.

I trembled in bliss as he shook over me. Endorphins surged through my blood stream, and I could barely form a thought, let alone a word. He leaned down to kiss me softly.

"Surprise," he said with a smile.

Mouth open, eyes wide, I was panting like a race horse ridden by a giant.

He settled beside me again, nestling me close to his body. "Clearly I was wrong about that magic," he said with a note of pride.

"Uh-hum."

"I have no control over it, though."

"Mm. Mhm." I swallowed and tried to get my bearings. "Saying that you're claim—"

"No, no!" He placed his hand over my mouth. "Don't say the C-word. It's like a shot of nitrous and I need to take you immediately. Not make love—take you."

He peeled his fingers off my mouth and paused, like I might say it again just for funsies. But honestly, this girl needed a break.

"Your C-word is a very different C-word than the one Mick at the bar always shouts out," I said.

He chuckled softly. "That bar…"

"Don't worry, I'm not going to sponge off of Miles, anymore. In fact…I *may* have burned that bridge. Though he thought he was having a heart attack, so maybe not."

"I've heard the lease on the building might be up for review soon," he said in a rough voice. "Would the neighborhood care if that bar shut down?"

The neighborhood, huh? I smiled to myself. He was so transparent it was funny. Too bad Miles wasn't a nicer person, because it looked like karma was about to deliver him a swift kick, courtesy of Kieran, and I wasn't going to do a thing to stop it.

"That particular bar shutting down?" I rubbed my hand up his chest before touching my fingers to his chin. I turned his face my way and strained up to kiss him. "No. But hopefully a new bar will take its place. One that isn't haunted, preferably. And still has a broken-down stool in the corner for Mick, though, because he doesn't like anything too new or fancy."

Laughter rumbled in Kieran's chest. He squeezed me against him. "Anything else?"

"The bartenders should get to keep their jobs. It isn't their fault Miles is a douche."

"Right. Hypothetically, if a new bar were to go up there, Mick's stool—"

"His whole corner. He's territorial about that particular corner."

"Mick's corner, including his stool, and the bartenders, would need a place in the new establishment?"

"Don't forget the bit about it not being haunted."

"Can't you take care of that now?"

"Yes, but I feel bad."

"Right. So Mick's corner and the bartenders get to

stay, and the ghosts have to take a hike."

I kissed him again, smiling as I did so. "Yes. Hypothetically, that's about right." I ran my fingers against his strong jaw. "So when are you going to clai—"

He slid his hand across my mouth. "Now you're playing with fire."

I peeled his hand away. "I like the fire. I like when you take me."

He chuckled softly. "Give me a few minutes to work up more energy. Otherwise I'll be a one-pump chump."

I laughed, squeezing him.

Silence gave way to the crash of the waves beyond the cliff. The room darkened around us as the brilliant colors of the sunset faded away. The mood changed subtly, more subdued, until he said, "When my mother went back to the ocean—which my father should've expected—he went crazy and ended up torturing her for the rest of her life."

I drew a line down the center of his abs. "Your dad is a shit-show, and I don't need to go frolic in the ocean."

He didn't seem to hear me. "He must've still loved her. I can't imagine this feeling will ever fade."

My stomach flip-flopped and goosebumps spread along my skin. I held my breath.

"Out of spite, he tortured her even though he loved her."

"Like I said, your dad is a shit-show. And unlike your mother, I'm not the epitome of a lady. If you fuck me over, I will wipe the world with your blood."

He huffed out a breath that didn't quite turn into a laugh. "That's the best news I've heard all day."

"Really?" I pulled back and leaned on my elbow, facing him. "I let you claim—"

He pushed his hand over my mouth and his cock straightened to attention. He squeezed his eyes shut and shook his head. "Not yet. Seriously, I'm not kidding. I won't last long if we go again so soon."

I laughed and pushed his hand away.

When his eyes opened, they were soft. He pulled me closer. "Ending up like my father is my worst nightmare."

"Well. Just don't lock me in a castle. My hair isn't strong enough for someone to climb up." I held up a finger. "But I'd be happy to *stay* in said castle, with unlocked doors, now and again. You know, in case you want to go back to visit."

"It's my father's property. I will inherit it should he die."

I didn't want to mention that there was likely a clause that forfeited the inheritance should the son kill the father. It seemed in bad taste.

"Listen…" I ran my fingers across his smooth skin. "Did you ever think of contacting the Fire Elemental in

Sydney? It seems like she'd have a vested interest in your cause." I shrugged, keeping it light. "Can't hurt at this point, can it?"

His breath rose and fell with his sigh. "When I learned my father had spies in the non-magical government, I worried he'd have them abroad, too, so I didn't contact her. And he probably does, but after checking it out, it seems Dara has seen through his tricks and blocked his attempts."

"So…that's a good thing, right?"

"Yes. Which is why I finally made contact." He stared at the ceiling. "She's a no-go. She wants what I want, but I don't think she wants to get in league with Valens's spawn. She was entirely professional about it, but I got the feeling that she didn't want to trade one tyrant for another."

A buzzing interrupted our conversation. Kieran rose a little, lifting me with him, looking beyond the end of the bed. He flopped back down.

"Go get my phone, will ya?" he said.

"No, thanks."

He sighed. "Worth a try."

I snuggled into the unbelievably soft pillows as he rolled out of bed and hunted for his phone.

"Well. To hell with her," I said to ease the blow, feeling the cool bedroom air drift across my skin. "Long story short, despite what people might think, you won't end up like your father. Not in anything you do. Even if I lost my way and allowed you to control me, Daisy would put her foot down."

A handsome smile lit up his face as he dug his phone from the back pocket of his discarded jeans. "I suppose that's true. I'm impressed with how she stands her ground against the guys. She's as strong as Mordecai is reasonable. They'll land on their feet. You've raised some good people."

"Thanks," I said, my heart full.

Kieran looked at his phone for a moment before his gaze came back up to mine. He slid back in beside me. "Speaking of the kids, they want to go home."

My heart sank. With all that was happening right now, home wasn't a good plan. I'd recognized the logic of that from the beginning, I'd just been wary about the strings attached to the place Kieran had bought. That ship had sailed.

"What about Henrietta's place? Will they stay there?" I asked.

Kieran's stare held mine. "That's what they meant by home." He paused for a moment, and I knew what was coming. "Will you accept it?"

A tear welled in my eye, though I wasn't sure why. "Yes," I said softly, and just like that, I knew everything between us had changed.

Chapter 18

KIERAN

KIERAN AWOKE AS light filtered into the room. A warm body snuggled up to his side and Alexis's sweet, feminine fragrance delighted his senses. He took a deep breath and let his head fall toward the window, listening to the soft crash of the distant waves. His body ached because of all the intense love making last night. He'd been a machine. Every time he'd so much as thought about the act of claiming her, all systems had fired up.

Arousal hardened his cock and a flash of desire stole his breath.

There it was again, the need to take his woman until she was panting in pleasure. It was more primal than the usual fire he felt for her. It was a fundamental need to mark the female he'd chosen. And that need had kick-started the foreign part of his magic that had exploded out of him last night. A magic he didn't understand the purpose of. After climax, it dissipated, leaving no trace of its use behind.

She had liked it, though, so he hadn't worried about it. Besides, she'd done her own job on him with her magic. She'd strengthened their soul connection. For a brief moment, a weird scene had filled the room—a midnight black line slashed through with glowing blue-purple, pulsing at him. It was Death, waiting to call him home. He could feel his soul's acceptance of it. Its need to be swept away. And though that should've scared him, he hadn't been afraid. The feeling had been welcoming, as though the great beyond were no big deal. It wasn't forever, it was just another area one could visit in life.

The logic made no sense, but then, that was often the case with magic.

He pressed his lips gently to her head and slid his fingertips over her exposed upper arm. He listened to her rhythmic breathing, nestled comfortably in his arms. Peace settled over him and the song of the ocean drifted through his blood. Their soul connection hummed softly.

Fuck, he was happy. Staying with her—lying with her—made him content in a way he hadn't known a man could be.

To love a woman is to admit your ruin, son. You'll lose your sense, and with it, your dignity. Don't be a fool like I was.

Kieran swallowed hard and pulled his arm up from

around Alexis. That was the warning his father had given him when he was young, one he'd repeated recently, after Kieran's mother died. He now understood the words in a new way.

Will that happen to me? Will I continue the family tradition by losing my sanity and imprisoning the one I love?

He pushed back the covers and climbed out of bed while grabbing his phone from the nightstand. A few messages waited for him. The first was from Zorn. The kids had settled into their new home easily and had met in Mordecai's room to discuss how to make the situation permanent. Then Daisy had disabled the monitoring device outside of her door, found the listening device in her room and taken that out, and proceeded to lock herself inside. She hadn't turned out her light until the small hours of the morning.

Zorn's message held some strong notes of pride. Apparently, he had installed the devices to see if she'd look for them, but hadn't actually expected her to find them. She'd proved to be a more cunning and insightful protégé than he'd originally expected.

The last message from Zorn made Kieran smile: She's plotting something.

The pupil was trying to out-do the teacher. That should keep Zorn on his toes.

He didn't bother replying. He didn't want to spoil

their games.

The next message was from Donovan: *One of the cameras was disabled at Lexi's house. Can't tell what knocked it down. Nothing seemed amiss around the property. Don't think there's anything to be alarmed about if she's staying with us.*

Donovan again: *btw—I bought the kids new laptops. Theirs was beyond shitty. You might get Alexis one.*

He frowned as he set his phone aside to slip on some sweats. Scenarios of his father's people knocking down a camera played through his head. Possibly someone of Flara's skillset might've resorted to such an obvious attempt to create a blind spot, but if that had been the case, Donovan would've noticed their intrusion on the property.

He snatched up his phone again, thinking it through as he headed downstairs. Jack waited at the island with an open laptop next to him. His phone sat off to the side and he had a half cup of coffee in front of him. He was manning the mobile security feed for Alexis's home house.

"Any news?" Kieran asked, heading straight to the coffee pot.

"Breakfast is in the oven." Jack absently gestured that way, his eyes not leaving the screen.

"I'll make something fresh, thanks."

"Did you get Donovan's message?"

"About the knocked-down camera?" Kieran waited

for Jack to nod. "How do you think it happened? Donovan said he didn't see any cause for concern."

"The camera caught a brief blur before it went out, like the flap of a wing or something." Jack scratched his cheek. "The moisture from the constant fog had weakened the bindings and the weight of the camera stretched 'em out. The other cameras needed to be resecured." He shook his head, frowning at the laptop. "They were high in the tree and nothing else was messed with—I agree with Donovan's assessment. I'm more concerned about Amber." He looked up at Kieran. "If Alexis is planning on hanging around here with us, of course."

Kieran filled the coffee pot and set it to brewing. He felt a smile as he placed a pan on the stove before opening the fridge. Despite the new threat and mountain of odds and ends he had to see to, at least Alexis would be close. It was one huge worry off of the table.

"She decided to stay," he said, and couldn't help the smug tone to his voice.

Jack nodded, going back to surveillance. "Good deal. What are your plans?"

Kieran gestured at the breakfast preparation, feigning a relaxed manner even though he felt anything but. He had to see how far Amber had gotten and try to head her off as well as he possibly could while he continued organizing a war effort with dwindling time and resources. Knowing Alexis could feel his inner turmoil, he needed her effectively distracted so no one would see her resulting worry, all while he played it cool to his peers.

He took a deep breath and focused in on the moment. "I'm making my lady breakfast in bed, what does it look like?"

Jack grinned and shook his head. "Late to the girlfriend game, and you're still going to make us all look bad."

Kieran laughed. "That's because I intend to keep this one."

He took the eggs out of the fridge, his thoughts slipping back to the danger at hand. "I need to figure out how far Amber has gotten," he said. "And I have to start putting things in motion. Ready or not, we need to move." He gritted his teeth. "I don't know where I'm going to find any more troops. We're going to be the underdogs in this one."

If Jack heard the uncertainty in Kieran's voice, he didn't let on. "We were always going to be the underdogs, sir. But that's just fine because the gremlin says we'll win so long as we have her family on board." He shrugged. "Thanks to you, we do. We're good."

The gremlin was what the guys and Bria had started calling Daisy because of her vicious fighting style.

Kieran wished he could believe Jack—he just didn't

know that they'd be enough. He needed a miracle.

"You and Zorn are on Alexis and the kids today," he said, cracking an egg. "She'll probably want to go shopping for the house, which is fine as long as she stays in the dual-society zone and you stay out of sight. We don't need to help Amber connect the dots. But the second you sense danger, get her out of there. My father is still following breadcrumbs, so I doubt he'll act just yet, but it's better to be safe."

"Yes, sir."

Kieran paused in whisking the eggs, a pang hitting him center mass. He had wanted to be there for Alexis's shopping spree, watching her eyes glimmer as she roamed her favorite stores without compromise. He remembered the way she'd argued with herself over that blanket she'd wanted to buy for Mordecai. She wouldn't have to hesitate anymore. Anything she wanted, he'd give her. Anything in the world. Except, at the moment, his time.

Fire burned in his middle, but he pushed it down. It couldn't be helped. He was too far on this path to walk away. It wasn't just about vengeance, anymore. His father needed to be stopped. A lot of people would die if his father's plans were realized.

Valens had to be stopped, and his allies needed to be torn down.

One thing at a time.

"So long as the coast is clear when she's shopping," he said, "let her take as long as she wants. I'll be furnishing her with a credit card. Make sure she has a good day of it."

"Of course, sir. She's great at spreading her good mood. A pity she couldn't go to better stores, though. Dual-society stores sell cheap crap. It all breaks too easily."

"Maybe you should be kinder on her things."

Jack smiled. "Maybe she should gain some muscle and feel my pain."

Kieran layered the pan with eggs. "You'll probably live to regret those words."

He sure hoped so, at any rate. He'd need all the help he could get.

Chapter 19

ALEXIS

"WAIT. STOP RIGHT there."

I barely heard Bria as I paused in the entryway of my new kitchen. I'd left Kieran's as noon waved goodbye. While part of me had hated leaving his warm body and exhilarating touch, another part of me was desperately excited to check out my new digs. Like this kitchen.

I had a new kitchen.

"I said stop right there."

I kept ignoring Bria as I swept my fingers over the kitchen table, then looked out the window at the windswept trees swaying in the backyard.

My backyard. My large, carefully tended backyard.

The crash of the waves pounding against the cliff face pulsed through the room and my body. The pull of the current tugged at my awareness, a strange feeling that I imagined would be ten times stronger and more useful if I were actually in the ocean.

Kieran had given me a bigger dose of his magic last

night, and my blood was singing. I'd also imparted a bigger dose of my magic on him—if the soul connection could be called as such—and could feel his tranquility and contentment as though it were my own. Or maybe it was.

I smiled and stopped by the sink as I felt the distance between us increase. He was on his way to the magical government building, then to the magical fair that was about to open in the dual-society zone. In other words, he was keeping up appearances.

Somewhere along the way he'd have to talk to his father, too. He hadn't told his dad, in person, that he was moving out.

My stomach flipped and I let out a breath slowly, aiming for calm.

Steady girl, we're not under fire yet.

I opened an empty drawer and stared at the interior blankly, willing my worry to drift away. I needed to furnish this kitchen. The guys needed to cook, and to do that, they needed appliances and kitchenware.

There has to be a better use of my time.

"I'm going shopping," I said, pushing for exuberance. I took another deep breath, ignoring the anxious feelings coming through the soul connection. It wouldn't be long now before the battle. It sounded like Valens was practically knocking on our door.

I wasn't ready.

It didn't sound like any of us were.

"I NEED TO GET THINGS." My volume had gotten away from me.

"You have bigger problems than a can opener," Bria said. "What's with—"

"Hey, Lexi," Jack said, sauntering in with his laptop under his arm. Zorn followed a moment later, his expression harder than usual. "You about ready?"

"No. Maybe." I patted my person, wondering if I needed to do anything before going out.

"Are you seeing this?" Bria gestured at me, her focus on Zorn.

"If it's what I think it is, it's an optical illusion," Jack said in monotone. "It shows the viewer whatever they need to see to get the message across." He paused for a moment. "Where's Mordecai?"

I took two distracted steps before I remembered this wasn't my mother's house, and my ward was no longer within yelling distance.

"That's going to take some getting used to," I mumbled as I brought out my phone. Then I smiled. "I can no longer hear them fighting. That *won't* take getting used to." I brought up the text message app, cluing back in to the conversation around me. "What's an optical illusion?"

"It's exactly what you think it is," Bria said tersely.

"What do you see?" Zorn asked her, his tone guarded. Jack shifted uncomfortably.

Bria shook her head, studying me. "It's done now, right? She can't undo this?"

"Undo what?" I put my hand to my chest. "What can't I undo?"

"I've heard that only death can strip someone of the mark of a Demigod," Jack said. "I'm not certain he knows he did it, though."

I frowned in confusion.

"Are you sure?" Zorn asked, stepping up to the island so he could get a better look at Jack's face.

"I can't be positive, but…" Jack switched the laptop to the other arm. "When they came downstairs, I didn't do a very good job of containing my surprise. Usually, if Kieran doesn't like my reaction to one of his decisions, he lets me know. In this case, I think he thought I was surprised he'd ignored his duties for half the day. He shrugged it off like it was no big deal."

"It's a very big deal," Bria said.

"What doesn't he know?" I demanded as Mordecai entered the kitchen wearing a sharp looking white button-up shirt and dark brown slacks that fit him perfectly. It reminded me of the outfit I'd wanted to buy for him, but couldn't, the day I'd met Kieran. Kieran hadn't just seen to my needs—he'd made sure the kids had new clothes as well.

"How could he not notice the effects of his handiwork?" Bria put a hand out toward me. "The warning is subtle, sure, but it's undeniable."

"You're anxious for your friend, but you believe in her happiness. That's why it's only a slight warning. It's telling you not to try and talk her out of this, or the mark holder will come for you." Jack studied me. "I see a glowing aura. It makes her look angelic, which makes me less afraid of what she can do. It'll make me better at protecting her."

"Seriously, what are you guys talking about?" I spread my hands and looked down at my body again, seeing nothing out of the ordinary.

"I don't see anything," Mordecai said in confusion. "But she smells more like Demigod Kieran."

"You already love and want to protect her," Jack said. "She's family, and your alpha, so that makes perfect sense. You're clearly happy with her connection to Demigod Kieran."

Warmth enveloped my heart. I still didn't know what everyone was talking about, but if Mordecai accepted my boyfriend now, after adamantly warning me away from him…that made everything so much better.

"What are you, an interpretative oracle when it comes to Demigods peeing on their booty of the month?" Bria asked, effectively ruining my nice little moment.

Jack laughed. "I'm a shifter. An ability to read the nuances of possession keeps us alive and our girlfriends ours."

Bria's face soured. "Because another man might move in on your girl if you didn't stake your claim like a barbarian? What, you figure he'd be able to take her from you because women don't have the brain power to choose for themselves?"

Mordecai took a step back like he was ready to flee.

Jack laughed harder. "You think men are the only ones who stake a claim on their significant others?" He jabbed a finger at me. "Don't you remember who started it? Alexis tied up the man's soul. His *soul*! That shit's cray-cray—"

"You're too old to say cray-cray," Mordecai said reasonably.

"Even if she was supposed to be a booty of the month," Jack continued, "and I don't think he ever saw her that way, she made that shit permanent."

"That soul thing isn't permanent," Bria retorted.

"It's permanent now," I muttered, my face heating. Bria's shocked face rounded on me. I threw up my hands. "I didn't mean to. His magic was searing across my skin and… I… It just felt right."

Mordecai stuffed his hands into his pockets. "It took me a while to come around, but not many men are strong enough to protect Alexis in a way she can't protect herself. And even fewer men are confident enough to accept her attitude and independence." Even though his voice was soft, it somehow cut through the room, keeping the rest of us quiet. "He's everything she's always asked the ceiling for after coming home from the bar. And even if he wasn't...he makes her happy in a way nothing else ever has. I want her to finally get her miracle." His intense and heartfelt gaze hit mine. "I think he's it, Alexis. I really do. I think he's the miracle you deserve."

Silence filled the kitchen and heat prickled my eyes.

Bria sighed and shook her head. "Do you know what's annoying? I can't form a rebuttal because then I'll just look like an unromantic asshole."

"If the shoe fits," Zorn murmured.

Her jaw dropped and she stared at him for one tense beat. "Really, Zorn?" she demanded, and my small hairs stood on end. I took a step away as Jack shifted uncomfortably. "Okay, fine. What do you see when you look at the magically shackled chick?"

Zorn's jaw clenched and his eyes glimmered defiantly. He focused solely on Bria when he said, "I see a woman who I will die to protect."

It didn't sound like he was talking about me.

"Whom," Jack mumbled.

Bria rounded on him. "Are you serious?"

He shrugged. "Grammar."

Bria narrowed her eyes, and another tense beat filled the space. I opened my mouth to make a light joke, but Jack shook his head at me.

Right. A lovers' spat of some kind. How awkward.

As if on cue, Daisy walked into the room wearing nondescript clothing that made her look completely out of place. Her jeans had no rips or tears, or any style whatsoever. Her black tank, though slightly faded, wasn't tied at her back to make it fit well, or ripped in a way that made it noticeable. I didn't see one pop of color. Her ponytail sat at normal height, neither low nor high. Her whole outfit just…was. None of her usual personality accented this look.

"What's up with you?" I asked as she stopped near the island. "Have you given up your love of flare?"

Her hip cocked out and her eyebrows lowered. "I need to be invisible. What's up with you?"

"Ha!" Bria pointed at Daisy. "I knew I wasn't the only one."

"Non-magical people can see it, too?" Zorn asked Jack.

Jack pulled his lips to the side in thought. "I think to an extent."

Daisy looked around the room and then back at me. Her expression flattened. "I'm not dense. I know about the morning-after glow, or whatever. Ew. Watch a movie and you know about that. But…did he get you new lotion or something? Your skin is practically glowing."

Bria's chin dropped. "Wait." She put out a hand to Daisy. "*That's* what you see? Are you saying you are cool with your parent hooking up with a possessive, stalking Demigod?"

"That's exactly what she's saying." Jack grinned. "She's happy about it."

"He wasn't stalking her when he first met her. He was trying to work out a potential threat," Mordecai said.

Indignation crossed Daisy's face. "Look. Do I think she should be shacked up with that guy? Obviously, no—"

"Liar," Jack whispered with a grin.

"—we all know that. He is the worst, even if he wasn't technically stalking her in the way we all originally thought. But clearly what I say has no effect on her actions, so I've moved on. Worry only about that which you can control. Learn how to adapt to everything else." Daisy paused and Zorn nodded, pride glimmering in his eyes. "I'm adapting. Usually she has a sort of...*air* about her—"

"It's happiness," Mordecai said as Bria said, "It's insanity."

"—but this time," Daisy went on, not hearing the others, "her skin is like...legit glowing. Like one of those filters on the camera that makes your skin really nice. Seriously, he got you a different lotion, right? I want some."

Bria put up her hands in defeat. "Alexis, honestly, just answer me one question: you're cool with being a kept woman?"

"Kept woman?" Daisy reeled back. "Are you kidding me? Ain't no one keeping my girl down." She gestured around us. "A Demigod with too much money wants to buy us a house? Um yes, we'll take it, thank you very much. He wants to buy us some new clothes, a bunch of shi...crap no one needs but is sure nice to have? Food? Yes, yes, and I'll take another helping, please and thank you. That motherfucker—sorry Lexi, but you know that swear was warranted—doesn't own us. If he thinks we can be bought, then he's the chump. We can and will leave at any time. We'll take the hand outs, but gifts with strings attached are for losers." She gestured to Mordecai, and then me, and then back to herself. "We ain't losers."

I nodded with my lips pulled to the side, thinking. "Yeah, that's about it. I don't mind people buying me stuff. I encourage it, actually. Why do you think I took drinks from Miles for so long?"

"It helps us save our money," Mordecai said, nodding.

"And it's not like he's in control," Daisy continued.

"We have all the paperwork on this house. If he tries to pull the rug out from under us?" She let the question hang in the air with her eyebrows lifted.

"We'll burn it down," Mordecai supplied helpfully.

Daisy's expression fell and she reached over to punch Mordecai in the sweet spot on his arm. "Thanks a lot."

"Ow! What?" he asked, rubbing the offending spot.

"You stole my thunder. *I* was going to say we'd burn it down."

"Then run off to Australia," he said expectantly. "I'm not stealing anything from you. Everyone knows that's the best plan."

A look of death crossed Daisy's face.

"I just…" Bria leaned against the counter, worry in her eyes. "Look, I know you guys swear by Kieran"—she glanced up at Zorn—"and everyone who works with him wants to stay working for him. As a boss and usually as a man, he's top notch. I'm a believer. I am. In almost all things, I am Team Kieran—"

"You worry that when it comes to a woman, he'll turn into his dad," Jack said quietly, all humor gone.

"Since day one, yeah," Bria said. "Look, genetics is a tricky bitch. Kieran got a *big* heaping of genetics from Valens. He has skills that not many possess. He stole Valens's prized possession out from under him, and after two months Valens still has no idea he was the one who did it. That takes a certain sort of a cunning. A Valens sort of cunning. And now here Kieran is, buying Alexis a new life, just like his dad did for his mom. He's also marked her without asking. Maybe he didn't do it on purpose, and maybe I'm in the minority here, but that's got me worried."

Silence fell through the kitchen, so thick I could barely breathe. She'd just dug up all the worries and concerns that had plagued me. Had this been a huge, irreversible mistake?

"I've known Kieran most of my life," Zorn said, his low voice filling up the room. "He found me in a gutter outside of a pub, beaten senseless. I should've been in the hospital, but my father wanted to get back to his pints and his dice. My attempt to drag him home hadn't been appreciated." He paused to take a steadying breath. "I was nothing. An unwanted nobody. There are very few high-powered magical people in the world, let alone in the magical elite, who would go out of their way to help a half-dead street kid. But Kieran ended his night out to take me home with him, and the Demigod's wife allowed her son to carry a bleeding pulp of a kid into her house and set him down on a spotless cream sofa in the living room. It wasn't a servant who nursed me back to health, though they had many. It was the two of them, taking turns. He might have a good helping of his father, but he was raised and nurtured by his mother."

Bria opened her mouth to speak, but Zorn wasn't finished.

"From that day forward, I've been a kept man. Kieran took me in, then bought me my first house. He bought the car I drive. He offered me a credit card, too, but by that time, he'd paid me enough salary, and taught me what to do with it, that I could stand on my own. He didn't do any of it to gain favor or loyalty. He wasn't attempting to buy me. He was offering to help me in the only few ways he knew how. I would go to the grave for that man and be brought back time and again to help him."

"But you're not a woman," Jack cut in. "Bria has a reason to be wary. There's a reason the Six is made up of all men, after all."

"Kieran's father did try to poison him to women, that's true," Zorn said. "He's never fully trusted himself to have power over a woman. He doesn't want to turn into Valens."

"What about Bria?" Daisy asked.

"She came on as a highly recommended outsider," Zorn said, "whom I personally interviewed—"

"He means banged." Bria's glimmer of mirth was short-lived. Her face soured again.

"You really shouldn't date people you work with," Mordecai said.

"No shit," Jack muttered.

"I was confident she would keep the relationship with Demigod Kieran professional."

"Kieran kept Bria at a distance, but Lexi reeled everyone in." Jack smiled warmly at me. "Thanks for that, by the way. This setup is way more welcoming, not to mention entertaining, than the sausage fest we had going on. I mean, the amount of unabashed farting would have made your head spin. I missed having a pack with women and kids. It just…evens everything out."

"Lexi doesn't succumb to his power," Mordecai said, understanding dawning in his eyes.

A wry grin twisted Zorn's lips. "He found a woman he can't control. Alexis is a strong leader in her own right, even if most of the time she'd rather not be bothered."

"Yeah." Jack nodded confidently. "My boy won't step out of line. His days of fearing women are not over, but his days of avoiding them long-term are dead."

Bria chewed her lip, her eyes on Zorn. "He did claim her, though."

"Yeah, but…what's a wedding ring, if not a claim on someone?" Jack put his hands out. "My boy is in it to win it, that's all."

Humor finally cracked Bria's worried façade as butterflies swarmed my belly at Jack's words. Her eyebrows lifted in defeat and she threw up her hands. "Okay. You win." She momentarily slipped back into seriousness and put two fingers to her eyes. "I will maintain my vigilance, but I guess we'll wait and see if the house needs to get burned down."

"Let's hope not." Daisy glanced around wistfully. "It's really nice. My room is *massive.*"

"If he doesn't know about the mark, can we risk taking her into public?" Zorn's gaze drifted down my body. "Only a Demigod can leave a mark like that. Even if people don't know what they're looking at, she'll stand out."

"Whoa, whoa, whoa." I put out my hands, suddenly anxious for a distraction. "I'm going to a forgotten part of nowhere. People make it a point not to notice each other in the dual-society zone. Unless you find a unicorn Burberry bag, no one so much as glances at you. I can travel under the radar, no problem."

"Except now you are a glowing angel," Bria said with a smirk.

"With a bitch face," Daisy said.

"Thank you, Daisy," I replied dryly. "But that's a good point. Anyone who notices me will get one look at my mug and then look the other way."

Zorn and Jack looked at each other, some silent understanding passing between them.

Jack shrugged. "If she gets undue attention, we'll

extract her," he said.

"If Valens sends someone worthy to tail her, I'll feel their soul," Bria said. "If they try to nab her, we'll make them disappear. The battle is coming, anyway—what's one misplaced stalker?"

Zorn's lips pressed together before he gave a curt nod.

"It'll be fine," I said, wishing I was a lot more excited about my chance to go spend money in my favorite stores. "I'm sure they'd go to my house first, anyway. There's no way they'd know I'd take today to go shopping."

Zorn nodded again. "Valens won't spare the resources to cover the area so early in the game. Still, with that mark…"

I shook my head helplessly. "I wish I could see what you guys did. I still have no idea what you're talking about…" Though something Kieran said tumbled through my mind.

There is no going back after this.

He'd meant that. He'd claimed me, as he'd promised, in a way he probably hadn't even realized yet—and I'd claimed him, too. Through the soul connection that was now permanent, I could feel his warm, steady pulse in my middle.

He'd claimed my body. I had claimed his spirit.

We were now connected, body and soul.

I didn't know if we had a future, given all we were up against, but I knew he was all I wanted in the present. He was my knight in shining armor even though I didn't need to be saved. He was a prince, asking me to help him steal his throne.

I chuckled to myself.

Now that was something I could get behind.

"Let's go shopping," I said, wondering what I could use instead of my fabulous handbag. I didn't need to draw notice. "If the worst thing that happens today is finding out a really hot Demigod wants to keep me around, I'd say I'm doing all right."

Chapter 20

ALEXIS

"I DON'T UNDERSTAND why I have to go with you when Daisy gets to train," Mordecai whined as we parked in my favorite dual-society zone shopping center. The location wasn't San Francisco proper, but rather a couple of small towns east, along the ocean and still within the San Francisco Bay Area, where there was a larger allocation of space for big stores. The town had a different and uninterested non-magical mayor than San Francisco proper, and given it was in the dual-society zone, Valens had no interest in it whatsoever. It was why I liked it so much.

"Because Daisy is training in the art of stealth, and you are not," I said, getting out of the car. Greedy anticipation ran through me. The rectangular piece of plastic burned hot against my upper thigh. I hadn't even put the credit card in my threadbare wallet, not wanting to soil it. "A large wolf wandering around in the middle of town might be noticed. A teen chick dressed in mundane clothes will not. Hence, here you are, in human form and about to have the time of your life."

"I doubt it," he grumbled.

The sea breeze drifted past my nose and a line of stores curved in front of me, beside a dirty sidewalk. Behind me, a couple of stores stood alone with the moderately busy street to the back of them. Busy for the run-down dual-society zone, at any rate.

"Okay." I adjusted the tweed shopping tote on my forearm, my inconspicuous handbag for the day, before smoothing my hair and straightening my very fine blouse. The guys had decided it wasn't a great idea for me to go home, where Valens's people might be watching for me, in order to grab cheap clothes that I wouldn't be noticed in. For the first time in my life, I'd have to "make do" with overly fine attire. What a strange situation I'd found myself in.

I pressed my key fob and locked my shiny and expensive car before bending to double check that my pants went down past my ankles. "I am looking fabulous, which would be really amazing if I weren't worried about Valens's people randomly showing up, recognizing me, and dragging me away to torture me for information," I murmured.

"When this is all over, I'm sure Demigod Kieran will take you out for a nice dinner or something where you can be dressed up," Mordecai said. "He seems to understand that you like that sort of thing."

Nervous flutters filled my belly. I'd just be happy with this all working out, period.

"First up, handbag shopping," I said, checking the time. Early afternoon.

Pressure settled on my chest. Half the day had gone by, and I had nothing to show for it. I should be training, not shopping.

I heaved a frustrated sigh. Kieran had suggested this shopping trip, which meant he really did want supplies for the house. He wouldn't send his people out on frivolous ventures, especially with Valens breathing down our necks. He wanted me here for a reason, and the least I could do was enjoy myself. This was a dream come true, after all.

"Come on," I said in a hush, veering us around a car, across an empty blue handicapped space, and onto the sidewalk. "This way." I tugged him right.

He resisted, looking down the narrow strip in front of the stores. "I smell a shifter."

"It's probably Jack."

"It's not Jack."

I paused for a brief moment before tugging him harder. "Valens doesn't employ shifters. He barely tolerates them. We're fine."

He came grudgingly but didn't stop darting glances behind us. "I've never smelled a shifter in the dual-society zone before."

"It's a shopping complex, Mordecai, with very popular, moderately priced stores. I'm sure there have been shifters in the area a time or two. I've never noticed any either, but that only means none of them have ever acted out of turn. It'll be fine."

"What if they know me?"

I scoffed. "How would they possibly know you? The alpha himself doesn't know what you look like now. What you smell like. And even if he somehow discovered where we *used* to live, we weren't there last night. We're safe. Both of us are." I pulled him toward the sliding doors. The glass parted like magic, welcoming us into the store's depths. "Besides, you only vaguely smell a shifter, right? That means the shifter is upwind and won't catch your scent. Given that you can't see them, they can't see you."

"I saw a few people walking, and one leaning against a pillar. Maybe there's more than one."

"Fine, but could you see their faces?" He didn't comment. "Exactly. You were too far away for facial recognition, and even if they had a picture of your face, they wouldn't recognize your build and your stride. We're fine, Mordecai. We've got the guys and Bria with us…somewhere. If something happens, they'll step in."

Mordecai blew out a breath and let me drag him toward the handbags. "I just don't know about this, Lexi. You've got that mark now…"

A splash of the normal excitement of the hunt rolled through me. "Please, *please*, let me see a Burberry. Let me see one," I said in a hush as I toured the round racks stuffed with purses. I didn't even care that it was a bad idea to snag a unicorn and traipse it through the shop—now that I had the means to buy one, I'd be hard-pressed to leave it on the rack.

"You already have a Burberry," Mordecai said distractedly. His phone vibrated, and he pulled it from his pocket.

"I have one style of Burberry, yes. I would love to have two. Or maybe a fun little Kate Spade. Or, oh my God, could you imagine me carrying around a Prada? Or a Gucci? I wouldn't even know how to act." I pushed aside some ghastly leather thing dotted with ridiculous rhinestones. "I'd settle for a little offbeat number that looks halfway decent."

"Jack is asking for our twenty." Mordecai's fingers tapped the screen. "I'm telling him that I think this shopping trip is messing with your decision-making skills."

"It's your attitude that is messing with my decision-making skills," I murmured, pushing aside a pink number. "That said, can you give a girl a little space, please? I need to concentrate."

But try as I might, I couldn't see anything worth buying. Not one thing. Every time I'd come in here without a penny to my name, the racks had been full of fun little ditties I just *had* to have.

Defeated, I grabbed his arm and tugged him toward the other end of the store. "Let's get you something."

A woman glanced up as I passed. Her eyes widened, then slowly began to sparkle. A wistful grin twisted her previously downturned lips.

"That's...weird," I whispered, hurrying Mordecai along.

His stare lingered on the woman, who didn't seem to notice him at my side. He bent back to his phone, clearly relaying the reaction to one of the Six, as we reached the men's section.

"Oh look, this one is nice." I pulled out a black button-up inlaid with shinier black squares. I held the shirt up to his frame. "Your shoulders are going to be a problem when you fill out."

"The wardrobe Kieran got me is better quality."

I put the shirt back, flicking my gaze back the way we'd come. The woman hadn't followed us, luckily, but she did keep glancing our way, leaning so she could see around Mordecai.

"That...might be an issue," I said softly, pushing a gap into the stuffed rack so I could distractedly assess the options. Mordecai was right—the shirt he wore was much nicer than any of the ones brushing against my fingertips. "Curses. Kieran's flare for quality has undermined one of my big dreams—"

"He's here." Mordecai's fingers curled around my upper arm. "Lexi, the shifter I smelled just walked in."

Mordecai's tone sent a thrill of adrenaline through me. The doors at the front slowly slid closed. The racks of clothes between us hid all but the newcomer's head and the tips of his shoulders. Given that he wasn't rushing forward to procure whatever necessity had brought him into the store, he was browsing. Except his square face and tight buzz cut didn't dip to take in the display of sunglasses at his right, or the belts and wallets a few paces to his left. He moved forward slowly, his eyes up, surveying. He was looking for someone.

"Mother trucker biscuit fucker," I said softly as I felt the stranger's magic pulse in his middle. Lower class three, I would guess. Nothing too fancy, but plenty fancy to ruin my shopping spree. "Are you sure it's the same smell?"

"Of course I'm sure." Mordecai turned to the side and held a shirt up to his torso, pretending to consider it. "When the doors opened, I got a blast of it."

I touched a shirt on the rack without seeing it, working with Mordecai to play the part. "Let's keep calm. We don't know that he's here for you."

"He's slowly veering in this general direction, Lexi, and this doesn't seem like a section that would interest him.

A sly glance up and it was easy to see Mordecai was correct. Taller than Mordecai, the middle-aged man probably clocked in at six-one, maybe six-two—Kieran's height. A plain, loose T-shirt stretched over his large chest and flowed down a flat stomach. Ratty jeans, run down yet stylish, hugged muscular thighs.

They were clothes a shifter wouldn't mind tearing apart. He wouldn't be interested in the business casual attire around us.

I noticed his movement. Sleek and graceful, though not as oiled or confident as any of the Six, this guy was probably a decent fighter. Being a shifter, no doubt he could run like the dickens. Surely faster than my two legs could carry me.

"There is no way he could've…" I let my words trail away as I thought back to entering the shopping complex. Our windows had been down, and the entrance was closer to the other end. With the funny microclimates in this area, and my accidental trailing of Mordecai's smell through half the shopping complex, this guy might well have picked up the scent. "Humpty bugger, fuck a tart."

"I haven't heard that swear in a long time," Mordecai said softly, a trace of sadness lining his words. My mother had been known for stringing curses together until she practically beat you with them. It had seemed like a worthy occasion to use one.

"Right. Okay. No problem. This store is a dud, anyway." I slapped the shirt out of Mordecai's hands and shoved him to the side. "Go. Head to the doors. We'll see if he follows."

I slipped my arm in his, a means of controlling his direction without looking obvious. "Oh look. These would really fit your face." I stopped to point at a horrible pair of sunglasses made for a woman. "Oops. My face, I guess."

The pause was for show, and Mordecai's stiffness didn't sell it.

"Loosen up." I pulled him forward again. "The worst thing you can possibly do is advertise your wariness. That just excites the predators. You need to think big. Act big."

"That guy would wipe the floor with me. He *is* big."

"That bastard won't even touch you. He's big, but he's not as powerful. I have no idea how that translates into claws and teeth, but it has to count for something. And I bet he feels pain a whole lot more than you do. Worst case, you take a few punches and beat him in the long game. Noses can be fixed."

"What if he has friends?"

"Mordecai, fretting is not a good look on you. Trust me, he doesn't have friends like we have friends. You think a wolf wants to mess with a freaking Kraken?" I lifted my eyebrows at him as the doors slid open in front of us. "A Kraken, Mordecai. No one wants to mess with one of those. They are legendary."

"And a Djinn," Mordecai murmured, allowing me to turn him right.

"Don't tell people we have a genie on our side. They'll just laugh and ask about the lamp." I pulled power from the Line to expand my magical awareness. Souls pulsed or burned around me. A spirit zipped from the edges of my vision, and I just barely noticed it slip beyond the veil. "That's…weird."

"What?"

"I've never seen a spirit slip beyond the veil like that. Run from Bria and escape behind it, sure. Stumble beyond it, yep. Lots. But that one seemed like a confident pro comfortable moving between the realms…" I barely kept myself from looking in the shadows away left. There, between a leafy tree and a grime-coated wall, I sensed Bria's soul. "Text Bria and ask if she is working Necromancy."

He bent to his phone for one beat before snapping his head back up and looking straight ahead. Every muscle on his frame popped tight. His phone vibrated in his hands.

There, leaning against a pillar, stood a man in a tight black shirt that did amazing things for his defined torso. His stylishly ripped jeans molded to his powerful legs and ended at brown, high-top boots with the laces undone. The silver watch encircling his wrist caught the light and gleamed. Power pulsed within him. A strong class four. I couldn't make out his exact facial expression, but it was clear he was looking right at us.

No, not us. He was looking at Mordecai. Without knowing how, I was confident this man knew who Mordecai was and meant him irreparable harm. I didn't know if he would challenge him right now, but he certainly intended to do so eventually, and was sure he would beat, and maybe kill, my ward.

"Wrong," I said between clenched teeth.

"What?" Mordecai asked, and I heard a quiver in his voice.

"I'm not going to let some sideburns-wearing doofus fucker threaten my ward. There is nothing worse than a pretty boy with an ego problem playing for the role of head dick."

"It's not ego, it's confidence, and he's probably near the pinnacle of his pack."

"But he's not near the pinnacle of mine. If he messes with us, I'll crush him."

The man pushed off the pillar, a contained movement that hinted at coiled energy straining at the confines of his muscular body. He looked almost amused, as though he'd found a fun little toy to mess around with for the afternoon.

My stare beat into the stranger, but I still hadn't

been noticed. That had to be purposeful.

"He's strong, Lexi," Mordecai mumbled. "I feel it. I feel the push of it. It's like an invisible force, shoving at me. He means to show his dominance over me."

In shifter terms, showing dominance could sometimes result in death. In this situation, given what I'd already concluded, it almost certainly did.

"Get behind me," I said, feeling the fire rise within me. I simply would not tolerate someone threatening one of my wards. Mordecai would have the future he deserved. If I had to rip off the legs of every pretty boy shifter I ran into for the rest of my life, I would. "We got this."

"Lexi, no. Let's just get out of here."

"Then what, Mordecai? If he knows who you are, and I think he might, this is just the beginning. These guys are predators. They'll hunt you down and take you out when you're vulnerable, just like they did with your parents. We cannot show weakness—"

Mordecai's phone vibrated and he brought it up to read the text message.

"What does it say?" I asked, willing the shifter to notice me. Clearly, he didn't think I was a threat. For some reason, that rankled.

"Jack says we have to handle this because he shouldn't be seen with us in public. He says not to run. The shifter will just follow. Also, you shouldn't use your wer on anyone but him."

"See that? We're on the same page. We'll just quickly show this sucker who the top dog is, and then we'll get to that home store and buy the place out."

The familiar souls on my radar moved locations behind the scenes—Zorn to the left among the cars, and the others fanning out right. They had faith that I'd send this guy running, and they planned to scoop him up after I did.

My confidence surged. They were no longer treating me like Kieran's girl pal who needed to be protected, but like one of their crew. I'd elevated my status in their eyes.

Warmth welled within me as the shifter sauntered out in front of us with easy movements and the self-assurance of someone who thought he owned the ground we walked on. He stopped in our path and smirked as he squared his shoulders. Violence crept into his eyes and raw energy throbbed in his middle, desperate to break free.

I didn't change pace or my path. We headed straight for him in a game of chicken.

"Something is wrong with this picture," the stranger said in a higher-pitched voice that didn't match his rough look. His gaze held steady over my left shoulder. He still refused to look at me. "You're alive."

My blood boiled.

I jerked my hand up like I had a knife, drawing his notice, then shifted to point at my eyes.

"Hey, pretty boy, eyes up top."

The man's gaze flicked over...then caught my hard stare. Confusion stole over his expression for a brief moment until the violence seeped back in. His boots slid marginally against the concrete as he ever so slightly repositioned toward me. He now knew who was in charge.

"Who're you?" he asked.

He *theoretically* knew who was in charge.

"It doesn't matter who I am," I answered, stopping out of striking range. "You're in my way."

His gaze slid over me and his eyebrows pulled down into a V. One of his hands closed into a fist, and the humorous violence in his eyes turned to unbridled hostility. Whatever the mark was showing him, he no longer thought the situation was funny.

"I'll say it one more time." I sucked power from the Line. "Move."

He bristled and his chin raised ever so slightly. The same fire I felt in my middle filled his gaze. He bunched, about to strike.

I whipped a line of spirit through his middle, snapping it against his spirit box. His eyes widened and his face went slack, stopping him cold. Pushing my advantage, I snapped his spirit box again, harder this time,

.ook a step into his space.

He staggered backward, clutching at his chest. Magic seeped out of him like he was a pierced balloon. He clearly couldn't get his bearings in line to change. It wouldn't have mattered if he had.

I increased the ferocity of my attack, battering his soul casing. He let out a high-pitched squeal before stumbling to the side. His knees buckled, as though he would kneel, but as soon as they touched down, he was up again.

I braced for his lunge, wrapping magic around his spirit box in preparation to squeeze. Instead, he spun—eyes wild, face drained of color—and sprinted toward the parking lot.

I felt Zorn's soul drag across the hood of a car and zip after him, faster than a person should be.

"Oh shit," I said, looking after the shifter darting manically between and around cars. It seemed he was aiming for the street. "Zorn must be in his gas form. That is a trip. I can't see him, but I know his exact location."

Mordecai's arm slipped into mine. He didn't say a word.

I heaved out a sigh as adrenaline shook my limbs. I'd barely gotten started and it was already over. I hadn't even needed to hurt him.

"He scared me shitless," Mordecai said with a trembling release of breath. "Excuse my French."

"That's not French, and it's all in your head. Remember when Thane turned? That scared *me* shitless. You just jumped right in."

"He didn't feel the same. He didn't…" He huffed. "It's hard to explain."

"We're good, bud." I patted Mordecai's hand and picked up the pace, leading him toward the home store. "If you can face down a class-five Berserker, you can do almost anything. A class-four wolf with fancy watches and stupid shoes shouldn't even register."

He was quiet as we reached the store.

When the doors slid open and a smile spread across my face, he said, "Lexi, even if Demigod Kieran does try to control you, you won't need any of our help. You'll handle him all on your own. He won't be a match for you."

Bless him, Mordecai was entirely naive when it came to the hierarchy of magic, but it was a nice sentiment, so I patted his hand, then pushed him away. If that shifter *had* known who Mordecai was, he wouldn't get a chance to tell his buddies. Mordecai was safe, and I had shopping to do.

Chapter 21

KIERAN

"**S**IR, WE HAVE a problem."

Kieran tore his gaze away from an email he could've never expected and that could change the tide and glanced at his office door. His assistant sat out front, within hearing distance. He picked up the telephone receiver of his office phone, silencing the speakerphone. "I'll call you back."

In a flash, he closed the office door and grabbed his cell. His office didn't have any foreign surveillance, but he wasn't sure about his phone lines. Couldn't be too careful.

He tapped Jack's name, surprised it wasn't Zorn who'd called. A quick internal check-in assured him Alexis was doing well, if a little frustrated. She wasn't under attack, and neither was Mordecai. At the moment, anyway. Something had happened about ten minutes ago that had almost alarmed him enough to dial Zorn's number. If it hadn't subsided quickly, he would've risked blowing their cover with a ringing cell.

"Sir," Jack said by way of answer.

"What is it?"

"Two of Will Green's shifters were hanging around the shopping complex. The first, low-level and fairly useless, followed Lexi and Mordecai into a shop at the end. He essentially flushed them out. A more powerful wolf was waiting for them. He knew who Mordecai was, but he clearly had no idea who or what Lexi was. She had to force him to acknowledge her presence as pack leader before she dealt with him."

Kieran leaned his elbow against the desk and directed his gaze out the window, not seeing the glistening ocean beyond. "What's the status?"

"Bria picked up the low-level member. He's restrained in the back of her stolen car. He doesn't know any particulars, which isn't uncommon for someone of his status in the pack, but he was given a picture of Mordecai, and told to call the higher-level wolf if he saw him."

"And the other?"

"Alexis scared him beyond rational thought. He couldn't even shift—he just took off running in human form. Zorn grabbed him, but he couldn't calm him down. The shifter changed, got stuck halfway through, and snuffed it."

Jack was breathing heavily by the time he'd finished relaying the events, and not because he was jogging.

√hat Alexis could do had clearly hit the enor-
, and powerful water shifter at his core. Even
ough he'd successfully trained with her, he was scared
it could happen to him.

"You've withstood worse, Jack, and not just from
Alexis," Kieran said calmly. "You've trained with me."

"Yes, sir. I know that, sir. It's just…she drove him to
hysteria. He couldn't even shift." Jack took a deep
breath. "I'll get on top of it, sir. If anything, it is a
reminder of how big of a help Alexis will be."

Kieran stood from his seat and walked to the win-
dow, looking out. "It can't be a coincidence that Will
Green's pack is looking for Mordecai directly after
Amber was assigned to this case."

"That's exactly my thought, sir. The low-level wolf
was the lookout. The higher-level wolf was the closest
muscle. They were looking for Mordecai as a team, and
I suspect they're not the only group in the area. They
can't be—there is no way they could've known we'd be
here today."

"My father still doesn't know that the breadcrumbs
lead to me, or he would've wanted Mordecai for himself, if only to see why I bothered fixing him up. No, my
father is tossing Green a bone. Or maybe he's simply
tying up a loose end without taxing his own reserves."
Kieran turned from the window as a shock of adrenaline zipped up his body. "How likely is it that the

higher-level shifter would've alerted Green to Mordecai's presence before he had the cargo in-hand?"

"I don't know enough about Green's pack to make that call. From what I've heard, the pack as a whole is deteriorating. That'll mess with their organization and chain of command. But as I was pulling out my phone to call you I smelled a faint whiff of blood, shit, and wet fur—what a wolf hunting pack smells like. It is impossible for me to be sure, but he might already be organizing."

Tingles of warning spread across Kieran's skin. "How many wolves do there need to be to elicit such a smell, generally speaking?"

"At the minimum, half a dozen dirty dogs, and a full dozen decent shifters who have temporarily given in to their animal."

"How sure are you about this whiff?"

"Fifty-fifty."

Kieran thought for a moment. He hated to ruin Alexis's big shopping expedition, but even if she could handle a group of wolves on her own, she'd draw a lot of notice. It was best to keep her under the radar for as long as possible.

"Pull Alexis out," he said. "Take them back to the house. Tell her I'll make it up to her. We'll draw Green out when there are less witnesses and take care of the problem then."

"Yes, sir," Jack said. "And maybe you can challenge her later and make a mockery of her magic. I'd love to put some nightmares to rest. The mark's effect only helps so much."

Kieran stilled as a soft knock interrupted the quiet of the office.

"The mark's effect?" he asked, ignoring Jack's hopeful tone. Kieran doubted anyone could make a mockery of Alexis's magic.

The knock hardened, the delay too short. Someone powerful and impatient was on the other side.

Only one person showed his impatience where Kieran was concerned.

"I have to go," Kieran said quickly and terminated the call. He dropped the phone onto his desk and hastened to the door.

$$\times \quad \times \quad \times$$

VALENS

IRRITATION ATE THROUGH Valens as the seconds ticked by. He turned to the composed but out of her league assistant, who was, for some reason, not reaching for the phone to see what was holding up his son.

"How long has this door been—"

The wood swung open a little too quickly before slowing, revealing Kieran in a suit befitting his position. At least that much Valens had been able to impress upon his son—the importance of dressing for his station.

"Father," Kieran said, a trace of anxiety in his eyes. Ah. He'd realized who must've been waiting outside and hurried to accommodate someone with higher authority. Which meant he'd originally assumed himself to be of higher authority, and had chosen to show dominance by keeping the caller waiting.

A thread of pride worked through Valens as he stepped forward. Good. His son was learning the importance of dominance and hierarchy. There was hope for him yet.

"Kieran." His son pulled out a visitor chair, looking at him with raised eyebrows. Valens slightly nodded, then took his seat. Kieran shut the door.

"To what do I owe the pleasure?" Kieran walked around the desk where his cell phone lay crooked just off-center.

Valens looked at it pointedly. Kieran promptly removed it from the surface and tucked it into a drawer.

Abstract paintings adorned the flat gray walls of the office. A fake plant sat listlessly in the corner, and the desk lacked a clean and proper shine. It was as if his son had no pride in his working environment.

Forcing that issue aside for one of more precedence, Valens crossed an ankle over his knee and leaned back. "I missed your company last night."

No emotion rolled through his son's uninterested blue gaze.

Valens hated that look—the look of a spoiled child who'd never known true hardship. It was as if Kieran expected the world to be handed to him, and when it wasn't, he whined about life being unfair. Youths were so tedious, especially in this day and age. Valens almost wondered if employing someone to run another territory would be better than grooming his own brood. If it wasn't for his son's impressive magic, he would without question.

Then again, maybe he ought to contemplate doing both. He certainly had the resources, and if he could claim Sydney, he would finally have the clout to pass his political proposals. Subduing the Chesters and establishing his power in their territories would then be a simple maneuver. He had already drafted out plans for the usurpation of over a dozen resource-rich areas. The Chesters had weapons, yes, but he had spies in powerful places and plans to cut them off from their war machines.

"Didn't Sodge tell you?" Kieran said in that lifeless monotone of his. "I finally closed on a house. I left him the details."

Valens entwined his fingers in his lap, fighting his annoyance. "Yes, Sodge mentioned it. He didn't indicate you'd leave so...suddenly, however. Your mother never taught you the value of respect and the importance of a proper farewell?"

Something flashed in his son's eyes, almost like the rolling turbulence right before a squall opened up on the sea. The next moment, it was gone.

"I apologize. I thought your assistant would've passed on the dinner invitation." Kieran entwined his fingers, not unlike Valens was doing. "I thought you might like to wait until the weekend so we can celebrate with a few too many shots of your favorite scotch. Early meetings aren't ideal when you can barely see straight from the night before." Kieran's smile didn't reach his eyes. "I can have her schedule it for earlier in the week, if you'd like…"

Anger simmered, but Valens kept his composure. This wasn't the first time she had failed to inform him of an important event on his social calendar. Usually it happened with regards to other women. The appointment would be grudgingly added to his calendar, though she'd leave it to his electronic devices to alert him when the date and time neared. Valens usually let those slide. Occasional jealousy could easily be reprimanded in the bedroom. But forgetting to mention his son's appointment, causing Valens to make a fool of himself, would require swift and harsh punishment.

"Forgive me," he said, the words tasting sour in his mouth. "I hadn't realized."

Kieran made a small movement, waving it away. Something hot and uncomfortable lodged in Valens's core—an imperceptible power shift?

"I've booked the Regency," Kieran said. "Sodge said that was your favorite."

Valens nodded. "Indeed it is. They consistently serve top quality food."

"Yes, I've enjoyed their lunches. Did you get a chance to look over the information I left with Sodge?"

Valens eased back, just a bit. That sounded more like the desire for approval.

"I did, yes. The manufacturer comes highly recommended. Their work generally speaks for itself." His pause was carefully chosen to convey disapproval. "The placement of their properties, however…"

A muffled vibration interrupted the ensuing silence. Kieran's brow pinched and he glanced down at the drawer in which he'd put the phone.

"There were options in more central areas," Kieran said, pulling the drawer open and reaching in to silence it, "but the comparable houses were just too…prominent. I apologize if I've read the situation incorrectly, but I thought it might be better to stick to fashionable lodgings on the outskirts by the ocean. That will give you the prominent placement within the city, and the ocean view will shield me from chatter regarding the proximity of the dual-society zone. It seemed like a win-win for my first step out on my own. I am of the city, but I do not speak for the city, as it were."

Valens stared at him for a speechless moment, his perceptions of his son shifting and changing. That answer had been perfect. Beyond perfect. It showed that Kieran not only understood his father's position, but that he could navigate around the potentially sticky situation of having two Demigods within one territory.

Pride flowered. Yes, there was hope for Kieran yet, and with it, hope for Valens's plans.

"Good," Valens said, taking his foot from his knee. "Yes, that sounds—"

The phone vibrated again, and Kieran glanced down at it. A spark of something lit in his son's eyes. Valens's chest tightened in response, but before he could identify the feeling, it was gone again.

"Well," Valens said, rising slowly.

Impatience soaked into his son's expression. He squeezed his phone and shook his head apologetically, war in his eyes.

"The house is *mostly* quality, but it seems the plumbing..." Kieran waved it away. "Please excuse me, Father. There is only so much I will tolerate. The service staff needs a lesson on their work ethic." Kieran saw him to the door in quick strides. "I'll see you this weekend, if not before."

As Valens walked out into the hall, he saw his son

myself from asking if he saw anything. Tight bands of warning wrapped around my chest before something akin to panic quickened my heart.

This wasn't my panic. It was Kieran's. What was he reacting to?

"Looks the same to me," Mordecai said, thankfully not able to see the anxiety collecting in my body. "Usually you stand in this section and drool. Shouldn't you know what you want by now?"

"I don't love that attitude," I said with a warning in my voice. "It's just…all my past favorites would easily work for our old house, but they'd look seriously cheap in our new house."

"Now we're in a rich man's house with a rich man's things—you need to shop at a better store."

I blew out a breath in frustration before moving along, knowing he was exactly right.

"Look, Mordecai, a lemon zester! I was hoping to find one of these. We can finally be one of those families that zests lemons."

"We are one of those families. Donovan brought one over to the old house. He's already used lemon zest in a few dishes."

I stopped with my mouth hanging open. "Why did no one tell me?"

"What's there to tell?" he said distractedly, meeting my gaze. "It's just lemon zest. I couldn't even taste it."

I gestured at the object in question, trying to maintain focus. Trying to remember that Jack and Zorn were in charge and they'd communicate if there was anything to communicate about.

So why did it feel like I was in a waiting room, expecting bad news?

"It's something extra that I could never justify buying in the past," I answered. "Like these napkin holders. Like most of this stuff. And come to find out we already had it? That's a big deal!"

Mordecai frowned in confusion right before his phone vibrated, taking away his focus.

My phone rang a moment later.

"Jack wants you to answer your phone," Mordecai said.

"I'm coming, I'm coming," I said, digging through my bag.

Bria's name showed up on the screen. I swiped and put the phone to my ear.

"Tell me we're in the clear," I said immediately.

"We're in the clear," she replied.

I froze for a second, hardly believing what she'd said. A relieved and slightly embarrassed laugh fought through my anxiety. I'd allowed Mordecai's paranoia to get me worked up.

"Good," I said with a sigh.

"Just kidding. Shit's gotten real. We got a pack of

wolves organizing. Where are you in the store, exactly?"

"Wait, what? But you said—"

"I lied to keep things light. Funny, right? Where are you in the store?"

Fear coursed through me, and it wasn't mine.

Not many things made Kieran afraid.

I grabbed Mordecai's wrist and yanked, leaving the cart behind. "I'm working my way to the back. We haven't seen anyone come through the front entrance. I'll have Mordecai sniff for anyone already in here with us. What's going on out there?"

"Good call. That's what I was going to tell you to do. Look at you, reading a situation and reacting appropriately. I'm attributing this to my outstanding merit as a trainer—"

"Bria, what is going on out there?"

"Oh right. Well, a big team of rough-looking shifters showed up, and they are amassing near the entrances. Will Green is on site."

"Will is...the alpha of Mordecai's old pack, right?" I'd appealed to Will's office years ago when I'd tried to get help paying for Mordecai's shifter serum. Will hadn't spoken to me directly, instead letting his secretary give me the bad news.

"Yeah. He's a nasty sonuvabitch. I can tell from here. And he clearly doesn't give a shit that it's illegal to challenge someone under eighteen years of age. This crew isn't looking to chat. They're here for business."

They were here for Mordecai, something I didn't dare say to the terrified teenager standing wide-eyed beside me.

My heart sped up. I'd easily taken out one wolf. I'd taken down a Berserker. But I'd only fought more than one person at a time in practice sessions.

"It's okay," I said, mostly to myself. "We can handle this."

"I love your enthusiasm," Bria said in approval. "The guys think Valens tipped them off, and if that's true, Valens has basically given Green his consent to kill a minor. I'm not going to blow sunshine up your ass— it's looking pretty grim. Jack is useless to us without water, I don't have the army of cadavers I would need to bail you out, and Zorn can only handle so many. Even with your help, we don't have the numbers. Zorn has called in the rest of the Six, and Kieran is on his way, but we're way the hell out here. It's a time versus numbers game. So just hang tight, and we'll see how it goes."

I stopped near a woman straightening a pillow on a display bed. "How many of them are there?"

Bria paused for a moment. "Two dozen shifters. They've been showing up in waves. Jack says they'll fight viciously, and they won't fight fair."

"How long before they make a move?"

A pregnant pause filled the line. "I don't know," she finally said.

She was lying. No time at all.

I turned and looked at Mordecai, studying the face of the boy I knew so well. I could remember all the times I had held him in my arms, begging the medicine to hurry up—terrified his sickness would take him. He'd depended on me to keep him safe, and even though I'd been up against the wire more times than I could count, I had always found a way to keep him alive.

I *would* always find a way. Somehow.

Chapter 23

ALEXIS

ONLY ONE PERSON noticed as I pushed open the scuffed beige employee door at the back of the store, and that person was no longer living.

"Stay close to me at all times, Mordecai," I said, still holding the phone to my head. I walked down an aisle of boxes and a rack of opened and probably returned items. Determination fought the fear coursing through me. I could do this. I had to. I could not let them get to Mordecai. "Do not change. That'll give us the edge. If we need to scale a fence or something, let *them* be fatigued from having made a quick change. And do not fight. A couple months of training hasn't prepared you for this."

"Okay," he said, following close behind me. Thankfully, he didn't point out that a couple months of training hadn't prepared me for this, either.

"Keep pace. Do not slow me down."

"Yes, ma'am."

"Do not shout out or yell unless you are in harm's

way. That'll only distract me, and it might de-rail…whatever it is I am doing."

"Kicking ass, that's what you'll be doing," Bria said. "Also, Jack forbids you to leave that store in this manner. He sounds like an old woman when he panics."

"What if they come at us from behind?" Mordecai asked.

"I don't need you to watch my six, Mordecai. I've got eyes in the back of my head and all the way around. I'll know who and what is coming for us at all times."

I sincerely hope.

"James Bond ain't got nothin' on you, lady." Excitement rang through Bria's voice, interrupted by the jabbering of someone who sounded angry. "Jack, would you back off? She's a type of Necromancer—we're born with the ability to take life by the horns. This is her calling, trust me—"

"Hey!" A man bending over a pallet of boxes wrapped in clear plastic straightened from his task. He looked our way. "You shouldn't be back here."

I veered toward him, knowing he must've received that pallet through a freight door. If the freight door wasn't open, there'd be a regular door nearby. All my experience working for retail stores was finally coming in handy.

"We're just heading out," I called as I neared him. Around a stack of boxes with pictures of flatware, I caught sight of what I'd hoped to find. Four floor-to-ceiling freight doors, all closed. Beside the last of them, a sliver of light cut across the floor from a regular door standing slightly ajar. "Bria, do you have eyes on the back of the building?"

"Most of it, why?"

"Can you see the freight door area?"

I heard scuffling, like fabric against concrete, before she said, "Yeah, barely."

The guy working on the pallet of boxes of what looked like pillows threw up a meaty arm covered in thick hair. I hated to think what his back looked like.

"You gotta go out the front. I can't have you back here. This is for—hey!"

I threw him a thumbs up to ease the blow of ignoring him. "Are the shifters waiting there?" I asked her.

"No. A dozen are waiting at the western corner so they can see two sides of the building. The others are up front with Green. Right now, all of them are wearing their skin. Wait…hold on…" Again, I could just barely hear Jack's baritone on the other end of the line.

"Lady, you can't go—"

I slapped a tiny sliver of magic through the worker, needing him to mind his own business. He gasped and grabbed for his chest, pausing with his mouth open and his gaze averted sideways.

"That guy looks like he's having a heart attack,"

Mordecai mumbled. "Did you just attack him?"

"I quieted him, not attacked him. What do you think I am, an animal?" Mordecai's lips tightened and I grimaced. "Sorry—I forgot who I was talking to."

"We've got movement," Bria said quietly. "Green and four others are heading into the store. Zorn thinks they intend to pull you out."

"They must know I dealt with their co-worker by now," I murmured, pushing my head to the crack in the door and trying to look out. Unsurprisingly, I couldn't see much.

"I agree," Bria whispered. "You need to get moving." Her tone had changed to serious and solemn. "Bring out everything you've got, Alexis. Shifters work together better than most magical species out there. They're strong and vicious. If you give them an inch, they'll rip you apart, and Mordecai after you. Don't give them that inch."

Nerves ate at me but I latched on to my determination.

"Here we go." I shoved the door open and stepped out into the bright day.

"She's live, she's live," I heard Bria say as I finally pulled the phone from my ear.

"Here." I handed it back to Mordecai. "Be the go-between."

I stepped down the stairs one by one, not rushing,

tapping into my power. Spirit crawled across the concrete and up along the buildings. Colors shifted as ultraviolet light filtered in around me. The Line materialized to the right and above me, its feeling comforting, its power infinite.

"Here we go," I said again, reaching the ground.

Just as Bria had said, a group of men and women stood at the far corner, backed away from the building so they could see clearly. Three of them started and the rest slowly clued in. A hand went up to a head, probably someone calling the crew upfront.

A man stepped away from the rest, headed in my direction.

"They heard from Kieran. He says to go back inside and take them in smaller groups until he can get here," Mordecai relayed. "But she says that if you do that, they'll catch everything on camera. This is a chain store, so she's not confident it's a closed loop. We'd risk revealing your magic." Mordecai audibly swallowed. "She said just to handle it."

"The freight doors and back entrance will have security cameras, too," I said, almost feeling the hard gaze of the man approaching us. His arms swung loose at his sides and his brick of a body swayed with each ground-pounding step. The rest of the pack followed behind him, power pulsing in their middles. Class threes and fours, all of them, and brick body was a lower class five.

Holy shit, they had a lot going for them.

"She says…you're welcome," Mordecai reiterated, having given her my message.

I spared a glance up at the freight doors, running my gaze along the top and then the sides. There had been three cameras, and now there were three fragments of cameras. Bria had prepared for an extraction.

I nodded as the shifters continued to stalk toward me. I knew it wouldn't be long before they got a positive I.D. on us. When they did, the rest would come running.

Something zipped by out of the corner of my eye. I started and jerked my head, but saw nothing, including the dead. A trick of the mind, or something else? Regardless, I didn't have time to worry about it.

The lead man kept reducing the space between us. His deep brown eyes came into focus, and then he nodded. But he wasn't looking at me. He was looking over my shoulder.

"Turn him over, wench," he said, slowing. "This is a pack matter. Our fight is not with you. You are free to go."

"Wench? What is this, a pirate ship? This isn't a pack matter. You fuckers killed a sick kid's parents, then tossed that kid out onto the streets to die. You forfeited your right to make him a pack matter. Now it's a bullshit matter…that I will be handling."

The group slowed further, then stopped, all acting on the leader's unspoken command. It was cool, I had to give them that, but it also made me want to start snapping my fingers and break into dance.

"Turn the Wolfram boy over, or die," the man barked.

"We've got incoming," Mordecai whispered behind me, his voice pinched with fear. "They're changing. The others—the ones still at the front the building. They're changing." He paused for a moment, and I could feel his arm trembling against my back. "Jack says they are getting into position for a kill." His voice turned urgent. "Kieran is still too far away. We don't have enough people, Lexi. Jack says to run."

"It's too late to run. Our only choice is to fight."

Chapter 24

ALEXIS

THE LEAD MAN lunged forward, still in human form. I took a step back to give myself more space while blasting a heavy dose of spirit and a whole lot of power, grabbing his spirit box and squeezing. He yelped, like a dog, but his hand kept coming.

I unlocked the gale force of the Line's icy wind, something I'd gotten better at directing since my last training. It blew through the group, flapping the shifters' souls wildly. Gasps and shrieks shattered the quiet of the day. Many staggered. One bent to a knee.

The lead man kept coming, as though attacking on muscle memory. Before I could dodge away, a dark arm came around me and whipped me to the side. The man's hand closed on empty air and his body kept going, staggering beyond me.

Mordecai released me, and despite my earlier instruction that he should do nothing and stay by my side, he stepped quickly after the man and elegantly wrapped an arm around his neck. He spun like a dancer before crashing two fast punches into the man's face. Between his attack and the effects of my magic, the man went down hard and fast.

I surged with pride. *That's my boy.*

Souls glittered and pulsed as they moved around the building. Two familiar souls followed them, one of which stole my breath.

"Goddamn that Daisy, she shouldn't be anywhere near this," I yelled.

A woman broke away from the others and ran at me. I punched her directly in the spirit box, making no attempt to ease her into it.

Her spirit box jolted back, dragging her body with it.

I widened my eyes. That was neat. I hadn't even known that was possible.

On cue, the rest of the shifters picked up speed, running at me now. Behind them, furry bodies turned the corner, the wolves from the front of the building.

"Act faster, Lexi," Mordecai yelled.

"Right, yes. Faster." I punched another, and another, hearing yells or grunts with each spirit assault. But I couldn't keep doing it one by one—it was letting the other shifters advance on me, and soon there would be too many for me to handle.

A man reached me and struck out. I bent back just in time, watching an enormous fist sail past my head in

HD. Mordecai's hand jutted out, just as fast. His fingers curled around the man's wrist. Using the man's lunge to his advantage, Mordecai spun and yanked, bringing the guy's body forward and meeting his face with an expertly thrown kick.

"Okay, yes, go ahead and fight," I said, slashing with spirit and taking two shifters down at once. But the wolves were almost upon us, running as a pack with perfect synchronicity.

"Focus on the living… Focus on the group…"

The voice was like a dying breath, rippling through the world of spirit. I barely understood the words while understanding them perfectly. I knew exactly who'd uttered each syllable while having no idea.

A shock of spirit blasted through the scene, bleeding away the colors of our plane a little more. Like an extremely heightened trance, time slowed down, then fell away all together. I felt tiny little strings connected to each of the souls around me, the ends all hanging loose. All inactive and waiting for me to grab them up.

A light breeze fluttered all the strings, and then I *saw*, abstractly, what I had previously only felt. Each string had a different hue, but they could be grouped into five overall categories—one for those without bodies, one for those with, and three more I didn't understand.

"Not yet…" I couldn't see a body, spirit or other-

wise, but it felt like the breath of a dying man had fluttered my hair.

Now I knew why people thought ghosts were so scary.

Fear jumpstarted my heart and suddenly I was falling. Rolling. Turning end over end.

The sun blasted my face. Someone yelled my name. A body flew to the side.

I blinked and wiggled my fingers, which felt strange. My body felt strange. Too…present, somehow. Too…substantial.

"Alexis," Mordecai yelled, terror in his voice.

I blinked twice, getting my bearings, only to realize I was standing stalk still while Mordecai spun and turned around me, grabbing people, delivering strikes, and throwing bodies out of the way. It turned out he *did* know what he was doing. He was utterly magnificent, and here I was, a dead weight.

"Alexis, what's happening?" Mordecai asked, thrusting his foot up and crunching a guy right between the legs. That's what you got for picking on someone who trained with Daisy—no rules.

"I freaked out, but I'm back. I'll—" I cut off as I realized the wolves had surrounded us in a large circle. Those in human form—the ones still standing, at least—slowed and took a few steps back, their postures changing. They were waiting for something. I could sense Bria, Jack, and Daisy lurking behind us a ways, and Zorn was following a moving soul that stepped out from around the far corner.

Tall and stacked with muscle, the man walked toward us with a slow, hunched-over gait, like a cage fighter entering the cage. His tight jeans must've cut off his circulation and his equally tight button-up shirt looked far too expensive to rip when he changed. Like the earlier shifter, he had a pricy watch on his wrist.

It had to be Will Green. His minions had secured his prey, and now he would show that he didn't need to change shape to finish the job.

"Look who it is," the man said as he entered the outer ring of wolves. The shifters in human form parted to the sides, giving him more space. "The little Wolfram boy. Amazing that you're still alive."

His pale blue gaze swung to me, the first of the shifters to voluntarily notice my presence. His twisted stare, filled with unhinged menace, hit me like a Mack truck, manifesting as a blow to my middle. I barely kept myself from stepping back with the force of it.

"And what have we here? I do believe you have the mark of a Demigod." His head tilted, surveying me, and his eyes lit with a vicious gleam that made my skin crawl. "You couldn't have been marked by the father, or I wouldn't have gotten the tip off. So that must mean you've been marked by the son." Greed filled his dead, pale eyes. "Does the father want you dead, too, I wonder? He learned his lesson the hard way—everyone knows he's tried to scare the son away from making the same mistake." A sickly smile spread across his thin lips. The scar running down his cheek and curling around his chin stretched grotesquely. "What would you be worth to the son, I wonder, if we were to let you live?"

"Wow." I blew out a breath and glanced to the side with dramatically played-up fatigue. "Do you always babble this much, or just when you're meeting new people?"

A vein pulsed next to his eye and his jaw clenched. A wave of aggression washed over me, and a manic light entered his hardening stare.

This guy wasn't right, in the way a circus clown with blood dripping from its mouth wasn't right. Something was *off* in his gaze, in his bearing, and in the way he was looking at me. Like his intellect had dimmed, making way for the rabid animal to take over.

I'd once overheard Jack warning Mordecai not to let his wolf strip him of his logic. It made so much sense now. Will Green had clearly lost that battle long ago.

"You need to learn respect, girl," he growled.

Goosebumps spread across my skin. Adrenaline surged through my blood.

"You don't teach people respect through violence, you fucked up, sad excuse for an alpha. You don't sneak-attack your betters when they are vulnerable, and you don't prey on minors. You stole your throne from the Wolfram family, and today I will help that family punish you for it."

The Line pulsed out a thick throb of power. My magic swelled beyond what I'd yet experienced. Time slowed down again and spirit spiraled around us. The little strings attaching everyone's souls glittered into view a second time, their ends resting at my feet and pulsing like beacons, almost urging me to grab them up. I started to collect them one by one, using my eyes, but then sank into the feeling of that other place—the place with no time, and no physical presence—and sucked them to me. I felt them, all of them, like balloons floating together from a festoon of ribbons. The souls were all connected to me, and mine was connected to the spirit around us, as if I stood in the middle of an intricate, glittering spider web.

Will snarled, a pure animalistic sound.

The world snapped back to full speed, and the alpha surged toward me in human form.

I plunged a thick cord of my magic through Will's middle and wrapped it tightly around his spirit box. Surprise lit up his face, quickly overpowered by that manic fire that wasn't controlled by rational thought.

Power throbbed through me and I *shoved* his spirit box with my magic. A sharp sound left his mouth. He barreled toward me, his momentum taking him the last couple feet, his arms reaching.

I pushed forward on the balls of my feet at an angle, easily stepping around his loose-handed swipe. I slapped his arms out of the air and then smashed my fist into his nose. My knuckles cracked and so did cartilage.

Souls throbbing within bodies closed in around us. I yanked that bundle of strings I'd sensed in my magical grasp, slamming souls against their suddenly tight housings.

Screams and shrieks and terrified panting filled the air, louder than before. I had their attention.

"You will leave this boy alone," I roared, shaking Will's spirit box. I tightened my grasp of the strings connected to the other souls. "You will forget he exists, or I will rip away your life essence and play puppet with your bodies, do you hear me?"

I shook all of their spirit boxes this time, in hard yanks.

"Do you hear me?" I hollered.

Someone broke off from the group, racing away.

Without thinking, I yanked the string and held fast. The force stopped him short and he bowed around his chest before falling to his knees, clutching at his heart. An inhuman scream erupted from his throat. He flopped around like a fish, completely lost to hysteria.

Another broke away. And another. I held on to their

spirit boxes, keeping them from running even though the sensation drove them to blind panic. If I didn't, Zorn and Jack wouldn't be able to catch them all. They wouldn't be able to keep Mordecai safe.

Screams turned to howls. Fear rose from the group, a palpable thing. Voices went hoarse.

"Uh-oh," I said, uncertainty pawing at me. I was handling this very badly and I wasn't sure how to hit the ejector cord without landing myself back in the middle of a bunch of angry or recently crazed shifters. "What do I do now?"

Will's power throbbed. A strange keening worked out of his mouth. He wobbled where he stood, but I could tell he would not take a knee. He would not submit, and until he did, Mordecai wouldn't be in the clear.

"You can end this," I said to Will. "You can end this at any time."

"Fuck...you..." he spat, his face red.

Clothes ripped as Will's body elongated, starting the change to his wolf. His spirit box altered with it, the hard outer crust changing density. The power I'd wrapped around it began to seep into the fibers. I brushed up against his soul.

"Oh gross," I uttered, freezing.

He froze as well, his magic swirling around him like someone had just kicked a hornet's nest. He abruptly stopped panting, now holding his breath instead. His eyes locked on mine and I recognized the utter terror swimming within them.

"For the love of God, don't latch on to that connection," I said, using spirit to delicately feel each little prong that secured his soul. That material hadn't changed, just the protective crust it was attached to. They would hold on if the change was quick enough. They would come loose if it wasn't, and his spirit would escape. He'd die. I said as much.

"Don't we want that?" Mordecai asked quietly, somehow cutting through the chaos around us.

"Fuck you, boy," Will ground out, his whole body straining. His maniacal stare clung to Mordecai. "You look just like your pappy, do you know that? Just as stupidly useless as that limp dick. He was worse than weak. He was soft. Spineless. He was bankrupting our pack. He was leading us nowhere." Drool escaped his mouth. "And don't get me started on that whore of a mother of yours. She spread her legs all over town. She—"

A low growl was the only warning I got before a shove pushed me out of the way. Mordecai smashed his fist into Will's face.

I staggered back, startled…and accidentally yanked Will's soul with me.

"Uh-oh," I said.

Chapter 25

KIERAN

HEART IN HIS throat, Kieran took a chance and bolted through the last few rows of the shopping complex parking lot to get around to Alexis. Using the service entrance would've drawn too much notice. All of his Six, other than Henry, should already be there, Henry having been the farthest away and the hardest to extract.

They must have arrived in time to help Alexis. They must have, or he would've gotten a call. He would've felt it through the soul connection.

Just like he'd felt her drift away earlier. He'd already been on his way to the shopping complex, racing through the hidden passageway behind her house to get to the dual-society zone, when a strange loss had niggled his awareness. It had felt as though Alexis had disappeared from this world. As though she'd died. If the feeling hadn't resolved quickly, he would have completely lost his composure.

Screams and yells sent cold trickles down his spine

as he raced around the corner. The cloud that was Zorn drifted not far away and Thane stood idle a few steps beyond him. Disbelief ran through Kieran. What the hell were these guys doing so far from the fight?

In a moment, he understood.

Furry bodies rolled around on the concrete, whimpering or howling. Human forms thrashed on the ground or bent over, clutching their middles.

In the middle of it all, her hair blown by some unseen force, cloaked in glowing white, stood Alexis, facing off against a badass shifter. She looked like a rampaging angel claiming her vengeance on anyone foolish enough to threaten her brood.

She was the most beautiful thing he'd ever witnessed in his entire life.

He jogged to a stop next to Zorn, his fear for Alexis dissipated like rain drops on hot cement.

"What happened?" he asked as Zorn materialized next to him.

"She's using her magic," Zorn said quietly, his voice somber.

"Yes, she is." Thane joined them, grinning. The glory of battle burned in his eyes. His Berserker side felt Alexis's call to arms and yearned to join her. It spoke to his unbelievable control that he had not. "I have been fucking vindicated for my reaction to her the other day. Fucking vindicated. I might've changed, but at least I wasn't reduced to *this*."

"She has a shaky handle on the situation, at best," Zorn said, his mind as quick and calculating as ever. "I have no doubt she can keep them down, but not long ago she asked what she should do next. If she releases her hold, more than half of them will take off running. There aren't enough of us to snatch them up before they escape. We need an end game."

Will Green spat a series of disgusting remarks about Mordecai's family, and the boy launched forward, throwing a well-placed and powerful punch at the older alpha.

"The kid was exceptional in the thick of it, sir—"

Zorn cut off as Alexis flinched back.

"Uh-oh," she said loudly.

Green collapsed. It wasn't from the punch.

Through his soul connection with Alexis, Kieran saw what happened next.

Confused and disoriented, Green's spirit form stood outside of his body, twice as muscular as his physical form and taller. Clearly he saw himself differently than he actually appeared.

Alexis had learned how to rip a soul out of a body, and she'd done it on accident.

"Sir—"

Zorn didn't need to finish his sentence—Kieran was already on it. He sent a thick blast of power into the scene, swirling around Alexis and Mordecai and rolling over the enemy. Their agonized screams and shrieks turned into squeals and grunts of pain. She might be able to frighten to the point of hysteria, but he could inflict pain to the point of unconsciousness or death. This time he aimed for the former. He needed to figure out what to do with all these shifters, and death was the last option.

He lifted his hand and called the fog, bringing it down in thick, fluffy sheets, a fog bank settling inland. It wouldn't be an abnormal occurrence out here.

Once visibility cut down, he wove air and dropped a thicker layer of fog beyond the small battle. That would keep people from wandering in and catching an eyeful, or worse, taking video.

If they hadn't already.

Mordecai stepped away from the limp body of Green, his eyes huge. "Did I do that?"

"No. I did that," Alexis said with a pale face. "I'm going to try and stuff him back in."

Green's spirit shook before reaching forward and grabbed an invisible line connecting him to Alexis. His spirit turned more translucent as he jutted toward her.

"Ew, no!" She waved her hands in the air before shivering. His spirit went flying, as though she'd flung him through the air. He landed on two wolves' bodies before rolling to a stop.

"I said not to latch on to the connection!" she yelled after him, her face screwed up in disgust. "That was your fault, and now look. You're all the way over there, wasting precious time."

"What's happening?" Mordecai and Thane asked at the same time.

"Growing pains," Kieran said, and started forward. Bria was already moving.

"Did you rip his soul out of his body?" Bria unslung a camo backpack from her shoulder, tiptoed through the downed bodies, and knelt by Alexis's side. "'Cause we can just shove him back in. Remember me teaching you that? No problem, remember?"

"Yeah, but will he come back to life as though nothing has happened?" Alexis blinked as she finally noticed the silence and lack of movement of those around her. Her expression fell. "Oh God, what did I do now?"

"It was me," Kieran said quietly, nearly at her side. "I finished the job. We needed to get this cleaned up so we can get moving. They aren't dead."

She jumped and her head jerked up. A look of supreme relief crossed her face and a gorgeous smile curved her lips. "Hi," she said, her voice breathy. "I didn't notice you there."

"Clearly," he said teasingly. Fire started in his middle and rose through him. Reaching Alexis, he touched her back, his attention wholly focused on her, and on the place where their two souls met and entwined, becoming one. "You okay?"

She shrugged with one shoulder. "I am, but he's not."

Bria bent down next to her and dug into her bag. "Let's see what's happening. We can't all see spirits."

But Kieran could. Green's spirit stood slowly, panic consuming his expression as his gaze lingered on his unmoving physical body. He walked to it, slowly, as though in a dream.

"I've accidentally broken the prongs in his spirit box," Alexis said softly, watching him make his way back. "I can shove him back in, and I'm pretty sure I can figure out how to make his spirit box return to normal, but those prongs..." With no warning, her eyes lost focus, and her body went completely still.

Kieran felt that same strange blankness through the soul connection.

"She did this before." Mordecai moved to her side. "Just went stalk still. Like she was in a trance. It seemed to help her, last time. We were under siege, and then everyone started dropping."

"Here we go." Bria rolled her thumb over the top of her lighter, then pressed the flame to a stub of incense. Red smoke curled up through the thick tendrils of fog. "The fog is not awesome."

Kieran flicked his hand and sent the moisture higher, blanketing them but not invading their space.

"Better," Bria said, looking around.

A strange *absence* could be seen in the gathering red smoke, like a person wearing black Spandex whose outline was fuzzy. It bent over Green's body, and Kieran got the distinct impression its arm reached into Green's chest.

"What in the holy fuck..." Bria's voice drifted away, her eyes widening as she watched the shape. "What is that? I can't feel a soul. Is it a weak spirit or something?"

"No." Kieran shook his head. "At least, it's not like any spirit I've ever seen. Though...that's not really saying much."

"Alexis?" Bria's gaze flicked up, but if Alexis heard her, she didn't acknowledge it.

He ran his hand down her back, comforted by her warmth. "Is it a deep trance?"

Bria shrugged, back to watching the figure bending over Green. Green's spirit had nearly reached his body, his expression urgent, as though he knew time was running out. "Quite possibly. She figures out the most stuff when she lets herself hang around in a trance for a while." Brow furrowed, Bria shook her head slowly. "I've never seen or felt anything like this. It's like...a blank patch in reality."

Kieran shifted from side to side, that strange feeling of *absence* between them gnawing on his nerves.

"Sir." Zorn stepped through the wolves' bodies. "We need to make some decisions and wrap this up. At this rate, we'll be noticed. It's a miracle we haven't been already."

Green's spirit reached his body and stared down at it. "I'm dying." His expression heated and he zeroed in on Alexis. "You filthy, soul-stealing bitch."

Green's spirit darted at her. Kieran reacted without thought. He sent a blast of his power, laced with Alexis's magic, through the center of Green's spirit. It sent the spirit staggering before jerking him to a stop and keeping him put.

The figure within the smoke—the hazy, blurred form—jerked up, and Kieran got the strangest sensation that it was looking directly at him. In a moment, Alexis startled, the sensation of her slamming back into him like it had earlier. The form blurred even more before dissipating entirely, and Kieran took a breath he hadn't realized he'd been holding.

"So it *is* your mark, huh, Junior?" Green spat, his face twisted in rage. "Does Daddy know, I wonder? We all know he's not the romantic type."

Kieran didn't have time to digest what Green was saying. His attention was on Alexis as she sucked in a deep breath. She blinked, and the haze cleared from her eyes—she was present in a way she hadn't been a moment before.

"I can put his spirit back," she said in a rush. "He—or it?—showed me. In that weird plane. I theoretically know how, at any rate. It seemed so easy."

"Who showed you?" Bria asked. "Where?"

"He said he's dying," Kieran said.

Alexis's magic slid across his, deliciously intimate and powerful, and his grip on Green was flicked away.

"He is," she said. "His body is, at any rate. There's a small transition time after a soul leaves. Usually, the body is dying, so the spirit can't go back. But if the body's healthy, I think the soul can be locked back in, however fragile the docking, and the person can go on living." She snapped, urgency riding her words. "It's like those people who have near-death experiences. You know, the ones who remember hovering above their own bodies or seeing a light at the end of the tunnel? Their bodies were mended enough to keep on trucking, and their souls hadn't given up. They were able to re-forge the connection." She blinked a few times in confusion. "Or maybe someone did it for them…" She shook her head and waved it away. "I don't know. This afternoon is super confusing. Bottom line, I think I can fix him."

"Do it," Kieran said before turning to Zorn. He sent another pulse of magic out to keep the downed shifters put. "But his reign of terror ends today. Get these shifters into a holding pen. Green has just lost his army."

"Okay. Okay, okay." Alexis braced like she was about to wrestle. "All I have to do—"

"You better make this right, you filthy whore," Green swore.

Kieran bit his tongue, barely keeping himself from cutting Green down a second time. Alexis needed to practice her magic, and in case all didn't go as planned, she had the perfect guinea pig.

"I bet you talk about women like that because you can't get any for free," Alexis murmured, yanking him into the air before stuffing him unceremoniously back into his skin. "You probably use your power to force them, you disgusting creep."

"Which is why it's so enjoyable to feel you manhandling his spirit." Bria rested her chin on her fist and wafted the smoke more thoroughly over Green's body.

Alexis's face closed down in concentration.

Zorn stepped closer. "I re-routed Henry to grab a van. He's not far out. Half-hour, tops. Daisy is working on re-directing people who want to get back here, but a delivery truck needs to unload."

"Just need to…" Alexis wiped her forehead while bending over the body of Green, not unlike that blurry figure that had appeared in the negative space of Bria's fog. "Two more…" She swore softly. "That one's fucked. My bad. That should be okay, though. The rest look good."

"What are you doing?" Bria asked, yanking up the sleeve of her shirt. Goosebumps covered her skin.

"I can braid my power and spirit together to fuse the prongs back into place." Alexis wiped her forehead again. "Then I just have to change the density of the spirit box back to normal, and we should be cooking with gas."

Bria held her arm up to be appraised by Zorn, silently relaying the presence of a spirit in their midst. His second should've been off directing the guys, but instead he stood there, half turned, his attention on Alexis. He obviously wondered the same thing Kieran did—could she fix a soul she'd previously torn out of a body?

"She's doing it," Bria mouthed to him, her eyes wide and excited. "How did you figure all this out?" she asked Alexis.

"Let her work," Zorn whispered.

But Alexis was straightening up, her face shiny with sweat and red from exhaustion.

"It's like I slip into this other realm where time and a physical presence don't belong," she said, out of breath. "And there's this...thing there. It's like a person without being a person. Someone I do but don't know." She shook her head. "I can't possibly explain it. It's a feeling, more than anything. Hell, maybe it's my subconscious. But this…thing showed me the strings connecting everyone, and then it showed me how to alter Green's spirit box and re-connect the prongs. It was like…instruction without words. Then, kinda suddenly, I was knocked back into my body."

"Riiiight," Bria said.

Green jerked and his eyes fluttered. His mouth opened and he sucked in huge breath. His body convulsed.

"He's going to change—"

A pulse of power cut Mordecai off. Green's limbs shrank and his face elongated. Fur sprouted over his body.

His spirit popped out of his body again.

"Crap." Alexis threw up her hands.

Chapter 26

ALEXIS

"**I** THINK I know what went wrong." Bria turned from the built-in grill next to the stove in my new kitchen. We'd had to steal most of the supplies from Kieran's house since my shopping had been cut short.

The guys were dealing with the shifter mess I'd created, so Bria was on dinner duty. I hadn't been allowed to cook for some reason, and given my afternoon, and my intense fatigue, I hadn't argued.

I wearily sank into the stool at the island. Wind howled at the window behind me, the wooden shutters drawn closed against the darkness beyond. The waves crashed wildly against the cliffs in the distance. I dropped my face into my hands.

"I know what went wrong," I said, my words muffled against my palms. "I've been thinking about it for the past three hours. Well...three and a half, if you count how long it took to get home from the store that severely disappointed my shopping appetite."

The BBQ fork swung to the side. "Oh yeah?" Bria

cocked a hip, something I now recognized as a signal she was thinking professionally.

"Yeah. I've been in and out of trances, I've been fiddling with my own spirit box—"

She sucked a breath through her teeth. "Until you get a firm handle on the whole situation, I wouldn't suggest playing doctor on yourself. You'll probably get marooned in the spirit realm, and Kieran will kill himself trying to drag you back out."

I waved the comment away tiredly. "I was just feeling around in there. But I'm pretty sure I know what went wrong. I mean…" I gestured with my hand. "Besides the fact that I keep getting shooed away from the spirit realm by some very pushy entity without a freaking body. I think the Line has its own minions or something."

Bria bent at the waist with a very intense look on her face. The black smoke billowing up behind her, caught by the hood over the stove, did not bode well for our meal. "I'm honestly not sure what to say. I've never heard of anything like that."

"Yeah, well, here's some more that you haven't heard…"

I paused as Mordecai slouched in, clearly tired but emboldened by his success. After Will Green lost his soul for the second time, and everything slowed down, the guys had all patted Mordecai on the back and praised him for a job well done. Even Daisy had dropped her competitiveness and given him a beaming high-five. After so short a time, his training was really shining through.

I waited while he opened the fridge door and stared into the depths.

I lifted my eyebrows after a moment when he didn't grab something.

I gritted my teeth when he shifted his weight and leaned on the door, still looking.

"Oh my God, how many times do I have to tell you?" I snapped. "Grab something and get out. You're wasting electricity."

He sighed, but reached for the milk.

"And don't you dare drink out of the carton," I added.

Bria frowned at me. "Since when is that a rule?"

There really were no words.

"Anyway," I said as Mordecai moved to get a glass. "I did repair the prongs after a fashion, and they would've held in a normal person, but shifters..." I formed a ball with my fingers, having no easy way to explain this to someone who hadn't magically seen and felt it. "When they shift, their spirit boxes magically change density. That's the moment I can easily seep in and mess around. The entity showed me how I can mimic that in a non-shifter." I dragged my lip through my teeth. "I'm pretty sure I can do it. Practice would really help, though. Because, I mean, I'd secured the prongs to Green's spirit box, but not well enough to withstand those few moments when the box changed. So, when he started to shift…" I let my hands drift through the air.

"You killed him," Bria surmised.

"Well…" I paused, remembering the fuming words Will's spirit had spewed after being booted from his body for the second time. Kieran hadn't even been able to shut him up. I'd had to shove him across the Line for some peace. "Yeah, but…"

"No, she didn't," Mordecai finally said as Daisy walked in with a ponytail on top of her head and a black exercise outfit. "I killed him. Alexis wouldn't have done any of that if not for me." His tone was bleaker than Green deserved.

"Well, yeah, but…" I squinted my eyes, thinking of a rebuttal he would buy.

"He killed himself," Daisy said, opening the fridge door and staring into its depths.

"Oh my God, if I have to—"

"Grab and go," Mordecai said over me urgently. "She's in a bad mood."

Daisy snatched out the orange juice container and slammed the fridge door.

"Apparently we're not supposed to drink out of the

carton anymore, either," Bria said dryly, and rolled her eyes.

Daisy looked at Bria for a long beat, glanced at the orange juice carton in her hand, and then put the OJ back in the fridge. Smart girl that she was, she'd realized Bria's backwash was probably in all of the cartons. She grabbed a glass and went to the faucet instead.

"He killed himself," Daisy repeated, firmly entrenched in her fifty-year-old persona. She turned and leaned against the counter as Bria rolled a blackened hotdog off the grill. "He wrote his own death sentence the day he murdered Mordie's parents. His pack should've taken him down long before now. And what is it Jack always tells you?" Daisy pointed at Mordecai, who was back to staring blankly. "If someone from one pack challenges a weaker member of another pack, the leader of the challenged pack can step in. Right?"

"The girl listens, I'll give her that." Bria nodded as she tore open a new package of hot dogs.

"I have to." Daisy slurped down half her water before continuing. "I don't have any magic. I need to figure out how magical people operate, learn their handicaps, and figure out the best time to attack. Jack has to repeat himself so often that it's pretty easy to get shifter info."

Mordecai's brows lowered. "I need to write stuff down, you know that! He never tells me these things when I have a pen and paper on me."

She put her hands out. "You're a bodily learner, like most shifters, and I'm an auditory learner, like most awesome people. I'm not complaining. Your blockhead helps me out." She raised her glass to him. "Cheers."

The shining moment of sibling love had been nice while it lasted.

"I'm technically in his pack, though," Mordecai said.

"Firstly…" Daisy gulped down the rest of her water. Rivulets ran down her chin and dripped onto the floor. My ire rose. "You weren't in his pack because he tossed you out for dead. He exiled you. You would've had to fight to get back in. According to shifter code, or standards, or whatever, you were no longer part of that pack, the magical governing body's paperwork be damned."

"That sounds like Jack," Bria said, rolling darkly scored hot dogs.

Daisy turned to refill her glass. "He said it when he was loading unconscious bodies into the van earlier."

"Is that what he was muttering?" Bria pulled over a bag of buns. "You listen really closely."

"To their every word, yeah. The Six are really powerful. Learning their secrets and weaknesses will put me above most of my competitors. Anyway, being that Alexis took him in, he was actually a part of Alexis's pack, and she had the right to accept the challenge. But, if we go a step further, Kieran accepted Alexis as his beta—"

"What's this now?" I asked.

Bria half turned and waved her BBQ fork in the air. "The mark he put on you. Some people would say it makes you co-ruler, but a Demigod will always rank higher than you. Which is why I said, in the very beginning, don't get involved. Remember that, when I first met you? I said don't get involved, and now look, you'll always be second best."

Mordecai huffed out laughter as he stared down into his nearly empty glass of milk.

"She's in a more powerful position," Daisy said with a smirk. "He gets all the attention, and she gets all the time in the world to stick a knife in someone's ribs."

"Wow." I dropped my face into my hands again. "What has become of my sweet family?"

"As the beta to Kieran's pack, that makes Kieran ultimately responsible for Green's death." Daisy put her glass of water on the counter. "Regardless, Green was the one who picked the fight. So you see, Mordie? You are doubly, or even triply, not responsible for this. But if you were... dude. Take it and run! That will really up your shifter points."

"I agree. You'll need to challenge into or create your own pack someday." Bria ripped open the bun bag. "It's time to harden up. Shifters aren't a soft group of people."

Mordecai slumped his shoulders. "I won't lie—I'll lose sleep over this, but… I know it wasn't wrong. He killed my parents, threatened my new family, and he threatened me… He couldn't have been a good leader. His days were numbered. I get that. It's just…"

"You haven't seen death before." Bria nodded. "It's jarring. Just think how it is for me—I deal in death all the time."

"And look how you turned out," Daisy said.

"Exactly." Bria lifted her hands in triumph, missing Daisy's point.

"It's not really death, as you think of it," I said as I heard the front door open. "He's still alive, it's just that he doesn't have a body."

"No, thank you." Daisy showed me her palm. "That's creepy, Lexi. I don't like hearing about that stuff."

"It's comforting!"

Both kids shook their heads.

"Eh." Bria rolled a few more blackened dogs off the grill. "Kids these days. Too soft, if you ask me. Here's a joke: what did the spirit say to the other spirit?"

"Stop," Daisy said, shaking her head.

"Mooove over. No, wait…" Bria looked upward. "That was the cow. What *did* the spirit say to the other spirit?"

"What's for dinner?" Jack sauntered in with Thane and Boman at his back. Crimson stained their shirts and fresh scrapes marred their bare arms.

"What happened?" I pointed at the red splattered across the dirty white fabric.

Jack looked down. "Oh, that. Yeah, you drove a few of them nuts, and Kieran only made it worse. When they woke up…" He made a circle at his temple with his pointer finger.

"It was crazy town." Thane rolled his shoulders. "A whole bunch made it through, though. You didn't drive them all crazy." He winked at me.

The front door opened and closed again, more of the guys coming in. I could sense Kieran, miles away, swimming in the sea. He was re-energizing in a way I wished I could.

"See there?" Bria pointed at the guys with her BBQ fork. "See what you'll turn into, Mordecai? Hardcore."

"That's not helping," Daisy mumbled, tucking her glass into the dishwasher and slipping to Mordecai's side. She laid a hand on his shoulder. "This was all Green's fault, Mordie."

"Nah, it was her fault." Boman pointed at me with a giant, glittering smile. The man was a looker when he rolled that smile out. "The secret weapon."

I frowned at him, but for the life of me, I didn't feel

remorse. Couldn't. That crew had been there to kill a fifteen-year-old boy. They didn't deserve remorse, nor would they get it from me.

"Nah, it was Green's fault," Jack said, stretching his hugely muscled arms out in the suddenly much smaller space between the table and the island. "All of this was his fault. He was twisted, and he accumulated a group of thugs who liked sick shit. They were half mad already— Alexis and Kieran just pushed them over the edge. That whole crew needed to be handed their hats. I wish I could've played a bigger part in it."

"I'm sure Daisy wishes you had." Donovan's nose crinkled as he laughed. He'd just filed into the kitchen behind the others with Zorn and Henry at his back. "She was a one woman show, turning people away and shutting down gossip. How did you get that woman to give you her phone so you could erase the video?" He leaned across the island, grinning at her. "I thought for sure we'd have to knock her down and steal her shit."

"A little too hardcore," Bria muttered, her back to the room as she worked.

"Yeah. I've never seen a person change personalities so many times in the space of twenty minutes." Boman peeled off his dirty shirt and tossed it into the corner. That was a habit that'd be short-lived, just as soon as I could work up the energy to yell at him. "That was a handy skill."

"You have to know how to talk to people to get what you want." Daisy shrugged, seemingly nonchalant, but her cheeks were noticeably red.

"That is just one of her many handy skills," Zorn said quietly, drifting to the corner of the room.

"Zorn is tired of everyone praising Mordecai, and not his pupil." Bria laughed as Jack joined her.

"What the..." Jack stepped back, outrage on his face. He gestured at the stove. "What the hell is this?"

Bria pushed a charcoal-encrusted bun off the grill. She flung another after it. "Dinner," she said without looking up.

"Dinner?" Jack motioned Donovan in for a look.

"No." Donovan looked over her shoulder, his good mood vanishing. "That's dog food."

"Mordecai, dinner's ready." Daisy gestured him on. Apparently, she felt she'd given him enough touchy-feely support.

"You wanted me to cook dinner, and so I cooked dinner. You didn't seem to care that I don't know how to cook, so..." Bria raised her eyebrows at them. "You get what you get, and you don't get upset."

Jack and Donovan's mouths dropped open. A small smile crept up Zorn's face.

"What happened?" Boman asked, his smile failing.

"How hard is it to cook hotdogs?" Jack asked with a raised voice. "They're already cooked. You're basically just heating them up. How hard is it to heat up food?"

The door closed softly and I zeroed in on the soft pulse in my middle letting me know Kieran was near. I looked up and my breath caught. All noise in the room dialed down to nothing.

He filled the entrance of the kitchen in a wet shirt that clung to his perfectly sculpted, powerful body. Ripped jeans hugged his muscular thighs, ending in sandy flip-flops. His raven hair fell across his forehead and his stormy blue gaze rooted to me with an intensity that gave me goosebumps.

"Alexis, may I speak with you?" he said, his voice thick and raspy, and fear crawled through me at his formality.

Chapter 27

ALEXIS

"W HAT, AND MISS the dinner I toiled to make?" Bria flipped another bun off the grill.

"You're not missing anything, sir," Jack grumbled, watching Bria's handiwork with wide, horrified eyes. He seemed powerless to stop the train wreck.

"Sure, yeah." I pushed up from the table as he glided through the kitchen, smelling of salt. His mouth-watering male magnetism tightened my core. His power and strength and intensity filled the space, sending out silent waves of explosive energy. The guys all turned, giving him their undivided attention. Daisy's face lost color again, and Mordecai looked down at his feet. Even Bria had turned, all serious, ready for a command to action.

The Demigod was in the room, more powerful than any pack leader could be, and he was owning his mantle. It didn't matter that everyone in the room was powerful in their own way and, besides Daisy, magical—he dominated their awareness and owned their focus.

I took his hand and melted at his touch, my legs going wobbly.

Without another word, he led me back the way he'd come and then up the stairs to my new bedroom. Once we were both inside, he shut the door behind us and motioned for me to take a seat on the couch by the window. The sound of crashing waves grew louder when he lifted the window. A wave of his hand, and his magic brought a gentle ocean breeze in, mussing my hair.

With serious eyes, he sat down next to me and silence fell over us. I couldn't read the surge of emotion coming through the soul connection. His stony face gave absolutely nothing away.

"I don't know how to begin," he said after a moment, his voice deep and thick.

"From the beginning?" I tried.

He looked at me for a long moment, and I thought I recognized uncertainty in his gaze.

"My father marked my mother," he started, and my heart skipped a beat.

He knew about the mark, and he clearly wasn't doing cartwheels about it.

"He has said, many times, that it was the worst decision he ever made."

Maybe the beginning wasn't the best place to start

after all. I couldn't comment on that, though. My heart was now firmly lodged in my throat, choking me.

"That when the woman wearing his mark walked away from him," Kieran continued, "it invited ridicule. He never said it, but it was clear that he thought the situation with my mother made him look weak."

"I don't plan on walking away from you," I whispered.

His eyes softened for a brief moment. Much too brief.

"What my mother did crushed his ego, and cracked his brain a little, I think, though it can be argued that he was always a little imbalanced."

It certainly could be argued, yes, and those with nerves of steel usually did.

"I was never taught how to mark a person," Kieran went on. "Or even what sort of magic goes into it. It is usually something a Demigod parent teaches their child. Kind of like a safe sex talk for those who can accrue diseases."

A chill spread across my skin because I knew what was coming.

"I didn't mean to mark you," he said. "I had no idea I was doing it."

My lungs burned from holding my breath, terrified he'd say he regretted it.

"A mark is forever," he continued, his face showing

no emotion. "Few Demigods still engage in the practice, and fewer still for love—my father can attest as to why." He shook his head slowly. "I am sorry, Alexis, please believe that. But I cannot remove it. I cannot alter it."

His voice held frustration, apology, and most of all, regret.

Swallowing was laborious. A tear escaped and dribbled down my cheek. I opened my mouth to claim nonchalance, but my lower lip trembled so much that I had no choice but to close it again. I managed a shrug before another tear followed the first.

I wiped them away, intense agony eating through me. I had no idea why this hurt so much. Why I was reacting this way. Of course he wasn't happy he'd accidentally made his claim permanent. It was purely logical for him to be freaked out about this. *I* should be freaked out.

But for the life of me, it felt like he'd just ripped a gaping hole in my middle, stuck dynamite in it, and lit the fuse. Something in me had thought—hoped—that even if he hadn't marked me on purpose, he'd be okay with the idea of the long haul. *I* had been cool with it, enough so that I'd created what I still thought was a permanent connection between our souls.

I'd been a fool. And now I was branded for all to see.

"Now what?" My voice was barely a whisper, and I

summoned all my strength to harden it. "Can we hide it?"

His demeanor changed, suddenly vicious and aggressive, even though he'd barely moved a muscle. "Do you want to hide it?"

"Well…" I wiped away another tear, confused. "Why would I want anyone to see a mark you didn't want to put on me?"

Silence ballooned around us.

"Damn it." He leaned back and blew out a breath before wiping his hand down his face. "Do you see what I mean?" He put his palms on his chest and I wiped away another tear. I most certainly did not see what he meant. I had no clue.

In a flurry of movement, he was up and pacing the floor. Panic gripped me that he might leave. That he might walk away, leaving me with this rejection and his unintentional brand. But when he reached the end of the space, he turned around and paced back.

"I'm handling this all wrong," he said, running his fingers through his messy hair. "I can't think straight. I'm trying to apologize for what I did—but everything in me wants to do it again. Wants to haul you over to that bed, claim you anew, and run my magic across every inch of your beautiful, intoxicating body."

I could only blink up at him, the mixed messages making my head spin.

He stopped in front of me, his expression frustrated. "Truth?"

"Yes, please."

He paced away. "There was a time when the mark was used to represent ownership. Prized harem members were marked. A favored king under a Demigod's control was marked." He turned and paced back. "The anti-slavery laws put an end to the practice of owning through a mark. That's when the marks became about love...about sharing power. A king in the magical world might mark his queen." He stopped and nailed me with a look. "I'm sure I don't have to tell you how infrequently Demigods choose to share their power." He started again. "Still, the practice occasionally works out. The Demigod of London and his wife rule together, for example. But what happened with my father and mother isn't an aberration."

Kieran sat onto the couch and bent over to rest his elbows on his knees.

"Marking someone is a huge decision. It's not like marriage, because it can't be undone." He turned his head to look at me. "We barely know each other."

I nodded, because he was exactly right. Regardless, my chest throbbed, another stick of dynamite exploding each time he said something like this.

He leaned back warily, his expression one of exhaustion. "I didn't give you a chance to say feck off. I did this without your permission. I locked you into forever…without even asking."

I nodded again, because that was true. Of course, I'd done the same thing by tying our souls together permanently.

"Everything points to my having made an irreversible error—one you should never forgive me for." He sagged. "But when you asked if there was a way to hide it… I lost myself for a moment. The thought tore at something deep in here." He pounded a fist to his sternum, the same place my dynamite kept going off. "I don't know that I could stop myself from marking you again. Even now, after I laid out what a terrible idea it was"—he shrugged helplessly—"I want to do it all over again. I want to sizzle my magic across your skin, and warn anyone else away from touching you. I want to share everything I have, and am, with you. I want you by my side in whatever comes next." He threw up his hands before letting them fall again. "I don't know where that leaves us, other than I'm sorry I didn't ask you, and I hope you can forgive me."

I stared at him, uncertain. "So…you wouldn't want to wipe away the mark if you could?"

His look was completely open. Raw. "No. Despite all the reasons I should, I don't. But depending on how pissed you are, I'll happily pretend."

A tear broke loose and tracked down my face. I

didn't want to let relief take hold of me before I could knock on something wooden.

He reached up and wiped my tear away. "I love you, Alexis. Each new thing I learn about you makes me want you more. This love may be new, but the roots have thoroughly taken hold. I have every reason to believe it'll keep growing until it drives words from the poets and makes even Ed Sheeran's love ballads pale in comparison."

I gave him a watery laugh. "And what if I do leave?"

Anger rolled across his face before he regained control. A heaviness filled the moment. He blew out a slow breath. "I'll take up yoga." A crooked smile tweaked his lips. "Honestly, it'll kill me. It'll drive me to rage. I do have my father in me, and I am possessive to a fault." His thumb trailed across my cheek. "But I do not own you. You are free to do as you please. I will not hurt you. I will never hurt you. I'll put checks and balances in place in case I should lose my mind. I will never make a woman suffer as my father made my mother suffer." His fist clenched. "Never."

I hadn't needed to hear any of that. I already believed it, or I wouldn't have let things go this far in the first place.

He looked at me for a long beat. Finally, he whispered, "I still don't know where we go from here."

I fought back laughter. As he sat there, looking to

me for guidance, he seemed almost like a normal man, sitting with the woman he loved, wondering if he was in the dog house.

"I thought Demigods were supposed to have all the answers," I hedged. I snuck my fist up and tapped the window sill. Just in case.

His mouth-watering smile made my stomach flip. "Sometimes we need a little help deciphering which way the wind is blowing."

I shrugged, finally letting relief take hold of me. He'd told me the truth of his situation, and now it was probably fair for me to be equally open with him.

"You had me going there. I thought you regretted the mark. I freaked out a little more than is probably normal."

He leaned closer and trailed his thumb across my jaw. "I will never regret that mark. Unlike my father, I don't see my connection to you as a weakness. I've just attached myself to one of the wildest, most unpredictable women I've ever met. It'll be a crazy ride, I have no doubt."

I narrowed my eyes at him. "You marked Bria, too? Because I'm not down with sharing."

He chuckled and brushed his lips against mine. "Tell me plainly, Alexis. Are you okay with my...accidentally marking you?"

I shook my head and the tip of my nose brushed

back and forth against his. "Accidentally? No. If you're going to do something right, you need to do it on purpose."

He pulled back a little, his eyes searching mine. Fire lit within them and eagerness crossed his expression.

"Claim me for reals this time," I said in a breathy voice.

Chapter 28

ALEXIS

KIERAN CRASHED HIS lips onto mine, needy and sensual. His sexy magic blistered across my skin before soaking down into me, driving out a moan. He ran his palm up my stomach and across my breast, but his fingers continued their upward path—wrapping around the back of my neck and then sliding down to my shoulder. He was backing off.

"Wrong direction," I said, nearly panting.

I tried to lean back and drag him on top of me, but he got to his feet.

"You said to do this right." He took my hand and helped me to stand.

My legs gave out and I tipped into him.

"You need to stand," he said softly, putting me to rights and steadying me.

His stormy eyes teased me as he clutched the base of my shirt and pulled it over my head. He tossed the fabric away.

"I'm not a true Demigod, did you know that?" he

asked, stepping a little closer. His heat blanketed me. His sexy magic vibrated across my skin, boosting my pleasure higher without him even touching me. "Demi is half, and I am but a quarter. Like you."

He lightly trailed his fingertips down my chest and over my budded nipples. A shock of pleasure zipped straight to my core.

"Oh Kieran, please, fuck me," I groaned.

"I will, love. Good and hard, believe me. But first…" He ran his soft touch down my stomach and then, with inhuman speed, flicked my pants open and pulled down the zipper. Moving slowly again, he slid my pants down over my thighs, following his fingertips with his lips, until my pants pooled on the floor.

"It is rare for someone like me to inherit a Demigod's magic," he continued, making his way back up my body in the same slow, sensual, worshipful manner. His palm grazed the inside of my right thigh. His tongue grazed the other. I couldn't breathe as he neared my apex. "I am the only Demigod who has access to my other parent's magic." His lips skimmed my left hip and his fingers caressed the other. "Even a true Demigod from two godly lineages will only manifest one god's magic. Yet I wield the magic of a Demigod, and that of a selkie."

Another wave of his sexy magic nearly drove me to my knees. He caught me and held me up, staring at me intently as his magic traveled across my body like two vibrating hands. It dipped between my legs and pushed up through me.

"Oh!" I clung to his wide shoulders, my eyes closed, gyrating my hips in time to the sexy magic massaging my core. "Oh holy fuck."

"Yes, exactly. I can fuck you anywhere, anytime, without even touching you." He bent and bit my nipple through my bra. The sensation blasted through me, and without warning, an orgasm swept me away. "Oh *God*."

I exalted in the pleasure, but the magic didn't let up. It kept pumping me higher still. Giving me no break.

"Of course, my selkie magic is minuscule compared to what I can do with Poseidon's lineage." The sound of crashing waves was so loud in the enclosed space that I jerked away from him, wondering if a tsunami had slammed into the cliff and was coming for the house. It hadn't, of course, but the room seemed to fill with the power and energy of the ocean—rip tides pulling, salt water bubbling, waves rolling. If I hadn't known better, I would have sworn water was pouring in through the windows.

My heart surged, blanketed by the sweet song of the ocean. In awe of its power. *His* power.

Kieran's warm palm slid up my suddenly chilled skin and stopped at my bra clasp. In a moment, the material was falling loosely to the ground. "Maybe it is because I am not a true Demigod that I want to share my power with you." He bent and then rose quickly, almost too fast to notice, and suddenly I stood bare before him. "More likely, it is because I trust you implicitly, and I know that giving you more tools can only help me in the long run."

"Always with a strategy." I had to yell in order to be heard over the noise of the rolling, tumbling chaos. Air swirled around me, fog so thick it was almost solid.

He grinned, and then he was gone, having disappeared into the swirling mists. A moment later he was back, completely nude and drop-dead gorgeous. His deliciously cut pecs led down into that devastating six-nearly-eight pack. His large cock stood rigid. But something told me he wasn't ready for me yet. He had an agenda, and I needed to let him set the pace.

Only as he reached me did I notice the needle in his hand. He held up one of his fingers, pricked it, and closed his eyes.

Power to a degree I could barely comprehend drummed around me, pushing against my body and electrifying the air. The tides ripped and surged around us. Fog rolled and boiled. The crash of waves deafening.

He held out his hand and the drop of crimson quivered on his finger. "Ingest this."

I barely stopped from recoiling—until I met his

eyes. The gravity I saw there, the openness, had me leaning forward. I trusted him with everything in me.

I wrapped my lips around the end of his finger and swallowed down the salty, metallic bite of his blood.

His magic burned a path across my skin, strangely pleasant and deliciously erotic. I moaned as I fell into the sensation, the feeling of his desire, and his devotion, evident through the buzz of our soul connection.

My magic surged out of me and the colors in the room changed. Spirit lined the walls and swirled within the fog. The Line pulsed, sending a shock wave of magic coursing through my veins.

"Yes," Kieran said softly, his voice a low hum. "Your magic feels so damn good."

His magic responded in kind and the pressure in the room built to a new high. The walls trembled. The ground shook. The fog swirled, so thick I felt the wetness slide across my face and coat my hair. I looked back again, wondering if I'd see that tsunami thundering toward us. I wanted to run. To hide. My primal instincts couldn't handle the onslaught of so much unbridled force and power.

Without warning, my ears popped, and then everything stilled. The fog dissipated and the crashing of the waves subsided until it was mere background noise. Silence drifted down between us.

It was as if nothing had ever happened.

I took a deep, shuddering breath, and though I stood naked by the open window, I no longer felt the chill of the night. My usual awareness of Kieran felt amplified, but that wasn't what had my eyes widening.

Power pounded through my veins. He'd increased the intensity of the mark, so I blanketed the already solid soul connection between us with more spirit.

"You have the gifts of my blood," he said softly, looking down on me with a gaze opened up all the way to his soul. "You will see it manifest in different ways. You will grow stronger, faster, and more capable. Your magic will…" His words stumbled, interrupting what had sounded like rehearsed information. "…might," he corrected, "see a boost in power. You will no longer feel temperature like a human, or lose your breath so easily. The pressure of the deep ocean will no longer trouble you. These gifts are bestowed so that you can better protect me…" He stopped altogether and ran his palms down my arms. "Sorry, that bit doesn't apply to you."

I shook my head, confused and feeling strange-ly…invincible. For some primal reason, I wanted to lift something heavy, like the couch, and then throw it through the window.

"What's happening?" I asked, feeling the throb of spirit. Feeling the call of the place where physical bodies weren't needed—the place that pushy jerk kept shoving me out of.

His smile tickled me way down deep. "I told you, I want to share everything I have with you. I trust you."

I slid my hands up his chest and stepped closer, smiling like a lunatic. "Does this mean I'm the first girl in your Six?"

His hands settled on my hips. "No. Because you haven't sworn to protect me. You're still just a girl. A super powerful girl with a Demigod's blessing, but a girl all the same. Tough luck."

I laughed and let my hands slide down his glorious pecs and hard stomach. "Freezing cold water won't affect me?"

"It'll be a nuisance, but you won't get hypothermia."

"And that couch...I could lift it and throw it through the window?"

One eyebrow tweaked upward. "Uhhm...maybe?"

"And I'd be fast enough to steal a cookie off of Daisy's plate without her stabbing my hand with a fork?"

His eyebrows lowered this time. "I may have made a mistake, here..." His eyes flicked up and slightly to the right. An unsettled expression replaced his bemused look. "I see it more clearly now. Did you strengthen our connection?"

"What?" I followed his gaze, but saw nothing out of the ordinary.

"The Line. It's clearer. It's...pulling at..." He took a hand from my hip and put it over his sternum. "Will its call ever win? Do you have to fight not to cross over?"

I glanced again at the spot he'd indicated, then shifted my gaze to the opposite side of the room, where *I* saw the Line. "Oh weird, I didn't know it would show up in different places for people sharing the same space." I shook my head, almost confusing myself with that one. "No, you'll get used to the feeling. It won't ever get any harder. While you have a body, at any rate. Your body will keep your soul contained in this world."

He nodded once, but he couldn't hide the soft fear still worming through our connection. He hadn't grown up knowing much about the spirit world—clearly it was the kind of thing a person had to get used to.

I reached down between us and wrapped my fingers around his hard girth. He sucked in a breath, his focus snapping to me like a rubber band. Any lingering fear fell away.

"I want to suck on this before you pound it into me," I said with an animalistic desire rising up in me.

Heat sparkled in his stormy eyes. He put his hand to my cheek before applying pressure downward, gently pushing me to my knees. He looked down at me as he fed me his large cock, and the power around us surged once again.

I slid my lips around the head and sucked him in as far as I could go. I watched as he took a deep breath and his eyes fluttered, lost to the sensation. I moved my palm along his shaft and pulled back before sucking him in again, harder this time. His tip hit the back of my throat and I picked up the pace, stroking and sucking in tandem.

"Oh yes, Alexis," he said, his head falling back and eyes closing.

He ran his fingers through my hair and made a fist, capturing me. Desire ran through me and I worked harder, cupping his balls and stroking his cock with my mouth.

"Yes," he said again, his body flexing. The sound of waves crashed around us. My skin sizzled with his magical touch. The power pumped in time with my mouth. "Fuck, Lexi, *yes!*"

He shuddered, his fingers loosening, and I took advantage of his distraction.

I stood so fast I dizzied myself—definitely faster than I'd ever moved before in my life—and shoved him toward the bed. His feet came off the ground and he all but flew backward, landing with an *oomph* on the mattress on his back. I could get used to the extra strength.

He didn't balk as I climbed onto the bed and crawled up over his body. It was my turn for dominance.

The Line pulsed again, and I realized I was making it happen. Power surged through me and I pushed it through the soul connection, dumping it into his body. He groaned and his eyes fluttered closed.

I licked his hardening cock—it was never long before he was ready again—before continuing up. If he could guide my head down, I could direct him where to lick. With slinky movements, feeling as sexy as all hell, I slid one knee to the side of his head, and lowered the other close to his ear, straddling his mouth.

His hands slid up the fevered skin on the backs of my thighs and over my butt. He sucked along my slit, finding my clit, and rolled it around with his tongue. His fingers trailed up my middle before dipping into my wetness, hitting me just right.

"Yes, Kieran, suck harder."

My eyes rolled back as he complied, his fingers moving in time to the glorious ministrations of his mouth. My body wound up and pleasure surged through me, strengthened by a boost from his sexy magic. Another wave of fire washed over my skin and I delighted in it.

"Yes, Kieran," I said, moving to his fingers. Tightening up in response to the pull of his mouth. "Oh God, yes. Almost there."

His tongue swirled and fingers wandered. His other hand gripped my thigh. I moved over him, lost to delight. So tight I couldn't stand it. Right on the edge—

"Oh!" I blasted apart, shivering with the orgasm that

tore through me. "Oh—*hmmm.*"

He picked me up in a dead lift and flung me beside him. I bounced on the mattress twice before he climbed between my spread thighs, his cock straining and eyes hungry.

"Pound my mark into you, isn't that what you said?" he asked dangerously.

"Yes." I ran my nails over his shoulders.

He reached between us and held the base of his sizable erection. "You can take more of me now. I won't have to hold back."

"Umm, yes." I slid my thighs up to his waist. "Fuck me, Kieran. Ride me hard."

He kissed my lips and his tip bumped up against my opening before he thrust. Color danced behind my lids as he filled me. I squeezed his middle while crying out.

"Fuck me," I uttered, pushing against him. Pulling at his body to get him closer. "Take me."

Without mercy, he pulled back and slammed into me. The slap of our bodies echoed through the room.

"You're mine," he said, slamming into me again. His magic burned across my skin and vibrated through my body. "You're mine alone."

It felt right to join our power together, so I pulled power from the Line and let the wind blow through the room. His soul didn't so much as flutter, held in place by mine.

"Yes, Kieran." I couldn't stop saying it, but I meant it. "Claim me."

Spirit throbbed around us. The veil shimmered not far away.

"Harder," I panted.

He rammed into me. The feel of him, and his magic, drove me to impossible heights. So good it hurt. Too much while not enough.

I pulled power from the Line again. And again. When his power rose, trying to dominate, I yanked on the Line for yet more power, my ability amplified by his blood offering coursing through my veins.

"*Hmm*, Alexis, more." He pumped faster, raw and ruthless. "*More.*"

So I listened. I gave him everything I had. Everything I was. Spirit washed through us as his magic enveloped our bodies. He groaned, and tightened his arms around me.

"I love you," he said close to my ear, and with one last thrust, I hit a height greater than any that had come before it.

My scream of unbridled pleasure filled the room. The tsunami had come after all, dragging me under to a place from which I never wanted to emerge. I shook with the orgasm, nearly blacking out, unable to do anything but repeatedly moan. He groaned above me, emptying into me.

As we came down, and the strength left my body, I still held on for dear life. For some reason, I didn't want to let go. I didn't ever want to let go.

Chapter 29

VALENS

VALENS SAT IN his son's favorite chair looking out the window at his son's favorite view. The glistening ocean usually calmed him, but something about his chat with Kieran yesterday niggled. On the surface, all was exactly as it should be. He'd left feeling elated and relieved. His son had it in him to be great, Valens could finally see that.

But something...was off. If he had the ability to be great, why only show it in fits and starts? It almost seemed like he only applied himself when it was necessary to appease his father, something that didn't match his behavior in the past.

At first Valens had thought it was simply a matter of Kieran trying to adjust to living in the territory of another Demigod, but he was no longer sure. Kieran had been known to rub the magical governing body in Ireland the wrong way from time to time. He'd had the habit of letting his presence be known, something Valens had needed to smooth out on more than one occasion. Not once had that been the case in these last eight months. Exactly the opposite in fact.

It could be that Kieran knew Valens was more dominant, whereas the governing body in Ireland wasn't, and was properly minding his manners. But again...Valens had always been in Kieran's life, and Kieran had often rebelled in various ways. Once, when he was fourteen, he tried to run away, refusing to let anyone rule him. His mother, land-bound, was beside herself distraught. She hadn't thought he could be found, not with his budding powers firmly taking hold.

The flight to Ireland had been longer than the time it took to traverse the waters, find the rebelling youth, and drag him back. Valens had been sure to make it a lesson Kieran remembered for years to come.

Men didn't change that much, even as adults.

"Sir." Sodge stopped near the entrance to the room. "Miss Amber has come to call on you. Shall I show her in?"

Valens frowned and checked the time. Lunchtime, if Valens were the type to worry about such things. Amber rarely disturbed him at home, especially without calling first. He'd be back at his desk in an hour, but clearly whatever news she had was too important to wait.

"Show her in," he said, not bothering to get up. He had more pondering to do, and this was a good place to do it.

"Sir." Amber stalked into the room, wearing leather from head to toe and light, rubber-soled boots. She came to a stop beside him, not hindering his view of the ocean. "Excuse the interruption, but I've come by…odd news. I thought you'd want to hear."

News she didn't want possibly intercepted over a cell phone line.

"Yes, what is it?" he said.

She shifted her weight. "Green has disappeared. He went after the Wolfram boy yesterday with his full fighting crew. Apparently, the boy was with his caretaker in the Serramonte dual-society zone shopping center. That was where Green directed everyone to amass. A few Chesters called the local precinct to report a large group of magical ruffians, but a squad car wasn't dispatched for some time—their district is overworked and underpaid. No official report was filed, but the description they were given fits Green's people."

Valens tore his gaze away from the glittering blue. "What of his crew?"

"All gone. No word was sent to the pack. Green had called a last-minute pack meeting before leaving, and never returned for it."

"How big is this crew?"

"Two dozen strong, sir. A force to be reckoned with. It's why he has remained in power for so long—he's got a lot of muscle on the payroll."

Valens steepled his fingers. "Can you find an explanation for where they might've gone?"

"Not one that doesn't include death, sir. There's more." She shifted again. Clearly something was really troubling her, a constant in the last couple of days. "There is surveillance on the caretaker's house—Miss Alexis Price. From what my people have seen, she hasn't returned to her residence since the day after being followed."

"She's expecting trouble, or her friend tipped her off they were being followed."

"Either way, Miss Price is poor. Or…she was poor. In the last few months, there have been uncharacteristically large deposits into her bank account. Now, she could still be someone's toy, but if she is, I can't figure out who's toy that might be. And very few benefactors would take in her teenage wards."

"The deposits?"

"Transfers from a dead-end account. In the last few days, she has made no withdrawals. Someone is paying for her lodging, and it isn't the Necromancer, who is seldom home."

Valens pinched the bridge of his nose.

"Several store clerks remembered seeing someone resembling the picture of Miss Price," Amber went on. "But the person they saw was much more beautiful, they said. Model material. They said she was radiant. One said she actually glowed. They described her with awe. I saw it myself, they had stars in their eyes. Their reactions were characteristic of…" Amber paused and Valens could swear she gulped. "Their reactions were characteristic of a Chester witnessing the recipient of a Demigod's mark."

Valens's stomach tightened up and the world froze around him, red tingeing the edges of his visions. Memories of Lyra and her radiant beauty bombarded him. He remembered the overwhelming need to own something so majestic, to showcase her on his arm for the world to see. She'd been more beautiful than any trophy in his trophy room, and more entrancing than any mortal, especially after he'd marked her as his.

He remembered people's expressions like it was yesterday. They'd fawned over her as though they were star struck. She had silenced entire rooms upon entry, lit up crowds with just a smile.

He'd given her that. He'd given her the ability to amplify her beauty. And what had she done in return? Humiliated him. Ran out on him right before the Demigod of London and his miserable wife were due in for tea.

"Are you certain?"

He could barely get the words out around his rage. He wished he'd been able to trap her spirit and not just her skin. His Necromancer could have stuffed her into bodies so Valens could personally mutilate her for the mortification she'd caused him. If she hadn't provided him with a Demigod heir, he would've treated her the same way in life.

And yet, for all that, he still wanted to look at her shining smile each day. He missed seeing her dancing in the waves, her flowing gown drifting in the ocean breeze.

She made him his weakest self, a disease for which there didn't seem to be a cure.

"No, sir," Amber said, cutting through the haze. "As of yet, I haven't come across anyone who took pictures, and no reports have appeared on the internet. It is hearsay at this point, sir."

Chesters were miserable wretches who hated the world and magical people especially. Their awe was rarely faked. Their insistence that it was the same woman, only more beautiful, spoke volumes. She'd now be the prize of the town.

His mind spun through all the details: the assessment a while back, the medical treatment for the Wolfram boy, the deposits from a dead-end account, his son's sudden move… Then there was the matter of his spirit trappers disappearing shortly after Lyra's death.

He struggled to breathe. How could he have been so incredibly blind?

"Your mother never taught you the value of respect and the importance of a proper farewell?"

Something flashed in his son's eyes, almost like the rolling turbulence right before a squall opened up on the sea. The next moment, it was gone.

Kieran had been unable to suppress his rage at first, hating the jab at his mother, but then he'd controlled it. Hidden it.

There were cracks in his son's facade. Tiny cracks. Miniscule.

How could he have doubted his son for one moment?

Anger rose through Valens. The fools in charge of monitoring Kieran had failed him. Their incompetence had left him blindsided. That would need to be dealt with.

"I received reports that yesterday Demigod Kieran left the building in a rush," Amber said.

"Yes, he mentioned he had an emergency with a plumber. Let me guess," Valens said. "He would've been just in time for the big shifter party."

"He did go home, but no one—plumber or otherwise—was waiting there to meet him. We suspect he left the house without anyone seeing him leave, though we cannot confirm." She paused for a moment, and they both knew she didn't have to say the next words. "He would've been in time, yes."

Valens laughed and looked out over the ocean. "Magnus has had the right idea all along, it seems. Take out the children before they become a problem."

"Sir?"

Valens waved it away. Another memory popped up.

Vengeance is a hardy pastime.

It had been staring him in the face all this time. He'd uttered those words himself about the silent benefactor of the Wolfram boy.

Jeffrey Smile.

Smile.

Kieran had been laughing at him. He'd moved into town, slick as they came, with a vendetta. He'd worn the cloak of weakness, showing off his bleeding heart, when all the while he was as cunning as Valens had ever been.

A note of pride disturbed his thoughts, but it couldn't smother his rage.

Kieran had been after vengeance for that whore. She'd probably filled his head full of lies and deceit. She'd programmed him to wreak vengeance for her.

"You were right to come here. Tell no one of this. We'll attempt to deal with the matter quietly. Get more information. Prove that your suspicions are true and my son is behind all of this. I don't want to make another mistake as it concerns him. I will not be made a fool of." He ground his teeth. "And get Vance. Tell him to meet me at Lyra's tomb tomorrow morning at sunrise. I want to make sure it is still intact."

"Yes, sir." She turned and strode out of the room.

His son could've been great, but now they would never know. He would destroy Kieran before the next Summit, proving once and for all that he could not be crossed. That he was the only Demigod capable of leading the magical world into its next phase of existence.

Valens sat quietly, simmering in rage. Far out at sea, he felt a storm brewing.

Chapter 30

ALEXIS

LIGHT BLARED DOWN from the noonday sun, glittering on the ocean as I fought for my life on the cliff near my new house.

I dodged a beam of light tearing through the air on my right side. Another raked the ground in front of me. It turned out Boman was a Light Bender, a really cool magic that gave him the ability to attack with light, or mask things by bending light around them. While I knew his position from being able to feel his soul, I couldn't anticipate the white-hot jabs that pierced my body and split my skin.

A fist sailed at me from the left, huge and white-knuckled, attached to a Berserker's enormous arm. From behind, a wave of mind-splitting power needled at my back.

"Not fair," I forced out through clenched teeth as I bowed back, barely ducking Thane's blow. "Three against one."

I slashed spirit at Kieran, trying to take out the leader of the training session.

He grunted before another wave of power slammed into me. Light cut across my shin, leaving a trail of searing pain. Thane roared, and I knew he was about to charge again. The guys were barely pulling their punches now that I had increased reflexes and healing abilities.

"Three against one will be nothing in the battle we're facing," Kieran shouted through the blasts of salty air and heady power.

"Yeah, but I'm not allowed to grab Boman and Thane's souls!" I punched Thane's spirit box to knock him off course and spun, facing Kieran, who stood at the edge of the cliff. An enormous wave rose behind him, building in height and power even as he thwarted my attack.

"That's because I want them alive for the battle." Kieran ripped his arms forward. A wall of agony knocked me back, nearly knocking me onto my butt.

I'd been practicing with souls all morning. The guys had brought by the most bloodthirsty shifters from Will Green's captured pack. Most of them had lost their senses and were trying to kill anything in sight, including me when they were unceremoniously released in the backyard. It was the only reason I didn't feel badly for practicing on them.

I'd gotten pretty good…except I still hadn't figured

out how to re-dock their souls well enough for them to survive a shift. I had no idea what I was doing wrong.

Which was why I was forbidden to mess with anyone else's. I was not trusted.

A ringing phone somehow cut through the commotion, and I could feel Kieran's confusion trickle through our soul connection. All his people knew we were training and not to be disturbed.

"Wait," I heard Boman shout from behind me.

The drape of light fell away from Boman, revealing him as he turned in the direction of the houses. Jack ran toward us, a phone clutched in his hand—my vision was now freaking amazing.

Something hard hit the side of my head, knocking me sideways. Thane roared and his feet thumped the ground. He was clearly intent on finishing our battle.

"Enough," Kieran shouted and a blast of power sideswiped me, cutting Thane down to his knees.

Stars swam in my eyes as Kieran's strong fingers wrapped around my upper arm and hoisted me up.

"You okay?" he asked as Thane rolled and screeched not far away, fighting the pain. His power didn't come with a handy off switch.

"Yeah," I said, still dizzy, as Jack yelled, "We've got word from Henry. Answer your phone."

The phone rang again as Kieran dug it out of his pocket. The rest of us had left our phones behind for the training session, but he'd insisted he could get a new one if it was damaged in the fight.

"Yes," he barked as Jack reached us, his eyes hard.

Thane groaned off to the side, finally changing back to human.

"How'd training go?" Jack asked me.

"She's ready," Boman said, his eyes on Kieran.

"I still haven't successfully re-anchored a shifter's soul, though," I said as Kieran turned away, bowing a little as he listened.

"We won't be fighting shifters, and you don't have to worry about keeping the enemy alive," Jack said. He made a claw with his hand and clutched the air. "You're good on ripping out souls, right?" He pulled his hand away. "This morning helped?"

He'd been in charge of making sure none of the blood-crazed shifters made it to me. He'd pulled up a chair and taken out a book. That had given me more confidence than anything.

"Yes. I can get at the souls just fine. I know how to alter the density of a spirit box in order to seep in and—"

Jack held up his hand. "I don't need the how or why, I just need a green light."

"She's ready, I said," Boman pushed. "What's the word?"

"She's only ready if she has the confidence to be ready," Jack replied. "And I don't know. Henry was keyed up. Something is happening. He wanted to talk to Demigod Kieran directly, so I got my ass out here as fast as possible."

"You think it's going to kick off?" Boman whispered.

Jack didn't answer as Thane lay back on his back and looked at the sky. "Ow. I hate when Kieran ends the fight."

Kieran pocketed his phone and turned back toward us, his eyes resolute. His gaze fell on me, and my stomach flipped. "Henry thinks they know."

A loud breath left Jack.

Kieran started off toward the house, leaving all of us to scramble after him.

"Amber tracked my father down for an in-person meeting in his house," Kieran said as he walked. "That's not usual. She has something she doesn't want spread around. Then she reassigned her whole team to hit the computers. Henry's contact thinks they're cyber-searching." He pushed a branch out of the way, paused until I'd passed by, and let it go. Jack barely caught it before getting thwacked in the face. "They're on my trail. Everything I did is hidden in layers of false leads and dead-ends, but the clues are there. With a lead, she's good enough to find it."

"Was it what we did yesterday?" I asked as we cut toward my house.

"Without question. Green didn't make that move without clearing it with my father first. Even if my father's people didn't find out about the mark, the way I rushed out of the office would've been enough to tip them off. My father got lucky with timing." I could tell Kieran was gritting his teeth in frustration.

Zorn met us as we emerged from the trees at the side gate to my yard.

"Their Necromancer has been summoned to the north end of Ocean Beach at sunrise tomorrow morning, where your mother's spirit was hidden," Zorn said without preamble. "He was heard complaining about it. Valens must have thought the spirit trap would hold beyond his crew dying. He wants to check it out."

"Their Necromancer probably knows what collection of smokes and whatever to use to verify the magic is gone," I said, thinking it through. "He'll know the magic has worn off, but will he be able to tell what happened to it?"

"The box is gone." Kieran pushed past Zorn. "I buried it deep in a cave in the ocean. He'll never find it. She's at rest. *All* of her is at rest, and that includes the fucked up shrine he made for her skin. He can go to hell."

"So Valens won't find anything there tomorrow?" I asked, following Kieran out of the side yard and to the grass.

"He will. But not what he's expecting," Kieran answered, slowing as he rounded the corner of the house.

My mouth dropped opened as I saw what was happening in my backyard.

Bria and Donovan each worked beside a pile of dirt, digging down through my manicured lawn. Judging by the two dead bodies they'd already unearthed, I had a pretty good idea what they were looking for.

"You stored bodies in my backyard?" I whined, putting out my hands. "How long have you had this house? Because the grass was perfect…"

"I had them get working, sir," Zorn told Kieran. "I figure we can always put the bodies back."

"We won't be putting them back. The time has come, ready or not." Kieran stopped near the others. "What's the time frame?"

"I have about fifty to go, but with your guys, it'll be quick," Bria said, eyeing the rest of my beautiful grass.

"Fifty?" I asked, unable to focus on the real problem at hand. I'd never had a lovely manicured backyard with lush green grass before, and come to find out it had been a crypt the whole time. "Why couldn't you leave them in the cemetery where you got them?" I paused. "You *did* get them out of a cemetery, right? You didn't murder them yourself?"

Bria glanced my way. "Of course I got them in a cemetery—we didn't need cops breathing down our necks. And they're here because your boyfriend wanted them close at hand. The grass is sod. It hasn't been down long." She straightened and put her fist to her hip. "You really know very little about home gardening, don't you?"

"I'll get the spirits assembled," Kieran said, ignoring our exchange. "You'll have your pick of everyone we could collect. I have personal artifacts of a few extremely powerful spirits beyond the Line. Lexi will need to control those."

My attention snapped to him. "You want me to fight *and* control spirits?"

"Yeah." Bria gave me a thumbs up. "Don't worry, you'll be great. I have all the faith in you."

"I don't think I can multitask," I muttered, following Kieran into the house like a lost lamb.

The kids sat at the table with tight eyes as we all filed in, leaving Bria and Donovan behind for obvious reasons.

"A couple days ago, you didn't think you could yank a soul out of a body, let alone put it back in." Jack patted my shoulder. "You work miracles under pressure. You'll do great, don't worry. Just don't take off running."

"Tell Henry to get all our forces mobilized," Kieran said to Zorn, the energy caged within him threatening to break free. His magic filled the room, materializing as heavy pressure. "It's finally here. Once we get that army of souls, we'll be ready to go."

"What about…" Donovan's words trailed away.

Frustration came through the soul connection. Kieran's gaze darted to Daisy and I had to wonder why. "We don't have any more time. We have to go with what we have and pray that it's enough."

Chapter 31

ALEXIS

A FEW HOURS of digging later, Bria put out her arms and looked over my horror show of a backyard. "First thing's first, let's look over our work station."

Some work station. My lovely grass was in shambles. Holes dotted the expanse in four neat rows. On one side of each hole sat a heaping of dirt peppered with clumps of grass, and on the other lay a dead body stolen from the peaceful resting place it had been lovingly placed by family members who'd thought the grave would be the end of it.

The joke was clearly on them. Or maybe me.

The bodies were in various stages of gross, from "fresh" (recently dead) to "corroded" (some stage of rot). A few were so far gone, the flesh barely hung on the dirty brown skeleton beneath it, not having received the benefit of being bleached by the sun. I had no idea how Bria was going to keep a soul stuck in there—or maybe that would be my problem.

I could feel the evening slipping by as the clock

counted down. We all understood that if Valens didn't make a move by sunrise, Kieran would. Worst-case scenario, we had a little over twelve hours to do a shit load of necromancy, take a power nap, and then I'd be plunged into my first real battle where my whole world was on the line.

To say I was nervous was like saying the ocean was a puddle.

I put a hand on my fluttering stomach as Bria turned to the table she'd set up, holding a plethora of Necromancer tools, from incense to candles to the really annoying bells favored by Mediums. Her gaze roamed the table and her eyes squinted as she noticed each thing. "All there. Good."

She pointed to the table set up just beyond it. Personal items sat in clusters, my aids in calling powerful spirits from the other side. Since the most powerful spirit I'd ever called was someone's stubborn grandpap, I really hoped it'd go well.

"Okay," she whispered, turning back to my devastated yard. "Good. Now, here's the plan. We're going to fill these bodies, one at a time, working together. I'll take a large section of the easier ones, since I'm the hack—"

"You're the only one with experience."

"Not for long, am I right?" She grinned at me before turning back to the yard. "I've placed the cadavers in order. We'll start on the left." She walked in that direction, pointing. "The top left, back there. These are sturdy bodies with a good deal of corrosion, which will help freak people out. We'll go down the column to here…" She stood at the foot of a large hole. "Then start back at the top of the next column, okay? Females go into a female body. Male into male. Otherwise it'll take longer for the spirit to adjust."

"You don't think this is a little…fucked up?" I couldn't help but ask. "I mean, who are these people? And what if they get loose or something, and some little kid sees Aunt Ethel running amok? They'll think she's a legit zombie. This is the stuff of nightmares."

She waved the comment away. "It's fine. All these people were donors."

"Organ donors. Not body snatcher donors. They were probably trying to help people, not have some rando stuffed into their body and forced to do our bidding."

She shrugged, moving back to the tables. "That's the risk you take. Now. Let's go pick our spirits." She paused by the Necromancy table. "I'm good to just leave this here, right? You can walk me through your readings?"

"What do you mean, readings?"

She made a *this is taking too long, hurry up* gesture. Another wave of anxiety rolled through me. "Their power, their skills, their strength—basically how good of a fit they'd be in a particular body. Just…" She pushed me in front of her. "I'll ask the questions. You tell me the answers."

"Okay." All I wanted to do was pop a Xanax and maybe take a bath in my new whirlpool tub, but instead I was ushered out to the front of the house. Boman had used his ability to conceal us from the nearer half of the neighborhood—and them from us.

My next shock of the night came quickly.

"Alexis! Where have you been?" Frank demanded with his hands on his hips, standing in front of a host of waiting spirits. "I was worried sick. Did you know someone broke into your house? I didn't see who it was, but I saw through the windows that he sure riffled through everything. And there are a bunch of mangy strays running around. The pound must've had a breakout or something."

"Hi Frank," I said, trying to edge around him. "You found me, huh?"

"I was worried about you." Frank scowled at me. "Your mother told me to keep an eye on you. I can't do that when you don't come home for days on end. Is this Mister Drusus's house?" His eyes narrowed and he lowered his voice, speaking out of the side of his mouth. "Don't give the milk away for free, girl. If you want to keep him, you have to keep him on the hook."

"Frank found us, huh?" Bria asked with a chuckle. "My lucky day."

"Yes." Frank's scowl hardened. "They said we'd see her." His gaze turned accusatory. "I had to ask these strange spirits where you'd gone. Thank goodness the timing was right, or I might've missed everyone entirely."

I blew out a breath. "Can it, Frank. We need to get people into bodies and go to war."

The anger and indignation quickly drained from his face. "Alexis, no! What would your mother say?"

I shooed him to the side. "She'd say, *Cut off their nuts and call them Sally.*"

"Yes, but you know she wouldn't actually mean it!"

I ignored him as I approached John, the tough guy I'd met in the ghost neighborhood. Behind them stood a line of grim-faced, tough-looking dudes with crew cuts and chiseled jaws. Backing them up was a gaggle of nutters milling around, bumping into one another and randomly screeching. The ghost house where they'd been imprisoned had driven the sense from their minds, and freedom hadn't returned it.

John, a barrel-chested guy with a wicked scar cutting across his cheek, nodded at me in hello. "I got the best I could. Some I lost to the Line. They couldn't resist the call. Or maybe didn't want to."

After what Valens had put them through, I couldn't

blame them.

Someone yelled from the middle of the throng. A commotion ensued as one of the spirits blasted through the others, dropping to his knees, and then rolled down the driveway like he was on fire.

"Some I couldn't seem to get rid of," John added. "They followed me like a bad smell."

I laughed and took a deep breath. "All right, where do we start?" I asked Bria.

We went through everyone, as quickly as we could.

"I can't imagine half these guys can fight," I murmured as Bria told me how to organize everyone in a line.

"Remember those animated cadavers in the ghost neighborhood, as you called it?" she asked. I pushed the spirits she'd deemed unnecessary (surprisingly not the craziest of the bunch) out of the neighborhood. The Line would probably call them home now that John wasn't around to anchor them in the turbulent world of the living.

I thought back, remembering how the reanimated dead had run at me, knocking me over and trying to rip and tear. They'd seemed more like zombies than anything.

"Even if they've never fought a day in their lives, somehow they know how to rip and tear their way to victory. I have no idea why that's the case, but I look forward to learning one day."

"If you outlive me, please don't shove me into one of these things after I die," I whispered, eyeing one of the worst cadavers. Three broken ribs jutted out through the decaying chest.

"No promises. I might miss you. I'll put your body on magical ice, though, don't you worry. Now." She stopped at the personal effects table. "Do you need some supplies to make it easier to pull these guys out?"

I fingered a small red die in one of the clusters before nudging a rabbit's foot. "Who are these people?"

"I don't know. Kieran brought in all this stuff. He said they were all high class fives in life, though, so they won't be easy to control."

"And I'm supposed to control all…ten of these, plus whatever leftovers you have for me, plus fight?" I was screeching by the end.

She patted me, as though that would help. I had no idea how she could be so utterly calm about our looming battle with a crazy and cunning and uber-experienced Demigod in his home domain. It was unnatural.

"Controlling them isn't that hard in and of itself. You just have to give them some gentle direction. You know, keep them from wandering. It's more like corralling. You're a natural. You'll do fine."

"But yet, you aren't doing the more powerful

ones…"

"I am neither a Demigod's daughter nor a Demi-god's shortsighted girlfriend." She patted me again. "Time to work. The faster we get these fuckers in bodies, the more sleep we can get. Oh, and I'm hungry. We'll need to fuel up after this is done. Lots to do, lots to do. Let's get some dead guys in bodies!" She slapped her hands together.

Butterflies filled my belly, but I didn't think about what was to come. I couldn't. If I did, I'd probably get cold feet and run off. Maybe lose it and roll down the driveway.

"Okay," I said with a sigh.

"John," she said, at her Necromancy table. "Come stand beside me. Yup. There you are. What a good, strong soul you got, huh, John?"

"I don't need to be corralled or controlled. I know what I'm about," John said. "Just put me in a body and stand aside."

Bria grabbed her supplies. "The strong and silent type, I like it."

I sighed and relayed what he'd said. This process would've been so much easier if she could see and hear spirits, too.

"That's a maybe, John," she replied. "I've found that even well-balanced spirits lose it when they get in a cadaver. But if you can manage, I'll leave you to it, how's that?" She paused and he stared at her. "Is he talking, or…"

"A woman like this could never work for someone like Valens, that's for sure," John muttered, following her toward a body.

I shook my head and nudged a small locket. Inside were two kids' faces, both sweet little cherubs, no more than four years old. I settled into a trance, picking up each item, one at a time, and closing my eyes. The Line pulled at my soul. Beyond it, I felt spirits moving around—not restless, but not content to stay put, either.

The die felt cold against my fingers. The rabbit's foot felt too soft. The image of the kids stuck in my mind.

That was the one to focus on.

After returning the other items to the table, I went deeper into the trance, sending a pulse deep beyond the Line to call the owner of the locket, the father of the two little kids. Surely he must be missing them. He would feel their absence. He would feel them in my hands. On my mind.

Slowly, a presence awoke.

I ran my thumb across the metal, picturing the kids in my mind. Tingles spread across my skin and my small hairs stood on end. A faint line appeared before me, connecting me to the soul.

"I'll be damned," I said softly. This was like the ribbons I'd used the other day to grab all the souls in the living bodies, only fainter.

I'd used this method every time I'd called a spirit from beyond, something I'd taught myself way before Kieran had come into my life. So maybe the epiphany with the shifters *had* come from my subconscious connecting the dots behind the scenes.

I pushed that thought to the side. Now wasn't the time.

The form materialized beyond the Line, blurry at first and then it resolved into the shape of a man. I kept pulling, dragging the spirit across the divide and into the world of the living.

Blinking groggily, a powerhouse of a man in his mid-thirties appeared beside me, his work boots scuffed, his cargo pants torn, and his shirt in tatters, revealing a hard body. He stared at me like he'd asked a question and was waiting for the answer. They all did, once they'd been beyond the Line long enough to let the sores of their past life fade.

"Hi," I said, flattening my hand. His locket lay open on my palm. "Is this yours?"

His dark brown eyes dipped to the locket, and a spark of recognition eased him a little further into the present.

"Yes," he said, his voice deep and rusty.

"Do you know who Kieran Drusus is? The Demigod

of…Ireland, kinda. He didn't rule there, he just lived there."

This wasn't going well.

"Why do you have that?" He moved to take the locket, and going by his speed—or lack thereof—I could tell he'd been out of the world of the living for at least a decade, probably two.

"Kieran Drusus gave it to me so I could call you. Do you know who he is?"

"Drusus?" Anger rose in his gaze, like a champagne bubble working up from the bottom of the glass. "Drusus…"

"Not Valens, but his disgruntled son. Kieran, the Demigod of—"

"Valens." More anger lit up his gaze now. Tensed his body.

"Right. So you have a grudge against Valens, I take it? He did something to you?"

"He killed me. He killed my whole family." His fists clenched and he took a step toward me, like he was contemplating grabbing my throat and lifting me into the air. In life, I have no doubt he could've done it. In death, he'd get an unwelcome surprise. "He blamed me for a fuck up that wasn't my fault."

"Yeah, he's a real dick." I checked my watch. I'd spent half an hour doing this so far, and I still had nine of these to go. I wasn't moving fast enough. "He tortured his wife, did you know that? Kieran, his son, who was trapped with her, had to watch her die slowly. So now Kieran is seeking revenge. He thought you might want to be in on it."

"Are you asking him to help?" Bria asked from the other side of the yard.

The man glanced up and the power within his spectral body kindled to life. It pulsed, then grew, then pulsed again, starting up like his brain had just done. When it was finished, I figured he was still damn near a class five. He must've been off the charts when he was alive. I had no idea why there wasn't a class six.

"I'm just letting him get his bearings," I said, leaning against the table.

"We don't have time for bearings. Slap him in the body and let him figure out how it works on his own time."

I crinkled my nose. I wasn't really comfortable with that. He'd been happily...sleeping, or whatever happened beyond the Line. I'd torn him away without asking, and now I was throwing uncomfortable memories in his face. It didn't seem right to force him into a body as a slave to my will. Besides, the guy clearly had a grudge. He'd probably love a chance to claim a little revenge, and like John, he'd probably want to do it on his own steam.

"Just pretend I'm putting you in a body right now,"

332

I whispered. "Anyway, Kieran is going to take on Valens and we could really use some help. If you're willing to strap on an old body, you can get your vengeance tomorrow."

"You're a Necromancer?"

"No. I'm a novice Spirit Walker." His brow furrowed in confusion. I sighed. "A Soul Stealer." Mistrust warred with the anger in his eyes. "Don't worry, I don't know what I'm doing."

"You work for…"

"Kieran. Valens's son. Who is going to try and kill Valens." I knew this was a huge jolt to the guy, but he really needed to get with the program. Time was ticking.

"You want to put me in a body…without controlling me?"

I made an irritated sound. "I could rip you back out in one second, no problem. I can send you beyond the Line again just as fast. It's not the stressful situation your tone suggests. Just get in the body, figure out how it works, and hang out until the fight. First one that gets Valens wins." I checked my watchless wrist and grabbed my phone. "I need to get going. I still have a body. It gets hungry and tired. I have to move."

Utter confusion screwed up his expression, and humor, of all things, bled into his gaze. "The Drusus child was newly born when Valens destroyed my family.

I wondered how it would play out with the mother."

"Badly. He basically tortured her until less than a year ago when she finally died."

He nodded slowly. "Sounds like Valens. And now the father will have to answer to the son."

"Yes."

"Tell me, is his son a good man?"

"Oh my God, seriously? Yes, he's a good man. I mean, I'm doing this for the guy"—I spread my arms to indicate the yard littered with bodies—"instead of taking him up on his offer to get safely away. Dealing with half decomposed bodies isn't awesome, in case you were curious." I was doing a bad job of selling his new home.

A wry grin twisted his lips. "You wear your heart on your sleeve. It's easy to see." He stuck out a hand. "Chad."

"No." I pulled back and waggled my finger at him. "No touching. You're a spirit now. If you touch me, you can siphon my energy. And it feels weird."

He pulled his hand back. "Show me to the body."

It turned out, he didn't much like the one he was supposed to fill. Rather than argue, or give Bria another reason to yell at me, I just let him pick another and then shoved him on in.

Once he blinked the body's dry eyes open, I paused. If Valens had a good Necromancer, he or she could just rip Chad out again. We'd lose a valuable fighter. But if I anchored his soul…

"Hold tight. This might feel weird." I lowered to a squat beside his borrowed body and built a prong from the spirit crowding the air. It wasn't great, but it would work. "If you don't mess too much with the body, that prong will hold, and so will you."

The mouth moved, but nothing came out. That was the problem with this setup—communication was lost. It was the only way they could fight, though.

"Okay." I moved to pat him, seeing the mouth move again, but held back. That would've been gross. "Head out of the line-up so we don't accidentally try to shove someone in on top of you. We're messing with Bria's system."

"You've totally fucked it up, and now I have to start over," she grumbled, a machine when it came to putting spirits into bodies. "You had better control that S.O.B. He's powerful, even as a spirit. He could inflict some serious damage."

It wasn't a great time to break it to her that I didn't intend to control him at all.

Back at the table, I grabbed the next cluster of trinkets, and set about calling the spirit attached to them.

Chapter 32

KIERAN

KIERAN CHECKED HIS watch as he exited his car, parked in his driveway. Nearly nine. It wouldn't be long now. The last eight months were winding down to a handful of hours.

He'd gotten word that his father was amassing his forces. Either he already greatly suspected Kieran was the snake in the grass, or he knew outright.

Nervousness churned Kieran's stomach. He'd accepted his father's invitation to join him in San Francisco with one thing in mind—revenge. Besides freeing his mother's spirit, that was all that had mattered to him. Now, however, he had found a reason to wake up every morning that didn't entail the destruction of another person.

"Sir, we're ready." Jack jogged up with damp clothes sticking to his body. "He doesn't have anyone waiting off the coast. The army he's amassing is all land-based, from what I can see."

Valens was confident that he could dominate in the

water. As well he should be.

But he doesn't have a team like I've put together, Kieran thought, steeling himself. *His people don't trust him, and they only respect him because they fear him. He has more power, but he does not have better leadership.* That *is what will win the day.*

"Henry can't get back, and Donovan is tying up some loose ends," Kieran said as he crossed the street to Alexis's house. A male spirit with a manic grin and tattered clothes stood in the middle of the street, eagerly waiting for something. A car to run him over, perhaps? "Besides him, you're the last in. I'm about to go check on the girls."

Kieran let himself into Alexis's backyard through the side gate and had to immediately control his expression. The strong cloud of incense did little to mask the odor of dead bodies in various stages of rot. The animated corpses jerked and staggered through the backyard, bumping into each other and occasionally swiping in aggression. Bria stood behind the Necromancy table with her head bowed amid swirls of colorful smoke. Wax dribbled from candles and bells lay on their sides.

"Those look like fucking zombies," Jack said in a rough voice. He'd followed Kieran through the gate in the fence, and the look on his face suggested he regretted it.

Kieran agreed. It was as if the zombie apocalypse had kicked off in Alexis's backyard.

"Over there…" Jack pointed to the far side of the yard.

A body with skin peeling off its chest lurched out of the way, giving Kieran a view of what Jack had spotted: Alexis, leaning against a table, arguing with empty space. A collapsed body lay at her feet with one of the arms bent back the wrong way.

He'd intended to collect everyone for a last meal, but he was quickly losing his appetite. He had a new appreciation for Bria's warped sense of humor.

"I realize it is super gross, but you wanted to help. This is how you can help." Alexis gestured down to the body. "We could sure use you."

As Kieran came closer, he could make out the form of the teen girl who'd stared at him in the government building every morning since he could see spirits. She picked at the buttons on her sweater, looking down at the body in disgust.

"I can move things in this form," the girl said, glancing behind her at a group of nine bodies in the corner of the yard. Though they were no less dead, their movements seemed more purposeful.

"Once, maybe twice. In a body, you can move things all day long. Regardless, I have one body left. If you want it, you can have it. Otherwise, I need to call someone else."

"What's going on?" Kieran asked, joining Alexis.

She looked overtired, badly in need of some down-time. "I summoned nine of your ten hopefuls. Before I summoned the last of them, I remembered Mia and wanted to see if she'd help out. She's insanely powerful." She gestured at the teen spirit, who was now staring at Kieran with her large, unblinking eyes. "All the other dead bodies are filled, as you can see. This one's the last, but Mia doesn't want to get in."

"Why is it...all broken like that?" Jack asked, edging away from the corpse at Alexis's feet.

"One nutcase who was supposed to clear off earlier snuck in here and waited with the others. Bria stuffed him into a body by accident. I had to wrestle him out and shove him across the Line. He'll probably weasel back out, though. He wants to stay in this world. Anyway, he was trying to choke me when I got him out, so..." Alexis gestured at the broken limb before return-ing her gaze to the girl. "Take it or leave it, in five...four...three..." She paused. "Two..."

"Claim your vengeance," Kieran said. "Set things right. Put yourself at peace."

"One..."

"Okay," Mia said in a humdrum tone.

In a blink of an eye, she was gone.

"Hang tight while I strap you in," Alexis said with a

focused expression. She closed her eyes. "This is the hard part."

The body jerked.

"Fuck it." Jack jumped backward.

The head rolled. An arm flopped to the side.

Jack took another step back and turned so he had one shoulder pointing at the sliding glass door.

"Done." Alexis heaved a weary sigh and kneaded her right shoulder. Kieran stepped in and gently moved her hand aside, taking over the massage. She leaned back against his body. "You did your research. All the people you called were plenty powerful and ready to tear Valens's head off. They'll manage themselves well."

A cadaver (Kieran now understood why Necromancers used that term—it was much nicer than dead body, corpse, or rotting zombie) broke free from the pack and rushed at Alexis's table. Jack shifted his weight, ready to react, but he didn't get the chance.

Alexis merely glanced in the cadaver's direction, rolled her eyes, and shifted her gaze to the left. The cadaver jerked to a stop with its limbs flailing. The shoulders turned, as though someone else had physically moved them. A moment later, the hips followed. The head whipped around last. The creature lurched forward, walking in the direction Alexis had gazed.

"Sorry," Bria called out. "That one has been dying to get away. He'll cause havoc when we finally set him free.

They'll stay put for now, though. I was just tying them all together and chaining them down."

"That's how Valens's old Necromancer was able to work with the Air Elemental to place the spirit trap," Alexis said tiredly, rubbing her stomach. He could distantly feel her hunger, half drowning in her anxiety and fear. "Bria has the power to trap the spirits for a short amount of time. Up to a day, she said. She always thought they'd have to be in bodies to be trapped, and for how she does it, I think she's right. But with an Air Elemental to carry and stabilize the magic, and a few tweaks—" She made an explosion with her fingers. "Now we know the exact magic used for the spirit traps."

"Could you do it?" Jack asked.

"Me?" Alexis rubbed her eyes. "I don't see why not. Other than morality reasons."

"Are you girls ready?" Kieran asked as Jack opened the sliding glass door. He soaked in the warmth of her body, the tantalizing feeling of her magic sliding across his skin. Was this the last time he'd get to head into dinner with her? The last time he'd casually drape his arm across her shoulders?

"It'll be okay." She rubbed his arm. "Daisy said so. Just don't ask her why. She gets violent, which means she's up to something."

"Oh yeah. She's up to something, all right." Bria

chuckled. "But damned if I can figure out what. She's taken Zorn's training to heart. I can't even get into her computer! A teen, keeping me out—what has the world come to?"

Kieran didn't comment. He knew exactly what she'd been up to, and if it hadn't been for a couple of crucial mistakes that had moved up the time table, Daisy's long game might've saved their asses. All the guys had heaped praise on Mordecai, but that young lady was a diamond in the rough. Zorn had been right all along.

"Anyway, we're ready," Bria said, and gave Kieran a thumbs up. "More than ready. We have a collection of cadaver power the like of which I've never even heard of. They're better than real forces."

"How is that?" Jack asked, leading them into the kitchen.

Delicious aromas swirled around him. Saliva coated his mouth and his stomach fought the churning to growl. Daisy and Mordecai moved around the table, placing the final utensils. Zorn and Thane chatted as they filled pitchers of water and what looked like iced tea. Boman transferred slices of meat to a platter.

"What do we need?" Jack stopped at the sink to wash his hands. Alexis headed upstairs with Bria to wash up and change.

"Grab the salad out of the fridge," Thane directed.

By the time they'd finished the preparations, the

girls were back.

"Because they can't be killed," Bria told Jack, acting as if he'd only just asked her about the efficacy of the undead army.

"What can't be killed?" Thane asked.

"Bria thinks the zombies in the backyard are better than real forces, by which I believe she means alive people." Jack shook his head, smiling.

"Zombies are better than people any day. Everyone knows that." Daisy straightened up to admire her handiwork on the table. "They're hard to kill."

"Right. Yes." Jack chuckled and placed the bowl on the table. "Except these aren't actual zombies."

"No, these are mind-controlled zombies, basically." Bria grabbed the salad forks. "You lop off an arm? Who cares. They won't feel it. You stab them in the chest? Great, they're good and close and can claw out your eyes. They aren't afraid of getting hurt, and they aren't afraid of dying. They'll do whatever I push them to do."

"But their magic isn't as strong." Jack lifted a brow before peering into the oven. He grabbed a pot holder and took out the aluminum covered baked potatoes. "And I don't care what you are, or who is pushing you—if you lose your head, your arms, and/or your legs, you're not going to do much good in the fighting ring. Not to mention that while their version of fighting might be ferocious, it's not actually good fighting. I could start smacking heads off, no problem."

"Lexi has a collection of highly powerful cadavers, who are actually trying to learn how to control their bodies. Usually a soul just gets in and flails around until they figure out how to move, but her people will be off the *chain* good." She grabbed the platter of green beans and headed to the table. "I'm stoked. Not to mention that if Valens uses his Necromancer, our girl can rip the souls out of his corpses." She clawed the air. "Rip that shit right out. Boy will they get a surprise."

"That's not the surprise I'm hoping she'll give," Kieran said softly, pulling the chair out for Alexis.

Bria took her seat as Donovan strolled in with a grim expression. He headed right for the sink to wash up.

"You good?" Kieran asked, taking his seat. The rest of the guys followed suit.

"It's all rigged up." Donovan leaned over his phone, which he'd set on the counter. "Three hours before dawn. They'll lose some really great magical war weapons in the blast. Fuck 'em."

"Agreed." Bria put up her glass.

"Wait, wait, wait…" Donovan slapped off the faucet, dried his hands, and hurried over. He sat, poured himself some tea, and put up his glass to join the cheer. "Fuck 'em."

"Fuck 'em," everyone chorused.

Kieran dropped his hand to Alexis's leg and gave her a light squeeze as food was passed around and plates were loaded. He wished Henry could've gotten away to join them, but Henry was running the surveillance team keeping tabs on Valens and his people.

"I came to San Francisco thinking I'd lost the heart of my family," Kieran began. "My mother. I had my Six, and Bria joined us, but in some ways, we were lacking a center. A hub to gather around." He rubbed Alexis's leg and looked on her beautiful face. "We found it here. With you." He looked at Daisy, then Mordecai. "With all of you. Now we're a stronger unit than we've ever been, and it's because of your willingness to include us. We won't go into this fight with only vengeance on the mind. Not anymore. We'll go into this fighting for a future. Fighting to secure happiness in this territory— for ourselves, and for everyone Valens has trampled and kept down. I'm honored to take this leap with you all."

"Fuckin' A!" Bria put her fist into the air. "I can't wait to unleash the dead with you all!"

Everyone paused with their glasses heading upward.

"You just couldn't give him the moment, could you?" Jack asked her. "You couldn't just be normal for two seconds."

"What?" She let her glass hover in the air. "Would it be better if I called them intensely powerful cadavers that will widen the eyes of our foe?"

Jack sighed and shook his head, clinking his glass off of Zorn's. "Odd taste in women, bro. That's the last word on it. Odd taste in women."

Kieran smiled, bittersweet. His gaze glued to Alexis's face. Tears shone in her eyes.

"It's not too late to get to safety," he said quietly, and almost believed it.

She glanced at Mordecai, and then Daisy. "I would've taken you up on that for them...if they would've let me." Her eyes hit his again and a tear trailed down her cheek. "I love you. I didn't say it last night because of all the stuff happening, but I love you. I wouldn't be anywhere else but at your side. We *will* live to see the sun set tomorrow. We will. All of us will."

"See that?" Bria said in the background. "See my restraint there? She said the L-word, and I said nothing."

"You're saying it right now. Not cool," Donovan said.

Kieran leaned over and kissed Alexis's sweet lips. He ran his thumb across the glistening trail on her cheek...and prayed she was right.

Chapter 33

VALENS

PINKS AND ORANGES exploded across the early morning sky, illuminating the trash-strewn beach. All of the fisherman and surfers had cleared away in anticipation of Valens's visit. Rocky sand crunched under his battle boots.

If Kieran's people were any good, Valens knew his son would confront him here, this morning. He no longer had any doubt that Kieran had taken down his spirit hunters and collected a ramshackle army, pieced together from old friends, cheaply hired guns, and men and women stolen from Valens's ranks. He'd be prepared.

So would Valens.

"Sir." Amber stalked up to him with her phone in hand. Valens's portly Necromancer followed her at a distance, his long beard swaying in the sea breeze.

First thing was first—Valens needed to make sure part of Lyra's ungrateful spirit, that of her selkie skin, still resided in that box, as it would for all of eternity.

Then he would deal with his son.

His heart beat faster than it had in…years. Decades.

Her skin's spirit better be in that box.

And the box better still be there.

"The Tunnel Street warehouse has been destroyed," Amber said as she reached him. "Exploded."

Rage bubbled up from deep within him. He didn't let it show on his face. He turned and faced the ocean, his eyes focused on the horizon. "That's unfortunate."

"The other warehouses have been secured."

"Those aren't of value in this situation. Clearly he knows that." Valens barely kept from grinding his teeth. "Find out who leaked the existence of that warehouse. When this is over, bring them to me."

"Yes, sir."

She waited just behind and to the side of him. Valens could hear the Necromancer breathing hard as he labored across the sand. The slob needed a better diet and exercise regime.

"Is everyone ready?" Valens asked, impatience clawing at him.

"Yes, sir. The beach and parking lot were cleared, as you see, and your teams are in position. Everyone is on hold. They're waiting for the go-ahead."

"Have you seen any of my son's embarrassing group of magical toddlers?"

"No, sir. If they are near, we haven't spotted them."

"They're near. He is the son I've always wanted. I see now what a mistake that was. Hindsight, as they say."

"Yes, sir. Should I leave you?"

"No." Valens waited for the Necromancer to reach him before moving forward. "Let me know when my son arrives."

✕ ✕ ✕

KIERAN

KIERAN STEPPED OUT of his car with a stomach of ice and mood of fire. Only two other vehicles dotted the large parking lot, both incredibly expensive—a rarity for this beach. When he neared the steps leading down to the shore, he took in the desolation. No fishermen dotted the water's edge, and no surfers rode the rolling waves.

His father had cleared the battlefield. He'd known Kieran would come.

"Is everyone ready?" he asked into the phone.

"We're good, sir," Zorn said. "Our teams are in position. Bria has spotted a team led by one of Valens's Elite. Valens's people are waiting, as we are."

Kieran blew out a breath.

"Wait for the signal," he said.

"Yes, sir."

Magic sang through the air. The ocean waves died down to nothing, and water pulled away from the base

349

of the cliffs as two figures walked out toward the rocks. A woman dressed in battle leathers waited near the old waterline, facing him. Closer, he realized it was Amber.

"Kieran, good to see you again," she said without a smile.

"Amber. Hello. I hear it took you some time to trace all my dead ends. Are you losing your touch?"

"Not at all. You're just that good." A tiny smile graced her lips. "Not quite good enough, though."

He smirked at her and continued on. "I bet you wish you believed that."

His father was standing at the box Kieran had planted, covered in pictures of Kieran's mother when she was in the hospital. One of Kieran's mermaid friends had waterproofed it.

Kieran stopped twenty feet away. His father could move fast, and he'd be hopped up on adrenaline. Kieran didn't want the meeting ending before it had begun.

"Not what you were expecting to find?" Kieran asked, changing the air currents so his voice carried.

His father straightened much too slowly, clearly fighting the rage that no doubt filled every ounce of his being. "Where is it?"

"Buried."

Valens turned to him slowly. "And the spirit?"

"Released. The magic had to be constantly reapplied. The spell would have completely dissipated after three weeks." Kieran widened his stance, something he knew would translate to his father as a show of power. "But I didn't need to wait. The Necromancer's magic was applied with air. Take away the air…"

Valens didn't so much as twitch. "Your Necromancer is a clever girl."

"Yes, she is. But she wasn't the one who figured it out. It was the woman who holds my mark."

There it was: tightened shoulders. Emotion had finally slipped into his father's bearing.

"Alexis freed my mother," Kieran pushed, anger rising. "Do you feel any remorse for what you did?"

"What *I* did?" Valens took a purposeful step forward. "And what did I do?"

"Trap her on that island without her skin. Torture her. Leave her to rot."

His father tsked. "I left her there with you. Is your presence really that torturous?" He took another step forward. His shoulders hadn't relaxed.

"I ask you again, do you have any remorse?" Kieran ground out, pain cutting through him.

His father smiled, an expression that didn't reach his eyes. "Remorse? Yes. I have a lot of remorse. Had I known the sniffling weakling you would become, applying a mark to a poor nothing who will only bring shame and ridicule on this family, I would've stomped on you as a baby and taken my sweet time making that bitch mother of yours suffer for what she did. Torture? She didn't know the meaning of the word. She had a cushy life compared to what I wished to do to her. I didn't get to dole out the punishment she so aptly deserved. Yes, I have remorse. Some of which I'll ease with your death."

Kieran couldn't help his mouth hanging open at the raw vehemence in his father's tone. At the harsh and brutal words he had for the people he'd once loved and cared about, Kieran included.

"That poor nothing keeps me level," Kieran forced out through suddenly numb lips. A strange ache formed in his middle, intensifying the pain from moments before. "She keeps me from turning into you."

His father laughed. "Then she keeps you at a disadvantage." Another step, closing the distance, fighting to keep his rage in check. The magical energy battering Kieran was almost a palpable thing. "It was a mistake, tampering with that box. I might've forgiven you for killing my men and corroding my staff. Your skills are impressive for one so young and inexperienced. I could've used you. But this…" He swept his hand to the side, indicating the box. "This is too far."

"Just think, I could've lived my whole life in your shadow."

Without warning, his father raced forward. The waters fell in behind him, the doddering old Necromancer forgotten.

Kieran barely had time to send out the blast of emotion that would summon his people.

It had begun.

Chapter 34

ALEXIS

KIERAN'S SIGNAL BLASTED through me. Adrenaline pulsed through my body.

"Let's go, let's go!" I slapped the side of the old yellow school bus filled with animated corpses before running to my BMW. We'd set up camp in the parking lot of a thankfully closed swanky restaurant, close to the beach.

"Show time everyone. Buckle up, it's going to be a bumpy ride!" Bria pulled the lever to close up the bus. Though she'd never driven one before, she'd offered to drive. She'd asked, "How hard could it be?"

I didn't know, which was why I was taking my car. I wanted to make sure one of us made it there alive.

"Kids, get clear." I pointed at Mordecai and Daisy, jogging toward my car. I'd told them we'd discuss the plan before piling into the car.

Now they were seeing the real plan, which was for me to leave them behind to make sure they were safe.

"Stay alive." I sat into the BMW, ripped the door

shut, and locked the car. Daisy reached the back door and yanked on the handle. I cracked my window so they could hear me but not reach in. "You have my bank account info." I started the car as Mordecai reached the other side, his face panicked. He didn't want me going off to battle without him.

Too bad.

"Raid the house. Kieran's, too. Sell everything of value. Keep your head down and keep training." Tears burned my eyes and terror filled my chest. What if this was it? What if I'd never see them again?

At least they'll be alive.

"I love you," I yelled, and peeled out of the parking lot.

The kids ran to the bus, but Bria was already lumbering behind me. They'd be fine. I'd made them survivors, and Kieran's guys had made them warriors. If any teenagers in the world could be orphaned...again...and still keep going, it was those two.

I stomped on the gas, not waiting for Bria. The spirits I'd anchored to bodies were autonomous, and she didn't need my power to control the rest of her smelly brood. My abilities would go to better use jacking up the living.

The car took the curves in the road without problem, so I pushed the speed well past the limit. Near the bottom of the steep hill, I sped through a red light before slamming on my brakes. A big black truck had pulled out of a side road, cutting me off. Hard brown eyes flashed in the side mirror for a brief moment before the trailer cut off my view.

The rest of the street was desolate, this wasn't our truck, and Kieran had wondered if his dad would be expecting him.

Clearly the answer was yes.

I slammed my foot on the gas pedal and pulled into the shared turning lane of the three-lane road. The truck's engine roared, the vehicle picking up speed to block me, but come on—out-gunning a new BMW? He was dreaming.

A second later, I took those words back.

A jet of pure white light blasted from the window and across the bumper of my car. Metal screeched and then clanged. My car bumped up and down, running over what was probably part of my bumper. Metal screeched again, dragging against concrete. Yup, definitely my bumper. At least my tires made it.

Valens had his own Light Bender. One who either didn't have the power to conceal the truck, or didn't think he'd need to bother.

But guess what Valens didn't have?

A Soul Stealer.

I reached into the driver's chest with a thick rope of magic. His scream reached my ears. The truck swerved wildly to the right and hit the guard rail. I yanked on his spirit box as I pulled ahead in the BMW. For a brief moment, I thought about letting him go with a busted truck. But if I did that, he'd just get out, run a few blocks to the beach, and kill our people. This was war, and I was either the predator or the prey.

I slowed my car to match the declining speed of the truck and soaked down into the guy's spirit box, disturbingly easy in a non-shifter, it turned out. I crushed the prongs and then yanked his spirit away.

Now what?

I slowed the car even more as I thought it through. Getting rid of him meant the other side was down one, sure, but what was he hauling in that truck? Chances were, Valens needed that rig, and we needed it gone.

"Plan B." I jammed his soul back in, keeping a hold of that sucker and pushing my will on him, like Bria had taught me to do in Necromancy. He needed to turn that truck around, head up the hill, and…

A crawling sensation overcame me. I fought it off.

This is war. War is brutal. I joined the fight. I need to commit.

I took a deep breath. He'd head up the hill, pull into the lookout lot over the steep drop leading down to the ocean, and hop the curb. He'd go for a lovely roll and finish it off with a nice swim.

Padding the horrible actions with happy words, that

was the ticket. I was sending him on a lovely little holiday.

The big yellow school bus slowed as it passed the now idling truck.

"Go." I waved my hand at her.

She stopped and opened the bus doors. "What's happening?"

"I've gotten control of the driver's soul and now I'm going to send his truck up to the top and over the edge."

A huge smile spread across her face. "Look at you! Donovan is gonna be pissed he lost the bet. I knew my girl had brutality in her." She put up a fist. "Go girl!" Her gaze flicked to the large rearview mirror. "Sit down in the back you crusty old fucker, this ain't our stop." She rolled her eyes at me before pulling the handle to close the door. The bus shuddered forward.

Without wasting time, I rolled forward to give the bus enough space. I gave the soul another mental push, almost like an Encourager. The guy inside, strangely not terrified but certainly pissed (he was clearly a professional and probably one of the Elite) cranked the wheel and increased his speed. The truck just barely made the U-turn. I closed my eyes and felt the spirit, connecting with him as he traveled up the hill. As he neared the top, I almost lost him, the connection too weak with the distance. I just barely had enough time to make him slam on the gas, plow across the curb, sidewalk, and through the guard rail.

"A lovely sail through the air. What fun," I mumbled, severing the connection. Blinking my eyes open, I started when I caught sight of the woman standing in front of me, dressed in some sort of red material, and holding a blow torch. "What the hell?"

I stomped on the gas pedal. She'd chosen a terrible place to stand.

Fire exploded across my hood and over my windshield, heat curling into the new crack in the window.

These people were seriously jacking up my car.

"Ouch. Ouch-ouch," I said, smacking her with my car. "I win."

Another two blocks and I saw the yellow bus pulled over to the side of the road. Nearly there, my heart lodged into my throat. Trucks like the one I'd just detoured were pulling into the parking lot up the way. Others had stopped on the road just outside it. Various men and women in black or red climbed out of them, and the troops jogged across the street to the beach.

Kieran had said that he'd collected nearly a hundred people. Judging from this crowd, Valens had organized a shit-load more, and who knew how many were hidden from view? How were we even supposed to get to him through all of Valens's people?

"Mother trucker biscuit fucker," I whispered, yanking the wheel sharply enough to screech the tires. I clipped the back of the school bus and a half rotted face tumbled into one of the windows. Thankfully, I couldn't see it smashed up against the glass from my vantage point.

I hurried out and around and helped Bria unload the bus. She was no longer smiling.

"Valens isn't fucking around," she said in an uncharacteristically somber tone. "Did you see all those trucks up there?"

"Yeah." I wracked my brain for something supportive to say. The battle was lost if fear had won. "The Six were closer than us, though. They must've gotten there in time to protect Kieran."

"And how the hell are we going to get them back out?"

I gestured at the rotting corpses.

"Are you serious? Look at these things. They're—"

One disappeared, then re-appeared ten feet behind me. Mia, obviously. "They're the stuff of nightmares, and they pack a helluva wallop. You said so yourself. Plus, you've got me. Ripping souls out is gross, but I bet I can get a few of their important people working for us. We got this."

She nodded as she organized the corpses. Her expression hardened into a determined look. She patted me on the back. "Thanks. I needed that. A punch in the face would've been quicker, but your softer approach won't shake a tooth loose, so that's cool." She unslung her backpack, reached in, and extracted a furry critter.

"What? No! Not the rats. What do we need with rats when we have the bodies?"

She set it down and took out a second, already animated.

"They are good scouts. If we need eyes on the ground, we got 'em."

"How about eyes in the sky? That would probably serve us better."

"That's on my list of to-tries. One day." She turned and motioned everyone on. "Here we go, everyone. This is where it gets real. Remember, you can't die again. But I can. Once I'm gone, your play day's over. So keep me alive."

"Does that work?"

"Hasn't yet—they usually don't give a crap about me—but I'm always hopeful."

I took the lead, my fists clenched and nothing on my person but my clothes. Around the bend up ahead, I knew orderly lines of men and woman were filing toward the beach. There was no way they'd miss us coming, and while I could cut several people down at a time, I couldn't withstand a magical attack. We'd be sitting ducks.

"We need another plan," I said, stopping dead. Bria ran a few paces past me before curling back. The line of corpses shuddered to a stop. "We need some cover. I should've saved that damn Light Bender. I could've used him."

"Now you're thinking. Too bad it came too late."

A grizzly hand nudged me, and my instinctive response was to grimace and move away. The corpse chosen by Chad, the guy I'd summoned with the locket, nodded jerkily. A long groan came from his throat.

"That is…off-putting," I said softly.

"What is?" Bria asked.

The currently trapped spirit was trying to communicate, but we didn't have time for charades.

I snapped his prong and yanked him from the body. The body fell into a heap next to his bewildered spirit. He blinked at me a few times, clearly dazed.

"What?" I barked. "We don't have much time."

"Run the bus through them," Chad said, his voice clearing. "Those lines are filled with grunts. They aren't trained to think for themselves. When they see danger, they'll freeze and wait for a command. That command will come quickly—Valens's people are highly organized—but we should have thirty seconds or so before they start retaliating. That's enough time to get the bus into the middle of their crew. When you do, make sure the doors are open. We can file out and get to work. We'll create chaos and hopefully they'll start accidentally killing each other in their haste to kill us. You can slip out through the crowd and hit the beach. Make a path for us and we'll follow. We can reassess after we rendez-vous with Valens's son and his men."

For one full beat, I did nothing but stare at him. Where the hell had Kieran found this guy?

"That's a good plan," I finally said. "A very good plan. You make it sound easy."

"It is easy."

"Right." I turned to tell Bria what he'd said, then started to jog back to the bus.

"Hey, aren't you forgetting something?" Chad called out.

"Oh yeah." I stopped and stuffed him back in the body, latching him in with the rickety prong. The limbs jerked to life.

"Chad, huh?" Bria said as we got everyone back into the bus. "Does his spirit look like a Ken doll?"

"What?" I shook my head in annoyed confusion as one of our crew tried to break free and run. I yanked him in the right direction and pushed him up the steps.

"Chad. That's such an eighties name. It reminds me of Ken, from Ken and Barbie?"

"Except Ken's name is...Ken."

"Right, yeah. It should've been Chad." She slipped in behind the wheel. "Behold," she yelled. "I have never, in my life, driven a children's school bus filled with cadavers into an enemy crowd in an epic magical battle." Judging from her smile and sparkling eyes, the thought pleased her as much as the prospect of a shopping spree would have pleased me. "This is going to be awesome!" She cranked the wheel. "Buckle up, everyone, we're headed for a wild ride!"

Chapter 35

ALEXIS

THE ROAR OF the engine and shaking of the old vehicle competed with my flip-flopping stomach and adrenaline-fueled anticipation. The cadavers crowded near both doors and some hung out of the windows, cocooning me in the grossest way possible. The John corpse waited by my side, not touching, thankfully, but hovering in what seemed like a protective way. I wondered if he'd assigned himself as my bodyguard.

"Yep, we're coming right for you," I heard Bria yell, laughter lacing her words. She was enjoying this entirely too much. "Ten seconds until impact!"

I grabbed onto the seats next to me. Yelling filtered in from outside. Shouts, then a scream.

"Boom, fuckers!" Bria shouted.

The bus jolted forward before bumping wildly. My vision jiggled as the frame shook. More screams, much closer now, some anguished. Hands came up to slap the windows. Glass shattered somewhere beyond the cluster of bodies to my right. Through the gaps between the bodies on my left, I saw glimpses of the crowd outside. They had showed up in dizzying numbers.

"Go, go, go, go!" Bria's voice rose over the din. "We're surrounded. Take 'em down!"

The throng of corpses began to move around me. Sparkles shone in through the window. The view suddenly changed, and I saw vivid blue waters and white sand that stretched for miles. It sure as shit wasn't Ocean Beach.

"They have an Illusionist," Bria yelled. "A damn strong one, too. Alexis, you gotta take 'em down."

The bus melted around me, the metal dripping down until it fell away. No heat kissed my skin, though. The drops of molten metal didn't splatter on my head. I was left standing on that beautiful, idyllic beach.

"Alexis," Bria shouted again.

Noise assaulted me from all sides. Yelling and screaming. Shouts and commands. A roar sailed past the right side of the bus, but I saw only limitless ocean. A blast shook the soft sand I stood on.

Corpses grabbed me, and suddenly Chad was by my side, groaning again. Trying to tell me something. He hustled me forward and gravity pulled at my feet. I felt a jolt and fell onto the hard, unforgiving…sand.

That Illusionist was messing with my head.

"Alexis!" Bria yelled again, closer now. She was barreling toward me. "You gotta get to work, girl. We need eyes."

"Okay," I said softly, stilling myself in the moment.

The hands around me fell away. Bria's voice quieted. The shouts and screams around me faded into the background. Spirit rushed in to cover the world, washing away the illusion that had blanketed it.

Bodies surrounded us in a circle, keeping us put as they waited for the command to action, just like Chad had said they'd do. There were so many of them, their souls throbbing merrily in their middles. Outlines flickered within the corpses around me, showing me the spirits in their temporary homes.

"Valens has a lifetime of wrongdoing to atone for," Chad said. The words were garbled within his decrepit body, but with all the spirit coursing around us, I understood them anyway, as though they'd been spoken directly into my head. Chad must've led people, because he'd noticed my hesitation. "His people have tortured and killed without concern. Innocents have died by the thousands under his rule."

The Mia corpse appeared on the other side of me. She was proof that Chad's situation wasn't an anomaly.

"If you do not act, they will take you as a prize," he continued. "You wear the son's mark, do you not? Valens will make you pay for that. He will make all of you pay. Only the dead are safe."

The fire of anger burned brightly in my middle.

"Not even the dead are safe from him," I said, feeling the faith Mia and Chad and John and the others had put in me. They were depending on me to set this to rights. "And it's the dead I've sworn to protect."

I sent a blast of the Line's magic out in all directions like a shock wave, punching through the middles of Valens's minions. Once they were down, I collected the little ribbons connecting everyone in the area, took a split second to grab them, and yanked them all to the ground.

"Here comes Johnny!" Bria shouted, quoting her favorite movie.

The illusion of the ocean cut out. Screams and hoarse yells rose around us as the enemy forces were brought to their knees. Some even tumbled onto their backs.

Through the din, one person rose. A woman built like a tank struggled up from the ground and staggered toward me.

"Kill the vile Soul Stealer," she yelled. "And save yourselves!"

"That was hurtful," Bria said as she ran forward to meet her.

She punched the woman square in the face, jabbed forward with her knife, pulled it back, flinging drops of crimson, and round-house kicked her in the head—all in one graceful series of movements.

The woman fell like a sack of bricks.

"That was overkill," Chad murmured.

I repeated it for Bria's sake.

"Can it, Chad, or I'll tell Barbie you cheated with Kimmy." Bria motioned us on. "Let's go. This is just a few of a great many. The boys are on that beach. We need to get to them."

She was right. Behind the group of peons kneeling around us, a sea of red and black moved toward the ocean. Magic flared and arched over the crowd, the battle raging and the Six clearly fighting for their lives.

Fear gripped me. I sent spirit through the connections I held, using it to seep past their spirit protectors. Without delay, I ripped out their life essences, the process easy now that I'd given in to the feeling of it.

Too easy.

Gritting my teeth, I yanked them all free.

Spirits popped out all around us and bodies fell to the ground. I didn't wait until the spirits regained their equilibrium from that harsh transition and started calling me names. I ran, cutting through the downed bodies and spirits alike.

"Follow Alexis," Bria shouted to our undead crew, purely for effect since her magic was actually leading most of them.

A group of people turned to face me as I reached

them, just within the large parking lot beside the beach. Hands came out and a sword rose. They weren't waiting for a command to attack.

I slashed through their middles and kept running, dodging between them as they froze or sank to the ground with wide, terrified eyes. A couple of them startled into action again, pushing past their fear or discomfort, but by that time the corpses had reached them. The army of the dead slammed into them, ripping and tearing with their hands. One dead guy bit someone's nose, losing a tooth in the process.

Another group of Valens's people waited beyond, shifting in their ranks, no doubt wondering what was coming their way. The organization made it clear who was in charge. I slashed at their spirit boxes while veering in the other direction, not wanting to barrel through bodies if I could help it. Group by group I took down whoever waited in my path, ripping the souls out of the leaders and leaving the others to be dealt with by the force at my back.

Kieran had been dead right to keep my magic a secret. My unfamiliar and deeply uncomfortable magic stopped them cold, and by the time the stronger, harder, more advanced soldiers regained their equilibrium, the dead were ravaging through them.

No one knew to target me until it was too late.

"Get to a place where I can work," Bria shouted,

slashing a serrated blade across someone's throat, turning in the same movement, and sticking it into the side of someone else's neck. "You've given me a lot of spirits and bodies to work with. I might as well make myself useful." She kicked a guy in the balls before ramming her knife through his breast plate.

"You're plenty useful now," I muttered in awe.

Amazingly not out of breath from all the running and magical fighting, I reached the barrier between the parking lot and the beach. A blotch of red drenched the first step and driblets ran from the bottom step out onto the sand. A body dressed in green lay facedown.

Glancing up, a shock of cold dread ran up my spine and fear pinched my gut. Greens and blues must be Kieran's colors, against the blacks and reds of Valens's people. They'd had to use colors to distinguish sides, but as I stood there, I saw a green-clad man turn and stab someone in blue. Likewise, someone in red flung out his hands and the woman in black in front of him sank down to her knees. Regardless of the turncoats, it was clear from the action spread across the beach leading to the water that Kieran's army was vastly, horribly outnumbered.

Beyond the turmoil, the ocean rolled and surged in unnatural ways. The natural waterline had been pushed back halfway to the spot where Kieran's mom's skin had been kept, and two figures fought on the hard-packed sand with a speed and ferocity that left no doubt as to who they were. The waves or foam swirled around them, sometimes nearly reaching one of them before being magically pushed away again.

As I watched, Valens glanced my way, and with my enhanced vision, I could barely see him do a double-take before Kieran stole his focus again. He'd seen the mark. Thankfully, he couldn't know what sort of power the mark-holder wielded.

With us on his side, he'll win.

Daisy had been entirely too confident.

Chad groaned beside me, and I swore I heard *stealer*.

Soul Stealer.

The magic that inspired fear unlike any other. Stories had been passed down of a single man walking through a raging battle and ripping the life from all he passed. Bodies fell around him and lay in piles in his wake. He was a living plague. No one was immune.

And then the horrifying inevitable happened: the bodies rose again.

The spirits passed through the fires of hell and were summoned back up to do the Soul Stealer's bidding. He was Satan's helper. He was a walking terror.

He was a she.

In order to save those I loved, I had to become the thing I most feared.

I pulled power from the Line. More than I ever had. It pulsed to the side, ready to welcome any souls I threw at it.

But I wouldn't be throwing souls. I would be recycling them. They would do my bidding and protect those who were trying to protect Kieran. He had always been right—I could turn the tide. And I would. I couldn't bear to lose the family I'd so recently let into my life.

Chapter 36

KIERAN

KIERAN DODGED A punch faster than any he'd ever seen. He managed to slam a fist into his father's side and then blasted him with a heavy dose of magic. Water crashed all around them, his father trying to knock him away with the surging surf.

But there was more than one ruler of the ocean in this fight.

Kieran waved away the white foam and shoved the waters, parting them on both sides of their fight. His father kicked his side just as a huge blast of air pushed him off his balance. Kieran tore down the air currents but took the kick. A dull ache spread across his ribs. Had he been a normal man, that kick might have cracked a few bones and maybe punctured a lung.

He blocked another kick and delivered one of his own, nearly reaching for Alexis's magic to push his father back. Not yet, though. She was coming—he could feel her power burning brightly through their connection, filling him up to bursting. He wanted Valens to see the woman he had chosen. The woman he had marked.

He wanted him to know he'd been wrong.

Zorn's cloud materialized into his physical form nearby, well within the water's natural edge. He surprised two of Valens's men who'd been running out toward the water.

"Need your lackeys to help you with your inferior son?" Kieran taunted, punching his father in the throat, then whirling just in time to miss a kick to his knee.

"Need my men to help fill your miserable excuse for an army?"

"Yes, actually. Thank you for that."

Magic surged and water rose back up around them. Kieran shoved it away.

"It seems you've developed a sense of humor. So have I." Valens swept his hands from the side and thick spikes of air bore down on Zorn and the guys he was quickly taking down.

Kieran gritted his teeth to tear down the spikes. The distraction gave his father a window. He blasted Kieran with a hot, stinging stream of magic that sent pain pulsing through his body. Black spots danced in his vision and his mind dizzied.

Valens hit him with another, stronger this time, and Kieran staggered back and bit down on his tongue. The rusty taste of blood coated his mouth.

"Weak," he heard his father say. A fist battered his

head, then a kick drove him to the ground. "The Elite are replaceable, Kieran, how many times must I tell you? Accrue many, bind them with their blood, and you need not worry if one or two goes down in battle."

"Have less, and you will achieve a stronger bond." He threw up his hand to block a punch but missed the fist. It smashed into his mouth, splitting his lip. Water crashed into his body, washing over him. A swell of magic rose. It would take him under and drag him out to sea, giving his father the upper hand.

He spat out blood and pushed to his hands and knees. He would not quit. He would not die, especially since he hadn't yet revealed his ace in the hole.

"What…"

His father's word was lost in the sudden gale force wind that fluttered their souls.

A smile curved Kieran's swelling lips.

"They will fight for you because they want to, not because they have to," he said, struggling up to his feet. "They will risk everything for you because you would do the same for them."

The battle on the beach, so clearly stacked in his father's favor, slowed. People clutched at their chests and howled in agony. A few broke away, like the shifters had done the other day, trying to escape the onslaught.

She had come.

The sea of black and red dotted with blue and green

opened up down the middle. A glowing woman dressed in black battle attire walked down the center, her arms held wide, her hair blowing from a wind every soul on the beach could feel. His mark had perfectly accented her magic's effects. She was a sight to see, hauntingly beautiful. An angel of death.

Warriors clad in black and red fell without warning, their lifeless bodies collapsing to the ground.

Behind Alexis lurched and jerked her army of dead, fearsome creatures with exposed bones, crooked jaws, and empty eye sockets. Even Kieran's men reeled back from them, except for four. The members of his Six who fought on land peeled away from the battle and jogged to her side, bloodied and dirty. They filled her flanks and headed up her army, cutting through the enemy like a sword through silk.

His heart ached. Alexis had faced her biggest fear. She'd embraced everything she was out of love for him. He didn't deserve it, but he was beyond grateful.

"A Spirit Walker," his father said softly, as though out of breath. He rubbed at his chest, like he was trying to wipe away a piece of dirt. "You've found a Spirit Walker."

"A poor nobody, as you said," Kieran replied, willing his body to heal faster. He pulled the water around his feet and up to his knees, soaking in its energy while his father was distracted.

His father's face came around slowly, and pride and envy warred in his expression. "I was wrong. You did well—she is worthy of a mark. A talent like that must be claimed. I hope you took her blood so as to control her."

"She's not the kind of lady who can be controlled." He swept his hand to the beach to prove his point.

The bodies that lay to either side of her began to jerk on the ground. A few started trying to get up. She was bringing them back from the dead in order to direct them. The sight was as gruesome as it was terrifying, and the enemy troops pushed away from her, terror-stricken.

"And if she'll ever forgive me for what I've made her do," he said, "I'll make her my wife."

Kieran blasted his father with his magic and fist both, pushing him back. Using Alexis's magic, he slashed through his father's chest.

"How…" His father grunted in surprise and fell back into the rising waters.

"When you show respect to those around you, and put others above yourself, they reward you in ways you could never imagine."

The waters rose around them before crashing down. His father took off like a shot, heading for the deep. Kieran had no choice but to follow, hoping the people he'd left behind could withstand Valens's army.

Hoping he could hold his own against his father. This was the part of the battle he'd always dreaded.

The part, he knew, his father would force him to do alone.

Chapter 37

ALEXIS

"WHERE IS HE going?" I screamed as anxiety and fear dumped into me through the soul connection. I sprinted to the water's edge, watching Kieran disappear into a crashing wave.

Zorn grabbed me around the waist and ran me up the beach. Another wave came in, and then another, huge and violent. They crashed down not far away, surging up the beach and around our waists. Another one crashed, right on top of the first two. Kieran and his father had kept the waters back, and now the ocean was resuming its normally scheduled program.

"I got her," Donovan yelled.

Before he could lift me with his magic, a corpse appeared beside me and wrapped its spindly arms around my shoulders. Lights and colors flew around me and my stomach fell through my feet, as though I were falling from a great height. A moment later, my feet hit sand and I stood in a pocket of empty space, looking at the resuming fight.

"Mia, no! I need to get out there to help Kieran!"

Lights and colors filled my vision again, and this time I found myself in an empty space just up from the natural water line. The small collection of souls I'd snatched and shoved back in bodies fought Valens's horde. The tales of yore had been exaggerating, it turned out. I didn't have the energy to steal the souls and reanimate the bodies of a large horde unless I did it one by one.

What a crock.

"His father is too powerful," I yelled at Zorn above the sound of battle and crashing waves. "Kieran has always been worried about facing his father at sea."

Zorn motioned for Donovan to grab me.

"Men are never worried," Donovan said in my ear, trying to pull me up the beach. "Though we may be slightly troubled from time to time. Come on. We'll get a boat."

"You get a boat. I need to help fight."

"You also shouldn't make a man spell out his weaknesses."

"I don't know what that means." I took a few steps forward as three people broke free from the fighting and charged at me.

Before I could react, a rage-filled howl rose up, turning my bones brittle. Thane, the Berserker, crashed through a line of enemy, flinging them to the sides.

Topping the crowd by four feet and swinging enormous arms packed with muscle, he was the super-sized version of the Thane who'd terrorized my backyard.

He lurched forward and grabbed one of the men running my way. With a swing of his shoulders, he flung the guy at a woman who was also charging me. They both went down in a tumble. Thane ran forward, so fast despite his size that I couldn't help taking a few startled steps backward. He smashed his fists into the people on the ground before grabbing up the remaining attacker.

"Go!" Donovan said, shoving me. "Hurry! Sometimes he gets confused and turns on his own."

I knew he was talking about Thane, and I didn't need to be told twice.

"You shouldn't make a man spell out his weaknesses," Donovan repeated, yelling over the roar of the battle as he steered me away from Thane, "meaning I need you to help me get up the beach and to some boats. I can't make it through this crowd on my own."

"Men have...such prickly...egos," I yelled.

The corpses filed in front of us. I used my magic to cut a path through the enemy as we made our way through, just barely noticing movement out of the corner of my eye.

"Incoming," Henry yelled, filing in behind me. "It's Amber."

A sleek body dressed in leather hurtled something. Donovan flung up his hand as a small ball whirled in our direction, spraying liquid as it came. Friendlies and unfriendlies alike jerked back, screaming and clutching body parts as the ball reached us.

It stopped mid-air, caught in Donovan's magic. Zorn pushed me to the ground and a few droplets of liquid flew over us.

"She's an Acidic," Henry said as Donovan lowered the ball into the sand. "She can create acidic saliva. Clearly, she made a slow-releasing ball of some sort to distribute it."

"She took off," Donovan yelled, yanking me up. "Come on. That was a distraction. She's getting out of here."

"She's not going to stay and fight for her boss?" I asked, running behind him.

"Yeah right," Donovan said, magically lifting some-one dashing toward us and throwing him to the side. A corpse barreled into a cluster of three fighters, one of ours against two enemies. Now it would be a cluster-fuck of body parts, some of them squishy. "Valens's people are highly intelligent, and their loyalty only goes as far as the blood oath he made them give. Those with loosened bonds will get out of here as soon as they can. Clearly, she has more freedom than most."

"Is the blood bond the reason you're still here?"

"No. And it's also not why we're going after Kieran when he told us to stay behind. We pledged an oath because we wanted to, not because we were forced to."

We neared the steps to the parking lot and had to slow as the corpses behind us stumbled and fell trying to keep up. Many of them still had very little working knowledge of the bodies they inhabited, and sand wasn't easy to traverse.

A group of fresh warriors, all in black, ran along the walkway above the barrier. I glanced back at the large host in black and red still standing their own on the beach. I'd severely helped, yes. Maybe I'd even turned the tide. But I hadn't come close to winning the battle for Kieran.

"Look!" someone said.

A large gray wolf with an odd spot near his left eye, one I'd come to know well, slipped around me and leapt over the stairs to the sand. It landed gracefully as another wolf followed. Then more. People behind me cheered. My blood ran cold.

"Mordecai, no—"

One of the other wolves, a bigger one, stopped beside him. Another, this time black. Another. They collected behind and around him, pushing back any enemy combatants who ran at our group.

For one solid beat, I stared into the striking hazel eyes of the boy whom I'd helped shape into a teen, and whom the Six would help shape into a man. He nodded solemnly, if a wolf can be said to look solemn, and joined the others. Snarling, they raced off toward the vicious battle on the sands, then slammed into the enemy warriors, tearing them to the ground.

"No! How did—"

"Let him go," Henry shouted and urged me on. "His pack will protect him. The youngest wolves will be shepherded out should the worst happen. They protect their future generation."

"They didn't do a whole lot to protect him last time." I would have run after him, but Donovan grabbed me with his magic and yanked me behind him.

"Trust," I heard Henry say as he followed.

The fresh group of warriors met us, swords or magic held at the ready. I slashed, punched, and cut, making them stagger, but my impact was waning. Clearly the tales of yore were *grossly* exaggerated. My magic was crazy, but I was still human.

"Save your strength." Donovan pointed, then fist pumped the air. "Yes!"

Henry gave a shout of glee. "They made it!"

A ball of fire punched a sudden hole through the fighting, throwing five black-clad people aside like dolls, and a petite woman with blond hair and a fearsome expression ran in the fireball's wake. The ground rumbled beneath me as fear once again swallowed me whole.

Right behind the petite blonde, dressed in black spandex and heavy boots and carrying two knives, ran my ward. Daisy.

"Get out of here," I screamed, running at her with abandon. I pulled a big surge of power from the Line, momentarily infusing my weakened body, and yanked a soul from a woman in red running at her with a glowing ball. I infused the soul with my desire, stuffed it back into the body, not bothering with a prong, and grabbed Daisy with a desperate grip. "Get out of here! There are too many of them!"

"Lexi, right?" the blonde woman said in an Australian accent. She said it casually, as if we weren't in the middle of a raging battle. "I'm Dara, the ruler of magical Sydney. Great to meet ya. I've heard so much about you." She smiled a flawless, white smile.

Something exploded on the ground—no, wait, exploded *up* from the ground—catching the fresh men who'd almost reached the steps. Rocks, it seemed, of all sizes, blasting up through flesh.

"I got your ward's note, and I have to say, she's very persuasive." Dara smiled down at a fierce-eyed Daisy, who held her knives at her waist, her gaze constantly moving. "She reminds me a lot of me when I was her age."

"But Kieran… Daisy? What?" I asked, out of breath

and torn.

"Sorry, Lexi," Daisy said, finally looking at me. "But we needed more people, and Zorn wouldn't listen, so I contacted Sydney on my own. Mordie helped. I told him that we'd make sure Kieran won this, and we needed more people to make that happen."

"You—*what*?"

"We have to go," Henry yelled in my ear. "Valens will be too much for Kieran!"

"Yup, you definitely need to head on." Dara grabbed my arm and helped Henry hurry me along. Donovan caught a collection of darts in the air and hurtled them back the way they'd come. "We need Demigod Kieran to win this. Our whole way of life is on the line. Don't worry—I'll watch Daisy. She's much too special to let anything happen to her. And non-magical! Amazing. Go on—you've already cleared the way for us. We'll just tie everything up."

"But Daisy—"

Air blasted the warriors who'd survived the rock attack, throwing them over the barrier and onto the sand below. Ten people ran out from around Dara, on the chase. Another group peeled away from behind her, taking off after the lingering clusters of Valens's people farther back in the parking lot.

"Good to have you," Donovan said to Dara, wrapping me up in his magic and dragging me behind him.

"I couldn't miss an opportunity to fight beside a Soul Stealer, now could I?" Dara shouted at our retreating backs. "I want to be in the history books with you!"

"That little gremlin saved the fucking day," Henry said, running beside me as I bobbed along. "She has balls of steel and a way with words. I have no idea how she did it when not even Demigod Kieran could, but she saved our fucking asses."

"No shit, right?" Donovan stopped at a sign post that showed a dog on a leash. He bent and half of his body disappeared into what must've been a hideaway concealed by Boman or Zorn. I hit the ground and staggered away, not ready for his magical hold to drop, and four small wooden boats lifted into sight. "She's a keeper, that's for sure."

We took off running back to the beach, the boats floating behind us. Once we were on the sand, a yelp tore my heart anew. I looked frantically for some sign of Mordecai. The wolves attacked with teeth and claws, taking down two to their one. Mordecai fought between two of his kind, both larger than he, but neither of his companions displayed the sheer fearlessness that came with an enhanced ability to tolerate incredible pain.

Arms wrapped around me and I found myself slung across Henry's wide shoulders.

"He'll be fine," Henry said as we ran. "You took down the people who wanted him dead. The people who were dragging that pack down. They're here for you, because of what you did, and they'll protect him as one of their own."

My chest throbbed at the thought of leaving the kids behind in the middle of a battle.

"You raised survivors," Donovan said as we raced toward the water. "When things go sideways, always put your faith in a survivor."

Zorn and Boman waited for us amidst a pile of bodies. Zorn cleaned a large, curved sword on the shirt of one of the downed men before sheathing it in an invisible scabbard on his back. The sword disappeared with it.

"What took you so long?" He grabbed one of the boats and pulled it closer. "Valens has the upper hand in both magic and experience. Kieran is running out of time."

"Dara showed." Donovan jumped into one of the boats.

A small smile pulled at Zorn's lips as he lifted me into one of the boats and jumped in after me. The rest of them each boarded a boat.

"You owe me a hundred dollars," Zorn said. "Now let's go. We don't have time to lose."

"Wait a second," I said, clutching the sides of the flimsy boat. There weren't even oars. "Are they magical or something?"

"No, but we are," Donovan called out and the boats rose off the ground.

Just beyond the waves, huge tentacles rose out of the water. They waved in the air until Donovan set us down. Four of the tentacles disappeared and suddenly we were moving, racing across the water.

"What's the plan?" I yelled over the rush of air. "How can we help—"

A stab of pain bled through the soul connection, and then the connection itself dimmed. Kieran was in serious trouble.

"Any way possible," Zorn shouted over the wind.

I could barely breathe, staring at the limitless ocean in front of us.

Would we even be in time to help?

Chapter 38

ALEXIS

"OH SHIT," I thought I heard before Zorn's words were ripped away by the wind and a roar I couldn't identify.

The boat slowed and slowly started to spin. I blinked tears out of my eyes, the result of hard, cold wind pounding into my face for twenty minutes, and leaned around Zorn. My mouth dropped open.

An enormous whirlpool, nearly a half mile in diameter, spun around a large central point. Way in the distance, a creature jumped out of the water, the shape resembling a mermaid. She landed farther away than she'd started, trying to get away from the funnel. She wouldn't be able to get in there and help Kieran.

"Valens is blocking everyone away." Donovan's boat rose up into the air and drifted closer to us. He hovered for a moment before the large tentacle took hold of the bottom of his craft and lowered him back down. "He knows he's stronger than Kieran one on one."

Pain drummed up through my middle. My connection to Kieran lessened a little more. We'd taken too long on the beach. He was drifting away. I had to do something—*anything*—or I knew without a doubt that he would die.

Steeling my courage, I pointed to the gigantic, terrifying pit of water. "Okay." I took a deep breath. "What's on the bottom of that funnel? Ocean floor, right?"

The guys exchanged looks and shrugged. Clearly no one had been at the bottom of an enormous sea tornado before.

My fingers gripped the edges of the tiny boat, my knuckles turning white as my mind conjured a mad plan. "That's usually how it works, though, right? The funnel goes to the bottom? And what's on the bottom? Rocks 'n' shit, right?"

"You're not thinking—"

"You're not jumping in there," Henry said over Boman. "That's suicide."

"Is it?" Zorn asked.

Henry lifted his open palm to face me. "He'd kill us if she died, Zorn, think it through. We should send Jack in. He's got the best shot of any of us."

"Valens will cut Jack down without a thought," Boman said.

"He'll cut Alexis down without a thought," Henry retorted.

"No, he won't," I heard myself say, dread filling me. I ignored it. "Valens has seen what I can do. He stopped fighting with Kieran to watch. He won't kill me—he'll want to capture me. That gives me time and security, at least in the short term."

I shook my head, and this time, it wasn't the wind causing my tears. I'd been scared a lot today, but never like this. This terror settled deep into my bones, freezing me from the inside out.

I heard my mother's voice. *Fear is but a speed bump on the road to greatness.*

"Let it take you," Zorn said urgently, leaning toward me. "Let the water take you. Don't resist it. You'll be able to see in it now. You'll be able to hear in it, too, like marine life does. But you still have to hold your breath. You should have…an hour, an hour and a half tops."

"This is madness," Henry yelled. "The waters will rip her apart."

"They don't rip, they pull." Zorn's eyes didn't leave mine. "You should feel a little rejuvenation. You're connected to him pretty tightly, so hopefully more than a little. That'll help. Wait until you get close. Work with Kieran. Between the two of you, you can bring Valens down. It was never supposed to be just him. It was always supposed to be the two of you. There can be no other explanation for how you found each other at the perfect time. You can save him, Alexis. I believe that.

With you, we can win this."

I nodded with each point he beat into me. I held on to each word for dear life.

"It was always meant to be the two of you," he reiterated.

I nodded again and looked away from the whirlpool, out over the amazingly tranquil waters. The guys argued around me—Henry and Donovan yelling and Boman peppering the conversation with swear words.

Without a word, I stood, took a deep breath, and let myself fall.

Immediately, the cold water of the ocean sucked me under. I closed my eyes, scared I would swim wildly to get back if I could see the boats. The Six. A feeling like hot tub bubbles drifted by my left side.

If I get bit by a shark before I do my part, I'm going to be so pissed.

Finally, I opened my eyes...into the deep blue of nothingness. Little fragments drifted around me, and some kelp, but other than that I was alone and adrift, hoping to hell the current would take me close to Kieran before I ran out of breath.

I closed my eyes again, wondering if I should swim. And then, just for kicks, and because I didn't have much else to do, I went into a trance. A deep trance. As I drifted down in the ocean, and I did the same within my own consciousness, wondering if the jerk in that other plane had any words of wisdom for my extremely stupid and half-baked plan.

Spirit swirled around me and a blurred form moved through it, shoving me. I smacked into my body and almost gasped.

Apparently the jerk did not want to be disturbed.

I continued to drift. And drift.

Don't fight it.

And drift.

A shock of pain nearly made me gasp again. The soul connection bled away even more, almost gone.

My heart sped up. Adrenaline dumped into my body.

I'd had to fight all my life, why would this situation be any different?

I oriented myself with the pull of the current and swam, cutting through the water like an Olympic swimmer. Strength coursed through my limbs. The harder I worked, the more it increased my energy. Zorn clearly hadn't known what he was talking about, and I was glad I never followed directions for too long.

The current pulled harder as I swam.

Now we were getting somewhere.

Another few strokes and a sea creature came into focus. It reached me, and thank heavens, it kept on going. With four heads and a beastly though serpentine body, I did not want to mess with that thing.

I swam farther, registering the dizzying effects of the whirlpool. That was good. It meant I was getting closer.

A hairy little sprite drifted toward me, swimming merrily, without a care in the world. I wanted to ask it if it was lost. It shot me a curious look as it passed by, and on impulse, I reached out and grabbed its foot. It thrashed, increasing my forward momentum.

Water streamed past my face as we rocketed around the funnel. I yanked the sprite, pointing him toward the center of the whirlpool. He cut through at an angle, unhappily dragging me behind him, so much faster than I could've swam.

Water sucked at us, turbulent now. The sprite finally realized what sort of mess he'd gotten himself into, and tried to turn in the other direction. A creature zipped by behind us, and another was pulled along over our heads. Currents dragged us, pulling us closer. We were near the vortex.

I yanked on the sprite and pointed in the direction I needed to go. It kicked at me, trying to get me off. I'd have to steal its soul to get it to help.

I paused for a moment…and let go of its foot.

It was an innocent. It wasn't right to kill it.

Pain ached through my middle, and the feeling of Kieran drifted away until I could barely feel him at all. I swam for all I was worth, fighting to get closer to that ripping and tearing water at the edge of the funnel. It was just there, right up ahead.

A strange high-pitched noise from the right grabbed my focus, and I turned just in time to see a huge gaping mouth with long, spindly teeth headed my way.

I screamed into the water and slashed out with my magic. The creature jerked and made that high-pitched sound again, but it kept on coming, slithering like a snake. When it tried to pull around me to attack from another angle, I caught sight of the rest of it. It looked like some sort of dragon from the blue lagoon, with sad excuses for wings, a dragon head, and a long shiny body.

It roared, a dismal sound compared to its land equivalent, and flowed forward to chomp on me. A spear cut through the water, zipping in front of me and skimming the beast. It recoiled and I magically dug through its chest, feeling for its spirit box. It roared again and rushed me, but I had it. I ripped out its spirit, held it for a moment, and stuffed it back in.

Another spear sliced through the water. A merman down the way with long red hair and a mustache fought the pull of the water, trying to get closer to the dragon-thing.

I waved my arms at him, trying to tell him to stop, and pushed my will on the dragon's soul. It jerked in confusion, but it had no choice but to obey. The merman threw another spear, retrieved from a pack on his back, and this time his aim was right. It skewered the dragon-thing's middle.

I didn't need a living body to work my magic. Thank you, Bria, for your excellent training.

I grabbed the thing's slimy tail, securing my hand against its fins, and held on as it moved into that funnel. Another spear poked through it, and I punched the merman's spirit box. He was probably on my side, but I didn't need him to accidentally stick a spear in my back.

The water churned, aerated as it slid against my skin. Messy white water announced the edge of the funnel. My energy still wasn't top notch, but the water had greatly replenished it. It was good enough to get the job done.

Summoning my courage, I urged the dragon-thing faster and closer, keeping us right next to that funnel, and then stuck my head through the side into blessed air.

Down about fifty feet, Valens and Kieran fought atop a surface of calm water, so flat it looked like glass. Their limbs moved at inhuman speeds, though Kieran was noticeably slower and clumsier. Blood smeared his chin and wet his clothes. He'd taken a lot of hits.

Valens whipped a pronged staff around and, as I watched in horror, stabbed it through Kieran's middle. Pain ached through the soul connection and Kieran sagged. His presence inside of me winked out, too dim to feel.

"What a fool, thinking you could best me." Valens ripped out the pronged staff and Kieran bent forward, panting. He put his hand to the glassy bottom, struggling to stay up. "I created you, in all senses of the word. Without me, you'd be nothing." He hefted the staff. "And because of me, you'll be no more. Say hello to your bitch mother."

Kieran struggled to get up as Valens took a step toward him, and I slashed out with everything I had, ripping through Valens's middle. He grunted and staggered backward, hitting the edge of the whirlpool. Water sprayed around him. Kieran didn't even look up.

"Hey dickface, up here," I yelled, pulling power from the Line and readying for another attack. I already knew he'd be too strong for me to best. Felling a Demigod was beyond my capabilities, something I knew from practicing with Kieran. But if I could just give him time to heal… "I got a little something for ya."

I wrapped spirit around his spirit box and gave it a good shake before trying to seep in.

A blast of power hit me that was so mighty it shoved me back into the water. Various sea creatures, including the spear-throwing merman, who apparently didn't hold a grudge, treaded water in a semi-circle around me, facing away. Guarding me. They were clearly Kieran's people, and had obviously figured out I was trying to help. Good news.

I urged the dragon-thing back to the funnel and stuck my head through again. Valens waited five feet from me, the glassy, solid looking water still under his feet. Kieran was now beneath the surface.

That was good. Water rejuvenated him.

"Well, well, well," Valens said, and the strength of his presence nearly pushed me back. His rugged features were just shy of striking, and a strange glimmer lit his turbulent eyes. It was clear Kieran had gotten the lion's share of his looks from his mother, but his large and muscular bearing certainly came from this man. "Look at this, the pretty little treasure has courage. You will make a mighty prize."

I rammed my power into his middle, trying harder to seep down in. He jerked back and released another wave of his enormous, heady magic, dunking me in a blazing fire of pain. It felt like it ate through my skin and dripped acid down my middle. Water closed over me, a tomb, and I started rising.

I squeezed my eyes shut and doubled down, battering Valens with everything I had. My dragon-thing swam furiously and its slimy surface slipped from my grasping hands. Mind-numbing pain consumed me, dripping down my esophagus, and jabbing white-hot spikes behind my eyes. Still, I kept at it, draining myself of energy and holding my breath, shaking and jerking and punching Valens's spirit box.

And then something wormed through the blinding agony—a comforting feeling, throbbing in my middle and cooling Valens's fire.

Kieran!

I blinked my eyes open and saw the most beautiful sight I'd ever set eyes on—Kieran streaming through the water with a glowing trident. Valens turned from me just in time for the sharp points to pierce his gut. The pain eating away at me eased. The water tomb pushing me upward vanished.

Kieran yanked the trident from Valens's body and struck again. Valens met the trident with one of his own, battering it away. The rest of his magical hold vanished from around me, and I swam in their direction. My energy increased with each stroke, though minimally. I didn't have much left, and not even the water and Kieran's magical gift could help me.

I summoned everything I had left and pulled magic from the Line for one final assault. Kieran barely dodged a strike and brought his trident down on his father. Valens ducked, taking the blow across the shoulder. He jabbed his pronged staff forward, grazing Kieran's side. Blood trailed into the water.

I struck again, intent on one thing. Getting to that soul.

Spirit wrapped around Valens's spirit box and started to seep in. A shock of power from Kieran barreled into him a moment later. Together, we converged, taking Valens from both sides. He was forced to split his defense and offense. I clenched my teeth, desperately trying to ignore the painful stabs.

My spirit kept seeping in, the progress painfully slow. Kieran battered Valens with his magic and stuck his trident in a second time. Then a third. The water moved around us—pushing me away (Valens), then pulling me closer (Kieran). I released myself to the currents, losing my bearings and closing my eyes, focusing everything I had on reaching that spirit.

Valens yelled, the sound twisting through the water, a frustrated and pained sound. Currents continued to shift and change around me, Father and son fighting over my proximity to their battle.

His spirit box's density shifted, then started the change. Valens froze for a brief moment.

That was the window Kieran needed.

A rush of his magic slammed into Valens, bending him in half. Backward. Valens's spine cracked, a fearsome sound heard throughout the water. The prongs of the spirit box loosened with the prospect of death, ready to let go. I reached in…and grabbed his soul.

Chapter 39

KIERAN

NEARLY SPENT IN a way he had never been before, every inch of his body aching, Kieran watched in utter shock as his father's body went limp. His head floated in the water. His legs drifted.

Valens's spirit blinked in utter confusion at Alexis.

The Line materialized and pulsed below them, and Alexis looked back and forth between the two, then at Kieran, needing direction.

The waters stilled around them as Kieran let go of his magic. Silence filled the space, expectant.

They'd killed his father. He was an orphan.

An unexpected sadness filled him. He'd hated his father for so many things, but now that he'd gotten vengeance…it had left him feeling hollow.

He had to remember this wasn't just about him. It was about his mother, and magical San Francisco, and all the people the Demigod had unlawfully killed for some reason or other. It was about the future, and the harmony between magical and non-magical societies.

Killing his father was bigger than him.

"Send him across—" Kieran started to say, but a strange blurriness invaded the water, like the figure he and Bria had seen in the smoke the other day while Green's body lay on the concrete. The soul connection weakened—and then began to blink out. The blurriness shot through the water and stopped by Valens's spirit, somewhat obstructing Kieran's view. Valens's face changed to one of shock, then anger, then fear, before his spirit started to dissipate. It didn't move toward the Line, it just...faded away.

"What's happening?" he asked, starting over.

The blurred form turned, and Kieran could swear it looked right at him.

Save her.

The words echoed in his head as the blurry form faded away with his father's spirit. A moment later, there was nothing left. They were both gone.

Alexis jolted. Her eyes snapped opened and she gasped, sucking in a lungful of water.

"Oh shit, no. Alexis!" Kieran could speak and pull oxygen from the water. This was his territory. But though his blood gift allowed his chosen few to spend longer than normal in the water, they couldn't subsist here. If he didn't get Alexis to the surface, she'd drown.

He rushed at her, dissipating the trident and wrapping his arm around her middle. She coughed and grabbed her throat, sucking in more water. Trying to get air.

He swam faster than he ever had in his life, straight up while parting the water at the surface to get her to the air faster.

"Hang on, baby," he said, sheer terror stopping his heart. "Hang on. Almost there."

He crested the surface he'd created, letting the water push him the rest of the way up to sea level. He pushed on her chest as she gagged. Water dribbled from her mouth. She coughed, clutching at him.

"Breathe, baby, it's over. We made it," he said, floating to the top and cradling her in his arms. "We made it. *Breathe.*"

Jack cut through the water, four boats held high with his tentacles. Each held a member of his Six, their faces pale, their eyes anxious. Zorn's gaze found Alexis, gasping for breath.

He readied to dive into the water, just as at home there as Jack, though not nearly as powerful. The brunt of his power existed on land.

"I have her. Stay in the boat." Kieran swam her closer and handed her up before climbing in himself.

She coughed and gagged, emptying the liquid in her lungs into the boat. She sucked in deeply, replacing the water with air.

"Is she okay?" Donovan brought his boat closer.

The way it shook in the air indicated he was tired. They all were.

"Yes," he said as a wave of relief washed over him. He hugged her close and looked up at the sky, a million emotions racing through him. "Yes."

Zorn was lifted away and dumped into Donovan's boat. "Sorry, bro. I'm about out of steam," Donovan said.

Kieran looked down at Alexis's beautiful face before brushing the wet hair off of her cheek. Her chest rose and fell, still gasping for air and coughing up water, but she was alive. They both were.

"Is it done, sir?" Boman asked.

Kieran looked at the shimmering surface of water, also calming, erasing the evidence of the enormous whirlpool and hard-fought battle. "Yes. It's over. His body is below."

"Will you leave it there?" Zorn asked.

Kieran shook his head and returned his gaze to Alexis. "It's tolerated, maybe even expected, for Demigods to fight one another for territory, but still, some may mourn him. I'll give him a proper burial so the people of San Francisco, and the world, can pay their respects, such as they are. But that can wait. My people below will guard the body, and his people have probably already taken off. Let's get home."

The boats started to move, propelled by Jack's Kraken form. He hadn't had much to do but swim. He'd be the only one with energy to spare when they got back.

Kieran sagged against the side of the boat, sitting on the bottom. He settled Alexis a little more firmly in his lap and sighed in relief when she curled up into his arms.

Earlier, when he'd felt her draw near, he'd been both scared she was in danger and incredibly relieved. His father had been too much for him. If she hadn't risked her life to save him, his body would be floating down deep instead of his father's. He had so much to be thankful for, and so much to apologize for, that he didn't know where to start. So he met her entrancing eyes, and said the first thing that came to his mind. "Will you marry me?"

Chapter 40

ALEXIS

"THERE SHE IS, the little heart breaker. My girl!" Bria put up her fist as I entered the kitchen. "Finally found sense."

Daisy and Mordecai looked up from their bowls of cereal. Thane sat at the island next to Bria, the only one of the Six who'd physically battled from start to finish, helping Bria, Dara, and the wolves clear the parking lot and the beach. He and Bria had gotten the week off to recuperate, like I had.

Kieran, the one who'd been beaten on the most, hadn't even allowed himself an hour off. The moment we'd gotten back to the beach, he'd stripped off his bloody shirt, tossed it to the side, and started to clean up the carnage. He hadn't done it to look good, either, like Valens might've done. There were no photo ops, and he refused to even let the news crews onto the premises. He was doing the right thing—cleaning up a mess he had created. The same mess he was now working tirelessly to set to rights at the magical government office.

With Dara's help to keep order, he hired and promoted people to fill all the holes he'd created in the magical hierarchy. He then created new holes, by firing those he'd found incompetent or untrustworthy before the battle. He was cleaning everything up and making things run smoother again.

And the people loved him for it. His levelheadedness, and kindness, and desire to honestly make a good change went a helluva long way toward garnering respect and goodwill. The people wanted to give him a job for it. *The* job. They didn't want the matter to be decided for them at the next Magical Summit.

He was adamant about not taking it, however. Donovan tried to bet Jack a hundred bucks that Kieran eventually would, but Jack knew better than to accept those odds.

I grimaced and trudged over to the coffee pot, my legs and arms finally not aching a full week after the battle to take down Valens.

"Soul Stealer?" Thane said, grinning at Bria and joining in the fun. He shook his head. "More like soul *crusher*. You are so cold."

I'd heard these jokes every day since the showdown. I guess I kind of deserved them. I *may* have accidentally blurted out "no" when Kieran had proposed. But honestly, he hadn't been in his right mind. You don't just accept the proposal of someone who was sitting in a small wooden boat covered in his own blood. We'd all had more than our quota of drama for the day, and no way was I going to start Round Two by accepting a proposal he hadn't thought through and didn't really mean. Besides, we needed to date and live together for a while before we decided on anything so legally binding. He might end up the Demigod of San Francisco. He'd need someone who was a little less of a shit show to help him run things.

"What's on the schedule today?" I asked the room at large. "Same as yesterday? And the day before that?"

"You mean, hiding out from the masses because Kieran doesn't want to make that mark public?" Bria lifted her eyebrows.

"That's not what he is doing, and she knows it," Thane said. "He just made the official announcement at the government building yesterday that the rumors were true, and there was indeed a Soul—sorry, a Spirit Walker at the battle. And that said Spirit Walker has been living in the dual-society zone, hiding from persecution, for years. He said it clear as day: she only used that side of her magic to save Kieran's life. He also said they're in a relationship." Thane nodded at me with a smug smile. "The most eligible bachelor in the city has thrown in the towel, and the girls are *pissed*."

I poured myself a cup of coffee. Kieran had told me

all about his announcement. He hadn't said so, but I knew people were freaked out beyond belief. They were scared I would be let loose on the city, ripping out souls wherever I went.

I was quite happy to hide from the magical world, just like I'd done all my life. The reasons might've changed, but the benefits stayed the same.

"We're going shopping," Mordecai said with a grin.

He and Daisy had gotten the week off, too. Mordecai because he'd taken some hard hits in the battle, ending up with a broken bone and few torn muscles, and then received my wrath for putting himself in danger. He wasn't allowed to leave my sight.

Daisy because she was grounded for going behind everyone's back, contacting Sydney with some damning secrets (my magic being one of them, Kieran's plans another), and then arranged for Dara to come without telling Kieran. If Dara hadn't contacted Kieran herself, the whole thing might've gone nowhere. Daisy had only gotten a week of punishment and a very soft chewing out by Kieran (or so the guys claimed—it had seemed pretty harsh to me with all of his magic being thrown around) because she'd saved the day.

"Rover!" A thunk and a grunt said Daisy had kicked him under the table. "That was supposed to be a surprise!"

"I'm not going shopping," I said, grabbing juice out

of the fridge. "My dream stores have crap in them. It's no fun anymore."

"Yes, you are going shopping." Thane slid off the stool with a wince and gingerly walked to the sink. He was still stiff. "There is one kitchen worth of utensils and gadgets spread between two houses, and it is annoying as all hell to cook."

"You're going shopping." Bria nodded solemnly. "Don't piss off the cooks."

"Are you seeing your people today?" I asked Mordecai. One day I hoped I could ask that question without sounding—or feeling—wary. They hadn't just joined the fight to help Kieran or me (he'd forwarded them a copy of the video of my showdown with Will Green), they'd also gone because Ray and Moesha's little boy was still alive. To them, he was still a member of the pack, and they'd wanted to help their own. His battle was their battle.

I was terrified he'd leave me for them, I had to admit, and even more afraid I wouldn't be able to fake being happy for him. Daisy said I didn't have to worry, but she did denial like no one else I knew.

"When is this shopping thing happening?" Bria pointed at Mordecai.

"You weren't in on this surprise?" I asked her.

She frowned. "They won't tell me anything anymore because *one time* I let it slip that Donovan was seeing two girls at once."

"Yeah, because you let it slip to one of the girls," Thane said. "Get a clue."

"Get some morals," she retorted.

"They weren't official. No one said anything about exclusivity," Daisy said, and took another bite of her breakfast.

"What do you know about dating rules?" Bria rolled her eyes.

"It's not very respectful to the women," Mordecai chimed in. "They aren't like ice cream. He has to pick a flavor."

"Not if they agree to be a double scoop to his cone." Thane fluttered his eyebrows suggestively.

"All right, all right, enough. Kids present." I frowned at Thane. He laughed and washed his plate.

"I'm never going to be tied down," Daisy said.

"That's because no one will have you," Bria replied.

Mordecai nodded thoughtfully. Daisy kicked him again. "Really, Mordie? You're going to agree with that?"

He shrugged. "You are a little terrifying. I doubt many men will be confident enough to think they'd survive one of your bad moods."

"He's too damn sensible for his own good." Bria shook her head. "Well, anyway, I'm going to go shower. Let me know when it's time to go shopping."

"You're not invited, I don't think," Daisy said as Bria walked out of the kitchen.

"Like hell I'm not," she called back.

It turned out, she wasn't. It would just be me.

Later that afternoon, I stepped out of the house in designer attire and my makeup and hair done. Mordecai had insisted that I should look nice, and Daisy had then picked out my clothes, because she didn't trust my sense of style (I wasn't complaining). A badly decomposing corpse sat off to the side, still filled with one of the nutters from the ghost house. He didn't want to leave the body, and because he'd helped out, I didn't want to make him. Still, it was getting a little gross.

The rest of the spirits had waited for the magical zone burial of Demigod Valens, held on day three after his demise, as a kind of celebration before moving on. They'd gone on their way, roaming to other places, or finally drifting across the Line. John had thanked me and said to call him back should we ever need anything. I got the feeling he wanted to go looking for Valens on the other side.

He'd never find him.

The strange presence without a real body or spirit form had shown me how to disintegrate a spirit by demonstrating on Valens. Clearly the...thing—being?—hadn't trusted me to get it right the first time around. At this point, I was pretty sure the grump in the strange plane wasn't actually my subconscious, though that left me with no idea who, or what, it was. Regardless, it was clear that even people in the spirit realm wanted Valens completely gone.

I couldn't say I blamed them.

"Well, don't you look nice," Frank said.

Frank had figured out a way to make this his new home. Apparently, this spirit wasn't attached to places, anymore, he was attached to people. Namely, me. Just my luck.

Kieran's red Ferrari rolled up the street, five minutes late. He pulled a U-turn and stopped by the curb before quickly getting out and hurrying up the walk. I feasted my eyes on that handsome face, letting myself fall into his stormy blue eyes, open all the way down to his soul. A soul I held firmly in my magical grasp. His perfectly tailored suit molded to his out-standing body, his broad shoulders leading down into trim hips.

"Hello, beautiful," he said with a mouth-watering smile. "Sorry I'm late. The treasury meeting ran over."

He put out his hand and I took it. Electricity sizzled up my arm and settled into a low hum deep in my body. Lord, I was smitten by this man. I wanted nothing more than to glue myself to his side and run, eyes open, straight at our future.

Whoa, girl. Learn to crawl before you walk. Then

think about running.

"You're finally letting me out of the house?" I asked with a smile, hiding the nervousness twisting my belly.

"It's time for you to finally join the magical world. I'll be your guide."

I took a deep breath as he opened the car door for me. "I don't really wanna."

He shut it and came around to the driver's side. "I'll happily live in obscurity with you after everything is all set up."

He still believed he'd turn the job down and walk away. Amazing.

My anxiety grew as we headed for the center of magical downtown.

"Are you going to hang me in the middle of Union Square to win the love of the people?" I asked as we slowed for the increased pedestrian traffic.

"And accidentally kill half the shoppers when you resist? Not likely." He chuckled and turned into an underground public parking garage under the square. Right out front, beyond the ticket booths, he pulled into a spot marked *Demigod.*

"You don't want the job, but you sure do enjoy the perks, huh?" I asked as he put the car in park.

"Yup." He walked around the car at a leisurely pace, slipping one of his hands into his pocket.

I stalled for a moment, collecting my thoughts. I

wore his mark—the people who saw us would know who I was. They'd know *what* I was. I did not envision this going well.

He opened the door and stuck out a hand for me, the turn of his shoulders and lean of his body indicating he was unimpressed with his surroundings. Here came the ego.

I allowed him to pull me out. "Should I be playing a part, too?" I whispered as he entwined his fingers within mine.

"Yes. The part of a woman confident in her own skin. The Alexis Price who grabbed ahold of my vitals, literally, and won't let go. Be her."

"Except she scares people, and I might make you look bad."

"Then be the Alexis Price who doesn't care when she makes a stalking, possessive Demigod look bad. It's the same Alexis Price, by the way."

I laughed and looked away. "I'm just worried I'll meet the lynch mob."

"You might, but it'll be because you stole my affections. They'll want what you have."

I rolled my eyes. "No wonder you're so strong. You have to carry your enormous ego around all the time."

"There she is."

We exited the parking garage into the sunlight, Kieran now in charge of maintaining the weather.

Instead of the perfect blue his father had favored, puffy white clouds drifted through the sky.

People had asked him if he didn't have enough power to keep the sky clear. He'd responded that true power lay in diversity. True proof of magical ability was the act of keeping constant change peaceful. A cloudy day would make people grateful for the sun, and would give a more interesting canvas for the sun to paint when it entered and exited the sky. It would give daydreamers shapes to picture when they stared at the heavens.

As one might expect, his answer went over extremely well.

Charismatic bastard.

"Here we go," he said with a strong, sure voice.

People passing by glanced over. Their gazes caught on Kieran, making them slow, then stuck like glue to me. Mouths dropped open and eyes widened. People started chattering.

"That's the Demigod!"

"Oh my God, that's the Demigod's girlfriend. Quick, get a picture!"

"I don't have a chance in hell with him…"

I laughed softly.

"What?" he asked as we crossed the street without waiting for a lull in traffic. Cars slammed on their brakes and drivers leaned forward against their steering wheels, watching us. More people waited on the other side, excitedly pointing at him or me.

"That woman thinking she wanted a chance in hell with you," I said.

"That's funny?"

"Yeah. You made me walk through my nightmare, then I nearly got myself killed. She should count her blessings."

"Ah." He was quiet for a moment. "Solid point. You're incredibly unlucky."

"Don't I know it."

We strolled up the sidewalk, and I felt the soul of Zorn lingering in an alley we passed.

"You have the Six on watch?"

He slowed as we neared a cluster of stores. People stopped walking and gawked. I half waited for someone to throw their underwear at Kieran.

"She is absolutely gorgeous," I heard.

Or me.

"She could've at least brushed her hair," someone else said.

"What I wouldn't give to hit that..." some douche said.

I gritted my teeth to keep from sucker-punching him in the spirit box. However well deserved, it wouldn't be great for public goodwill.

Kieran turned slowly, his face a terrifying mask of viciousness. Magic seeped around him. His gaze hit Mr.

Douche with a force that had the other man stepping backward.

"Sorry, sir," the man mumbled, his face paling. "I meant no disrespect."

"Subtle," I said as Kieran turned back.

"You wear my mark. Disrespecting you is disrespecting me."

"You sure didn't seem to mind the hair comment, though…"

"The which?"

It hadn't even registered.

He gestured around us. "Where shall we go first?"

I finally clued in to my surroundings. Top of the line stores crowded the streets, everything from domestic items to expensive lotions to handbags.

"We can't shop here," I said quietly.

He looked down at me, and I saw the love in his eyes. "This is the best this town has to offer. We'll start here. When things with the government are resolved, we'll hit Italy and France. We'll visit the castle in Ireland. I have all the money you could want, Alexis, with more on the way. You can have it all. I just want you."

"Did you hear what he said?" someone asked wistfully.

"She is so lucky," someone else said.

"I would give my left arm for that man."

I quirked an eyebrow. "Gonna let that one go, too?"

He gave me a crooked grin. "That's your department. I just take care of the guys."

I shook my head and noticed Chef's Kitchen just up the way, a store that I'd never dreamed, in a million years, I'd ever have the money to shop in. It wasn't even a big dream, it was a dream for another person in another life.

A strange nervousness washed over me, and suddenly I wanted to run. To hide. This was all too good for me. *He* was too good for me. I was the nothing daughter of a nobody, having grown up in the crack of nowhere. I didn't belong on one of the most expensive streets in magical San Francisco about to go into a bunch of top-of-the-line stores. That wasn't my MO!

My phone vibrated and I distractedly fished it out, aware that I was stalling. That people were staring at us expectantly.

A text from Bria: *I see you left without me, you dick. I would've bought that store out, too. Make good choices.*

I couldn't help responding: *I'm about to bolt. I don't belong down here. Everyone is staring.*

Kieran lightly moved my hair over my shoulder before stepping closer and sliding his arm around my waist. He wasn't in any hurry, and he wasn't concerned about showing affection in public. He was backing up his mark.

I leaned into him, relishing his comfort and support. Wishing it could only be him and me.

> **Bria:** *Just wait until you walk into Prada with me by your side. They'll be following you thinking I'm a shoplifter. Been there, done that. Stole the purse to prove it.*

I spat out a laugh and then wiped down Kieran's shirt.

"What's up?" he asked softly before kissing my temple.

"Bria is talking me down from freaking out."

"She's worth three million dollars, did she mention that?"

I reeled backward with wide eyes. "What's this now?"

He smiled and I swear every woman in the area swooned. "She lives frugally and saves like hell. She's worth a lot of money. Zorn nearly blew a gasket when he found out. If she can waltz through here, with her metal shirts and dog collars, so can a hard-working woman with floodwater pants and messy hair."

"You *did* hear that comment." I playfully slapped his chest and he laughed.

"Be you, Alexis," he whispered near the shell of my ear. "I love you, in every way. No one else's opinion will change that. Just be you."

"I love you, too," I said, and pointed at Chef's Kitchen. "We might as well get some good materials for the guys."

"Good thinking. I hear that store has one hell of a lemon zester."

As we entered the store, I squeezed his hand and leaned my arm against his. "The kids wanted me to get my miracle. They both thought they'd already received theirs, and wanted me to finally get mine. I never thought I would. Not in my wildest dreams. And yet, here I am, living a fantasy with a man I love. Everything I've done has been worth it. I'd do it all again. You are my miracle, Kieran."

He lifted our joined hands and kissed the back of mine. "You are my salvation."

Happiness tingled from my head to my toes, and I realized that on the walk over here, no one had stared at me in hatred. No one had turned away in fear or unease. No one had mentioned my magic at all. They'd been far too concerned with who I was with, what I looked like, or my position by Kieran's side. It calmed me in a way nothing else could've. My life wasn't perfect, but I wouldn't change a single thing.

I had my miracle.

I patted his hand, then pushed him away. I also had shopping to do.

Epilogue

MAGNUS STEEPLED HIS fingers as he watched the images flash across the TV. The likeness was astonishing. She looked almost exactly like her mother. Beautiful. Gorgeous, even. But there were a couple of differences.

The magic, for one. Patrice had been a mutt, but her power had sprung from Zeus. This woman wielded the magic of Hades.

"The first Soul Stealer the world has seen since…"

The words of the *Magical World Wide News* faded away to the back of Magnus's thoughts.

So. After hiding for her first quarter century, the Spirit Walker had decided to declare herself in magical society. With an upstart Demigod's son, no less, who'd somehow inherited Poseidon's magic without a properly forked family tree. Amazing. Surprising, even.

Fated?

Magnus touched his fingers to his lips, sifting back through his memories. Back through time.

Maybe.

The other Demigods of Hades would be eager to

shepherd her under their umbrellas. They'd be frothing at the mouth to snap a chain around her neck. This girl was mostly untrained. She was malleable. Powerful to no end. She'd be an unstoppable addition to their inner circle.

But there was one problem: she wore the mark of Poseidon, and the upstart mark holder had been good enough to fool Valens for nearly a year before tearing him down.

Magnus laughed softly and shook his head. He never would've thought that possible. Some rulers, maybe. But not Valens.

Valens had seemed unstoppable.

It just went to show—your brood is your blind spot. Valens had learned that lesson too late.

Miss Price was already under an umbrella. A powerful one. And if Magnus read the situation correctly, the mark-holding upstart was about to be crowned the king of an extremely influential city, with the blessing of Sydney, a growing up-and-comer on the magical scene. Together they held enough cards to be left alone. For a time, anyway.

Magnus studied the girl's face. He studied the eyes.

His eyes.

There was no question—he'd need to pay her a visit. He had a reputation to uphold, after all.

THE END

About the Author

K.F. Breene is a *USA Today* Bestselling and Top 10 Kindle All-Star author of paranormal romance, urban fantasy and fantasy novels. With two million books sold, when she's not penning stories about magic and what goes bump in the night, she's sipping wine and planning shenanigans. She lives in Northern California with her husband, two children and out of work treadmill.

Sign up for her newsletter to hear about the latest news and receive free bonus content.

www.kfbreene.com

CPSIA information can be obtained
at www.ICGtesting.com
Printed in the USA
LVHW052043050422
715338LV00005B/548

9 781732 798991